P₁
SELENE (

M000279153

"Readers will be captivated. Fans of Gillian Bradshaw's classic *The Beacon at Alexandria* may especially enjoy *Selene* and find a promising new historical novelist who shares the same gift for wonderfully researched, vividly evoked, good old-fashioned storytelling."—*Historical Novel Society*

"*Selene of Alexandria* is pure fiction magic...I couldn't put this book down... [It] made me laugh and cry, hope and despair."—*Story Circle Book Reviews*

"This book is outstanding, not just for a first novel, but for any novel. Once you've read it, I'm sure you'll join me in waiting impatiently to read Justice's next project!"—*Lacuna: Journal of Historical Fiction*

"*Selene of Alexandria* does what historical fiction does best—weave historical fact, real-life historical figures, and attention to detail with page-turning, plot-driven fiction."—*The Copperfield Review*

"The author has weaved a brilliant tale that brings to life this fascinating era, complete with never-to-be-forgotten characters, unrequited love, and the desire of one woman to overcome adversity. It is a story that picks up momentum with each page until it reaches a very explosive ending. Highly recommended."—*History and Women*

"The characters are well-drawn, the plot propels us forward, and the writing carries us easily throughout the story. Even the antagonist comes across as a fully fleshed out person. The depiction of all the historical figures we see through Selene's eyes and the level of authenticity is remarkable."—*Historical Novel Review*

"I am enthralled with the work of this author... [She writes] with beauty, brilliance, and brutal honesty. Run to the bookstore and buy this for yourself."—*BookPleasures.com*

Books by Faith L. Justice

Novels

Selene of Alexandria
Sword of the Gladiatrix (Gladiatrix #1)
Twilight Empress (Theodosian Women #1)
Dawn Empress (Theodosian Women #2)

Short Story Collections

The Reluctant Groom and Other Historical Stories
Time Again and Other Fantastic Stories
Slow Death and Other Dark Tales

Non-fiction

Hypatia, Her Life and Times

Children's Books

Tokoyo, the Samurai's Daughter (Adventurous Girls #1)

SELENE
OF ALEXANDRIA

FAITH L. JUSTICE

RAGGEDY MOON BOOKS

SELENE OF ALEXANDRIA

First published in 2009

Copyright © 2009 Faith L. Justice

Reprinted 2020

10th Anniversary edition

All rights reserved

Raggedy Moon Books
Brooklyn, NY, USA
raggedymoonbooks.com

Paperback ISBN: 978-0692356982
Hardback ISBN: 978-0917053191
Epub ISBN: 978-1452336015
Audio Book ISBN: 978-0917053184

Library of Congress Control Number: 2020906192

Cover design by Jennifer Quinlan
historicaleditorial.com

In memory of

Mary Ann Justice, beloved mother and first reader.

ACKNOWLEDGMENTS

IT HAS BEEN MY PLEASURE to write this story and bring these characters and this time to life. Among the many people who helped and encouraged me, I want to particularly thank the members of my writer's group *Circles in the Hair*. For over twenty years, they have been there for me; reading drafts, providing insightful feedback, and encouraging my dreams. Special and loving thanks go to my husband Gordon Rothman for supporting me in countless ways; and to my daughter Hannah J. Rothman, who grew up sharing me with this book and showing no sibling rivalry whatsoever. No historical fiction acknowledgment would be complete without thanks to the many librarians and collections that tirelessly answer questions and find obscure documents. My special thanks go to the New York City Research Library—a world class institution.

Characters in Order of Appearance

(Historical persons in *Italics*)

Selene, a young Christian woman of the ruling class
Nicaeus, Selene's older brother
Antonius, Nicaeus' friend
Rebecca, a Jewish servant
Calistus, city councilor and Selene's father
Phillip, Selene's oldest brother
Hypatia, Lady Philosopher, astronomer and mathematician
Theophilus, Bishop and Patriarch of Alexandria (385-412)
Orestes, Augustal Prefect (governor) of Egypt
Abundantius, Roman General and military *dux* of Alexandria
Demetrius, slave and secretary to Orestes
Timothy, Archdeacon (second in command) to Theophilus
Honoria, Selene's friend
Cyril, Theophilus' nephew, Bishop and Patriarch of Alexandria ((412-444)
Aaron, Rebecca's brother
Auxentius, medical history and theory scholar
Haroun, anatomy teacher
Paulinus, bishop's chief steward
Hierex, Christian teacher and Cyril's right hand man
Lysis, Antonius' father
Jesep, leader of the Jews
Ammonius, Nitrian monk
Arete, Honoria's mother
Ision, Honoria's father
Urbib, Jewish physician
Mother Nut, Egyptian herbalist and healer
Thomas, Imperial agent
Melania, Christian midwife
Peter, Christian presbyter

SELENE
OF ALEXANDRIA

FAITH L. JUSTICE

CHAPTER 1

Alexandria, Egypt, AD 412

B LOOD POUNDED IN SELENE'S EARS, beating to the rhythm of her bare feet thudding on the hard beach scrabble. Her breath came easy as she crested a low ridge and took a moment to glance back. Through the deep shadows of early dawn, she saw her older brother Nicaeus and his best friend Antonius struggle out of a shrubby wash at the bottom of the ridge. She threw her head back and shrieked a triumphant ululation. Arms wide, she hurled herself down the slope with wild abandon.

Running filled her with joy. The feel of her body working smoothly—legs striding, arms swinging, lungs pumping—put her in supreme awareness of her senses. The sky seemed bluer, the briny tang of the breeze sharper, the cry of the seagull more exquisite. Selene never felt more alive than when she ran.

At the stone marking a mile from the city of Alexandria, she skidded to a halt. Selene took a goatskin bag from her belt, unstopped the neck, and poured water into her mouth. Her sweat evaporated in the morning sea breeze, leaving a gritty rime of salt under her breast band. Selene pulled her clammy linen tunic away from her body. Several black curls escaped her braid and lay plastered to her forehead and shoulders. She pushed the hair behind her ears and waited for the two boys.

Antonius arrived first, staggering down the scree-covered slope to collapse at Selene's feet, his breath coming in ragged gasps, his dusky skin ruddy with exertion. Nicaeus was behind him, blowing like a hippo. Her brother leaned over, hands on knees, trying to catch his breath. Selene laughed and sprinkled them with water. The boys scowled at her. Her brother made a half-hearted swipe for the goatskin but she danced out of the way.

"Who's fastest?" Selene teased.

Her brother lunged after her. "You won't be if I ever get hold of you. Gazelles can't run with broken legs."

"You'll have to catch her first. That doesn't look likely," Antonius said between wheezes.

Nicaeus collapsed next to his friend, laughing. "You're right. Whatever will we do with our wild little Selene?"

"Not so little any more. I'm nearly as tall as you, brother." Selene's lithe body seemed to have skipped the awkward-colt stage common to fourteen-year-olds and moved smoothly into graceful young womanhood. She cast a critical eye at her brother and his friend, who at sixteen and seventeen still had an unfinished look; their proportionally larger feet held the promise of more growth—longer limbs and deeper chests. She walked back to the boys and offered her goatskin.

Nicaeus poured water over his head. "My sister, the Amazon." He looked at her and grinned. "But even Queen Hippolyta had her Theseus."

"And fleet Atalanta had her golden apples." Antonius leered. "Maybe I should bring one the next time we race. Would you marry me, Selene, if I beat you on the course?"

Selene snorted. "Why would I want a husband with wits as slow as his feet? Besides, I heard your esteemed father was planning a match for you with Honoria."

"Honoria of the horse face and cow hips?" Nicaeus laughed and punched his friend on the arm.

Antonius' leer turned sour. "Where did you hear that?"

"From Honoria, last week after Sabbath services. She wants hordes of children and thinks you will sire beautiful ones." Selene brushed the dust from her short undertunic and tied the goatskin to her corded belt.

Antonius groaned and reached for Selene's ankle. "Save me, O Amazon Queen, I would much rather marry a friend than a brood mare."

"Honoria is my friend and a perfectly nice young woman. You could do worse in a wife."

"Besides, it will be at least two years before Father finds a likely husband for my wild sister." Nicaeus rose and offered Antonius his hand. "You wouldn't want Selene anyway—too bony. Now Honoria has breasts like cushions—something you can sink your face into."

Both Antonius and Selene scowled.

"As if you would know anything about it," Antonius muttered. Nicaeus turned a brighter shade of red.

Selene tossed her escaping curls over her shoulders and strutted in front of the boys. "I won't need to catch a husband. I plan to convince Father to let me stay unmarried, like Lady Philosopher Hypatia."

The boys snorted in unison, laughing at the unlikely idea that the esteemed City Councilor Calistus would let his only daughter go unmarried. Antonius squinted at the rising sun and grinned at her. "Come, Nicaeus. We need to get your sister home, before your father comes looking for us. It wouldn't do to miss the new Prefect's welcoming procession."

Her brother and Antonius linked arms and strode toward the city, which was becoming visible through the dawn mists.

Selene dawdled as the boys picked up the pace. The subject of marriage disturbed her acutely as she approached betrothal age. It hadn't always been so. Her mother had been happily married to her father for over twenty years. She bore him six children, three of whom still lived. As a little girl, Selene assumed she would marry, have children, and run a household as her mother did. That changed the day her mother and infant brother died of a fever, two years ago.

At the funeral, Selene rejected the comforting words of the priest and vowed to thwart death any way she could. She would become a healer, a physician. As she grew from child to young woman, Selene realized death was inexorable, but the urge to become a physician strengthened. There were a few women healers, mostly holy women and pagan medica, who ministered to the poor. Selene knew the main obstacle to her ambition was her father. No upper class man would willingly allow his daughter to engage in any profession. Calistus would have to be persuaded by someone he respected.

"Who's fastest now?" Her brother's taunt broke into her reverie. She sprinted to catch up, a plan forming in her mind.

"Nicaeus, I need your help."

"Oh ho, the mighty Amazon Queen seeks the help of a lowly male." He bowed, brushing the dusty road with the back of his hand. "How may I be of assistance?"

"I want to meet Lady Hypatia. She teaches in the public forum on Mondays. Would you take me there?"

"If Father gives permission."

"You know he would never do that!" Selene wailed.

"No, I don't. He's indulged you in everything else—tutors, gymnasium-training, attendance at council meetings. I know no other girl your age that has had your experience. Why wouldn't Father allow you to go?"

"Lady Hypatia is a pagan. He might not want it known that his daughter attends lectures by the infamous female philosopher. Please, Nicaeus, help me."

"Poppycock! Lady Hypatia is well regarded by the city fathers and the Church. I won't go behind Father's back. Ask him. If he says yes, I'll accompany you."

"But…"

"I said no."

Selene looked at Antonius. He grinned and shrugged his shoulders. He would not get between her and her brother.

It was true that her father admired the Lady Philosopher of Alexandria. He had attended her lectures, as had most of the men in positions of power in the city and the Church. It was also true her father allowed Selene much freedom in private, but she doubted he would approve such a public departure of decorum. Selene needed a plan to get Hypatia on her side. Once she was accepted as a student, her father would surely give his permission to continue her studies.

The stench of a long-unwashed body assaulted Selene's nose as they rounded a ragged limestone outcrop. She spied a wizened man perched on a pile of rocks. His matted hair hung in clumps like a sheep's fleece. His stick-like limbs sported grotesquely swollen joints that must have cause considerable pain. The man's hooded eyes bored into Selene's with an intensity that sent her cringing against her brother.

"Repent. Let the Lord Jesus enter your heart, for He died upon the cross to deliver us from evil. Give up worldly pursuits and join the One in Grace for He will soon return and rise up the righteous to heaven. Heathens and nonbelievers will be destroyed by fire and suffer the tortures of the damned. Repent. Let the Lord Jesus enter your heart." The holy hermit waved a knurled stick, barely missing their heads.

Antonius knelt before the old man, grabbed Selene's hand, and hauled her down beside him. A rock pierced her knee. "Ouch!" she cried.

Antonius hissed at her to be silent and dug his elbow into her ribs. He addressed the holy man with bowed head. "Holy Father, will you give us your blessing?"

4

Nicaeus knelt by her other side. The old man shrieked more prayers, and then put his hands on their heads for a final blessing. Selene shivered. She hoped he didn't have lice. More and more ascetics left the cities to infest the cave-pocked hills and stony deserts. They fervently believed the Second Coming was imminent and prepared to be uplifted to heaven through fasting and hardship. The general populace revered the hermits, feeling the ascetics' holiness reflected on the city. Selene never understood why the Lord Jesus Christ would require anyone to stop bathing in order to be saved.

The three rose from the ground, Selene rubbing her knee. They bowed to the hermit and then sprinted toward home, scuttling through the western necropolis inhabited by the dead, and those living ascetics who took up residence in the tombs. Selene's family had a fine tomb farther to the south, but they were not here to feast with the ghosts of their ancestors as many did on the anniversary of the deceased's death. Selene hurried, ignoring the sense of loss that crawled up from her stomach to choke her throat anytime she neared the tomb.

She squinted to the east. The sun glared through a haze, promising a hot July day for the new Prefect's investiture. The city's white limestone walls rose slowly from the low-lying Mediterranean shore. Alexandria sat on the westernmost part of the rich Nile delta, sandwiched between the sea on the north and the immense Lake Mareotis on the south. The Great Alexander had chosen this spot for his Egyptian capital because the breezes saved it from the desert's desiccating heat. Selene welcomed the coolness on her fevered skin.

A short distance from the Gate of the Moon, set in the city's west wall, they retrieved a small pack hidden under a rocky shelf. Selene swaddled herself in a long white linen tunic, gray wool cloak and laced leather sandals. She pulled the cloak over her head to hide her dusty hair and give her relief from the sun. She whirled in front of the boys. "Do I look respectable now?"

Nicaeus struggled with his traditional cloak, which was bordered with a narrow band of embroidery proclaiming his status as the son of a councilor. He swore fiercely until Selene took a hand.

"Let me." She settled the wrap in folds across his left shoulder and right hip, around his back, over his head, and down to his right arm, where she wrapped the end so it dangled nearly to his knees. She looked him up and down, then glanced at Antonius adding finishing touches to his own fine cloak. "You'll do. Maybe you should get Antonius to teach you how."

5

"Why should I, when I always have a servant or you around to do it for me?" Nicaeus' grin disappeared, not at Selene's frown, but at the sound of church bells marking the time. "Come. If we're late, Father will tan our hides. He wants to make a good impression on the new Prefect."

Selene sniffed and wrinkled her nose. "We'll make a better impression after we bathe. We have but a short time to go home and make ourselves presentable." The boys followed her lead with no grumbling.

They entered the gate with an ever-increasing crowd, past city guards. The common people came from the countryside to join the public feasting and perhaps pick up a coin or two from the Prefect's coffers or the Patriarch's appointed almsman. The three proceeded onto Canopic Street, the vast main thoroughfare bisecting the city from east to west. The magnificent Church of St. Theonas, sometimes called the church of a thousand pillars, anchored this end of the boulevard, while the Church of St. Metras greeted travelers from the east as they entered the Gate of the Sun. Selene's father had been a boy when St. Theonas had served as the Episcopal residence. The former Patriarch Athanasius needed ready refuge in the necropolis and desert monasteries during his ongoing battles with the Emperor's choice for the Patriarchy. Calistus occasionally spoke of those bloody times with a fierce desire never to see them repeated.

Those dark days seemed long over on such a festal occasion. Flowers wreathed the church in all its glory. Garlands twined about the columns, bright hangings shaded the doors, and streamers waved gaily in the windows. All the buildings along the processional route would be similarly adorned.

Selene glanced down Canopic, assessing the crowds and their chances of making it home on time. Other wide boulevards branched off at regular intervals, leading to spacious homes clustered in residential districts—the sign of a planned city. The wide straight streets were bounded with shaded colonnades. Brightly painted statues towered over squares or peeked from carved niches.

Sharp cries drew Selene's attention. A group of men in rough brown robes, armed with heavy wooden cudgels, emerged from the church and forced their way through the crowd. A woman pulled her children out of their path and drifted off into a side street. Others suddenly found their errands took them in opposite directions, leaving Selene and her companions in the middle of the wide boulevard. The glowering men headed straight for them, brandishing their weapons.

CHAPTER 2

"SELENE!" ANTONIUS YELLED.

When she remained rooted to the spot, he grabbed her arm, sprinted toward the church and yanked her onto the steps. She stumbled against the wide marble slabs, banging her shins, and yelping in pain. "Are you trying to get your head bashed in? Those men are dangerous!"

Antonius' face was pale except for two hectic red spots high on his cheekbones. Was he angry? Frightened? She would have stepped out of the way in another moment. There had been no need for him to treat her so roughly.

She shook off his hands in a pique and reached down to rub her shins. "The only wounds I have sustained today are those you gave me. First you force me to kneel on sharp rocks and crack my rib with your elbow. Now you practically pull my arm out of its socket and cause me to scrape my shins. May the Good Lord save me from your protection!"

"Why, you ungrateful, stubborn, donkey-headed—," Antonius paused, grasping for words, "—child! See if I save your precious hide again. Let your brother do it. That's his job, not mine."

His unkind words stung, because they were close to the mark, but Selene felt wronged by his attack. She yelled back. "I don't need either of you to protect me. I can…"

The shouts of the armed men drowned out her final words. They boiled by the steps, then halted to insult the vastly outnumbered gate guards. One guard, pale face sweating under his helmet, stayed close to his post, looking as if he would bolt for the guardhouse any moment. The second man, older, maintained a cooler head. "It's a feast day, good brothers. I'm sure your patron, the Patriarch, would not like to hear of disturbance by his chosen ones. Go about your business and leave the travelers in peace." The guard's friendly smile and affable manner disarmed the unruly men who, finding no fight, drifted off in another direction.

"Let's go home." Nicaeus grabbed Selene's arm and escorted her firmly down the steps to a side street. Antonius sulked behind.

"Who are those men?" Selene asked her brother. "Where do they come from?"

"They're Patriarch Theophilus' parabolani, his personal body guard. He recruits them from the hospital guild. Only those strong of back and light of purse will work lifting the sick and carrying the dead. The Patriarch offers them good money, and the protection of the church, if they become too zealous."

Selene craned her neck to look back at the parabolani. "I don't see the Patriarch. Why would his bodyguard patrol the streets? That's the city guards' duty."

She observed the two boys exchanging glances over her head. Her anger flared anew. She shook off her brother's hand and stamped her foot. "I'm not a child to be cosseted and protected. What do you know of this?"

Nicaeus sighed. "Patriarch Theophilus is building a private army in the city. Father believes he wants to suppress the Novatian Christians. The council fears riots if he attempts to purge the city of rival Christian sects."

Selene, at first irritated that she had been kept unaware of these developments, sobered. She was not yet born when the Patriarch had suppressed the last public vestige of the pagan cults. After murderous rioting on both sides, he closed the Great Temple of Serapis and reconsecrated it as the new Episcopal residence. Her father said smoke had fouled the air for days as the Christians burned the tens of thousands of books housed in the public library there. When she questioned the tears in his eyes, he said they were irritated and would talk no more about it.

She took him at his word. Her father was a good Christian. Why should he mourn the passing of the last pagan temple?

"The parabolani are most diligent in their policing," Antonius added. "Student friends of mine came home with cracked heads when the Patriarch's men caught them drunk outside a tavern. Their fathers protested the treatment, but the deacons quoted scripture and admonished the men to keep their sons under better control." He rubbed the back of his head as if in sympathy for his friends' pain.

Selene, remembering him complain of a sore head two days ago, asked, "How are your 'friends' doing now?"

Antonius had the decency to blush. "They are on the mend." He looked ahead. "I see no meddling parabolani in our path. We should hurry." He grabbed Selene's elbow and the two boys hurried her toward home. Noting the angle of the sun, she did not protest their haste.

SELENE AND NICAEUS entered their father's home bickering. "Please, Nicaeus, I need longer to prepare. Let me have the baths first?" She looked at her dusty feet, sniffed her armpit, and wailed, "I stink as bad as the holy hermit!"

He seemed to relish her minor tragedy. "I'm sorry, little sister, but I'm older and have precedence. You'll have to wait your turn."

"But there won't be enough time!"

"Remember that the next time you beat me at a race," he teased.

She flounced off to her room with his laughter echoing in the stone halls. Her room was tucked away on the second floor in a warren of small private bedrooms. She opened the door, threw herself on the bed, and planned a number of petty revenges on her selfish brother. Perhaps a purgative in his soup? A knock at the bottom of her door interrupted her plotting.

"Enter!"

Rebecca, her personal servant, backed through with a basket of clothes balanced on her head and a pitcher of water in her arms. Although but two years older than Selene, Rebecca had the composure and easy confidence of a much older woman. She had been Selene's primary teacher in how to run the household. Selene jumped to help, taking the pitcher and placing it on a small table next to a wash bowl and sponge.

"Rebecca, you are an angel in disguise. Whatever would I do without you?"

Rebecca looked at her disheveled state and pursed her full lips in a moue of distaste. "We haven't much time to get you decent, Mistress. First we wash off that dust, next arrange your hair, and then fresh robes." She grabbed Selene's hands and clucked over the bitten nails. "I don't know if we can soak out that grime, but I can at least smooth those ragged edges."

Selene stripped and kicked her dirty garments to a corner, while Rebecca poured warm water into the wash bowl and laid a thick reed mat on the stone floor. Selene closed her eyes and sighed as Rebecca gently sponged the dust away, wrapped her in a linen towel, and started to comb her tangled hair. "Rebecca, what's the gossip about our new Prefect?"

"My friends say their masters are apprehensive. He is unknown. They speculate on whom he will support in the disputes among the Christians, much less the other factions. He is also unmarried. There is much talk about which of the local maidens might be a suitable match." She stopped to separate a particularly bad tangle. "Selene, what do you do to your hair, let birds make nests in it?"

"Ouch! If you can't be more careful, I'll comb my own hair." Selene reached up to grab the tortoise shell comb from Rebecca. The servant girl slapped her hands away.

Rebecca took a blue glass bottle from a pouch tied to her belt and poured the contents into a shallow bowl. "Here. If you need something to do with your hands, soak them in this oil."

Selene obediently put her fingertips in the bowl. The oil smelled faintly of roses. "Where was the Prefect posted before Alexandria?"

Rebecca finished combing and started to smooth Selene's nails with a flexible piece of horn. "He served in the army, but left to take provincial posts. For the past several years, he served in the Emperor's court under the sponsorship of Anthemius, the Regent."

"I suppose he worships Mithras, like most of the army?" Selene dried her hands on the linen towel and dropped it to the floor.

Rebecca shrugged. "Come, Mistress, time grows short. Let me see what I can do with your hair."

"Something simple, Rebecca, I don't want to be pushing curls off my face all day. If I had my way, I'd cut it short like the holy women."

Rebecca gasped. "Cut your hair? Oh, no, Mistress! It's so beautiful." She pulled the hair back from Selene's face, secured it with bone pins, then twisted it into a compact bun. Silver combs held it in place. Rebecca teased two small tendrils into curling in front of Selene's ears, then handed her a polished silver mirror. "Here, this is a simple style."

Selene looked at herself critically. "Nicely done. Go as lightly on the cosmetics and I will be most satisfied."

Rebecca smoothed lotion on Selene's face and neck. "You really should stay out of the sun. You're scandalously brown. Before you know it, your skin will look like cracked boots."

"I like being scandalous. Besides, powder should make me suitably pale."

Rebecca applied a light dusting of powder and shaped Selene's eyes with kohl. A thin red paste for the lips finished the picture.

Rebecca laid out her clothes: a long-sleeved, full-length linen undergarment to be covered by a lightweight, cream-colored wool dalmatica. The voluminous garment was cut in the simple style of the day: a wide, straight sheath for the body with generous sleeves that came to the wrist. This one had green and blue embroidered strips depicting fanciful sea creatures bordering the sleeves and appliquéd from both shoulders to the hem. The crowning touch: a filmy blue-green silk wrap for shoulders and hair. Rebecca draped Selene in her various layers and stood back to judge the effect.

Selene fussed with the swaths of material belted with a silk cord under her budding breasts.

"Stop trying to improve on perfection, Mistress. The stripes are aligned." Rebecca settled the silk wrap in wispy folds over Selene's hair and shoulders.

"With all this cloth, I feel like I'm wearing a merchant's tent," Selene complained.

Rebecca smiled, showing small, irregular teeth. "Would you wear less and be taken for an actress or acrobat, men vying for your favors?"

Selene blushed at the thought, mumbling, "At least they're comfortable."

"The tent looks quite elegant with your height."

Selene took a second look in the mirror. "Now for the jewelry and I'll be ready to greet the new Prefect…as if he will see me in the crowd." She put on the heavy silver bracelets and faience earrings, which had been her mother's, bringing back bittersweet memories.

Rebecca nodded approval. "You look much older than your fourteen years."

Selene preened. Since she had the responsibilities of the household, she could at least be treated as an adult.

"There's one thing missing," Rebecca added.

"What? I'm wrapped, draped, and pomaded. What more can you do to me?"

Rebecca opened a carved cedar chest sitting under a narrow window and pulled out a pair of clean sandals. The blue leather enclosed the toe and heel, leaving the arch free. "We can't have you padding about the city barefoot like a beggar."

"Of course not." Selene giggled and sat on the bed so Rebecca could lace the sandals. There was another knock at the door. "Yes?"

"It's Nicaeus. Father waits. Are you ready?"

Selene's heart quickened. She glanced at Rebecca, who nodded. "I'll be right out."

Selene strode across the room, then moderated her gait to the feminine glide her friend Honoria had worked so hard to teach her. The astonished look on her brother's face was worth all the fussing. She kept a serene mask as she took his proffered arm and they descended the stairs.

Their father waited in the vestibule. Calistus was of unremarkable height, with the stooped shoulders and small rounded belly of a man who spent more time at his books than in the gymnasium. Today the full regalia of a city councilor disguised his physical imperfections: full length white tunic, topped with a voluminous toga bordered with the thin purple stripe denoting his class. He wore rings and medals, denoting his various civic offices and honors, and carried a mahogany staff capped with gold.

Selene's heart swelled as he smiled at her, his eyes lighting with joy and his face creasing with laugh lines.

"I see you both will do me proud today. Let's be on our way."

They exited onto a broad residential street and proceeded toward the agora. The streets in their quarter filled with families of distinction—councilors, lawyers, rich merchants—making their way east. As they approached the agora, the crowds became more varied with churchmen, sailors, shop owners, apprentices, teachers, beggars, and pilgrims all heading in the same general direction. Wine shops and fruit merchants did a brisk business. Other enterprising men and women hawked baskets of dark brown rolls, flat bread, and grilled meat and onions on a skewer.

The smell of cooked onions and garlic vied with that of unwashed bodies and urine. The workers who cleaned and stocked the public privies seemed unable to keep up with the crowd. Or possibly many people, unwilling or unable to pay the small coin for use of the privies, relieved themselves where they willed. Selene wished she had brought a perfumed cloth to hold to her nose as they passed one particularly noisome alley.

She stopped to look over some vases showing the profile of the boy-emperor Theodosius II on one side and, purportedly, the new Augustal Prefect on the other. Other merchants sold bronze coins, plates, glass beads, goblets, and all manner of wares adorned with the stylized faces of the emperor and the prefect. Her father called to her and Selene hurried along, not wanting to lose him in the crowd.

The street emptied into the spacious open square where Canopic Street met the equally wide north-south street of Sema. Porticoes and public buildings surrounded the vast agora. Wooden stands, erected at one end, held city officials and offered a platform for the speeches. A freestanding monumental arch stood opposite the podium through which the procession would arrive. Selene could feel the crowd's excitement heighten. Her own pulse raced.

Her father took her arm and pointed toward the wooden stands. "We'll be over there." The three picked their way through the crowd towards their designated spot. Calistus sat with the other city councilors in a place of honor on the platform. Selene and Nicaeus stood with the councilors' families on the steps of the law courts, above, and a little to the right of their father.

From that height, Selene could make some order of the crowd below. She spied Lady Hypatia, made conspicuous by her gender, sitting among the city nobles. The Patriarch Theophilus and his immediate staff occupied a dozen of the seats. The tall man in full army uniform must be the Egyptian dux Abundantius. The Jewish council of elders completed the platform contingent. Behind this first rank, families and staff ranged up the steps, each in the place designated for them by religion, birth, age, and profession.

"Can you see anything yet?" Selene asked her brother.

The sun was just past its zenith. Nicaeus shaded his eyes with one hand while looking eastward along the boulevard. "Nothing yet. We'll probably hear it before we see anything."

"I suspect it will be an hour or more before the procession makes it to the agora," a deep voice said behind Selene. She turned and looked into the bearded face of a man with brown eyes and black hair, much like her own. His lips turned up in a smile. Selene put a hand to her mouth, then gasped, "Phillip!" She greeted her oldest brother with a leap into his arms. Phillip grabbed Selene in a bear hug, then put her down with a grunt. "My baby sister isn't such a baby anymore." He looked her up and down with a wistful smile. "In fact, you've grown into quite a lady."

"Phillip! It's been three years! You've grown a beard. Why did no one tell me you were coming? When did you get home? What was the court like? You must tell me all about Constantinople! Does Father know you're home?"

At the mention of Calistus, a shadow passed over Phillip's face. "Father doesn't know I'm back. I decided not to finish my law studies, and had the good fortune to travel home with Orestes and his escort. We took the overland route and became great friends on the journey."

"Orestes?" Nicaeus blurted. "Our new Augustal Prefect? You're friends?"

"Close your mouth, brother, or you'll catch flies. Yes, the new Prefect and I are quite good friends." The next hour passed quickly as Phillip regaled his small but attentive audience with the exploits of his fellow law students, the wonders of the royal court, and his adventures traveling with Orestes.

Selene's breath came quick as Phillip described a narrow escape on the trip. "We chased the bandits into a blind canyon where they fought for their lives. Just as I thought they were finished, the leader…" Phillip's words were drowned by the blare of a hundred trumpets playing a fanfare. They all looked up in surprise. "I'll finish the story later."

Selene's deep disappointment at the interruption of the story must have shown, because Phillip chucked her under the chin and said, "Don't worry, little sister. I lived." She punched him in the ribs and turned to watch the procession.

It took the better part of another hour for the whole parade to wend its way into the agora. First units of soldiers from the garrison at Nicopolis, followed by all manner of conveyances fantastically decorated by the city's guilds and youth groups. Most were wagons decorated with flowers and streamers, containing people acting scenes from the Bible relating to their professions. The shipbuilders provided Noah and the Ark with several real animals. The bakers chose the Sermon on the Mount and tossed free bread to the crowd, to the disgust of the food vendors.

Selene gasped when a lovely painted plaster statue of what seemed to be the Virgin Mary was revealed to be the goddess Athena. Several pagan students from the association that provided it accompanied the statue. They marched in silent defiance when they entered the agora, then broke into a hymn of praise to the goddess in front of the platform. The Patriarch rose and pointed a staff at the students, as if to strike them down. "The laws are clear forbidding public worship of idols. Stop this abomination at once!"

Immediately a pack of parabolani attacked the students with clubs. The students fought fiercely in defense of their goddess, kicking and punching their attackers, but were no match against beefy men with cudgels. Selene heard the sickening crack of wood on bone and shrieks of pain that turned to shouts of anger as the parabolani broke through to topple the statue. It shattered into a thousand pieces and a cloud of dust. The troops from Nicopolis drove a wedge-shaped formation through the melee and started separating the combatants by hauling them to opposite sides of the agora.

The soldiers' quick action forestalled others from joining the fray, but the mood of the moment turned sour. The crowd milled and muttered on the edge of violence. Suspicious glances, and not a few provocative remarks, flew from group to group. Selene's heart fluttered in fear. Phillip pulled her close and looked around, as if scouting for an escape route. Nicaeus blocked her view as he moved in front to protect her, but she heard a commanding female voice cut through the mutters of the crowd.

"Peace, my friends and fellow citizens. Let us not spoil this celebration by committing bloodshed over the foolishness of a few youths. We are here in fellowship to welcome our new governor. It would be a poor welcome indeed if he met with riot and disorder on his first day. My friend Patriarch Theophilus will join me in this plea for peace; will you not, Good Father?"

Selene peeked around Nicaeus to see Hypatia holding out a hand to the angry Patriarch. A few ragged cheers started on the edge of the crowd. "Heed Hypatia. Peace for the Prefect."

Theophilus spread his arms to address the crowd.

CHAPTER 3

ORESTES, AUGUSTAL PREFECT and Governor of all Egypt, chafed at the slow pace of the procession. He made a striking figure, his military bearing belying his civilian purple and white ceremonial robes. Orestes had toiled for years in provincial towns to reach this appointment. This would be the culmination of his career. If he were successful, the rewards would be substantial, both in terms of power and esteem. The Praetorian Prefect and Regent Anthemius, his patron at the court, had warned him this appointment would be a difficult one. The city had been quiet for several years, but had a reputation for riot and disputation with imperial authority, particularly as the Patriarch grew in power.

Orestes nodded and waved from his burnished chariot, handling the four white mares himself. An aide stood at the back, tossing coins to the tightly packed crowd; more coins in this poorer section of the city close to the walls, fewer as they neared the agora where the more privileged awaited him. Orestes would have dispensed with the whole celebration, if he had a choice, but the fractious people of Alexandria did not give him one.

His good friend Abundantius, posted here for several years as the Egyptian military commander, made it clear what the people of the city expected. "One of my predecessors had to accompany a new Patriarch into the city to protect him after he had been tossed out," he had told Orestes. "The good father was humble and most holy, but he was the Emperor's man, not theirs. The new Patriarch came into the city with little fanfare and compounded his error by shortening the investiture ceremony. The good citizens of Alexandria drove him out of the city until he did it right. 'Right' meant a full procession with troops, clergy, and—most important of all—a feast day for the city."

Orestes laughed at the story, but took Abundantius' point. Alexandria was the third largest city in the Empire and the major supplier of grain for Constantinople as well as the army. Peace in the Empire depended on bread from Egypt. Peace in Alexandria depended on a shrewd mind, an adept hand at the helm, and a lavish welcome complete with free food and drink.

Orestes watched closely the faces of the people he had been sent to govern. They changed dramatically as he approached the agora, from the dark pinched countenances of the Egyptian peasants flooding the city, looking for work, to the olive-toned descendants of Greek and Roman conquerors. The crowd had a fair sprinkling of black Nubians and an occasional startling blond barbarian, both usually towering over the people of this region. Alexandria was a crossroads for trade and pilgrims. People from all over the Empire, and beyond, traveled its streets and did business in its shops and offices.

Orestes sensed a change in the crowd's mood as he approached the agora. They looked uncertain, muttering and straining to hear voices trickling from the open space in front of the triumphal arch. He motioned to the decurion of the mounted escort Abundantius had provided. The grizzled man approached, horse skittering from the chariot wheels.

The soldier snapped a salute. "Can I be of service, Sir?"

"Do you know what is going on?"

"No, Sir, there's been no word."

"Then carry on, but prepare your unit for trouble."

"Yes, Sir!" The decurion rode from mount to mount giving orders and watching the crowd carefully.

Battle senses alert, Orestes rode into the vast square. He saw several people cleaning a pile of rubble from in front of the viewing stand. A diminutive woman in scholar's white, and a frail man in full Bishop's regalia, harangued the crowd. He immediately recognized the famous Lady Philosopher Hypatia and Patriarch Theophilus. Whatever the problem, they had it under control.

The crowd roared his name. The roar devolved into a chant: "Orestes. Blessed be your name. Just be your rule." The chant continued as he circled the agora, descended from the chariot and ascended the steps to the podium. His escort took positions ringing the platform. He raised his arms for silence. The crowd gave one final roar and quieted in expectation of the speeches.

Orestes sat on a cushioned chair left conspicuously vacant. He faced a tedious afternoon and was pleased to see the dignitaries well served with food and wine. Numerous scribes stood ready to record the speeches. Copies would be posted throughout the city tomorrow. A sailcloth canopy gave some relief from the sun, but Orestes soon felt sweat trickling down his back to be absorbed by his wool tunic. He resisted the urge to doff his full toga.

The Patriarch took the podium first. He welcomed Orestes to the city, then conducted a lengthy prayer and homily admonishing him to do God's work. A number of nobles, councilors and elders followed Theophilus, each expressing their gratitude to the Emperor for sending such a wise and just man to rule over them. One by one they pledged their undying support. After three hours, Orestes asked a servant to escort him to the facilities and excused himself to visit the private privy built under the reviewing stand for the comfort of the dignitaries.

He returned in time to see Lady Hypatia take the podium. She nodded as he seated himself, and launched into her speech. He listened with interest, never having heard a woman speak in a public forum. Her intense form and commanding voice seemed to cast a spell over the crowd. They had been shuffling noisily and talking among themselves, but now they quieted, occasionally laughing at an amusing story or punctuating her speech with shouts of agreement. Anthemius had recommended Orestes seek the Lady Philosopher's advice and now he understood why. Hypatia seemed to have astute insight into the history and workings of the city.

The rhythms of her speech kept him enthralled until the use of his name startled him. "Orestes, I ask you to lead the city well. Remember, a leader is best when the people feel a firm hand helping them along the road, not when they feel a heavy foot upon their necks. Beware of false obedience and acclaim. Listen more than you speak. Honor the people and they will honor you. When your work is done and your aim fulfilled, the people should say, 'We built this,' and honor you for letting them. Welcome to our fair city, Orestes. May you—and we—prosper."

Hypatia bowed to Orestes as the crowd started chanting his name. It was his turn to take the podium and greet the people. He straightened his shoulders and strode to the lectern with his head held high. The chanting filled his chest with pride until he remembered Hypatia's words on false acclaim. These people knew nothing of him except that he represented the Emperor. He would have to prove himself worthy of their regard, as he had with his army commands, through hard work and wise decisions. He felt a momentary hesitation, then let it pass.

"My fellow citizens," he began in slightly accented Greek, "I greet you on behalf of the Most Pious and Beloved Emperor Theodosius II. In this, the fourth year of his reign, the Roman Emperor of the East extends to you his blessings and assures you of his love and justice." Orestes continued in the same vein, as customary, acknowledging the warm welcome and elaborately praising the city and its people. "The Emperor knows of the great work you do here in Egypt, laboring to feed the Empire…" There were a few mutters and dark looks, so he hastened onto another topic. "In appreciation, the Emperor has increased the bread dole by one-half portion for three months."

The crowd roared its approval, stamping their feet and clapping loudly while calling his name. When they quieted, he continued. "The Emperor provides a thousand head of cattle for your feasts." More cheers rippled through the crowd as the word spread beyond his voice.

Orestes noted the lowering sun, the restive condition of the crowd, and concluded, "In light of the advice given me by the wise Lady Hypatia to listen more than speak, I'll conclude by saying it is an honor to serve my Emperor in this fairest of all cities. Enjoy this feast day, good citizens, and may God bless us all."

The crowd indulged in one more round of chanting before dispersing to the various celebrations sponsored by the city, professional guilds, and the church. Orestes, girding himself for a long night of banquets in his honor, turned to the city and church elders, and surrendered to his fate.

"WHICH GROUP IS THIS?" Orestes asked Abundantius as they ascended the stairs to their third reception. The dux had volunteered to escort his old friend around the city and make sure Orestes got to the Prefect's mansion in time to bathe before starting his duties early the next morning.

"The city councilors."

"How many?"

"Only about thirty…with their families."

Orestes groaned. "I'm getting too old for this. My shoulder is bruised from so many vigorous salutations, my ears numb from the incessant requests for an audience, and my face will likely crack if I have to smile one more time." He ran his hand through his close-cropped auburn hair. "I would rather march thirty miles, in full pack, cross-country, than spend another day such as this."

Abundantius roared and pounded Orestes on his reportedly sore shoulder. "You're the one who gave up military life for civil service, my friend. Now you must live with it. Come, the councilors wait."

The City Council building housed the banquet. They ascended the marble steps, past a row of columns, into a massive hall. Internal columns held up a vaulted ceiling, painted deep blue, with the twelve constellations depicted in gold leaf. Painted plaster walls gave the illusion of looking out into a formal garden. About seventy temporary couches lined the walls, many accommodating two or three occupants. A leather couch strewn with red and purple silk cushions was reserved for him to the right of the entrance.

Orestes took his place and waved off the servants bringing food, although he did accept a goblet of cold white wine. The councilors approached him one by one, according to rank and seniority. Abundantius introduced each and provided amusing stories about some as they left earshot.

"This next one is a solid fellow," Abundantius said in low tones. "Honest. Has a good head on his shoulders and is well respected by his colleagues."

Orestes looked up. A familiar face grinned at him behind a dignified old councilor's shoulder. "Phillip! Is this your family?"

Phillip bowed low. "Yes, Honored Prefect. This is my father Calistus, my brother Nicaeus, and my sister Selene."

Orestes clasped Calistus' arm. "Well met, Sir. Your son has told me much about you. I look forward to knowing you and your family better." The younger brother stepped forward with a bow. "Nicaeus, is it? I hope you've been staying away from the green melons."

"Yes, Sir." The lad blushed to the tips of his ears and glowered at his brother.

Orestes' eyes widened at the sight of Selene. Taller than most women by half a head, she had strong features: sweeping eyebrows, a nose a bit too long, and a generous mouth. Not daintily pretty, but handsome in a way that lasts well into old age. "Phillip, this lovely young lady surely cannot be the madcap child with skinned knees you told me of?"

Selene curtsied low and flashed a smile as he offered his hand to help her rise. "I see my brother has been most generous with his stories. You must not believe everything he says, Lord Prefect. He is a most notorious teller of tales.

He honed his gift through the study of law."

"Ouch!" Phillip mimed pulling a knife from his heart.

Calistus frowned at his oldest son and said, in frosty tones, "You must forgive my unruly children, Sir. Although it might not be in evidence, they were taught how to behave on formal occasions." All three offspring lost their smiles at their father's rebuke. Phillip's face settled into careful neutrality, only the tightness about the mouth betraying tensions between father and son.

Orestes pushed away unwanted memories of his own stern father and said with a smile, "They are a pleasure, good Calistus. In a long day of ceremony, levity with friends is welcome. And Phillip proved himself a most worthy friend on the journey."

Calistus' countenance softened at the praise for his son. "I'm pleased Phillip was of service to you."

"I hope you will be of service, as well. I wish to consult with you on a number of matters."

"At your convenience, Sir." Calistus bowed.

As the family retreated to their couches, and before another could approach, Orestes mused, "Phillip proved himself a most capable and resourceful fellow on our journey. I believe I have a special appointment for him."

Abundantius raised a goblet. "What? When?"

"That depends on the next few days. I have much more to learn before I can tell what tasks to set him. But I will need people I can trust in sensitive positions." Orestes raised a glass of wine. "We'll see what opportunities present themselves."

AFTER RETURNING THE JEWELRY and fine clothes to their chests, Rebecca cleaned the cosmetics from Selene's face and combed her hair. "What is the new Prefect like, Mistress?"

"He's magnificent, Rebecca! When my gaze met his, I had trouble breathing. My heart fluttered; I thought it would stop. His eyes are clear green, like gems on an expensive ring. They seemed to see into my very soul." She sighed dramatically. "He's a full head taller than Phillip, with hair that shines like gold streaked with copper. He held my hand." She cradled her right hand against her chest. "Where he touched me, my skin yet burns."

"Perhaps cold water would relieve the discomfort." Rebecca combed the curls out of Selene's hair.

Selene laughed. "To soothe my hand or douse my dreams?"

"It is not my place to douse your dreams, Mistress. I caution you not to lose your heart at first glance. How old is the Prefect?"

"Younger than Father and older than Phillip. He's not decrepit, if that is what you're hinting."

"No. I find it strange that a man in the prime of life, and in such a powerful position, has never married. Surely there were opportunities for an advantageous match over the years?" Rebecca pulled the loose hair back and quickly braided it to keep it from tangling during the night. "Is there anything else you require before you retire, Mistress?"

"No, Rebecca. Wake me in the morning, no later than the third hour."

"As you wish, Mistress."

Selene turned Rebecca's words over in her mind as the servant girl exited. It was indeed strange for a man of Orestes' position to be unmarried. Perhaps he had made a vow to the church or had lost a true love. Or maybe he preferred boys.

What was this unwanted feeling Orestes stirred in her? How could she find out the truth about him? What difference would it make, if he were unavailable? Why was she thinking such things when that morning she vowed she would remain unmarried? The thought shook Selene out of her romantic reverie.

A sudden restlessness took over her body. Selene picked up the small alabaster oil lamp Rebecca had left burning on her cosmetics table, and left her room. She didn't know where she was going until she found herself before Phillip's door. Light spilled across the threshold. Selene knocked timidly with her foot. "Phillip, are you still awake?"

She heard a groan and a faint, "Come in." Her brother lay face down on his bed, a male slave massaging his body. Lamp light rippled off corded muscles and flowed across brown skin. A faint scar ran up his backbone from his waist to mid-back. As a boy he had fallen from a wall, scraping his back raw. One of Selene's first memories as a toddler was of their mother soothing her brother's pain with a poultice of wet leaves that smelled of mint. Tears stung her eyes. She missed those simpler days, before her mother died and her older brother went to finish his education at the capitol. Phillip turned his bearded face toward her. There were dark circles under his eyes. "What is it, Selene?"

She collapsed on a bench against the wall, scrubbing her face with both hands. "Nothing. I'm tired, is all. You look exhausted as well. I'll not keep you up." She rose from the bench to leave.

"No, don't go." He reached out to stay her. Selene gave a significant glance at the slave putting away the oil. Phillip nodded. Most people treated servants like pieces of furniture, but Selene knew how the silent shadows gossiped in the kitchens and the marketplace. They provided much information to her.

"Marcus, you may go now. Attend me in the morning," Phillip commanded. The slave bowed as he left the room. Phillip sat up, wrapping a linen sheet around his middle. "Now, little sister, what can I do for you?"

"Hold me a while." She sat beside him on his bed and nestled into his side, his arms snuggling her close. They sat quietly. Selene's breathing slowed and her eyes drooped. A sudden shift of her brother's body brought her out of a half doze.

"You're too old for this type of cuddling, little sister, and I'm too tired." Phillip stifled a yawn.

"I know. I came by to see if the servants had cared for you properly and..." she hesitated.

"And to see if I might arrange for you to see Orestes again?"

"I came for no such thing!" Selene exploded off the bed, her recent lethargy forgotten in a surge of pique.

Her brother laughed. "I'm not blind. I saw how you looked at our Prefect all during his appearance."

"I did not!"

"Yes, you did."

She stamped her foot and turned her back on him. He stood and took her by the shoulders, turning her around. "Orestes is a good man, Selene, but he's not the one for you."

"I don't want him! I didn't...I don't want any man. At least not for a long time. I...he just..." Her words stumbled to a stop. She stood in her brother's arms, trembling.

"He what?"

"He makes me feel strange—like I've never felt before. I can't talk around him; I have trouble breathing, my ears ring. I feel so...so...stupid! Maybe he's bewitched me."

Phillip laughed, hugged her briefly, and then stepped back, holding her at arm's length. "You've been spending too much time with the servants, picking up their superstitious ways. You're fourteen. It's natural you would be attracted to a man, especially one as handsome and powerful as Orestes. Don't worry, little sister, you'll get over it. Things will be better in the morning."

He turned her around and gave her a little shove toward the door. As she left, she stuck her head back in. "Promise?"

"Promise."

"Phillip?"

"Will you leave and let me go to sleep?"

"It's good to have you home again." She ducked out before she heard his reply. Content, she would sleep now and leave the mystery of the Prefect for another day.

CHAPTER 4

O RESTES WOKE JUST BEFORE SUNRISE. He always did, no matter how little sleep he had the night before. When on active patrol, he used this predawn time to walk the camp perimeter, check on troop readiness and have a quiet word with the foot soldiers. In his administrative roles, he used this precious private time to exercise and prepare for the day.

He rolled over in bed, sat up, and groaned, slightly disoriented by unfamiliar surroundings. The night before, Orestes poured as much drink into potted plants as he had consumed at the banquets, but still his head ached. Abundantius, less circumspect, had consumed all the fine wine the good city fathers presented. Orestes rubbed his cropped head ruefully. His friend had always been able to drink and be cheerfully free of ill effects the next morning.

Orestes shook the cobwebs from his mind and surveyed his sumptuous room with a frown. The profusion of bright silk hangings, lustrous gilded wood, and painted statuary offended his ascetic tastes. He should have known the Alexandrian Prefect's quarters would reflect the Oriental splendor of the Constantinople court. A wealthy benefactor had willed the estate to the Emperor after the destruction of the Ptolemaic palace district during Diocletian's reign.

The mansion, situated south of the agora, crowned a low rise of limestone built up into an artificial hill. From the loggia, one could look over the whole city, yet have easy access to the governmental and commercial heart directly north. Orestes' suite of rooms looked out onto a central garden of neatly clipped bushes and banks of flowers. His personal quarters took up the top floor of the entire east wing.

As Orestes stood, a muscle spasmed in his back. His in-drawn breath hissed as he bent halfway over, hand on a gilded chair. The servant who'd seen him to bed a scant two hours before had informed him a slave had been assigned to see to his personal needs. "Demetrius!" he shouted.

The slave, a compact man of uncertain middle age and probable Greek heritage, entered immediately and rushed to Orestes' side. "Master, what is wrong? Should I call a physician?"

Orestes waved him off. "No. My head is the worse for the celebrations and my back rebels against this soft life." He rubbed both hands on his lower back as he straightened, and surveyed the room. "Get rid of that nest of cushions masquerading as a bed. I require a platform of cedar, built to half again my length and my arm span wide. Have a mattress made with close woven cotton and stuffed with something solid—straw or feathers, not down."

He made a sweeping gesture with his right hand. "Remove all statues, except three of the smallest; all chests and tables, except the largest; and that chair." Orestes pointed to an ugly throne-like affair sitting on a raised platform against a wall.

Demetrius bowed. "At once, Master."

"It can wait a little," Orestes replied in an ironic tone.

Demetrius discreetly cleared his throat.

"Yes, man. Speak up."

"Would the Prefect care to be shown the mansion? The steward awaits your pleasure."

Orestes groaned at the prospect of another round of introductions and insistent importunities. "The Prefect wishes a tour of the baths and a massage before facing the steward."

The one luxury he did approve of in his new home was the gymnasium and baths. All upper class homes had running water, and most had baths, but the majority of the populace frequented public facilities, hundreds of which dotted the city. The more luxurious baths charged fees and were frequented by the city elite.

Demetrius led Orestes through the colonnaded outside passage, past several carved mahogany doors, to a narrow staircase in the rear of the complex. Orestes felt the humidity increasing as they descended to a chamber with vaulted ceilings. An exercise pool stretched before him. His footsteps echoed off the stone floor with a wet slapping sound. Two slaves stood at attention beside a bench piled high with thick towels.

Demetrius pointed to a series of doors on the left. "This way we have the cold, warm, and hot rooms, all furnished with pools, benches and tables. The attendants are skilled in all the usual services: massage, barbering, hairdressing, skin waxing."

"Is there an exercise yard?"

"Through that door at the end of the room. There is a full complement of weapons and a weapons master could be employed if you wish, Master. The guards use the yard for practice when the Prefect is not in residence."

"Good. Arrange for the best wrestler to work out with me in the mornings. Once a week I'll want a swords master to attend me. My custom is to arise before dawn, exercise, and bathe before attending the office."

"Might I suggest the Prefect plan to attend the public baths on occasion? Much important city business is conducted as the city fathers take their ease."

Orestes rubbed the bridge of his nose. He intended to add frequent trips to the public baths to his schedule. The imperial court had been much the same. "That is sound advice. When is the most auspicious time of day to arrive at the baths?"

"After the afternoon council session and before the evening meal."

"I'll enjoy my own facilities this one day." Orestes surveyed the beckoning rooms then started for the one with steam pouring from under the door. "I'll soak in the hot pool, have my massage, and finish in the frigidarium." He snapped his fingers at the body slaves. "Attend me."

ORESTES LAY ON A MARBLE TABLE draped with a warm towel of soft combed linen. The material felt silky against his skin. A slave pummeled his sore muscles, kneaded sweet-smelling oil into his skin, and scraped off the oil and sweat with a strigil, a small curved knife. Orestes caught a whiff of wintergreen under the heavier scent of sandalwood.

Demetrius stood against the wall, an unobtrusive shadow, sparking Orestes' curiosity. "How came you to this state of servitude, Demetrius?" Orestes asked.

A blank mask settled over the slave's face. "It's a common enough tale. My widowed father drank heavily and ran up debts against his shipping business. A run of bad weather and spoiled cargo ruined us. My sister and I were seized and sold into slavery to pay the debts. My father died shortly after of a wasting disease of the liver."

"And your sister?"

Small lines of bitterness puckered the corners of Demetrius' mouth as he replied in a low, flat voice, "She was put to work in a brothel. She died a year later in childbirth, as did the babe."

"I see. No patron? No business associate of your father's to look after you two?"

The slave stiffly shook his head. "His business associates pressed the magistrate for our enslavement."

"And what path were your feet set upon before this tragedy?"

"I was a student of history and languages. The former for my pleasure. The latter to be useful to my father in his business."

Orestes had observed Demetrius during the morning, carefully testing his abilities as a body servant and his knowledge of the estate. His tone toward his master was always deferential, his advice well considered. Demetrius took no notes, but made quiet requests of waiting servants. The others accorded the slave a level of respect not usually offered to one of his rank. Orestes did not doubt his every wish would be dealt with efficiently and to his satisfaction, but hoped Demetrius might prove of higher worth in another capacity.

"Based on your study of history, what do you recommend I do first as Prefect?"

Demetrius blanched and bowed his head. "I would not presume to advise you, Master."

"Come, man," Orestes said. "You have already given me excellent advice. I am new to this city and require people I can trust to give me assistance."

"I'm a slave."

"Precisely. As a slave, you go places I cannot. You hear things I do not. You do not have the same interests as the nobles or councilmen who try to influence me. I need someone to balance their views."

"My first advice is to take your time finding advisors. You know nothing of me. You do not know if I am wise or trustworthy."

"By your very words, you prove both." Orestes smiled. "Most men would cut off a finger to be a privy advisor to the Prefect. What else would you advise?"

Demetrius squared his shoulders. "A close relationship with Patriarch Theophilus. He is the spiritual leader of this city, and most influential. You can do little without his approval. Hypatia, the Lady Philosopher, is also an able advisor. Her wisdom has guided several of the Prefects, although the last gave her words little heed."

Orestes sat up as the body slave toweled off the remaining oil. "Any others?"

"Many to be wary of, a few to listen to." Demetrius frowned in concentration. "I will make a list for your perusal. I also advise a tour of the province and as many public appearances as you can. The people need to know their governor and feel they can appeal to you."

"My private life will become the stuff of gossips and dinner conversation."

"As it would anyway. Your history is already making the rounds of the salons, Master. If the gossips do not get something new to talk about soon, they will make up their own stories."

"Very well." Orestes dropped his feet to the floor. "Let's go to the frigidarium. A cold dip should be the thing to prepare me for the day."

"At your pleasure, Master." Demetrius bowed low.

LATER, AFTER DISAPPOINTING THE HAIRDRESSER ("I've worn short hair all my life"), the barber ("I know beards are fashionable, but I like to be clean shaven") and the cook ("Water to drink in the morning, bread and soup at midday, simple fare for dinner"), Orestes retired to his office.

On the way, Demetrius commented softly, "The staff is most eager to serve you in any way, Master. They feel your refusal to use their services is a reflection on their abilities."

"You mean they fear they will be dismissed."

Demetrius shrugged. "If the Prefect has no need for a service, it is logical to conclude the Prefect has no need for the servant."

"I have no time or inclination to indulge in the elaborate rituals of a nobleman. However, I will be entertaining many local and foreign guests, who will require the services of a skilled staff. The cook will yet get to dazzle me with his art." Orestes rubbed his smooth-shaven jaw. "Arrange for suitable gifts to be distributed to the staff in honor of my arrival, and assure them of their positions."

"Yes, Master." As they approached a mahogany door, Demetrius informed him, "Isidore, the steward, awaits you in your office."

One corner of Orestes' mouth quirked upward. "The first in a long line of appointments, I suppose. I hope it is an auspicious one."

They entered the room, Orestes in the lead. An officious little man, whose thin beard failed to cover the blemishes from a past disease, rose to greet them. The man's sallow skin was not enhanced by the garish yellow-orange of his robes. "I hope everything is to your satisfaction, Augustal Prefect." Isidore minced forward, hands fluttering. "Would you care to inspect the grounds now?"

"I've seen what I want of the estate. I've left instructions with Demetrius for ordering my quarters and my schedule. Give him all due assistance."

Startled, Isidore cast a suspicious glance toward Demetrius. "Your Excellency will need assistants. I've taken the liberty of recommending three young men for the position of personal secretary. They come from the best families and await your pleasure, Sir."

Orestes put on a polite smile. Isidore might be overly efficient and trying to please the new Prefect, but more likely he was taking gifts from the fathers or patrons of the young men. Many would give good money to know what business the Prefect conducted in private, what decrees would be made...and when. "Thank you, good Isidore. As I am new to this city, I would not give offence by elevating one family above another by taking a son into my employ."

Isidore hid his disappointment with a bow. "As you wish, Excellency. Should I seek others more to your liking?"

Orestes turned to his body servant. "Demetrius, you read and write, do you not?"

"Yes, Master. I speak, read and write Greek and Latin. I also speak the local Egyptian dialect fluently and know some Hebrew."

Isidore's head bobbed. His eyes grew round with consternation. "But..."

"Good." Orestes interrupted. "Until I can better assess my situation and choose for myself, Demetrius will be my personal secretary." He ushered the steward out of the office with a firm hand on his back. "Thank you again, Isidore. I expect regular reports from you on the running of the household. I would see the accounts tomorrow, and once a quarter thereafter."

After the door shut on the outraged Isidore, Orestes surveyed his office. This room was more to his liking. It had a functional lived-in look, though still ornate. A massive table with legs carved in the shapes of fish dominated the room. Orestes' feet sank into a rich carpet woven in greens and blues as he approached the table. He ran his hand appreciatively over the highly polished surface inlaid with various types of wood and ivory showing scenes from life along the Nile.

"Should I arrange a suitable gift for Isidore, as well, Master?"

"What?" Orestes looked up. He thought a moment, then smiled. "Would I be mistaken in thinking Isidore has been helping himself to 'gifts' from the estate for years?"

"That is not for me to say, Master. I know only that he purchased a large villa in the outlying precincts last year. He has many business interests, all profitable. The last Prefect seemed satisfied with his service."

Orestes' smile turned sour. "My predecessor was satisfied with a great many things that I am not. That is why I am here—to rectify his mistakes. I see no need to enrich Isidore further. I want you to point out the excesses in his accounts."

Orestes lowered his lanky body onto a green leather chair behind the table. Four smaller matching chairs sat along the wall. Fresh sheets of papyrus, quill pens, bottles of ink, and wax for seals sat at the ready on a side table, along with initial reports on the city. "Well, Demetrius, let's begin."

THE NEXT DAY, Orestes, accompanied by Demetrius, journeyed to the Prefecture where he had another set of offices. The cavernous seat of provincial business was located next to the city council building. In an endless round of introductions reminiscent of his first day, Orestes met dozens of civil servants, both permanent and temporarily elected to preside over the vast and intricate bureaucracy of the city and province.

Unlike his servants, these men seemed confident in their roles. Prefects came and went, but civil servants held their positions through connections with powerful city patrons. Many of those patrons paid handsomely to have a son, nephew, or client installed in an office that collected taxes, regulated trade and workshops, or engaged in public works. Orestes found it prudent to maintain good relations with the nobility by allowing them some profit from such lucrative appointments, if it wasn't too excessive.

The lowering sun found Orestes with his entourage of city officials and their assistants on the bank of Lake Mareotis. Mud brick buildings sprawled along the shore behind them and stone docks thrust into the lake. The harbormaster, a bluff man with graying beard, barrel chest, and the bandy legs of a sailor, greeted them with a bow. "Lord Prefect, welcome! All is ready for your inspection."

Orestes looked around curiously. Trade was the lifeblood of Alexandria. All the goods to and from the Egyptian hinterland went through this city. Dock workers swarmed like ants to discharge the cargo: amphorae of wine and oil, barrels of fruits and vegetables, bales of wool and linen, stone from the quarries, pottery from the kilns. This bustling freshwater harbor saw as many boats, and more barges, than the seaward harbors. Orestes marveled at the sheer volume, as well as the variety of goods that moved through this port, but his primary responsibility lay with one particular export.

"I should like to see the granaries first."

The harbormaster bobbed and waved a hand to the east. "This way, Your Excellency. This month of July the Mother Nile begins to rise, bringing life to the land. Last year's harvest is arriving from the central granaries established along the river. We are in the middle of our busiest season." He waved toward the lake. "See, even as we speak, barges arrive from the south."

Orestes squinted at a small fleet of nine barges crawling across the horizon toward the grain docks. The flat-bottom boats wallowed with their heavy loads. Bargemen strained at their oars. The last barge straggled a distance from its fellows.

Orestes and his entourage continued down the docks toward the towering stone granaries. The harbormaster explained the intricacies of wheat inspection to insure its quality was "unadulterated, with no admixture of earth or barley."

As they approached the docks in front of the granaries, a shout went up.

"There, Master." Demetrius pointed to the incoming barges.

A dozen men in small flat-bottomed boats attacked the straggling barge with spears and slings. The other eight raced for shore, leaving their companion to its fate. One bargeman was in the water. Two others fended off the punts with their oars, but there were too many. A pirate climbed over an undefended side, clubbing one bargeman, before the others tipped the marauder into the water.

"You!" the harbormaster shouted at several lounging sailors. "Take The Egret and go to their aid." He pointed to a trim little sailing vessel tied to the dock.

One of the sailors stood up, spat something dark on the ground, before putting his hands on his hips and cocking his head. "It's too late. By the time I get 'er under sail, the pirates will be back in the reeds."

The harbormaster's face turned red. "There might be survivors, man!"

The sailor spat again, this time marking a stone bollard.

Orestes stepped forward and flipped a silver coin at the sailor's feet. "Another one for every live man you bring back. I'll make it gold for a live pirate."

32

The sailor picked up the silver coin and tucked it into a pouch. "Yessir." He turned to his crew and cuffed the nearest one on the head. "You heard the man. Git!" They raced to the end of the dock, jumped aboard, loosened the lines from the bollards, and raised sail. The crowd watched helplessly, as The Egret sped away.

The pirates grappled the barge, pulling it toward tall reeds screening the bank.

"If the pirates make it to the reeds, they will disappear into the hidden by-ways. The barge will be lost, its cargo disappearing into the villages on the shores," the harbormaster explained. "My apologies, Augustal Prefect. I've asked for shore patrols, but the council has yet to hear my petition."

"Do you lose many ships?"

"More as the season waxes. Mother Nile was not generous last year and the harvest was thin. There is hunger in the hinterland. Desperate men do desperate deeds." He bowed his head as if expecting a blow for his honesty.

"I see." Orestes gazed out at the concluding drama. The pirates made the reeds ahead of The Egret. The crew tacked back and forth, sending the odd arrow into the waving reeds, but to no avail. They stopped their useless pursuit to pull bodies from the water.

Orestes detached a pouch from his belt and handed it to the harbormaster. "See that this purse goes to the families of the lost men. I'll take up your petition with the council."

"Thank you, Excellency. Your help and generosity is much appreciated."

"We will postpone our tour of your fine facilities." Orestes nodded toward the returning ship. "You have other duties to attend to." He spoke briefly to Demetrius, who departed with haste. Orestes then made his roundabout way home via the agora, dropping off members of his entourage as he went.

DEMETRIUS AND PHILLIP WAITED for Orestes in his private sitting room. Phillip's bearded face split into a dazzling smile at the sight of his traveling companion, and he rose. They clasped shoulders, thumping each other on the back. "Well met, my friend! How go your first days?"

Orestes motioned him to sit and took a comfortable couch next to a cold brazier. "It is much as I expected: too many people to remember and too few I can trust. Thank you for coming at my summons, Phillip."

"It is my pleasure to serve." His friend shrugged. "How can I be of assistance?"

Demetrius left, presumably to fetch refreshments. Orestes suddenly became aware of the emptiness of his stomach. It had been a long day, with little sustenance.

"I saw something disturbing at Mareotis harbor today." Orestes described the pirating incident. By the end of his tale, Demetrius returned with servants bearing platters of steamed fish wrapped in grape leaves, grains and vegetables cooked with a rare yellow spice from India, fresh breads of a light delicate brown sprinkled with sesame seeds, and a generous flagon of strong red wine.

"Join me, Phillip. The cook will be most disappointed if I return this savory food barely eaten."

"My pleasure." Phillip's eyes sparkled at the delicious smells emanating from the various platters.

Demetrius sent the others away and served the food. Orestes raised a spoonful of grains and vegetables; the spicy scent tickled his nose. He hoped the cook had not put too much yellow powder in the dish. The last time he had this spice, the food left a fiery taste that no amount of water seemed to quench. He tasted the grains and chewed with satisfaction.

"I asked the cook for simple fare." Orestes admitted, "I'm glad he ignored me. Try the grains, they are quite good."

Phillip tucked into his food. After many compliments, he returned to their previous topic. "I've also seen disturbing things."

"Such as?"

"On the trip home, people clogged the road. Not merchants or pilgrims, but whole families with bundles on their backs, heading for the cities. I've traveled these roads to visit my father's estates. I have never seen such sights. There must be famine in the land." Phillip paused. "And the brigands we encountered! The countryside used to be safe for unarmed pilgrims. Now all must go armed or escorted."

Phillip stared into his cup, swirling the wine into a miniature whirlpool. "My friends tell me the mood in the inns is sour and black, as if an evil spirit sucked all joy from life. Old women on the street cry doom, young women and men openly sell their bodies. I'm afraid your predecessor did little to keep such sights confined to the poorer neighborhoods."

"I've found little to impress me about my predecessor's practices. He seems to have let the church keep the peace and used the money allocated for that function for his own comfort. One of my first tasks is to build up the guards. I will call on General Abundantius for military troops till that is accomplished. How do you think the city nobles will react?"

"To troops on the streets? As long as they can do business as usual, they will care little." Phillip finished his wine and set the empty cup on a low table. "They will probably welcome the additional security."

"And the council? I will need their support."

"They're a pricklier bunch." Phillip scratched at his bearded jaw. "I don't know. My father would be a better judge of that."

"I would like to meet your father and talk with him at greater length. Do you think you might return the favor of this meal and invite me to your home?"

"Consider it done." Phillip smiled. "Selene will be pleased."

"Your sister?" Orestes was startled.

"You made quite an impression on her at the reception. She'll be mooning about you for weeks, along with every other eligible maiden in Alexandria. You may have to arrange a marriage to escape constant pursuit."

"I shall never marry." A shadow of pain flitted across Orestes' face. "I enjoy the company of women from time to time, but have little patience for their intrigues and wiles. The court in Constantinople overflows with the plots of women, priests, and eunuchs. The Emperor's sister Pulcheria is chief among them."

"She's a year younger than Selene! What plots could a girl concoct?"

"Children grow up fast in the royal palace or they sometimes do not grow up at all." Phillip looked thoughtful as Demetrius poured him a second cup of wine. Orestes commented, "Selene did not strike me as the type to plot. She seemed altogether too straightforward and innocent."

"Selene was always headstrong, but never devious." Phillip shrugged. "But I've been away three years. Much has changed—in my family and in the city." He sipped his wine pensively. "I fear we have troubled times ahead and would do all in my power to avert it. How may I be of service, other than arranging dinners?"

"My immediate needs are for information. I need people who can walk in all parts of the city and report to me what they hear and see. Can you do this?"

"It seems a noble cause, and more intriguing than running my father's estates."

"This assignment is not without its dangers, my friend. Think carefully before you decide. I have no wish to impose on our friendship in this way."

"It is no imposition." Phillip gave him a crooked smile. "I think I will enjoy such work."

"Who else might we enroll in our intelligence gathering?"

"I know some trustworthy fellows who would be glad to do the Empire a service."

Orestes raised his cup in a salute. "Good. I've already given thought to your first assignment."

Phillip leaned forward as Demetrius cleared the platters.

CHAPTER 5

S ELENE HURRIED DOWN the broad avenue from Honoria's house. She had stayed far too long, but they had had little time together of late and there was much to speak of. Rebecca had finally sent Nicaeus to escort her, saying she was urgently needed at home. Nicaeus seemed annoyed at his task and answered her questions with grunts, leaving her to speculate on the nature of the urgency. He at least told her no one was ill or dying.

She tossed her outer robe to a servant waiting in the vestibule and immediately headed for the kitchen at the back of the house. She entered the room to the sound of people shouting and pottery shattering. Slaves and free servants rushed from one room to the next, carrying pots of water, baskets of vegetables and live fowl. The savory smell of baking bread conflicted with that of briny fish. A corpulent cook turned suddenly from a table where she was cutting cubes of meat and collided with a skinny servant carrying a basket of eels. The eels cascaded across the tiled floor to Selene's feet. One had the temerity to snap at her dusty toes. At least they were fresh.

The cook and the servant started shouting at one another.

The burdens of being the lady of the house settled heavily on Selene's shoulders. She longed for the freedom of her runs on the beach, but this was her responsibility. She picked up a wooden spoon and banged it on a copper cauldron, sending a hollow boom throughout the room that stunned the panicked servants to silence.

"You, Cook," she pointed the spoon at the red-faced servant, "tell me what is happening."

"I turned around and this clumsy son of a three-legged camel dropped a basket of eels—"

"What?" the skinny man protested. "If this female hippo didn't take up the room of five people, I could have easily—"

Selene banged on the copper cauldron again. "Quiet! I don't give a fig about the eels. I want to know why you are all in such a panic."

Rebecca entered the kitchen on the heels of Selene's tirade. Taking in the disorder, she said, "Your esteemed father sent word he was bringing guests for the evening meal and asked that you oversee the preparations. With you gone, we were trying to arrange the evening ourselves, but," she paused, shrugging her shoulders, "you know the old saying about too many generals."

Momentary panic seized Selene, followed by a rush of gratitude for the work the servants had already done. She had become more adept at this type of entertaining since her mother died, but still relied heavily on Rebecca and the others to see to the details. "How soon will they be here and how many are we to prepare for?"

"Shortly after sundown. Your father is bringing the Prefect and Archdeacon Timothy to the evening meal. Phillip, Nicaeus, and you are also to be in attendance."

"Orestes? The Prefect is coming tonight?" Selene squeaked, her panic returning.

Rebecca held her gaze, saying in a calm voice, "Six is an auspicious number. I'm sure we can avoid disappointing your father's honored guests."

Taking a deep breath, Selene girded for battle. "Of course. We have Father's good name to maintain. Rebecca, take two servants to the main quarters and see that the vestibule and dining area are in order. It wouldn't do for guests to stumble over loose tiles or foul their garments with dust. When you have set them their tasks, meet me in my quarters. I must prepare as well. Nicaeus?" Her brother stopped his surreptitious progress through the back door. "Would you see what wines we have available?"

He bowed low. "Of course. Anything else, Mistress of the House?"

She threw an over-ripe kumquat, which he ducked. "No, dear brother, check the wine and get yourself cleaned up." She turned back to the servants with a sense of purpose. "Cook, what do you have in mind for the menu tonight?"

*****

SELENE WATCHED IN THE MIRROR as Rebecca tucked in the last curl and secured it with a jeweled comb. She stood and Rebecca tied a gilded cord around her wine-red gown so as to best show off Selene's slim figure. Rebecca always knew the perfect decorative touch to elevate a good presentation to an exquisite one, whether it was clothes, food or statuary. Selene turned for a last inspection. Rebecca nodded her approval as someone knocked at the door.

"It's Nicaeus. Father approaches. Are you ready?"

"Yes." Selene opened the door and linked arms with her brother. She looked over her shoulder at Rebecca. "Go to the kitchen and make sure all is ready. If there are problems, come get me."

Rebecca gave her a short bow. "Of course, Mistress."

Selene and Nicaeus strolled out of the cramped warren of bedrooms on the top floor and descended a broad marble staircase into the spacious public rooms. Most homes of the rich celebrated open communal space, and theirs was no exception. Built in a rectangle with blank walls facing the street, colonnaded public rooms on the ground floor opened onto a central courtyard. The rooms held little furniture, but the floors and walls sported lavish murals of country scenes and colorful mosaics commemorating Greek and Egyptian legends.

Selene checked the arrangements in the courtyard garden. Aromatic torches kept insects at bay. Water trickled from a fountain surrounded by green shrubs. In the triclinium, where they took their meals, green and red striped cushions adorned the couches. Someone—Selene assumed Rebecca—had arranged a spray of lilies to complement one of her father's favorite fishing scenes on the wall. Oil lamps depending from a chandelier shed a soft glow, creating an air of intimacy appropriate for discourse.

Nicaeus and Selene arrived in the vestibule to see the impressive figure of the Prefect conducting an animated conversation with their father. Archdeacon Timothy, a barrel-chested man who seemed totally unencumbered by a shriveled left leg, thumped Phillip on the back as the latter finished a story.

Selene made a deep curtsy.

"Lady Selene." Orestes took her hand and raised her to her feet. "It is good of you to receive me on such short notice."

When her eyes met his cool green gaze, she stopped breathing. She felt a blush rising and ducked her head, unable to meet the eyes that seemed to see into her soul. "Th-thank you, sir. Welcome to my father's house." She retrieved her hand and turned to the rest of the party. "Archdeacon Timothy, it's so good to see you again. I'm pleased to welcome you to my father's house." She bowed slightly to her father. "I hope the preparations are to your satisfaction, Sir. Shall we repair to the courtyard?"

Her father's eyes glowed with pride. "I'm sure all will be perfect, my child." He took her arm and gestured to the rest of the party to proceed. "Please, let's see what miracle Selene has wrought."

COOK DID WELL, Selene thought as she surveyed the remains of the feast. The lamb spiced with cardamom and the marinated palm hearts were particularly fine. The bones of the fowl stuffed with liver and onions littered platters. She had not tried the eels, but the men seemed to enjoy them. She would have to commend Cook for her efforts. Selene reclined on her couch, sipping watered wine, listening to Orestes and Phillip regale the dinner party with stories of adventure and piracy.

They seemed easy with each other. Her father watched Phillip with barely concealed surprise. But her brother always mixed well in whatever company he found himself—high or low. It was the low company that sparked Calistus' stern disapproval.

The conversation turned to council business—increasing disorder in the city and the need for more guards—as servants removed the platters. The house staff looked fine in their matching livery of white with a deep blue stripe on their tunics. Rebecca, in a fresh robe and neatly dressed hair, exchanged a few pleasantries with Phillip, then continued to carry a bowl of rose-scented water and linen towels to each guest to wash their hands.

Another servant stood ready to serve candied figs and dates stuffed with nuts. Selene gave him a hand signal to offer the treats to the guests. Orestes chose one of each and nibbled in a peculiarly dainty manner. Selene noted with annoyance that Nicaeus took a more than generous share. She waved the servant past her own plate to make sure there was plenty for the others. Concentrating on the logistics of the meal, Selene was taken by surprise by the sound of her name.

"Selene, I understand you are quite an athlete." Orestes smiled at her. His slightly parted lips revealed a crooked front tooth. Her breath caught in her chest. She opened her mouth to reply.

"She's faster than anyone I've seen, especially over long distances," Nicaeus broke in. "You should see her leap a wash or take a hill. The gazelles can't keep up with her. She's good with a javelin and sling as well, but I can outshoot her with a bow."

Selene felt heat rising in her face and was grateful for the lamp's flickering shadows. The uncertain light also hid the murderous glance she sent her brother, but did nothing to leach the warning tone from her words. "Nicaeus, I'm sure our honored guest doesn't want to hear about me."

"On the contrary, I admire women who can take care of themselves. The native women in Britannia are superb athletes. Many are warriors, and leaders of warriors, more feared by the Roman troops than the Celtic men. My grandmother was reputed to have led a chariot charge in one of the last battles beyond Hadrian's Wall one month before giving birth to my mother."

That explained his height and coloring, Selene thought, he was of barbarian stock! "And what of your mother?"

"She died giving birth to me. My father was Prefect to Londinium. He remarried to a proper Roman lady." A shadow crossed Orestes' face. Selene, unsure if it betokened grief or the wavering light of the lamp, preferred the more romantic explanation.

"I understand you served in Britannia as well," Calistus said, raising another cup of wine and admiring its deep red color through the translucent glass. "A tragedy for the Western Empire when it lost that colony but, given the current state of barbarian-benighted Rome, it's as well the troops were recalled. It's impossible to keep order so far away."

Selene glanced sharply at her father. How unlike him to make such an impolitic remark, especially after the Prefect revealed his own barbarian ancestry. She motioned Rebecca over and, under the guise of giving her more directions, asked that her father's drink be well watered.

Orestes sipped his wine and said, in a regretful tone, "I'm not sure Britannia ever was Rome's, Calistus. As with many provinces, their roads may be straight and paved, their harbors bustling, but underneath is a stubborn wildness that yields not to outside influences. Egypt, in a strange way, reminds me of my homeland."

Selene laughed. "I have heard Britannia is a land of cool mists, magic trees, and strange bogs. What about such a country could remind you of our blazing desert and meandering Lady Nile?" She tried to imagine cool wet wilderness, but her experience failed her. She had hazy notions of reed-filled swamps and familiar crocodiles.

Orestes looked directly into Selene's eyes. "Both have been conquered but have taken on only the trappings of their conquerors. Britannia pretended to be Roman, but is quickly reverting to petty kingdoms, as Roman troops are recalled to the continent. Egypt absorbed the conquering Greeks with barely a ripple, and bowed to Caesar, while changing nothing but the names of its gods."

"Surely in four hundred years there has been change! We are a Christian nation," Selene protested.

"The Empire has broken in two, but Christianity is splintered in pieces. There are nearly as many sects and cults now as before. The old gods vie with the new and their disruption is stamped on this city. My work here will be quite… challenging."

Selene, caught in Orestes' intense gaze, turned her sight with difficulty to Archdeacon Timothy as he spoke. "Some would say the troubles in Alexandria are due to malignant demons or the 'disruption of the gods,' as you put it. If the truth were told, it is the lack of work and the heavy taxes that leads faction to fight faction. A few men are amassing wealth and power, while the ordinary people become ever more burdened."

"A few men have always held wealth and power, Timothy." Calistus snorted. "There is nothing new in that."

"But there has always been enough left over to care for the rest." Timothy shook his expressive face. "Soon Alexandria will be no better off than Rome after that Visigoth Alaric sacked it."

"I have every intention of forestalling such a calamity," Orestes said. "I hope your Patriarch will assist me in this. How is his health? When my secretary inquired about an appointment, he was told Theophilus was indisposed and receiving no visitors."

"It is but a cold on the chest. The Patriarch works too hard, and has become frail of late, so the physicians advise him to rest and build his strength. I do my small part as his eyes and legs during this time of confinement."

"The Archdeacon is being too modest," Calistus interjected. "He is the Patriarch's successor, as have been all Archdeacons."

Timothy raised an eyebrow. "Not recently. Patriarch Athanasius fostered Theophilus and chose him as successor."

"The Emperor has seen fit to appoint his own from time to time," added Phillip.

"Theophilus served in all levels of the church first," Calistus protested, waving his hand dismissively at Phillip, "and the imperial appointments—disasters, one and all!"

Selene noticed her brother's mouth tighten at his father's correction.

"I assure you this Emperor will take no hand in the succession," Orestes said.

"And let us not forget Cyril. Theophilus is grooming his nephew for the Bishopric. No," Timothy shook his head. "My succession is much less than assured."

"In ten years, Cyril might be ready. A Bishopric is not an empire or business to be handed down from father to son or uncle to nephew." Calistus reached over to pat his friend on the arm. "The clergy would never propose, and the people would never affirm, a Patriarch so young and inexperienced."

"Let us pray this discussion is premature." The Archdeacon raised his goblet in a toast. "To the Patriarch's health!"

Orestes finished his drink and Selene motioned for a servant to refill his goblet. Orestes put his hand over the mouth of the cup. "No more. This is excellent wine, but I fear I must leave. Tomorrow I have much work to do and I have no wish to make decisions with a sore stuffed head."

The company rose, rearranging robes and making small talk on the way to the vestibule. Selene accompanied her brother Phillip, clinging tightly to his arm. Calistus held Orestes' elbow as they walked. "Who else are you calling on in these early days?"

"Other city councilors, the Patriarch when he is well, and, of course, Lady Hypatia."

"A wise choice. Any man of substance who visits our city should wait on Hypatia. She is much respected by the city fathers as well as her fellow philosophers."

A slave held out Orestes' short military-style cape. He shrugged into it, addressing Archdeacon Timothy. "And how fares the Lady Philosopher with the church elders?"

"Theophilus has the highest praise for Hypatia's intelligence, wit and good will for this city. Although a pagan, she has remained above the fray." Timothy chuckled. "Indeed, the good Patriarch's only complaint is that he has been unable to convert her. She remains stubbornly convinced that philosophy transcends all religions. And Hypatia, when arguing philosophy, is a most formidable lady. If not for my faith, she could almost convince me."

Orestes and Phillip clasped forearms in a farewell grip. "Thank you for inviting me to your father's home, my friend." He bowed to Selene and took her hand for a kiss. "And you, gracious Selene. Thank you for accommodating us on such short notice. I hope to see you soon."

"Thank you for the good company, sir. I most enjoyed your stories." Selene raised shining eyes to his. "I should like to see your island of mists and fierce women warriors."

Orestes shivered slightly and the light in his eyes turned inward before he dropped her hand. "I believe you will, my dear."

Timothy captured Orestes' arm. "Well, my good sir, let me accompany you to your quarters. My home is but a bit farther and I would be glad of the companionship."

Orestes' small escort joined the Prefect and Archdeacon from the anteroom, where they had lounged during the dinner. The company parted, murmuring polite good-byes and fond wishes.

After the company had left, Selene excused herself to oversee the cleanup while the men readied themselves for bed. When she finally made it to her own mattress, Selene collapsed, bone tired. Her earlier euphoria over the flawless evening soured to a black mood. She fell asleep comparing her closely proscribed life to that of the British women Orestes spoke of—leading armies, making decisions, driving chariots—and found her life wanting.

In her dreams, a tall red-haired woman with tragic green eyes lashed four black horses across a battlefield littered with the dead of her clan. By the time the warrior woman reached the end of the field she became Hypatia, resplendent in scholar's white, expertly guiding her horses and chariot through the crowded streets of Alexandria.

Selene smiled in her sleep.

CHAPTER 6

THE NEXT MORNING, Selene groggily groped for fading dreams as Rebecca prepared her for mid-week church services. No cosmetics, jewelry, or fancy clothes today. The presbyter castigated any woman exhibiting her wealth and status at the services. Selene donned her most comfortable sandals, knowing she would be standing for a considerable length of time. The whole family gathered in the vestibule, exited to the street and paraded to the local church with all their neighbors.

The Church of St. Athanasius, built by Theophilus in honor of his foster father, the previous Patriarch, stood with open brass doors, welcoming worshipers into cool dark stillness from the heat of the streets. Selene loved the church with its high vaulted ceilings. It was a small jewel of its kind; with beautiful painted murals of the Ascension in the nave and ivory inlaid screens sheltering the sanctuary. Intricately embroidered silk altar cloths glowed white in the dim light.

The current Patriarch built nine churches during his twenty-seven years as bishop, sparking his critics to call him a litholater, a stone worshiper. Calistus had once told Selene a story about the divine guidance that led the Patriarch to such extravagant actions. There had been a marble slab inscribed with three thetas, and a further inscription which promised: 'Whosoever shall interpret these three thetas shall receive what is underneath this stone.' Theophilus said the thetas stood for 'Theos, Theodosius, and Theophilus.' Under the slab, he found a treasure which he immediately spent on church construction. Calistus had laughed and remarked, "The Patriarch has sparked much controversy during his tenure, but he is always supported by the construction guilds."

Today, as they ascended the steps, Selene saw the sub-deacons greeting people and showing them inside. They kept out scoffers and those who were denied the sacraments as penance. One deacon engaged in a vociferous argument with a well-dressed man over whether it had been three or four weeks since his penance was imposed. The deacon motioned with his arm. Two burly gatekeepers came down the steps and, not-too-gently, escorted the well-dressed man away. Inside, Selene and her family journeyed to the front of the church to stand with others of their rank.

An hour later, Selene shuffled from foot to foot. The marble floor was beautiful but hard on the legs and back. Her attempts to offer her discomfort to God as penance for her sins, failed to bring any relief. Selene glanced at her father. He didn't seem to be in any distress. A small stir rippled through the congregation as a deacon removed a crying child, but settled as the presbyter made an announcement.

"Pray with me for the recovery of our beloved Reader." Readers, the lowest rank of the church orders, read the gospels to the congregation. Selene brightened; maybe the presbyter would dispense with that part of the service. Her hopes were dashed when the presbyter continued, "Please welcome the Patriarch's nephew Cyril, who will read the gospel of St. Luke."

Small groups of men and women started for the doorway, as was their wont during the reading. Many people left to talk with neighbors and friends during the service and returned later for the sermon and blessings. One presbyter was known for leaving the church when the gospels were read so he could "go with his flock" and learn the latest gossip.

Selene forgot her minor pains. Having heard her father and his guests discuss Theophilus' nephew the night before, she listened with renewed interest. Having a guest reader could be a treat—or not—depending on the reader's skills. She watched a slight young man with a curly beard and sloped shoulders ascend the steps to the Bishop's chair. Cyril, taller than most men, surveyed the congregation with piercing black eyes.

Once he started reading, the exodus stopped. Most returned to their spots. Selene found Cyril a superb rhetorician. His voice seemed too deep to come from his skinny chest. He cast his fervor over the crowd like a net, drawing them closer, entangling them in his passion for the words he read.

A palpable restlessness rippled through the crowd when Cyril finished. The people wanted more. Instead, the presbyter took the chair and railed against the latest heresy from Antioch on the nature of Christ and the divinity of Mary. Some Antiochines evidently refused to call Mary "Mother of God," substituting "Mother of Jesus" in their sermons.

Selene stretched her aching back and stifled a moan. She compared the presbyter's admonitions to the thought problems her math tutor set her— interesting intellectual exercises but of little value in the real world. Her indifference made her feel vaguely guilty, because Selene knew people such as her father thrived on intellectual disputation. She could understand nursing people, providing food for the hungry, and shelter for those without, but she failed to see the importance of how people referred to the Virgin Mary. Deeds, not words, were the essence of Selene's faith.

The presbyter rose from the Bishop's chair to lead the congregation in prayer. "Thank the Lord," Selene muttered. She lifted her arms, palms facing out, head bowed in an imitation of Christ on the cross. The rest of the worshipers did likewise, then broke into a beautiful rhythmic chant. Selene could feel her spirit lift to the sound of the psalm set to music. The beauty of the words and intricacy of the rhythms made her body ache to express the sound in passionate motion, not stand in static obeisance.

After the presbyter delivered his final blessing, the congregation stirred. Selene spotted her friend Honoria with her mother and sisters. They resembled a flock of peahens—short, plump, and twittery—heads bobbed and hands shaped the air as they conversed. It was well that Honoria's father was one of the richest men in the city. Honoria was the oldest of seven daughters for whom he must provide dowries.

Selene turned to her father. "May I walk with Honoria a while?"

Calistus surveyed the crowd flowing toward the door of the church and spotted a small knot of church elders congregating in a corner. "Yes, go ahead, child. Nicaeus can escort you and your friend home."

Selene caught the sour look on her brother's face, but he did not dare protest.

Calistus took her other brother's arm. "Phillip, come with me. I want to introduce you to people you should know. Maybe we can talk the deacons into providing a few benches for the older members, eh? My bones aren't what they used to be." He clapped his son on the shoulder and guided him toward the men, who seemed in deep debate.

Nicaeus trailed behind as Selene approached her friend's family. The tallest of the round sisters bounced over to her. "Selene! I was hoping we would meet!" Honoria rose on tiptoe to kiss Selene's cheek, then tucked an arm under hers. "What a lovely gown. That shade of green suits you. Did you find the material at the Syrian's booth in the market? He has the loveliest things..."

Selene listened to her friend chatter about her clothes, last night's heavenly dessert, and her youngest sister's annoying habit of leaving sticky hand prints all over anyone who picked her up. As they left the dark coolness of the church for the reflected brightness of the colonnades, Selene looked over her shoulder at Nicaeus and motioned him closer. "You needn't stay with us all the way home. We'll be perfectly safe."

"But Father said..."

"I won't tell if you won't." Selene motioned to a group of three young men hovering by the steps. Antonius smiled at her and she waved back. "Go with your friends."

"You could invite Antonius to join us on the walk home." Honoria smiled up at Nicaeus and fluttered her eyelashes.

"I'm sure Antonius would be delighted to join you on a stroll." Nicaeus bowed over Honoria's hand, converting a look of pure glee to one of appropriate regret. "But I know for a fact he is otherwise engaged today, as am I." He looked over his shoulder, saw no sign of Calistus, then admonished Selene, "Be sure to walk straight home."

Nicaeus headed toward the other boys.

As he left, Honoria pinched Selene. "Ow! What was that for?" Selene rubbed her bruised flesh.

"That was for letting your brother and Antonius get away. They could have escorted us home. You know I rarely have the opportunity to be in his company."

Selene took Honoria's arm, steering her down the colonnaded street toward their homes several blocks from the church. She asked gently, "Is Antonius still your choice for a husband?"

"Of all the matches father has proposed, he is the only one I would gladly accept. Father is obsessed with allying with a political power, and a councilor's son would be a more than suitable son-in-law." Honoria hesitated. "Father feels the sting of being new to his wealth, but in this case it works to my advantage." Her eyelids drooped and a soft smile lit her face. "Antonius is well favored and, I believe, kind. I think I could be happy with him." Her eyes widened. "Does he talk about me to you or Nicaeus?"

Selene hesitated, not wanting to hurt her friend by repeating unkind remarks, but unwilling to give false hope. "Antonius does not know you, Honoria. He has nothing on which to base either affection or aversion." She squeezed her friend's hand. "I'm sure when he gets to know you he will find you as fine a friend as I do—kind, loving, and sweet-tempered."

"Do you think so?" Honoria shook off her dreaminess and raked Selene with an appraising eye. "What of you, my dear? Does your father fancy you as wife to the Prefect or has he another match in mind?"

"The Prefect? Orestes?" Selene looked at her friend in astonishment. "Where on earth did you hear that?"

"Everyone knows the Prefect is looking for a wife to cement his appointment here." Honoria smiled slyly. "Why else would your father invite the Prefect to your home, if not to show you off?"

Selene shivered in the heat. She didn't want to be married, did she? Selene decided to deflect the subject.

"What else do 'they' say about the Prefect?"

"That he's tall and straight, like a cedar tree. That he rides a horse so well he is taken for a centaur. And," Honoria surveyed their immediate surroundings and, satisfied, whispered, "his green eyes can bewitch any woman."

"Is that all?" Selene laughed. "Did they not mention that he breathes fire, can understand your unspoken thoughts, and sleeps on a bed of iron spikes?"

"Oh, Selene, don't be such a tease." Honoria withdrew her arm and stamped her foot. Selene laughed and tucked her friend's arm back under hers. "I'm sorry, Honoria. I am constantly amazed at how rumors spread. Didn't your father tell you about Orestes?"

"You know my father never talks to me about anything important."

"Why hasn't Ision proposed you as a match for the Prefect?"

"A merchant's daughter and the Egyptian Governor?" Honoria laughed. "Father aims high but even he knows better than to propose such a pairing."

Selene smiled. One of the traits she found most endearing in her friend was Honoria's frank appraisal and insight into her own precarious social position. Honoria didn't preen or fawn over the other girls of their set, as one uncertain of her rank, but acted as if she belonged. She was well aware that she would belong only so long as her father had money or until she could marry into status.

"Which brings me back to my original question. What marriage plans does Calistus have for you?"

"Me?" Selene tossed her head, dislodging the cream-colored veil protecting her from the sun. She readjusted it around her shoulders. "I do not care to marry."

"And how much influence will you have in that?" Honoria wore a sorrowful look. "The holy societies take only widows, and your father will provide a fine dowry. You will not have much choice in the matter."

"I don't wish to be married and I will have a say in my life." Selene leaned down to whisper into Honoria's ear. "I already have a plan. I'll study with Lady Hypatia. She is a woman of many talents and great respect."

Honoria gasped. "Your father will allow you to study with the Pagan Philosopher?"

"He hasn't given his approval—yet. I plan to attend one of Hypatia's public lectures and approach her. If she accepts me, how could Father refuse?"

"By saying no?"

"It is a great honor to be a student of Hypatia's. Many of our esteemed councilors, the Governor of Upper Libya, the Bishop of Ptolemais, even members of the royal court, studied with her."

"And how do you plan to attend this public lecture? You have to go through the market and close to the docks to get to the Museum. It's dangerous for a girl to travel the length of the city without escort."

"I have a plan for that as well."

The two girls whispered and giggled their way home.

Chapter 7

ORESTES RUBBED HIS TEMPLES, trying to forestall a headache. He closed his eyes to shut out the sight of the enormous stacks of reports and petitions mocking his efforts to master his appointment. As a field commander, he had only to show personal courage and enforce discipline to bring order out of chaos. His brief experience at court did not prepare him as well as he hoped to face the bewildering array of possible allies and enemies in Alexandria. He struggled with how best to sort them into camps, learn their strengths and weaknesses, evaluate their strategies, and deploy them in his cause.

Demetrius entered his office with another armload of scrolls. "More matters for your attention, Master."

The dull throb lurking behind Orestes' eyes became a stabbing pain. He drowned in paperwork from officials gauging how much latitude he would afford them. Did he hold the reins of state tightly or loosely? Until they knew, every decision would be forwarded to him. This mountain of minutia sapped his time and energy.

"Can't the administrative staff take care of those?"

"I believe these will be of interest to you, Master. More allegations of civil disorder, assault, and destruction of religious property."

Orestes frowned as he scanned the reports. "We've been getting a half dozen a day. This is a fair city, a prosperous one, far from the dangers of the barbarians in Gaul and Italy. I don't understand this destructive urge of the good citizens of Alexandria."

Demetrius shrugged, moved behind Orestes to massage his master's neck and shoulders. "Alexandria has a history of perverse violence. Greeks, Egyptians, Jews, Romans—many peoples—each with its own language, customs, gods. A century ago the good citizens killed a Roman trader who accidentally harmed a cat. It's been but twenty years since they rose up and murdered two holy men, representatives from the Church in Constantinople. A mob dragged them through the streets, hacked their bodies to pieces and burned them on a pyre."

"A gruesome death, for sure, but this is mostly a Christian city now." Orestes winced, then relaxed under the tender ministrations of his slave.

"An opposing Christian faction murdered the monks. Patriarch Theophilus united the Christians to break the back of the pagan cults early in his episcopate. But lately, with the Patriarch's illness, and their common enemy suppressed, the various sects have begun squabbling."

"So much for 'love thy neighbor,'" Orestes muttered as Demetrius kneaded the knots in his shoulders. After a few moments, he shrugged off the gentle hands. "That feels better."

Orestes tapped his front teeth with the tip of his reed pen. "Patriarch Theophilus sent word he was too ill to wait on me after I first arrived. I think it is time I paid my respects to the Bishop of Mark. See if he will receive me." He eyed the stack of papers. "Today, if possible."

Demetrius bowed from the door. "As you wish, Master."

ORESTES WAS PLEASED at the courtesy shown his office. The Patriarch responded immediately that he would welcome the Prefect's presence and asked him to come at his convenience after noon. Orestes arrived with Demetrius and two bodyguards at the sprawling complex that housed the Patriarch and his staff. Theophilus had converted the Serapeum, a former pagan temple compound located on a prominence in the southwest Rakhotis district, to the Episcopal Palace. Orestes thought it significant that he and the Patriarch occupied the two highest points in the city.

A deacon met them at the gate and escorted them across the grounds to the administrative offices and personal residence of the Patriarch. He pointed out the Library of St. Mark and several houses for presbyters and visitors as they progressed. Arches supported the whole edifice, with enormous windows above each arch. Sitting courts and small chapels occupied the highest level. In the middle stood the Church of St. John—on the site of the former temple of Serapis—built on a magnificent scale with an exterior of marble and faced with columns.

Orestes, familiar with the imposing imperial and religious architecture of Constantinople, recognized the symbolism of converting this center of pagan worship to the seat of Christian power throughout Egypt. It was a most awe-inspiring sight and befitted the rank of the See rivaled only by Rome in prominence.

A large number of young stalwart men dressed in rough brown robes guarded the gate to the Patriarch's compound, congregated in the courtyard, and filled the halls. They carried themselves more with the swagger of soldiers than the piety of priests. Orestes knew fighting men when he saw them, whether they wore the breastplates of the Roman army, the furs of the northern Germanic forests, or monks' robes. Why did the Patriarch need an army?

According to Demetrius, Theophilus avoided the more brutal actions of his mentor Patriarch Athanasius, known for beating and imprisoning his rivals. However, a dispute over the anthropomorphic nature of God had inspired riots soon after Theophilus' elevation to Patriarch. Theophilus sided with the more intellectual monks of the city who believed as the philosopher Origen believed, that God was incorporeal, not shaped like a man. When desert monks invaded the city and threatened to put him to death as a blasphemer, Theophilus quickly changed his mind. Since that time, the Patriarch united the desert monks and reigned unchallenged, but perhaps in his illness Theophilus felt threatened.

The deacon led them through a maze of rooms filled with secretaries interviewing supplicants, then past hordes of clerics reading and responding to neatly stacked correspondence. They overtook several monks carrying household goods up the stairs—rich carpets, embroidered hangings, altar cloths, silver goblets—gifts from the spiritually faithful and others hopeful of more earthly assistance.

They arrived at a plain oak door, where the deacon bade Demetrius and the bodyguards wait on a bench. Orestes entered the room and stopped to let his eyes adjust to the dimness. Heavy draperies shadowed the windows and only two lamps relieved the gloom, one on a wall and a second on a modest wooden table piled high with papyri. An old man wrapped in many layers of robes sat at the table, scribbling with a reed pen.

Orestes was shocked. At his investiture a week ago, Theophilus seemed frail, but now his skin was the color and texture of old parchment, brittle and creased, pulled tight over fine bones. A blue vein throbbed erratically in the old man's temple. His nearly translucent eyelids fluttered up to reveal dark eyes, startling in their vividness, with a hint of pain in their depths. Theophilus started to rise in a generous act of courtesy, for Orestes was obliged to stand in the Patriarch's presence unless bid to sit.

"Please, Father, don't trouble yourself." Orestes strode forward.

The Patriarch murmured to a servant, who immediately produced a chair for the Prefect. Theophilus nodded his approval and spoke in a cracked voice. "Be seated. Your presence gives me a break from the tedious duties of my office." He swept his hand toward the piles adorning his desk. "I've been ill for several days and much of this work has gone unattended." He sat back and gazed at the papyri with a rueful smile.

"I left a similar situation in my office." Orestes chuckled in sympathy. "What did man do before inventing paper?"

"We have an insatiable need to record the most mundane details of life." Theophilus lifted one substantial pile. "These are mostly lists: how much grain, cloth, and wine in storage; who has tithed what to the church; charitable accounts; names of new penitents." He sighed. "As if this has anything to do with the grace of God."

"My reports are of a similar nature, but one among them, the impetus for my visit, disturbs me."

Theophilus frowned. "Not more taxes, I hope. The people do suffer greatly under the current burden."

"Not taxes, Patriarch." Orestes smiled at the familiar refrain. "I wish it were that easily dealt with. This has to do with reports of attacks on citizens and religious property."

"Then it is likely still a matter of taxes. When I process, I am besieged by families looking for alms. One poor soul, but two weeks ago, told me a typical story. It is a lean year, yet his landlord demanded nearly the whole of his meager crop for taxes. The man could not feed his family and they came to the city looking for work. Unfortunately, there is little for them here. They and their neighbors crowd the tenements, beg for food, steal when they are desperate."

He indicated the leaning tower of papers. "Many of these reports are from Christian charitable societies—our poor houses, orphanages, and hospitals are all overflowing. Our stores of food and clothing are low. If you wish to settle the unrest, Prefect, lighten the levies or give some back in the form of food for the poor. Your gracious increase of the bread dole was a start. Perhaps that could be extended?"

"Our most generous Emperor believes the substantial amount of grain diverted to the Church for distribution is sufficient." Orestes avoided pointing out not all who received the dole were poor. The Church, and those who served it, were not only exempt from taxation, but also received grain subsidies. The list of non-church receivers had several prominent names on it, presumably in exchange for past services rendered.

Orestes spread his fingers in a gesture of helplessness. "Unfortunately, I have little control over imperial levies, except to see they are collected and speedily shipped to their destinations."

Theophilus shook his head. "Maybe it is the Lord's work, for the poor and the wretched do convert in greater numbers. The well-content see no need for change. After the sack of Rome, only the Christian communities were able to organize to provide food and shelter. Soon the whole town was firmly and devotedly Christian. A little more misfortune and perhaps Alexandria will be likewise."

The Patriarch's words disturbed Orestes. He did not want to believe Theophilus would manufacture troubles in order to extend his power. But in his experience, cunning ambitious men more likely served the Church as Bishops than in more humble roles, and Theophilus had a reputation as both.

A servant put a silver tray on the table and poured two goblets of wine. Orestes noted the fine workmanship—a clear glass to show the ruby depths of the drink, the rim banded by chased silver. Theophilus reached for the one nearest him and raised it with a trembling hand. "Do join me in refreshment."

Orestes lifted his glass, smelling the sweet heavy wine. The taste sparked memories of blazing afternoons; dark purple grapes ripening on the southern slopes of Gaul.

Orestes watched surreptitiously, and with some alarm, as the old man attempted to drink without spilling. Theophilus' hands shook and he soon gave up the effort, sighing sorrowfully as he contemplating the full goblet.

"Thank you. A most satisfactory vintage." Orestes placed his cup on the table. "I will take up little more of your time. I came to pay my respects and ask your advice."

A sparkle of humor showed in the Patriarch's tired eyes. "I pray my words are informative, if not useful."

"I am new to my office and thank you most heartily for your insight, but the reports I referred to earlier are about more than theft. There is also disorder and destruction of property—usually religious in nature—sometimes committed by men dressed as monks. This does not seem the act of hungry people, but those of differing convictions. The Emperor expects order in the cities, but I do not want to place soldiers on every corner. What might I do to bring about accord?"

Theophilus eyed Orestes with satisfaction, as if this awkward inquiry into his affairs was precisely what he wished to discuss. "I understand you are of the Christian faith."

Orestes, taken aback by the abrupt change in topic, confirmed, "I was baptized by Patriarch Atticus in Constantinople before making this journey."

Theophilus steepled his hands, touching the fingertips to his lips. "Ah! You are new to your faith." Flames of passion animated the old man's eyes. "What do you believe, my son?"

"I fail to see what my religious beliefs have to do with bringing order to this city."

Theophilus leaned forward and slapped both hands on the table. "Then your eyes see dimly. This city needs a strong Christian leader. One who is public in his faith in the way of the good Emperor Constantine. One who will show strength to the non-believers, support the church in its endeavors, and enforce the imperial laws against heresy."

The Patriarch's thrust became clear to Orestes. He parried. "You will have my full support in upholding the laws."

"But what of your soul? You should have instruction. I would be happy to have my nephew, Cyril, attend to your needs."

"Your offer is most kind, but I could not consider taking your nephew during your illness." Orestes bowed his head. The last thing he wanted was a churchman—and the Patriarch's nephew, at that—to have regular access to his clients and offices. "I will attend services, as you advise, and in all ways try to be a model for the citizens of this city. But surely there is more I, or possibly we, can do to help bring peace to the populace."

Theophilus stroked his chin. "There is another source of discord which you can influence."

"And that is?"

"There is a class of disreputable entertainers—actors, dancers, mimes—who soil our city with their wicked ways. The women are little better than prostitutes, inflaming men by showing their bodies and freely giving their favors. They are a temptation to men and an affront to our mothers, sisters, and daughters. It is in your power to shut down the theaters and expel these vermin from the streets."

Orestes was dubious. When one of his superior officers had been newly baptized, he instituted flogging and demotions for soldiers visiting brothels. That action brought about resentment and mutiny among the troops. Perhaps some middle ground might be found.

"I will look into the matter. Is this a problem for your flock? Do many stray?"

"Not many." Theophilus coughed, hacked briefly into a cloth, then managed a sip of wine. "We have strict penalties for those congregants found frequenting theaters and brothels. I fear for the souls of those poor unfortunates without the benefit of our moral guidance." The Patriarch raised a knowing eyebrow. "This disreputable element is a threat to peace in our fair city."

Orestes mused on whether the entertainers were the Patriarch's true target, or a means to an end. "If I can curb these performances, do you think you could control the more violent elements among your followers?"

"That is my mission." Theophilus put his hands together as if in prayer. "Only when this city is of one mind and one heart, dedicated to the One True God, will there be common cause. I've been striving for twenty-seven years to make this a Christian city and bring peace to our bodies and souls. It is a difficult struggle."

"Is that why you surround yourself with armed monks? I have always felt it better to convert with words and deeds rather than cracked heads."

"You speak of the parabolani? They are my bodyguards. You should be aware there have been threats against my life over the years."

"Yes, but it is my understanding there have been none of late. You could always call upon me to supply city guards, if you feel the need. I would be honored to accommodate you."

The Patriarch started to cough again and, gasping, took another sip of wine. Servants hovered near his elbows, throwing worried looks at each other.

Pity dampened the frustration building in Orestes. The old man may be clever in his machinations, but his body failed him. His empire slipped from his fingers and he still had to account to God for his actions. Orestes concluded he need do little more than bide his time and be gracious.

"Thank you, Good Father, for your time and advice. With your blessing, I shall take my leave. I fear I've overtaxed your strength."

Theophilus put a shaking hand on the Prefect's bowed head and croaked, "Go with God, my son, and may He light your way."

Orestes straightened, murmuring his thanks. A violent spate of coughing and wheezing followed him out the door. Relief mixed with guilt and pity. Orestes resolved to make his case more forcefully with Theophilus' successor. Archdeacon Timothy seemed a more reasonable man.

THEOPHILUS WATCHED THE PREFECT LEAVE. "Did you hear, Nephew?"

"Yes, Uncle." One of the servants detached himself from the shadows and took the chair vacated by Orestes.

"What are your thoughts?"

"His lack of conviction troubles me." Cyril frowned. "But he is newly baptized. Perhaps Bishop Atticus is not as strict in his requirements as you."

"Many at the court are convenient Christians," Theophilus nodded, "outwardly conforming to Christianity because it is the religion of the Emperor, maintaining the old ways in thoughts and deeds. But I spoke more of his purpose here in Alexandria than of his belief in God."

"From his words, he wishes peace." Cyril shrugged. "Doubtless a peaceful, prosperous city would put him in line for further promotions."

"Yes. He cannot attain his goals without our help. That is why he is so deferential."

"But you are the Patriarch! How else would he treat the Father of our Church?"

"I did well in sending you to the desert monks in Nitria for your spiritual education, my son." Theophilus chuckled. "But you have much to learn about dealing with men of power. Orestes is backed by the imperial troops at Nicopolis. We must be subtle in our approach, support the Prefect, put him in our debt until the time is right to rid this city of non-believers. If we push him too early, he might turn against us, as have other Prefects."

Another paroxysm of coughing doubled over the old man. Coming out of his fit, he noted the drawn look on his nephew's face and reached out a hand, which Cyril clasped in his own. "You have been a good son to me. Better than one from my own body. I regret leaving this task to you at such a tender age."

"You have time yet to oversee my education, Uncle. God would not take you from me, or your people, so soon." Cyril leaned forward, earnest eyes raised to his uncle's faded ones.

Theophilus extricated his hand and patted his nephew's cheek. "My days on this earth are nearly finished. God has set you a trial. You must carry on in my stead. Purge the city of the heretics, Jews, and pagans. Lead Orestes to the light."

The old man coughed again, bright blood showing on a fresh kerchief Cyril supplied. Tears blurred the younger man's eyes. "I will do your bidding, Uncle, for it is also God's."

"I know you will, my son. Tomorrow we start planning. There are many things I must tell you, many pieces to move on the game board, if you are to succeed me."

CHAPTER 8

THE NIGHT BEFORE HYPATIA'S PUBLIC LECTURE, Selene retired to her room to prepare. She had taken Nicaeus' third best tunic, ostensibly to repair an embroidered neckband. The bleached linen garment lay, arms outspread, on her bed. Except for its length, the tunic was not much different from her daily wear: a basic "T" shape decorated with two red and blue embroidered strips from shoulder to hem and two smaller strips banding the edges of the full sleeves. Given the warm summer weather, she could forego a mantle.

Sandals proved a problem. Nicaeus' feet had grown large over the last two years. Her own dainty footwear would be inappropriate for a boy, so she sent Rebecca to the second-hand market to find a suitable pair in stout ox hide.

Selene seated herself before her silver mirror and combed her hair. It rippled in silky waves down her back and across her shoulders. She raised sewing shears and cut off a hank at her left ear. It dropped to the floor in a dusky heap. The remaining hair bounced back in a loose curl.

"I have the sandals. Is there anything else before you retire, Mistress?"

Selene started. She was so intent on her task she had not heard Rebecca enter the room.

Rebecca's gaze darted from the shears to the hair on the floor. Her eyes grew round. She raised a hand to her mouth to stifle a moan. "Oh, Selene! Your beautiful hair!"

"Rebecca! Just in time to help. I despaired of being able to cut the back straight."

The servant shook her head in wonderment. "What do you think you are doing?" She approached Selene and took the shears.

"I'm going to disguise myself and attend public lectures tomorrow. I hope to obtain a prominent teacher as my patron. I should go unnoticed among the young boys."

"And what is to stop me from going right to your father and revealing this foolish plan?"

Selene looked at her servant in shock. "Rebecca! You would betray me in this? How many times have we kept secrets from Father? No harm has come of it. I will tell him myself, once the deed is done and I am approved to study."

"Those were minor matters: the loss of a coin, climbing a forbidden tree. Those things your father could readily forgive. But this," Rebecca swept her hand from the shorn lock of hair to the tunic on the bed, "is against your father's express wishes!"

"Father has never forbidden me to cut my hair or walk to the agora or attend lectures." Selene raised her chin defiantly. Rebecca looked at her with a sorrowful expression. Selene turned back to the mirror and crossed her arms over her chest. Rebecca's accusing image still showed over her shoulder.

She slumped.

"You're right. Father never said I could do any of those things." She raised her eyes to plead with Rebecca's reflected ones. "I want to be a physician. I need a patron, Rebecca, someone who can convince my father to let me follow this dream."

"You were never one to shrink from a difficult task." Rebecca sighed and laid her hands lightly on Selene's shoulders. "But I think you underestimate your influence with your father. He loves you deeply. Why not approach him?"

Selene shook her partially shorn head. "In this, he will not indulge me. His love will tell him to keep me safe at home until he can find a suitable husband." She reached up and covered Rebecca's hand. "I truly believe this is the best way."

"Do you have a patron in mind?"

"Lady Hypatia."

"The foremost philosopher in our city?" Rebecca shook her head. "I fear you have set yourself not just a difficult task, but an impossible one."

"I can do it, Rebecca, with your help." Selene turned again to plead with her servant. "Help me be a boy tomorrow and all will be well. I know it."

With a look of resignation, Rebecca picked up the shorn lock of hair. "How do you intend to keep this a secret from Calistus? Don't you think he will notice at first meal tomorrow?"

Selene frowned. "Maybe I could wear a scarf or veil?"

"Indoors? Your father will be suspicious."

"Tell my father," Selene drooped against the cosmetics stand with a limp hand to her forehead and half-closed eyes, "that I am indisposed. Ill. Afflicted with my moon time." She 'recovered,' giggling with relief. "That should stop all questions."

"Perhaps." Rebecca tugged at her lower lip while she surveyed Selene's ragged locks. "I'll braid your hair before we cut it, and use the braids to dress your hair while it is growing out. With pins, ribbons, and veils, we might make you presentable. Or I can take your hair to a good wig maker?"

"No. I'm sure you'll do fine with braids and pins." Selene inspected the first cut in the mirror. "Will you do the back?"

Moments later, four thick braids of hair coiled on the wash stand. Selene ran her hands through closely cropped curls. "My head feels lighter. What do you think, Rebecca? Do I look like a boy?"

Rebecca looked her over critically. "A fine-boned one, yes, if no one looks too closely."

"Good. After the servants leave for the market, I will slip out the back and proceed from there." Selene took Rebecca's hands in her own. "Thank you. This will work out. You'll see."

"I hope so, Mistress. For your sake and mine. Sleep well. I'll wake you in the morning. Perhaps by then you will have returned to your senses."

SELENE FELT EXPOSED and vulnerable in her brother's tunic. It fell midway down her calf and startled her whenever the hem flapped on her legs. She wore brief tunics while running, but her public attire always enveloped her from head to foot. More discomfiting was the lack of company. Only scandalous women appeared in public unaccompanied by mother or servants.

She pushed at the fabric around her waist and readjusted her belt, trying unsuccessfully to cover more of her legs. Realizing her inward unease might be reflected in her appearance, Selene tried to relax. She focused her senses outward. There seemed to be a general flow in the direction of the agora. Once she was beyond the quiet neighborhood of her home, her nervousness transformed to anticipation and a delicious feeling of freedom. She could do as she pleased and there was no one to say her "nay." Tomorrow she would be Selene again, but today she was an unknown boy, free to explore the city.

Selene drifted with the current, taking in the smell of frying fish and the sound of merchants hawking their wares, as she moved through the marketplace adjacent to the agora. The sun shone high overhead. She bought a fig leaf stuffed with mashed beans and roasted garlic for a bronze coin, scooped the aromatic paste into her mouth with her fingers, licked the remains from the fig leaf, and discarded it on the street.

A public fountain, shaded by a tree, gushed water from the mouth of a demon into a trough embedded with seashells. Before the Romans introduced inexpensive concrete, such mundane objects as troughs were laboriously chipped from stone in treeless Egypt. Selene joined a line of women with jars, and stuck her face in the flow for a drink and a cleansing splash of water. The warm sun quickly dried her face and damp hair. She ran her hands through her short tresses, amazed at the ease of its care.

She reluctantly left the anonymity of the marketplace and entered the agora. The huge square was only moderately crowded. The viewing stand for the Prefect's investiture had been taken down days ago, and the streets swept clean. Selene stayed to the left. She wanted to avoid the law courts and city offices, where pronouncements were posted and friends of her father were likely to congregate.

She headed for a complex of buildings containing lecture halls, baths, and a small theater, sandwiched between the agora and the ruined palace district. The men she encountered paid her no attention. The crowd was a shifting mosaic of light colored robes, punctuated by the glint of polished armor or the occasional brown or black of a strolling monk. One of the latter approached her now.

Selene stiffened, then relaxed. This monk was unarmed, but who knew about the next one? She rubbed her head in unconscious imitation of Antonius when telling his tale of cracked pates. Selene surveyed those closest to her and edged toward a band of youths. They cut through the crowd to the main north-south thoroughfare, the Street of the Sema. The Great Alexander's body had been removed from his magnificent tomb, and the building destroyed centuries ago, but the street still bore its name. The secret of his final burial place had been lost with the ages. The boys headed out of the agora, leaving Selene in the shade of a stoa, plotting her next move.

"Selene! What, by all that's holy, are you doing here? And dressed like that!" A young man's fingers dug into her arm. She looked up into Antonius' concerned dark eyes. They grew wider in shock. "What did you do to your hair?" he nearly shrieked. Several people turned their way with curious looks.

"Shush." Selene shook off his hand and rubbed her arm. She would have bruises as well as short hair to explain the next day. "Tell the whole city and disgrace me, will you?"

Antonius' face turned several shades redder than normal. "What are you up to? Don't you know it's dangerous for women to travel in the city alone, especially in these times? I should take you straight home."

"Antonius, please don't take me back." She clutched his arm. "I wanted to hear Hypatia speak. Once! I promise I won't do this again." She looked up at him through her lashes. "Besides, with you here, I'm not alone."

Antonius gave her a skeptical smile. "Once? Well, why don't we find Nicaeus? He can decide what to do with you."

Selene relaxed slightly. Antonius linked arms with her in the way of students. They followed the sheltered stoa around the periphery of the square to the eastern exit, then headed south. They left behind the somber atmosphere of the agora, which was afflicted with the weighty issues of government and law, and entered a more carefree environment.

Selene tried to look at everything at once without seeming to. Boys, both younger and older than she, hurried along the streets carrying wax slates, or lounged under shaded stoas talking with friends. The occasional older man passed by in white scholar's robes, sometimes accompanied by students, sometimes with a colleague. They passed a silent theater and several loud taverns, young men spilling from the doorways, laughter wafting over the walled courtyard.

As they came opposite a public bath, four boys swept past, jostling Antonius and knocking Selene to her knees as they pelted down the street toward an intersection. Antonius pulled Selene to her feet and yanked her into a doorway. A larger number of students—she guessed about a dozen—followed closely on the others' heels, shouting taunts and waving sticks at the fleeing youths.

"I told you this wasn't safe! Those were philoponoi chasing those other students. I recognized their badges."

"The 'zealous ones'? Why would they attack other students?"

"The students being chased are pagans. The philoponoi have been more zealous since the pagan students slipped their float into the Prefect's investiture procession. They seemed to have taken that action as a personal affront." Antonius grabbed her arm and tugged her around. "I'm taking you home."

The blood had drained from Selene's face but now came back with a rush.

"I'm not a pagan and have nothing to fear." She yanked her arm away. "I am not going home. I've come so far and I'll see this through."

Antonius clenched his jaw and narrowed his eyes. Selene felt her opportunity slipping away. She had counted on his sense of public decorum. No well brought-up boy would dare cause a scene by hauling a girl screaming through the streets; harmony and moderation were the mark of their class. But the resolve in his face boded ill for her plans. Antonius might ignore convention if he felt she were in true danger.

A knot of unshed tears tightened her throat. She put a hand on his arm and spoke softly. "Please, Antonius, it was a minor clash. Just boys chasing each other. The streets are calm now." She looked up at him with glittering eyes. "You don't believe I would chance my father's disapproval on a whim, do you? I want this so much. Haven't you ever felt like that? Wanted something so badly that life without it would be ashes and dust?"

His face softened and his eyes took on a haggard look. "Yes, I've felt that way." He looked around the street, sighed, and linked arms with her again. "The lecture halls are this way. Maybe we can catch up with Nicaeus there."

They crossed the street and turned the corner from the baths. Two halls sat side-by-side, sharing a solid wall and a flat roof. Tall windows provided air and light to the interior. They entered the building through an off-center opening. Four tiers of stone seats were set stepwise against the side and rear walls. Hypatia sat on a double-height seat in the center rear of the room. The space at the front and down the length of the hall between the seats was empty. There were about forty students, but the tiers could accommodate three or four times that number.

Selene plucked at Antonius' sleeve and whispered, "I want to sit close."

They edged to the back of the hall; taking seats on the bottom row, about one quarter of the way past Hypatia's left hand. This was the closest Selene had ever been to the great lady. She had always seen her from a distance; heard her voice carry across crowds. Now she could see the laugh lines at the corners of Hypatia's eyes. Dramatic streaks of white hair flared from her temples, striping the tidy bun at the nape of her neck.

The students stilled as Hypatia called, "Come to order."

Selene listened closely. Hypatia might have an old woman's face, but her voice vibrated with life, a clear alto. Selene, realizing she had been holding her breath, let out a long sigh.

"We've studied the ancients and their philosophy. Today we will discuss the modern thinkers, in particular Plotinus. Our subject today is the nature of beauty and its relationship to the soul. What is it that attracts the eye? Color? Symmetry?"

Hypatia looked toward a boy seated to her right, almost directly across from Selene. He lowered his face, as if afraid of being called upon.

"Agrippa?"

All heads turned as Agrippa stood to declaim. Selene saw why he tried to hide his face. A large birthmark marred his right cheek, spreading like red wine splashed from forehead to neck. The kitchen servants would call it the mark of a demon. Selene wondered if Hypatia had intended a special message for the afflicted boy through her choice of topic.

Agrippa cleared his throat and started in a near whisper that gradually became louder. "Many declare that the symmetry of parts delights the eye; that the beautiful thing is essentially symmetrical, patterned. Yet Plotinus points out that using this criterion excludes color, sunlight, the stars at night or a lump of gold. Faces are symmetrical, yet can be accounted beautiful or ugly." His hand crept up to the birthmark. Agrippa looked around self-consciously, then abruptly sat.

"Thank you, Agrippa," Hypatia said in kindly tones. "So beauty is more than symmetry. Is beauty eternal?"

Her piercing gaze settled on Selene, who rose to her feet as if compelled. Selene, vaguely aware of Antonius' frantic whisper and tug on her robes, ignored him as she took a breath and dropped her voice several tones.

"Beauty cannot be eternal, for natural processes ensure decay. The flower wilts, skin and limbs wither. Even man-made art chips, weathers, and falls to ruin," Selene answered confidently.

Hypatia's lips pursed as she tapped her chin with one finger. "And your name is?"

"Sele...uh...Selonius, Honored Teacher." Selene bowed, partly to hide a blush.

"Those things of and made by man do indeed fall into decay. But what of those things of and made by God? The stars? The soul? Are they not eternal and therefore eternally beautiful?"

"The stars sometimes fall from the sky, so they cannot be eternal. As for the soul?" Selene shrugged. "The presbyters tell us it is eternal, but I have no way of knowing its beauty."

Murmurs rippled through the students. Selene heard a hissed "blasphemer!" as well as several comments in her favor.

Hypatia's eyes narrowed as she raked the crowd. "Take your differences outside. This is an open forum for reasoned discourse, not a gymnasium for pugilists. Selonius is correct. We do not know. Yet, the search for knowledge is the essence of divine philosophy, that most ineffable of ineffable things."

She pointed to another boy further down the row from Selene. "Clement, take us back to Plotinus. What does he say of beauty and the soul?"

Selene took her seat as the boy rose. "Plotinus urges us to seek the spark from the One. He says the fount of all that is good or beautiful is within us and not of this world. The beauty we experience with our senses is but a hazy shadow in twilight compared to the beauty we can find through the examination of our mind."

Clement looked at Hypatia as if for confirmation.

"Yes! The mind contemplates the ultimate Beauty and Goodness and not the contrived shifting and ephemera that man beholds in the material order of existence. Life lived according to reason is the purpose of men. Let us pursue that life. We must, through strenuous effort of mind and heart, extract from our inner selves the eye buried within us. This intellectual eye, this luminous child of reason, allows the individual to burst the shackles of matter, where beauty cannot remain."

Selene flushed, breathing hard. The words rang in her ears, but did not resonate with her heart. She did not want a life of contemplation, but of action. She gloried in the world of the senses. Would Hypatia understand that? Was she the wrong person to help? Disturbed, Selene continued listening to the discourse.

When Hypatia called an end to the lecture, Antonius dug his elbow into her ribs and hissed, "Ready to go now?"

"No. I have to talk to her."

"But you said…"

Antonius' words were drowned by the voices of other students as Selene pushed her way toward Hypatia. She crept closer as the crowd thinned. Antonius caught up with her, but she ignored his threats to drag her back to her father's house by her hair. He hadn't earlier, and she doubted he would at this late date. Being so close to her goal, Selene redoubled her efforts. She needed to petition the great lady and determine her fate.

Hypatia rose, dismissing the remaining students in preparation for leaving. Selene, her heart in her throat, stepped into Hypatia's path and bowed gracefully. "I wish to speak to you, Honored Teacher."

The diminutive woman looked her up and down, starting with the dusty sandals, dwelling on her bitten fingernails, and finally searching her face. Selene put her hands behind her back and shifted from foot to foot.

"Many wish to speak to me, but I have time for only a few. Who recommends you to me?"

"I come on my own behalf, at great personal risk." Selene's voice edged up in her nervousness. "I will take little of your time, Lady."

"I think I see." Hypatia reseated herself and patted the stone next to her. "Please sit. I'm straining my neck looking up at you." Antonius stood back several paces, a scowl marring his dark good looks. "Antonius, isn't it? Don't stand there. Come join us."

Selene perched on the edge of the tier. Antonius approached, bowed, and murmured, "Thank you, Honored Teacher," then took a seat on the other side of Selene.

"Now, my dear, what is so important that you must risk disgrace and your family's displeasure roaming around the city in that costume?"

Blood rushed to Selene's cheeks. "You knew?"

"Not for sure until now. You are tall for a girl and chose your draperies well to disguise the most obvious features of your sex. But there is a certain fineness of bone and variability of voice that give you away to any keen observer."

"I tried to get her to go home," Antonius grumbled.

Hypatia smiled. "I'm sure you did. Now...Selonius?"

"Selene."

"Selene, the changeable moon. Calistus' daughter?"

Selene nodded.

"You have not answered my question." Hypatia sat patiently.

"I wished to hear you speak. I wanted to see you."

"Why?"

Selene sat silent, staring at her hands clasped in her lap without seeing them. She raised her head and looked steadily into the questioning eyes of the older woman. "Soon I will be of an age to marry. My father will choose my husband. My husband will choose where we live, what social relationships we honor, how we educate our children. The Church will dictate my conduct in public and private. I want to make some choices for myself. I wanted to meet a woman who made choices for herself."

"Ah, my child, that is where you are wrong. I did not choose this life. I was born to it, as you are born to yours. My father Theon was a mathematician with the Museum. He was graying when I was born, and my mother died before my second birthday. I grew up reading from his texts, listening to his scholar friends arguing over meals. The Great Library was my playground. In form, I am a woman, but in the content of my mind and the nature of my soul, I am a philosopher. This is not a life you choose, but one that chooses you."

Tears threatened to spill from Selene's eyes. She blinked them away. "But I do feel chosen. I want to study." She hesitated before telling her innermost secret; afraid Antonius would laugh, or, worse, Hypatia would. She took a deep breath. "I know you feel philosophy is the highest calling of man, nurturing the soul. I wish to follow a humbler path and study medicine. Not just midwifery, or the herbals and nostrums the wise women sell in the market. I want to study anatomy, surgery, and the works of Galen and Hippocrates."

"Philosophy is a fit subject for men or women of your rank, but medicine is work for freedmen. Why would a girl of your birth wish to study to be a physician?"

"I want to know 'why.' Why do some wounds heal and others don't? What is the function of our organs: heart, brain, lungs, muscles? Why do some of our parts get diseased? Why do we have hot fevers, but shiver as if we are cold? I want to know and I want to help people with what I know. I've already been practicing."

Antonius snorted. "Splinting a bird's wing or tending a sick kitten doesn't make you a physician."

Selene rounded on him, chin high. "Who sewed you up when Nicaeus clouted you on the head with a practice sword last year? You almost fainted at the sight of all that blood. I didn't even twitch." She grabbed him by the forelock and pulled his head down. "Show Hypatia your scar."

"Ouch!" He batted her hand away and rubbed at the stinging spot.

"Children!" Both sets of eyes turned to the stern voice. "I've never been one to discourage a true calling, even for one of the humbler arts. If your soul leads you to this, it is a powerful force for learning. Most people with a passion will not be denied. They find a way to live their dreams or they turn into bitter, destructive people."

Hypatia cupped Selene's chin with her hand. "We are so different, yet in this I think we are alike. 'Why' is the great question of scholars. Most people leave that question behind in childhood after being told 'it's God's mystery.' But a few search beyond and find answers for the rest of us. You will find your way, I'm sure of it. Come tomorrow after mid-day meal to the Great Library. I'll show you where to look for the texts you need and introduce you to possible teachers. Antonius," Hypatia snapped her fingers, "you needn't look like a fish out of water." He closed his gaping mouth. "Please see that Selene makes it home safely."

"Oh, thank you!" Selene clasped Hypatia's hand. "I'll be there. Nothing could keep me away."

Nothing except her father.

CHAPTER 9

I SEE YOU ARE FEELING BETTER, SELENE." Calistus stood by the fountain, arms folded across his chest. "I went to your room before mid-day meal to inquire about your health. Rebecca—reluctantly—told me you were out. She didn't tell me of your costume."

"I, uh…" Selene's hands fluttered between her brief tunic and her shorn locks, her mouth dry as dust. Antonius backed toward the door.

"You." Calistus' eyes speared the boy into stillness. "What have you been doing with my daughter?"

"He had nothing to do with this, Father." Selene stepped in front of Antonius. "He found me in the marketplace and offered to escort me home."

Calistus scowled. "You may go home, boy, but tell your father to expect me to call upon him tomorrow. I'll send a slave to inquire as to his pleasure and convenience."

"Yessir." Antonius bowed, then lunged for the door.

Calistus turned to his errant daughter and shook his head. Some men went into fiery rages when angry, turning red, eyes shooting sparks. Selene's father became sorrowful, as if the punishment he meted out truly hurt him worse than it did his child. Selene trembled under his quiet censure.

"I have allowed you altogether too much freedom: lessons with your brothers, running outside the city. It's more than time you started acting like a young lady. Your punishment for this outrageous behavior is to remain in this house until the next Sabbath. No trips to the market, no visitors, and especially no running. For her part in this deception, I've dismissed Rebecca from our service."

Selene was stunned. "But, Fath—"

"Do you question me?"

"No, Father." Selene approached him, throat constricted, blinking back tears. She sank to her knees, head bowed. "I justly deserve any punishment you mete out. I deceived you, but do not put my sins on Rebecca. She did what I asked and tried mightily to dissuade me."

Calistus bent and tipped up his daughter's chin. "I cannot have a disloyal servant in my house."

"Father, I know no one more loyal than Rebecca. What she did, she did out of love for me, at my request." Tears streamed down her cheeks. "Please let her come back."

"My child, it is a hard lesson to learn, but you must know that your actions affect others. When you made the decision to deceive me, you not only put yourself in jeopardy, but all those who helped you on the wrong path, regardless of their motive."

"Even Lady Hypatia?"

"What has she to do with this?"

"It was she I went to meet at her public lecture. She agreed to be my patroness and teacher."

"You dare compound your lies?" Calistus looked as if his heart had broken. "You hold me in such low esteem, you expect me to believe you had an audience with the Lady Philosopher?"

"But—"

"Go to your room. At once."

"Yes, Father." Selene walked stiffly from the courtyard, stifling thoughts of her father's unfairness, knowing, but denying, she was at fault.

SELENE SULLENLY PICKED at her food that night. Her father ate his meal in silent disapproval. Phillip was out, which seemed to upset Calistus even more. Nicaeus, after his first joking comments drew icy stares from his father, gave up his attempts to start a conversation.

After dinner, Selene rushed to her room, threw herself on the bed and cried herself into a sweaty, restless sleep. In her dreams Rebecca starved, begging on the streets; a disdainful Hypatia denied their meeting; Nicaeus, Antonius, and Phillip surrounded her, pointing and laughing while her father stood in rigid disapproval.

"Mistress Selene?" She heard a knock at the bottom of the door. "Are you awake? I've water and dates for you." It was Anicia, Cook's youngest daughter.

Selene rolled over and groaned. There was another knock at the door. She pulled a cover over her head and mumbled, "Go away."

"Mistress Selene, are you all right?"

In a louder voice, "Go away!"

Today should have been a joyous one, her first as a student with Hypatia. She sat up. Lady Hypatia. Waiting for her at the Great Library.

"No, wait, Anicia." Selene leapt to her feet, opened the door, and yanked the girl into the room, overturning a jar of water on her tray.

"Oh, Mistress! Look at this mess!"

"Never mind. I need you to deliver a message for me. Go to Lady Hypatia, she lives in the scholar's quarter on the Road of the Peacock..." The servant girl's eyes grew big as pomegranates. "Anicia, what's wrong?"

"The Witch. You want me to take a message to the Great Witch?"

"Philosopher Hypatia is no such thing. She's a scholar and a teacher."

Anicia's jaw set in a stubborn line. "It is well known the Pagan Philosopher practices sorcerous astrology. The presbyters have forbidden such magic."

"Astronomy. She studies the positions of the planets, not their influence on our lives. Patriarch Theophilus does not condemn her. She is held in high esteem by all in the city."

"Not all." Anicia cowered at Selene's scowl. "I only repeat what I have heard in the markets and streets."

The girl's fear jolted Selene. After what happened to Rebecca, how could she think about entangling another servant in her schemes? But what should she do? Selene couldn't let the Lady Philosopher believe she was uncertain in her will. Neither could she let Rebecca go without a word of apology or recompense. Selene sat chewing a nail while the servant unsuccessfully attempted to clean up the spilled water with a sopping rag.

Suddenly, Selene lay back on her bed, moaning. "Leave it, Anicia. You do not have to deliver any message. I have a severe headache and wish to be left alone today. Please tell all the servants I am not to be disturbed."

"As you wish, Mistress." The girl bowed out the door, closing it softly after her.

After Anicia left, Selene rolled off the bed to paw through the pile of clothes on the floor. She found Nicaeus' tunic and shook it out.

*****

SELENE CAUGHT HER BREATH. Her heart thudded in her chest so loud she was surprised no one heard it. It had been difficult getting out of the house unseen, but once in the streets she made her way quickly to the scholars' quarter. If she were caught, her father would have every right to beat her or send her to live with the holy women. Selene silently bargained with God, promising never to disobey her father again if she could do what she had to and return without his knowledge.

Modest houses lined the streets south and east of the harbor. Most were three or four stories high, with families living in one or two rooms on each floor. Small shops selling leather, glass, jewelry, and embroidery fronted the streets, living quarters perched above. Public baths, bakeries, and cookshops adorned every street. Selene couldn't picture Hypatia living in such an ordinary neighborhood.

Selene spied a young boy coming out of a bakery, with the day's bread tucked under his arm. "Boy! Can you tell me where Lady Hypatia lives?"

He looked at her with suspicion. "You don't know? You're not from around here, are you?"

"No, but I have a message for her from a student. Can you tell me the way?"

With her explanation, the boy seemed to lose interest. He pointed south. "Cross two streets; at the third, turn right. Her house is second on the left, by the almond tree."

Selene bowed her thanks and strode down the street. The shops thinned to single story houses on tree-lined streets. Where Hypatia lived, blank walls faced outward in a more compact version of Selene's neighborhood. She knocked on the second door. The carving over the doorway had been hacked out and a crude cross painted in its place. Selene had heard some Christian youth gangs engaged in this sort of vandalism, but wondered that Hypatia let it remain on her door.

A middle-aged woman with a pinched face answered the door, looked Selene over with a critical eye, and sniffed. "What's your business here?"

Selene bowed, acutely aware of her rumpled appearance. "I have an appointment with Lady Hypatia."

"The Lady sees no one before noon except special personages. Be on your way." The woman turned to go.

"Wait! My appointment is for later today, but I cannot make it. I want to explain to Lady Hypatia my circumstances. Please let her know Selonius would wait on her for a few moments. She will be most displeased if I fail to make our appointment."

"She will be most displeased if I interrupt her studies."

"May I at least leave her a note?"

The woman nodded stiffly and allowed Selene inside.

"If you would be so kind as to provide me with a wax tablet and stylus? I'm afraid I forgot mine."

The pinch-faced woman led Selene to a small office inside the door where she indicated the needed supplies on a plain wooden table. Scrolls and books towered in stacks against the walls, some threatening to topple. Selene had never seen so many books in a private residence. Most wealthy households kept a copy of the gospels or a book of psalms. Others, who fancied themselves patrons of scholars, might collect a few dozen manuscripts in a chosen field. Few collected so many. Selene speculated this was not the only room stuffed with books.

The woman cleared her throat. Selene stopped gawking and moved to the table. She took a few moments to carefully word her message, then wrote in a fast, clear hand:

"Honored Teacher,

I beg your forgiveness, but I will be unable to meet with you at our appointed time and place. My esteemed father, Calistus, has seen fit to restrict my movement to his home for the period of one week. He is unconvinced of the veracity of my words concerning the events of yesterday. Unless I can persuade him otherwise, I fear I will be unable to pursue your generous offer to sponsor my studies. It is with much hope for your understanding and a heavy heart that I close.

Yours in truth,
Selene."

Selene fought back tears as she left the tablet in the hands of Hypatia's servant.

She took her bearings after exiting the quiet house, heading further east. This next task would be much harder. Rebecca's family lived in the poorer section of the Jewish quarter, but Selene had no idea where. She had but a few hours to find Rebecca before returning home. Selene didn't want to risk her father's wrath a second day, but her obligation to Rebecca weighed heavily on her heart.

Selene entered the quarter with a sense of despair mixed with apprehension. She knew of the turbulent fortunes of the Jews of Alexandria. Brought here by the early Greek kings as mercenaries and scholars, their population waxed and waned with the political tides. Today they seemed a multitude thronging the streets, Rebecca but one among them.

This neighborhood was much like others Selene had visited. The shops contained the work of silver smiths, incense makers, perfumers, and gem cutters. One merchant promised to repair damaged clothing "as good as new," and, indeed, Selene could not tell where the sample had been rewoven. But, unlike the neat and spacious homes in her quarter, these buildings tumbled on top of one another, like an overgrown termite hive. The narrow roads filled with carts selling vegetables, cloth and other everyday goods. Gangs of small children raced up and down the streets, kicking balls, hauling baskets, or minding even smaller children. She wandered past cookshops, bakeries, and baths. Normally the scent of fresh bread made her mouth water, but today Selene's stomach knotted and denied hunger.

The street she followed emptied into a square with a fountain in the middle. One side was taken up by a magnificent building, several stories high, fronted with blazing white limestone. From the solemn attitude of the men coming and going through its various doorways, Selene surmised it was a synagogue. No matter the god or goddess, all places of worship seemed to exude a sense of holiness, reverence, and peace.

The feeling did not reach beyond the pillared steps of the building. Color flowed past Selene's eyes in the form of striped cloth and garish jewelry; sounds assaulted her ears. On one corner, a young woman danced to a drum and tambourine. On another, an old man played a pipe in high fluting tones that rivaled the nightingales. Over all this, voices rose in an intricate rhythm: women shouting to one another at the fountain, prayers floating from the open doors of the synagogue, children screaming as they played.

The pulsing life lifted Selene's spirit. She approached the women at the fountain and gave them a short bow. "Good day. I'm looking for a friend; a young woman named Rebecca. Her mother, Miriam, lives in the neighborhood with her four sons. Could any of you good ladies tell me the way?"

A lean woman, with graying brown hair and a droopy right eye, straightened from her task. "What kind of friend are ye, who don't know where she lives?"

"Rebecca lived and worked in my father's house. I've never been to her mother's home."

The woman's mouth hardened. "We don't need your kind around here, boy, chasing after our daughters. Be gone."

Selene blushed furiously. "But, you don't—"

"Be gone, I said!" The woman threatened her with a fist. "Before I call my son to thrash you!"

The other women muttered and gave her dark looks. Selene decided to move on. Where moments before the bustle of the square excited her, now it felt threatening. She retreated to a side street, leaned against a wall and watched a group of children play, trying to decide whether to continue. Suddenly she straightened and called to the children. "I have a bronze coin for information."

The children streamed to her and crowded about, shouting. She asked for quiet, then repeated what she had said to the fountain women, this time not claiming to be a friend. "Do any of you know her?"

They looked at one another and shook their heads.

"A bronze coin for the child who brings me someone who knows Rebecca. Another coin to the child who leads me to her home. I'll wait in the inn around the corner." The children scattered in all directions, shouting to their friends.

Selene entered the stuffy darkness of the inn and ordered watered wine from a thin girl who looked too frail to carry the heavy wooden platters of drinks and food ordered by the other patrons. Sitting at a rickety table in a corner, Selene listened to the conversations around her. One group of men vigorously debated the merits of various dancers they had seen perform at the theater. A man at her right bargained with another for the rental price of a shop. Another group, across the room, huddled over drinks and talked in tones too low for Selene to understand.

Before she could finish the thin vinegary stuff they called wine, a small boy with crusty sores on his legs sought her out. "I've found someone, Master.

Roua's outside. She can take you to the one you seek."

Selene pushed her goblet aside. "Let's go." They stepped from the drowsy darkness of the tavern into the sunshine.

She didn't notice the tall bearded man rise from a table across the room and follow her out the door.

CHAPTER 10

THE BOY LED SELENE around a corner. There a thin girl, about eight, gripped the hand of a two-year-old wearing an outsized tunic with a deep hem and rolled up sleeves. The girl's black hair trailed in a neat braid down her back, but her tunic was worn and patched. Selene wrinkled her nose at the faint stench of urine wafting from the toddler.

"Roua, tell what you know," the scabby boy encouraged.

The girl looked at Selene with hungry eyes. "You'll give me a copper?"

"If you can take me to Rebecca's house."

"There's a young woman named Rebecca on our street. She has four brothers. Her mother sometimes gives us food. She's not in trouble, is she?"

"No." Selene smiled. "Rebecca's my friend. I want to find her and make sure she's all right. Can you take me to her?"

"This way." The girl picked up the toddler, who peeped over her shoulder with large round eyes, thumb in mouth. Selene had an urge to make faces at the boy to see if he would smile, but resisted. It would be unseemly for a boy of her station to play with a baby. Instead, she noted where they were going. She would have to return on her own.

They wended their way through several narrow streets and came on one that looked little different from the others. "She lives up there, on the corner, above the shop." Roua indicated a five-story building with a tannery on the first floor.

"Thank you." Selene gave the scabby boy and Roua each a copper coin. They scampered off with their treasure. They might have led her astray, but she didn't care. She had known hunger, but by choice. The pinched faces and gray skin of these children were new to Selene, and disturbing.

Selene shook off her troubled thoughts and entered an open door to the right of the shop. This led to a dim narrow courtyard between buildings. The tannery opened onto the courtyard, filling the narrow space with rank fumes. Blank windows, like eyes, stared out into the empty space. Crumbling brick stairs zigzagged up the walls to narrow balconies that rimmed each floor.

Selene ascended the stairs to the first doorway. The opening was covered with a woven reed mat. She heard someone stirring inside. Two low female voices exchanged words.

Selene rapped on the wall next to the doorway. "Rebecca? Are you there?"

The voices stopped.

Selene heard bare footsteps slap the floor. Rebecca pulled the mat aside and looked at her in astonishment. "Selene! What are you doing here?" Her eyes flicked over Selene's shoulder.

Selene hadn't realized how much she wanted this to be the end of her quest. Relief at seeing Rebecca's face almost overwhelmed her. "I've come to beg your forgiveness," Selene rasped around the tightness in her throat. "May I come in?"

"Of course." Rebecca backed away, holding the mat open. "This is my mother Miriam and younger brother Aaron. Mother, this is Selene."

It took a few moments for Selene's eyes to adjust to the dimness of the room, but she finally made out two shapes sitting by a window. One, an older and plumper version of Rebecca, sat on a three-legged stool, spinning wool on a drop spindle. She looked Selene over from head to foot, the corners of her mouth slightly down-turned. The other, a boy of about ten with curly brown hair and an open friendly expression, sat on the floor twining the finished yarn about his hands. He jumped up, dropping the yarn in a tangled heap.

"Did Selene come to play, Becca? I got a ball." Aaron snatched up a stuffed leather ball; similar to those she had seen the other children playing with.

"No, Aaron, Selene did not come to play," Rebecca said gently. "You must help Mother with the wool. Remember?"

A confused look came over the boy's face. Then he thumped his chest and looked at Selene with pride. "I'm Mother's helper. She can't spin without me to hold the wool." He dropped the ball, which rolled to a corner, and sat back at his mother's feet to wind the yarn on his outstretched hands.

Selene raised her eyebrows at Rebecca. Most boys Aaron's age would be working or studying.

"Aaron had a fever as an infant," Rebecca said in low tones. "The doctor told us his body will grow, but his mind won't. He will be a child forever."

Stricken, Selene murmured, "I'm so sorry."

"Don't be." Rebecca smiled. "He is a sweet child and a comfort to Mother."

Miriam looked up from her task. "I'm afraid we have little to offer you in the way of refreshment, Mistress Selene." She angled her head toward a shelf on the opposite wall while her hands continued to spin. "Rebecca, see if we have any figs left. There's water in the cask."

"No. Thank you, but I can't stay." Selene reached out to touch Rebecca's sleeve. "May we speak?"

Her former servant indicated a corner occupied with another three-legged stool and a small carved chest. The single room was almost bare. Sleeping mats, two baskets, and a plain pottery jar lined one wall. Two spare robes hung from pegs next to the door. Selene sat on the chest, leaving the stool for Rebecca.

The older girl sat, folded her hands in her lap, and asked, "Was your plan successful?"

"Yes. No. I never meant..." Selene stumbled to a halt, took a deep breath and started over. "I saw Hypatia and she agreed to sponsor me. When I returned, Father was so angry, he didn't believe me. He said he had dismissed you for helping me. I begged him to let you come back, but he was adamant." Selene bowed her head. "I had no idea Father would blame you for my misdeeds. Can you forgive me?"

"Your father had every right to dismiss me." Rebecca shook her head. "I should never have helped you do something so dangerous. I'm older than you and should have more sense."

"But I would have done it with or without your help. If not yesterday, then next week. It's not your fault!"

"What's done is done." Rebecca sighed. "There is little use in blame and recrimination."

"I know. That's why I brought this." Selene reached in her pouch and took out a bracelet. She ran her fingers over gold coins showing the profile of a long dead emperor, set in lacy gold filigree. "I want you to have this."

"Your mother's bracelet!" Rebecca gasped. "I can't take such a thing from you."

"I have little coin of my own, but this is mine, and I give it freely. I think Mother would approve." Selene looked around the bare room and thrust the bracelet into Rebecca's hands. "Take it for your mother and brother. You can sell it for a good price."

The skin tightened around Rebecca's eyes and mouth. "My brothers will be back from their trading voyage in a fortnight. They will take of care us. In the meantime, I will seek other work."

"Please keep it against need. It is the least I can do."

Rebecca let the bracelet drop to her lap. "Does Calistus know you are here?"

Selene blushed. "No."

"Oh, Selene, you compound your error by this reckless action." Rebecca rose, looked out the window, and sighed. "At least you are not running around the city unaccompanied."

"Are the children still there? I thought they ran off as soon as they had their coins."

"Children?" Rebecca shook her head. "I was speaking of Phillip. He awaits you in the courtyard. I saw him before…"

"What?" Selene jumped up and strode to the window. A tall, bearded man lurked in the shadows. He had her brother's form, but wore the rough clothes of a workman.

Rebecca turned to her brother. "Aaron, go invite Master Phillip up."

"Phillip's here?" The boy's eyes shone with delight. "Will he play ball?"

"I don't think so, but you may ask." Rebecca smiled and tousled her brother's hair. "Be a good boy and fetch him." Aaron scrambled out the door, shouting for Phillip.

The man in the shadows stepped forward. Selene tardily recognized her brother. What was he doing here, and in such clothes? How had Rebecca known him? When had he met Aaron? And the biggest question: Would he tell Father of her latest escapade? Selene's mouth went dry and palms slicked with sweat at the thought of her father's reaction to this jaunt.

Phillip ascended the steps, laughing, with Aaron. His face was carefully neutral, but when he met Selene's gaze his eyes were as full of questions as her own. He bowed to Miriam and Rebecca. "Mistress Miriam. I'm delighted to be invited back to your home. I hope you and your family are well?"

"Well enough, Master Phillip." The older woman inclined her head. "It is good to see you again. Will you stay for a meal?"

"I would, Mistress, but I must return my sister home. Thank you for your kind offer." He turned to Selene. "Have you concluded your visit, sister?"

"Uh, yes," Selene stammered. "I'm ready to go."

Everyone made polite good-byes. Selene and Phillip started down the crumbling stairs.

Rebecca called, "Phillip, I forgot. I have something for you."

"I'll be a moment." Her brother bounded back up the steps, spoke briefly with Rebecca, and returned.

When they reached the street, he asked, "Do you care to tell me what's happening? It's most confusing to leave home for a single day and return to find my sister magically transformed into a brother."

No recriminations. No condemnation. How she had missed the comforting presence of her older brother! Selene poured out the story of the last two days, her hopes, dreams, actions, and their consequences. By the end of her tale, they were nearly home. She felt flooded with relief at unburdening her heart.

"A physician?" Phillip whistled. "You aim high, little sister. Can you not tend the sick in charity hospitals with the other Christian ladies?"

"No." Disappointment marred her face. "This is not a trivial matter that will fly out of my head when I have more important things to think of."

"I know you are not light-minded, Selene. It's just," Phillip scratched his beard, "couldn't you choose something more suitable to your station? Women of our class don't enter professions. Are you sure this is what you want?"

"Women of our class marry and have babies. I want more." Selene eyed her brother. "Men of our class don't run around in worker's garb."

Phillip had the decency to blush. "Becoming a physician requires hard work, years of study, and apprenticeship."

"I can work hard and I will, if I can convince Father to let me. Will you help?"

"Father and I aren't on the best of terms."

"He is unhappy because you didn't complete your law studies?"

"Among many things." Phillip smiled ruefully. "I can talk to him, but I don't know how much good it will do."

"Thank you, brother." She glanced up at him shyly. "Could I ask one more favor of you?"

"Keep your little trip today a secret? I might forget to mention it to Father."

"That and…"

"I wouldn't go to the well too often, Selene. It might run dry."

"This isn't for me." She put a hand on his arm. "Well, it's mostly for someone else. Could you talk to Father about Rebecca? I don't know what I'll do without her."

"I would have spoken to Father about Rebecca without your plea." He tousled her shorn hair. "With me gone so much, we need a cool head to look after you." They reached the door. "I'll go first and make sure Father is engaged so you can get to your room."

Selene tiptoed past her father's office and raced to her room to change. When she emerged, the household staff deluged her with details about meal preparation, petty disputes and assignments. After dinner, she returned to her room to find her mother's gold bracelet on the cosmetics table.

Selene sat with the rebuffed gift in her lap, thinking of Rebecca. They had been together since before her mother died, but she had had no inkling of Rebecca's life outside this house. The girls had talked about their families, but Selene had never imagined the harsh reality of Rebecca's existence. She prayed Phillip would be more successful than she in arranging Rebecca's return.

Phillip: missing for a whole day, mysteriously showing up at Rebecca's in workman's clothes, obviously familiar with Rebecca's family.

"Stupid me." Selene slapped her forehead with the heel of her hand. "Phillip wiggled all my secrets out of me and told me none of his. He'll have a lot to answer for next time I catch up with him."

CHAPTER 11

ORESTES WAITED UNDER the covered walkway in the Museum precincts for Hypatia; his curiosity about the Lady Philosopher mixed with a touch of trepidation. For two generations, the elite of Africa and the East had come to study with the famous philosopher/mathematician. He looked forward to a private audience with the woman who commanded such respect in her city and abroad, but feared she might find him wanting.

To soothe his unaccustomed nervousness, he studied an exquisite wall mural showing Narcissus at a pool with Egyptian reeds and crocodiles. Throughout the city he found this curious mixture of cultures: Greek columns and their capitals decorated with the likenesses of Egyptian plants and animals, Greek clothing adorned with Egyptian jewelry, Greek tapestries showing ancient Egyptian gods and myths. Even in families, the mixture was evident in the use of names from both cultures. Rome had stamped its likeness in more subtle ways upon the city, in the form of government, taxes, and the ubiquitous use of concrete.

Voices raised in excited discussion drew his attention. Hypatia, surrounded by a flock of students, approached her offices. She moved with the grace of a young woman, although white liberally streaked her black hair. Her former beauty showed in the fine bones of her face and the sparkling of her dark eyes, but time had added the inevitable creases to her brow and sagging flesh about the jowls and throat.

He watched her shoo the boys away and stride briskly toward him, hands outstretched. She took both his hands in hers and smiled up at his towering form. "Lord Prefect! You shouldn't be loitering in the hallways. Did none of the students offer to show you into my rooms?"

He smiled back. "They did, Madam Philosopher, but I declined. I wished to observe the coming and goings of the most famous school in the Empire." He indicated bustling students carrying the tools of their trade: books, wax slates, musical instruments, paint pots. "This is truly a shrine to the Muses."

"The Museum still has its heart—students, teachers, books—even if the physical buildings no longer exist." Hypatia made a sweeping gesture. "These public rooms are our home now. The Ptolemys built a magnificent Museum and Library as part of a palace complex that covered almost a third of this city, but that was destroyed over two hundred years ago, along with the gardens and zoo. The scholars saved much but, from the surviving inventories, we know much was lost as well."

Orestes watched a knot of boys pass by laughing. "The students seem content."

Hypatia stared after the boys with a fond look, then shook her head. "I am also content to live in these modern times. The ancient kings and emperors kept their scholars close and used them for their own ends. Our Alexandria is a city of learning available to all: the Museum, the Great Library, the Christian Catechetical School, the Jewish Shul." She patted his arm. "To the business at hand. Would you care to see the Library or stroll the neighborhood?"

"A walk sounds delightful. After only a few days in Alexandria, I see far too many scrolls."

Hypatia tucked his arm under hers and strolled down the corridor toward a patch of green. "What is the nature of these scrolls?"

"Lists and accounts, petitions for action: granting contracts for hauling grain, settling disputed inheritances, building public works. More than a few ask for restrictions on one group or another: banning mimes and street dancers or a tax on the wool merchants. One suggested a ban on chariots in the city streets."

Orestes smiled at the look of mock horror on the learned scholar's face. Hypatia was famous for her chariot rides through the city.

"The gods forefend! Someone is trying to deprive me of one of my most cherished activities? Let me guess." Hypatia put a finger beside her nose, sunk in thought. "The vegetable merchants! I accidentally overset a cart several months ago and the purveyor of greens threatened retribution."

86

"No, my dear Lady. The vegetable merchants are one of the few groups I have yet to hear from. If I remember correctly, it is the litter bearers who protest the use of private chariots on the basis of public safety."

"I suspect their motives have more to do with restricting competition, or the need to clean their sandals frequently."

Orestes laughed out loud—a rare occurrence.

Hypatia's face dimpled like a young girl's when she smiled up at Orestes. "I am quite a good charioteer. Let me demonstrate my skills." She scanned the crowd of boys and men until, apparently satisfied, she startled Orestes by shouting, "Gaius, come here." A gangly boy with protruding front teeth swiveled his head, spotted the source of the command and headed their way.

Gaius sketched a bow. "May I be of service, Honored Teacher?"

"Yes. Tell the stable master I will require my chariot within the half hour."

"Yes, Lady."

Hypatia turned back to Orestes. "Now, Orestes, back to your paper predicament. May I presume you faced similar problems in your former assignments?"

"The army runs on paper as well as on its stomach."

"How did you handle those dilemmas?"

"My aides and the quartermaster handled most of it."

"Exactly! Entrust routine matters to assistants. Let them deal with the paper. You deal with the people. Spend your time and effort on issues more critical to the functioning of the city."

"What do you see as most critical?"

"There is a rising tide of hate and violence in the city which mirrors the schisms in the Empire." Hypatia's tone turned somber. "With a boy Emperor in Constantinople, many see an opportunity to take power locally. You can provide a force for bringing these factions together, but you must be strong and, above all, be perceived as impartial in your dealings."

"I concur." Orestes nodded. "This city seems more fractious than most. Like a high-strung horse, it needs a strong hand to thoroughly train it. But first I'll have to gain its trust."

"An apt metaphor! After our tour, you must tell me what you think of the wild steed you've been sent to tame." Hypatia pointed out buildings and people of interest as they walked toward more utilitarian buildings clustered on the edges of the sprawling Museum compound.

Orestes marveled at the magnetism of the woman on his arm. He barely knew her, yet talked as easily as if they had grown up together and shared life's secrets. He tried to be suspicious of this power Hypatia seemed to have over him, but failed. He genuinely enjoyed her company.

The pungent smell of manure announced their approach to the stables. A chariot with a pair of handsome bay geldings awaited them. Hypatia went to the fore and rubbed the horses' noses. Orestes looked over the rig and nodded his approval of the maintenance of the chariot and harnesses.

"They belong to a former student, who makes them available to me." Hypatia slipped two pieces of apple from a hidden pouch and fed the animals. "One of my few indulgences. I hold a teaching chair from the city but the stipend would not allow me to keep such lovely creatures and provide for their upkeep." She moved around the chariot, nimbly jumped into the car before Orestes could give her a hand up, and gathered the reins. "Are you ready for an adventure?"

"My life is in your hands, Lady Philosopher," Orestes said grinning.

He took a position to the left of, and behind, Hypatia. She slapped the reins and shouted "Hie!" to the horses. They tossed their heads and took off at a quick trot. Orestes grabbed for a handhold on the edge of the chariot and settled his weight on the balls of his feet, glorying in the rushing wind.

Hypatia provided a fund of historical information and contemporary gossip as they toured her favorite parts of the city. Orestes found he had much in common with this lady scholar: a disdain for formal trappings, a leaning toward an ascetic life. It was the same easy relationship Orestes had shared with his fellow army officers, a bond of trust and common purpose. Something he never expected with a woman.

As they approached a crowded market street, the horses slowed to a sedate walk and picked their way gingerly through the shifting hordes of people and carts. Orestes marveled at their steadiness in the midst of chaos. He was about to compliment Hypatia on her skill when an old man hastened out of the crowd, followed closely by two men dressed in rough monk's robes and waving cudgels. The men ducked under the horses' noses, causing them to snort and back up. People behind the chariot shouted and made a sign to ward off evil. Others yelled curses, making the horses skittish.

The crowd closed around the monks and their quarry, blocking the chariot fore and aft. Orestes saw the cudgels come down and glimpsed a body fall to the ground. A woman screamed and the crowd milled, deadlocked by those moving toward the commotion and others trying to flee. The horses' eyes showed white; sweat darkened their necks. Hypatia's eyes darted over the crowd, looking for an opening while she crooned to the horses to soothe their nerves. Orestes feared they might take the bit and run, which would surely cause injury and possibly death to some in the crowd.

"Good people, back away!" Orestes shouted in his parade ground voice. "Make way for the Prefect and Lady Hypatia." He continued shouting until the edges of the crowd thinned.

A shoving match at the center of a tight knot of people concluded as bystanders pinioned the arms of the combatants.

"Bring those men to me," Orestes shouted. The curious crowd pressed close as the men were brought to the chariot.

"Why were you pursuing this man?" Orestes looked directly at the monks. They seemed to be of that rough element—the parabolani—he had spoken to Theophilus about. The old man had a lump rising on his forehead under a bloody cut.

The smaller of the parabolani spat on the ground. "He is an Origenist heretic and spreads his untruths by preaching in the streets. We will take him to our bishop for examination."

The old man struggled briefly in his captors' hands. "Theophilus has no jurisdiction over me. I follow my own bishop, who teaches the truths of St. Clement and his student Origen."

"See? He admits his heresy." The parabolani shook his arms free and crossed them in satisfaction. "The laws are clear. You must turn him over to us."

Orestes bristled at the man's easy assumption of power. "I hear no words of heresy from this man's mouth. Any disputes should be worked out between your bishops, not taken to the streets. I am responsible for public safety and you, sir, have caused a disruption. Be warned and take these words back to your superiors. I will not tolerate attacks on private citizens by criminal or monk. You," he pointed to the old man, "be gone. The monks will abide with me a moment."

The Origenist fled through the crowds, looking fearfully over his shoulder. The parabolani scowled at Orestes, but held their tongues. When the old man escaped from view, Orestes sent the parabolani on their way with a final warning. The crowd, realizing the show was over, turned away, muttering their dissatisfaction that no one had been punished.

As the people dispersed, the horses tossed their heads, but seemed visibly calmer. Orestes was impressed Hypatia had kept the horses under control during the entire incident. He turned to her. "Do you have any insight into this dispute?"

"It's a complicated matter, these disputes among Christians." She shrugged. "On the surface are genuine disagreements about scripture, the nature of God and Christ, the fallibility of the human soul. At the core, I suspect a struggle for power and influence. One sect gains ascendancy with the Emperor and all others are outlawed. In Africa I have heard of whole congregations jailed and their lands and goods confiscated because they followed a Bishop named Donatus."

"The Emperor does not make my job easier." Orestes sighed. "Every dispatch brings new laws enumerating more heresies and their punishments."

"It's my understanding the Origenists have a more liberal view of Christianity than my friend the Patriarch can tolerate. They believe our souls are fallen spirits and this life but a trial which a soul experiences as many times as necessary to find God and holiness." Hypatia smiled ironically. "According to their beliefs, such as Socrates and Heraclitus were Christians before the time of Christ. They practice Christianity as true philosophy—love of wisdom, a search for God within. In another time, they would have been my students, not the Church's."

Orestes, keeping an eye on the lathered horses, said, "Do you often run into disturbances of this nature?"

"Rarely before, but twice in the past year. I've thought about altering my route, but…" Hypatia raised her chin. A stubborn light glinted in her eyes. "I've driven through the city for decades and am loath to change my ways because of a few rough characters."

"I believe you should avoid this part of the city, Lady." He noticed her mouth set into a grim line. "At least let me provide you with an escort."

At that she laughed. "No, my good Orestes, I will not accept an escort in my own city. Come. I have a special place to show you."

Hypatia slapped the reins and guided the horses through the straight streets toward the Mediterranean Sea. The horses' hooves crunched on the oyster-shell road as they turned onto the seven-stadia Heptastadion Dyke toward the famous Pharos lighthouse. Orestes marveled at the ingenuity of the ancient engineers, who had connected the island of Pharos to the mainland and divided the natural harbor into two sheltered bays. Pleasure boats floated in the eastern harbor like a great flock of birds on a quiet pond next to the navy docked below the ruined palace complex. The western harbor held barges and merchant ships.

Orestes had arrived by land and missed seeing the famous lighthouse from the sea. This was his first opportunity to view it up close. It was built in three sections: the lowest a massive square, the middle octagonal and the top cylindrical. A bronze statue of Neptune holding a trident adorned the top. The towering structure dwarfed the buildings clustered around its base.

"Magnificent, isn't it? It's the symbol of our city. It's nearly as tall as the Great Pyramid." Hypatia shaded her eyes from the sun glare as she looked up. "An amusing story tells that the king who commissioned the lighthouse wanted only his name on the monument. The architect craftily inscribed his own name in stone and covered it with plaster on which the imperial inscription appeared."

"Clever man." Orestes laughed. "Over the years, I assume the plaster peeled, leaving the architect's name?"

"Of course! Would you like to see the inscription? We can climb to the top. The lighthouse affords a wonderful view."

They hitched the horses to a post and approached the massive monument. The bottom portion contained fifty rooms packed with harbor officials, tradesmen, and the odd rough seaman. A senior administrator recognized Orestes and started in his direction. The Prefect waved him off. The man's face fell at the lost opportunity to meet with Egypt's governor.

"Administrators are an important part of your power in this city," Hypatia gently chided. "It would serve you well to get to know them and attend to their needs. Nothing happens without their cooperation,"

"I hoped to keep this a pleasurable jaunt." Orestes frowned. "I'll meet with the bureaucrats another day."

"Don't wait too long. Small slights build fast into large resentments." Hypatia took his arm as they ascended the leftmost of a broad set of helical ramps winding up the interior walls, passing mules burdened with the wood fuel for the lighthouse fire. In the top sections, the ramp gave way to steps and the mules to human slaves carrying the fuel to a storage platform. They passed the piles of wood and came out on a narrow balcony ringing the section below the huge mirror that amplified the light of the fire. They exited, looking out to sea. Hypatia pointed over the door. The wall contained a carving eroded by time and weather. Orestes read:

SOSTRATOS SON OF DEXIPHANES OF KNIDOS
ON BEHALF OF ALL MARINERS
TO THE SAVIOR GODS

Hypatia led Orestes to the rear of the tower, overlooking the buildings and industry that made up the bustling metropolis of Alexandria. Sunlight glinted off white marble and gold domes, color rioted in the streets, but no sound reached them on the freshening wind except the screech of sea birds.

"This is what I wanted to show you." She leaned against the railing, arms outflung. "Beautiful, isn't it? My students have traveled wide. They write to me of the wonders in other cities, or urge me to retire to their country estates, but I could never leave this. Alexandria is in my heart and bones. I wanted you to see it as I do, in all its glory. Keep this vision in your mind as you make decisions and take action. It is your home now."

"It's been a long time since I called any place home." Orestes looked over the teeming city. "In the army, home is where you retire, not where you are born or serve. I have a job to do here, a difficult one, in which I fervently hope you will assist me, but I have a feeling my bones weren't made to rest in this land."

"I've found it prudent to pay attention to inner voices." Hypatia nodded soberly. "Some say they are the voices of gods or demons, but I believe anyone trying to bring order to the chaos of his life does well to seek his satisfaction from within. Our inner spirits guide us truly; where mortal advisors distract us into thinking we can impose an abiding form on this changeable world."

They stood in companionable silence. Orestes initially rejected Hypatia's belief that it was impossible to imprint a permanent stamp on the world. Why were people put on the earth if not to shape it? Yet the cityscape gave him pause.

He faced two towering obelisks, memorials scavenged by Emperor Augustus from an ancient Egyptian Pharaoh. The striking columns guarded Cleopatra's monumental temple to the divine Caesar. The Caesarion, built on a low rise overlooking the harbor, was surrounded by a vast precinct of porticoes, libraries, chambers, groves, and open courts. The temple was now the Great Church. The unknown pharaoh, Caesar, Augustus, Cleopatra—all turned to dust centuries ago and their monuments rededicated to Christ. How long will Christianity last? The gods seemed to come and go with the ages.

Maybe Hypatia made sense. Orestes had learned early to seek satisfaction from within, rather than approval from a harsh father or distant god. He would build no monuments of stone; seek no physical legacy. He held himself accountable only for a task well done: a peaceful city, a steady flow of grain to the empire and, perhaps, the approbation of the woman at his side.

Hypatia stirred. "I have to call upon someone. Would you care to join me?"

"What's the nature of your appointment?"

"I met a most remarkable young woman, who wishes to study medicine. Her father is reluctant. I am going to try to sway his thinking."

"Are women allowed to study at the Museum?" Orestes asked, before realizing to whom he spoke.

"They are few, and none in the last generation, but," she added dryly, "a handful of us did—and still do—study, as well as teach. There are no women physicians in the city at this time, so the girl needs a patroness."

They wended their way down to the waiting chariot. Orestes offered Hypatia his hand on the steep stairs. "Who is this lucky girl who has attracted your interest?"

"Selene, daughter of Calistus. Have you met her father? He's one of the more moderate voices on the city council."

Orestes snorted in surprise. "I met Calistus and his daughter at their home a few days ago. His son Phillip is a great friend of mine. I would be more than happy to revisit the family."

He had thought there was something special about Selene. She had a confidence seldom seen in one of her youth or gender.

SELENE MOPED ABOUT HER TINY ROOM, nursing a headache and trying to work up the energy to call Anicia for cold cloths and willow bark tea. The child was nearly useless. If only—Selene's throat constricted as she fought down tears brought on by the reminder Rebecca was gone because of Selene's rashness. She flung herself on the bed and buried her face in the covers.

Anicia opened the door and timidly whispered, "Mistress Selene, your father wants to see you as soon as you can present yourself."

Selene sat up, then clutched her head as pain shot from the base of her skull into her eyeballs. "Oh!" she moaned. "I don't think I can see my father this morning. An army of demons has taken up residence in my head. Please, Anicia, cut it off and spare my father the trouble."

The servant girl squealed in horror and backed into a corner, a tray held stiffly in front of her as if in defense. "Mother has charms against demons. Please, Mistress, do not let them out!"

Selene rolled her eyes, which agitated the girl further. "I'm not possessed, you ninny, I have a headache. What have you on the tray?"

Anicia tentatively stepped forward. "Here's something Mother prepared for you." She looked at Selene from the corners of her eyes as she placed the tray on a stand next to Selene's bed. "Mother has charms for headaches, too. She says they work miracles."

"The only miracle I want is Rebecca back," Selene muttered under her breath. She reached for a sweating pitcher and held it to her forehead. Its coolness penetrated and soothed her brain, allowing her to pick at the melon and bread. The headache subsided to a dull throb between her eyes.

Anicia sniffed and backed toward the door. "Will that be all, Mistress?"

"No, that will not be all. Father wishes me to attend him. Find me some clothes."

Anicia sorted through a chest for a suitable day robe. She pulled a comfortable blue linen tunic with matching over-robe from the stack. "Will this suit?"

"Yes." A sour smile quirked Selene's lips. "At least it won't take us long to dress my hair." She ran her hands through her shorn locks. "There. All done. Help me with the robe and I'll see what tortures Father has in store for me. I have no idea what could be worse than being confined to the house. It's the second morning and already I'm half-crazy with boredom."

Anicia helped her dress. Selene looked in her mirror. Her face was pale and there were dark smudges under her eyes. She decided not to apply cosmetics. Her haggard appearance might engender a crumb of sympathy.

Selene dismissed Anicia and went in search of her father. She found him in his workroom, reviewing accounts with his steward. He seemed deeply worried. Selene had never thought of her father as old, but he suddenly seemed aged; hair thin and generously salted with gray. Deeply etched lines ran from his beaky nose to his kind mouth, and his eyes held a rheumy cast.

Selene's chest filled with remorse for the heartache she had caused him. She rushed to his side.

"Father, I'm sorry for the trouble I've caused you. Please forgive me."

He patted her bowed head. "I cannot stay angry with you, child. You bring me too much joy." He eyed the stack of papers and motioned the steward to leave. "Even your willfulness will serve you well in the coming times." Calistus flinched, caught his breath, and gripped the arm of his chair.

"Father, are you unwell?" Selene noted with alarm the gray tone to his skin, and forgot her own physical discomforts.

Calistus indicated a pitcher and goblets on a side table. He gasped, "Water."

Selene flew to the table, slopping water as she poured a generous glass and brought it to her father. He took several sips. The color returned gradually to his face. "I feel better now. Just a passing pain and shortness of breath. It goes quickly."

"How long has this been happening?"

"Only the last few months. Don't worry, Selene."

"Let me brew you willow bark tea for the pain, Father." She turned to leave but Calistus stayed her with a hand.

He leaned back in his chair and closed his eyes briefly. "Later, child. I asked you to meet me this morning because I received a message…"

"Master Calistus, you have visitors." One of the house servants bowed in the doorway.

"'Visitors'? I expected only Lady Hypatia."

"The Augustal Prefect accompanies her, Master."

Selene gasped, looking at her worn clothes and bare feet. Hypatia and Orestes! She looked like something dogs had worried in the street. She tucked in a stray curl and wet her lips. There was nothing to do but to make the best of it. Her father's words cut through her chagrin.

"I'm sorry I doubted you. As I started to say, Hypatia sent me a message this morning asking if she could wait on me to discuss your education. I have no idea why Orestes is with her."

They both stood as the guests entered, escorted by Phillip. Selene noted her brother wore appropriate dress this morning.

Calistus approached, took Hypatia's hand and bowed. "Lady Philosopher. An honor to have you in my home." Hypatia murmured polite phrases. Calistus turned to the Prefect. "Orestes, welcome again. To what do I owe this honor?"

Orestes clasped his outstretched forearm. "I had an appointment with Lady Hypatia this morning. She gave me a grand tour of the city from her chariot and asked if I minded a brief stop. I was delighted to find she intended to pay you and your lovely daughter a call." Orestes bowed in Selene's direction. She returned the bow, wishing desperately for a veil, or at least sandals.

"Let me see to refreshments for our guests, Father." Selene started to slip out the door. Her father's hand on her arm stopped her.

"No, my dear. This discussion is about your future. You may as well stay and hear. The servants will take care of our refreshments."

"No need for such courtesies, Calistus. We intend to take up little of your time." Hypatia waved off the servants and seated herself on the bench Selene had vacated. Orestes took a chair in front of the worktable while Phillip leaned against the wall, his arms crossed. Calistus resumed his chair, Selene standing at his shoulder.

"Your daughter came to my public lecture day before yesterday without your knowledge." Calistus nodded at Hypatia's words. "She approached me afterward concerning her wish to continue her studies. I was impressed by the depth of her desire and the persistence with which she pursued her goals, and offered to help her find appropriate teachers. In this, I was sorely remiss. Of course, you are the one to make this decision for your daughter. I will abide by your instructions, but I feel Selene would benefit greatly through study." Hypatia folded her hands in her lap and regarded Calistus with a level stare.

He coughed, glanced briefly at Orestes, then took up the challenge. "Thank you, Lady Hypatia, for making this effort on my daughter's behalf, but, saving yourself, I know of no other woman or girl who has been educated beyond her household."

"It is rare among your class and becoming rarer, but not unheard of. In the generations just past a number of high placed and learned women were teachers and philosophers. My contemporary Plutarch, Master of the Athenian Academy, has trained his daughter in philosophy. She is achieving some celebrity in her own right."

"Selene is a capable young woman, Father. Our tutors always held up her diligence as a model for my own behavior." Phillip chuckled ruefully. Calistus quickly smoothed a scowl.

Orestes chimed in. "Rome and Constantinople have their educated women, both those who patronize the philosophers and those who send their daughters to study. The Emperor's own sister, Pulcheria, is most learned. She is, I believe, younger than Selene."

"Enough, enough!" Calistus raised his hands in surrender. "How can I resist the foremost Philosopher in our city and the Augustal Prefect? I'm surprised you didn't enlist the Patriarch in this crusade."

"Theophilus sent his regrets, but ill health kept him home," Hypatia said with a straight face. Calistus gave her a sharp glance, but she maintained her bland expression with only a hint of a smile at the corners of her lips.

Calistus leaned back in his chair and spread his hands on the table. "I suppose it would do no harm for Selene to study Philosophy, if she is sufficiently chaperoned."

Hypatia gave Selene a sharp glance.

"Uh, Father?"

"Yes? Don't tell me you wish to go unchaperoned, because I absolutely forbid it!"

"No, Father, a chaperone is fine. It's...I want to study more than Philosophy. I want to study medicine and become a physician."

"What?" Calistus spluttered. "That is entirely different." He motioned to his guests. "You made no mention of learned women physicians among our class. I can't have my daughter entering a profession."

"Christian women of all classes practice medicine. I met a most remarkable physician—the daughter and widow of a nobleman—in Constantinople." Phillip came to her defense. "She trained a number of young girls to work in the Christian women's hospital."

Selene threw her brother a grateful smile, then knelt at her father's feet. "Please, father. I will abide by any restrictions you wish. Let me follow this path. I have a true calling."

Orestes approached and put a hand on the older man's arm. "Calistus, a talent for healing is a true gift from God. If Selene has it, she should be allowed to learn and use it wisely."

Hypatia rose and joined the trio at the table. "I will personally see to her teachers. Only ones of the highest honor and reputation will be recommended to you."

Selene looked up at her father with shining eyes and hopeful face.

Calistus glanced at the accounts stacked on his desk. The gray tone returned to his complexion. "You are too much for me. Selene may study medicine, but not until next week. She is confined to the house till next Sabbath."

"Oh, Father, thank you!" Selene flung her arms around her father and hugged him till he grunted.

"Be careful, or your first patient will be an old man with cracked ribs."

She let him go, rose and bowed to her guests. "Thank you. Both of you. Honored Teacher," she turned to Hypatia, "when may I wait on you after the next Sabbath?"

"This day next week after the mid-day meal will be fine, my dear. I'll send word where we may meet. Come, Orestes." She linked arms with the Prefect. "We must complete our tour."

A discreet servant showed the guests to the door. Selene left to make the long overdue willow bark tea, but not before she overheard Phillip saying. "Father, with Selene studying, we'll need a housekeeper, one experienced with our staff…"

CHAPTER 12

THE FOLLOWING WEEK, Calistus personally escorted Selene to the scholars' precinct south of the Caesarion to meet with Hypatia. They found her in a scriptorium where dozens of men, old and young, hunched over tables copying texts for use in the Library or sale to private collectors.

After greetings, Hypatia asked Selene, "Do you write a fair hand, child?"

"Yes, Lady. My tutors gave me high marks in writing Greek and Latin."

"Good. All students and apprentices do work in the scriptorium. We've lost thousands of volumes through the centuries to war and fire. We want to preserve the rest."

"The public library at the Serapeum burned in my youth." Calistus shook his head. "A great loss."

"That was a terrible time." A sad look stole over Hypatia's face; then she brightened, gesturing toward a small group of men piecing together a deteriorating papyrus scroll. "Here is preservation rather than destruction. The copies are written on parchment and bound in codices. The book is a much more durable and convenient form than the papyrus scroll. Come, I'll show you the main parts of the Library, then introduce Selene to her teachers."

Hypatia glided down the main aisle of the scriptorium flanked by the scratching of reed on parchment. Selene and her father followed closely. They exited into a maze of covered walkways where bound codices and older scrolls wrapped in leather sleeves rested in row after row of recessed niches hidden behind the columns. Dangling tags identified the contents of scrolls organized in collections of literature, philosophy, and science.

"Here's where the medical texts are housed." Hypatia indicated a side aisle. They turned the corner to see an ancient man sorting through dusty scrolls and large bound books. His fringe of white hair floated like spiders' webs around his dried-apple face.

"I know it's here somewhere," the old man muttered. He replaced a scroll and stretched to pull down another. He couldn't reach the shelf and gave a little jump, his robes hiking up to show skinny ankles ribbed with blue veins.

"Auxentius, why don't you use a stool? I'm not sure your frail bones will take the beating you're giving them." Hypatia indicated a short wooden stool at the side of the aisle. Selene went to retrieve it.

"My dear Lady Philosopher, what would you know about bones? I promise to leave things of the mind to you if you agree to leave things of the body to me." Two red spots stained the old man's cheeks as he gasped for breath.

"Here, Master." Selene approached with the stool. "Or I could get the scroll for you?"

Auxentius blinked up as if trying to bring her into focus. "What? Oh, er, the third one from the left on the second shelf from the top." Even with her height, Selene had to use the stool. It would have been totally beyond the old man's reach.

He snatched for the document like a magpie going for a shiny trinket. "Thanks, child. Now where is that reference?" Auxentius sat on the stool and spread his treasure on his lap. "Damn pests!" He shook the scroll, releasing a cloud of tiny desiccated insect bodies. Selene saw several holes in the fragile papyrus. "We lose more books to bugs and vermin than to fire or theft," the old man muttered.

"Auxentius!" Hypatia's tone turned sharp. The toe of her sandal tapped the marble floor with a hollow slapping sound.

"What, Hypatia? Can't you see I'm researching something important?"

"This is City Counselor Calistus and his daughter Selene, the new student I told you about."

"Oh? What day is it?" He peered more closely at Selene. "Hypatia, this young person is female."

"Daughters usually are," Calistus said dryly.

"It's just after noon on Monday," Hypatia said with a touch of asperity. "We discussed all this last week."

The old man bobbed his head. "So we did, so we did. I forgot. Which reminds me…" His muttering subsided as he stroked his beardless cheek. After a moment of blankness, he became aware of them again. "Did you say it was after noon?"

Hypatia nodded. Selene spoke up. "Master Auxentius, have you eaten your mid-day meal? I've found the mind works better when the stomach is well fed."

"Food? I think I had fruit this morning. Or was that yesterday? No matter. We can go to the dining hall and I can examine you there. Hypatia told me you have already studied using unorthodox methods. Let's see what you really know." The old man hobbled down the aisle.

"Don't worry, my child," Hypatia said. "Auxentius is a most learned teacher in medical history and theory. He wants to test your knowledge so he can plan your studies. I'll come to the dining hall in an hour and take you to meet your anatomy teacher. Come, Calistus, I wish to talk to you about the council's latest decisions concerning public water."

Selene glanced at her father, who smiled his approval. Auxentius led Selene down the corridor, occasionally murmuring something incomprehensible. She assumed he was not talking to her and, since he did not wait for a response, she followed quietly.

When they reached the common dining hall of the scholar's quarter, he seated himself at a long stained wooden table and waved over a youngster carrying a heavy load of used dishes. The child tottered over and stood sweating beneath his burden. "Boy, get me wine, fruit, and meat rolls from the kitchen. Anything for you, my dear?"

Selene shook her head.

"Good. It's difficult to talk with your mouth full. Tell me what you know about Aesculapius, Hippocrates, Herophilus, Galen, and Pliny. What were their major contributions to medicine? Discuss their seminal texts and contemporary criticisms of their beliefs."

Selene sat frozen with mouth agape, her mind temporarily blank. She had not prepared for an examination. Auxentius peered at her with heavily lidded eyes that didn't blink. He reminded her of the small lizards that sunned themselves on the rocky beaches where she ran. The absurd thought broke through Selene's panic. She took a deep breath. "Aesculapius is the Greek god of healing. The pagans call his daughters Hygieia and Panacea goddesses of…"

"Wrong! Ancient people ignorantly believed them to be gods." Auxentius snorted. "They were real people like you or me. Continue."

101

Selene wished she had ordered watered wine from the boy. Her mouth felt dry and her nerves jumpy. She rushed ahead, storing the implications of Auxentius' statement about two famous women healers away for later contemplation. "H-Hippocrates was one of the first physicians to describe his patients' illnesses in detail. His writings are still in use today. Several of his sayings are everyday knowledge, such as 'When sleep puts an end to delirium it is a good sign.' "

Auxentius nodded in grudging approval as his food arrived. Absently, he started stuffing himself, breadcrumbs dropping into his robes. A dribble of fruit juice leaked from the corner of his mouth but stopped halfway down his chin. Selene tried to concentrate.

"Herophilus is not familiar to me, Master."

"Ignorant child!" the old man muttered, devouring the last of a meat roll. "Herophilus wrote the first anatomy text based on real observations. Damn churchmen won't allow us to do dissections on humans now. Not even criminals!" He rambled on, proving it was difficult to talk, much less be understood, with a full mouth. Selene dropped her head in despair at keeping up with his seemingly inexhaustible store of knowledge. In the middle of a rant about the absurdity of an obscure author, he suddenly took note of her again. "Continue. What of Galen and Pliny?" He waved a pomegranate vaguely in the air.

Selene forged ahead in a tentative voice. "Galen of Pergamon was a physician to the Roman Emperors. His writing on anatomy and treatment of diseases is considered the definitive text in modern medicine."

"Galen studied here in Alexandria, as well as Pergamon and Rome," Auxentius muttered into a bread roll. Selene waited for him to embroider his comments, but he seemed satisfied.

"Master, did you want me to address the works of Pliny the Elder or his nephew Pliny the Younger?"

"Impudent pup! Pliny the Elder, of course."

Selene nodded. "Pliny wrote Natural History, an encyclopedia of science. I've read all 37 parts…"

"What is your opinion of his work?"

She hesitated, not wanting to offend the old man.

"Your opinion, girl." Auxentius tipped his head to the side. "If you want to be a physician, you must have an opinion and not be afraid to tell others."

Selene intuitively knew the truth of his words. All good physicians exuded a sense of confidence, inspiring people in their ability to cure—whether justified or not.

"I found much to admire in Natural History, Master, but also much that was fantastical. In particular, I doubt the existence of a race of headless men, or another with feet so large they use them to shade themselves from the sun."

"Absolutely right! Rubbish! How any intelligent man could swallow such donkey dung, I don't understand." He wandered off into another lecture, this one on the uselessness of cataloging information without testing its veracity.

"Auxentius, are you quite through?" Selene heard with relief Hypatia's amused tone over her shoulder.

"Yes, the meal was quite satisfying. I'm not sure what kind of meat the cook uses in the rolls, but they are tasty."

"I mean with Selene. Are you finished testing her?"

"Oh, the girl. Yes, yes. Quite satisfactory. Knows her Pliny. Heard of most of the classic writers. Much better than the usual student. She'll do. I'll make up a list of readings for her this afternoon." He noticed the scroll lying ignored during his meal. "Now what is this doing here?" Auxentius scratched his head. "Oh, yes, the reference!"

"Come, Selene. I'll take you to your anatomy teacher." They left Auxentius poring over the text, oblivious to their exit. "I'll remind him later to prepare a syllabus for your initial studies." They continued out of the eating hall and walked to a small stone building set back from the street. As they came closer, the sweetly sick smell of decaying meat caused Selene's stomach to clench. She glanced quickly at Hypatia. The older woman seemed oblivious to both the odor and Selene's reaction.

They ducked through the open door. Light filled the inside from several high wide windows. The walls were lined with shelves. Some contained books, others covered jars, another a collection of sharp instruments: knives, bone saws, awls. Dust motes floated in the streaming sunshine, lighting a battered stone table dominating the room. Selene stifled a gasp. The body of a small ape lay spread-eagled on the table, its internal organs heaped in piles around the still figure. Small channels allowed blood and body fluids to drain through holes in the table into buckets set below. Selene batted at the flies that infested the air and struggled to keep her stomach under control.

A tall man of obvious Nubian stock separated from the shadows in a corner. He wore a rough brown sleeveless tunic and leather apron, stained from his bloody exertions. His smooth ebony limbs and shaved head glistened in the light. Selene particularly noted his large blunt hands, the nails pared short and rimed with blackened blood.

"Master Haroun, here is the new pupil we discussed last week, Selene, daughter of the Counselor Calistus."

He peered at her closely. Selene felt like a prize racehorse up for auction. He finally spoke. "Has old Auxentius been at you yet?"

Taken aback by the unexpected question, Selene stuttered, "Wh-Why yes. I just left Master Auxentius."

"Did he regale you with Galen and ply you with Pliny?"

"He mentioned it would be wise of me to know the masters and their writings."

"Dead men gone to dust centuries ago can't teach you to see living flesh and know healthy tissue from diseased. Look at me." Haroun waved his hand from head to foot. "What do you see?"

Selene inspected him in the same way he had her, noting various scars, his well-muscled body, and one sandal thicker than the other. "Your skin, teeth, and breathing indicate good health. But you suffered from an animal attack in your youth. Your left leg—the one with the scars—is shorter than the other by far, probably due to damage to the muscles or tendons. From the look of your shoulders, I guess you wrestle, throw the javelin or the discus."

Haroun smiled, showing two gold canines. "She has good eyes, Hypatia. Promising." He turned back to the girl. "It was a jackal and I wrestle. But it takes more than good eyes to see what is. You must also use your hands to feel the difference between broken and straight bone; your ears to hear the difference in humors in the lungs; and your nose to smell health or disease on flesh, breath, or urine. Are you up to the task, girl? I can't have you fainting or fluttering in my classes."

"Yes, Master Haroun. I don't faint at the sight of blood or flutter in distress." She bowed to the tall man, desperately hoping she could keep her promise. "I want nothing more than to study with you."

"Hypatia speaks on your behalf and you've proven to have some talent in observation. Can you draw?"

"With ink and charcoal, Master."

"You may come to my anatomy class three days hence. It starts at dawn, before the heat of the day makes it impossible to work. Wear clothes you don't mind getting stained." He bowed to Hypatia and turned back to the ape. The two women beat a hasty retreat.

Hypatia took Selene's arm again. "You are doing well, child. Let's return to your father. Of course, I expect you to attend my lectures."

Selene tried to keep a neutral face as she contemplated hours of obtuse philosophic discussion, abstract mathematics, and calculating the rotation of the planets. "I would be honored to attend any classes you recommend, Lady."

Hypatia laughed knowingly. "Natural history, my dear, science. Of course, I believe the study of philosophy is the highest calling a person can have. Philosophy encompasses all the lesser subjects. But I think your interests are more of this world than the next. When you need it, you will seek out philosophy and higher mathematics as well."

Selene relaxed and, at Hypatia's urging, chatted easily about her experiences of the day and her excitement about her studies. They continued to a spacious public garden, Hypatia greeting people along the way. Selene's head swam with names, specialties, and relationships. When they reached her father, she forgot all decorum and threw herself at his chest.

"Oh, thank you, Father. I couldn't be happier." She hugged him tight in an explosion of emotion. "You won't regret this. I won't shirk my duties at home. All will be as before."

He caressed her hair. "I'm not worried about the household, my dear; Rebecca's been doing a fine job since she returned. I'm worried about you. Will you be safe? Will you be happy? This is a difficult choice you're making."

"It's not difficult, Father. It's the only choice for me."

Hypatia cleared her throat. "Selene did well today, Calistus. I'm sure she will fulfill her promise. Now I must be off. I'll expect her at my lecture, two days hence."

Selene watched the diminutive woman disappear into a hall, then guided her father toward the garden exit. The sweet scent of lilies replaced the faint odor of death lingering about her clothes. She felt as if she could float home on her happiness.

ON THE MORNING of her first class, Nicaeus' surly mope and belligerent pout spoiled Selene's ebullient mood. It wasn't her fault Father assigned him as chaperone. The third time he scuffed a rock, it ricocheted off her ankle.

"Ouch! You did that on purpose!"

His eyes shifted from her angry gaze, as he muttered, "Did not!"

She rubbed her ankle to remove the sting. "Listen, Nicaeus, you're stuck with me three times a week for the next several weeks. You might as well make the best of it. You might learn something."

"I doubt it." One side of his mouth turned up in a lopsided grin. "I've never liked to study."

It was true their tutors sometimes despaired of Nicaeus. When they were young, a teacher resorted to a cane to encourage the boy to apply his wits. Calistus dismissed that man, saying a stick never taught any lesson except that the strong can beat the weak bloody. Nicaeus was not a stupid or light-minded youth, but seemed directionless, like a piece of wood adrift on the Nile. That's why Selene was startled when he said, "Luckily, you don't have to be smart in the army, just fast and strong."

Selene grabbed his arm and pulled him around to face her. "Nicaeus, not the army! We might not see you for ten years. Father would never give his permission."

"He wouldn't? Phillip got to escape to Constantinople. You get to follow your heart's desire to study medicine. What possible excuse could Father have for keeping me out of the army?" Nicaeus scuffed at another rock. "It's not as if I'm needed here."

His flat tone belied the pain showing in his face. Selene reached out to cup his cheek in her hand, but he turned his head away. Staring at a middle distance, he continued, "It's an honorable career. Phillip told me he would ask Orestes for a commission. I would go in as an officer with the Egyptian Prefect's recommendation."

"But they don't post troops in their own provinces." Tears shone in Selene's eyes. "I don't want to lose you! It was hard enough with Phillip gone for three years, and he was safe in a city." She dashed the tears away and said, in a bantering tone, "Besides, you are needed here. Who will accompany me to classes if you go?"

He folded her into his arms and patted her back. "I won't go for several months. By then you will have a new chaperone."

"Are things so bad you feel you have to leave us?" She leaned into his shoulder.

Nicaeus' face took on the grim lines of a much older man. "It's time I made my own way. Phillip will inherit when father passes on. I don't have the patience for a civil appointment or your thirst for knowledge. This is best for me."

She had watched without comprehension as Nicaeus grew older and more restless. Selene assumed their father would chart his younger son's course or Nicaeus would find something or someone to anchor him. Selene never expected he would run off to the army.

"We have a while to figure this out." She straightened in his arms, heaviness temporarily lifting from her heart. "I'm sure I can come up with a way to keep you happy at home. Maybe we can find you a rich wife."

"You don't understand, Selene." Nicaeus pulled back, laughing. "I want to go. Don't try to come up with a romantic scheme to keep me here." He wagged a finger at her. "I don't want to see a parade of rich, empty-headed girls traipsing through our house."

"We'll see. Maybe I can find one with a few brains to make up for your lack of wits." She turned and started toward her classes at a brisk walk, counting off on her fingers. "There's Harmonia, Eudoxia…"

"Selene!" Nicaeus shouted after her. "Don't you dare!"

CHAPTER 13

OUR FATHER, WHO ART IN HEAVEN, have mercy on my uncle. Restore him to health so he may take up the staff again in Your name and lead Your people to righteousness." Cyril prayed with fervor and despair in the private oratory connected to the Patriarch's bedchamber. Theophilus' health had steadily declined over the past two months. A constant stream of clerks carrying letters and gifts now flowed to the bedroom where the Patriarch conducted most of his business. He grew weaker each day and soon would be unable to see anyone other than physicians and close aides.

"Master Cyril?" a servant boy asked tentatively from the door. "The Patriarch is asking for you."

"Thy will be done. Amen," Cyril concluded. A spike of irritation at the interruption jarred with the peace prayer always brought to his soul. When he became Patriarch…

Cyril cut the thought short and shrugged his shoulders to rid himself of the knots. If God could be persuaded by the number and fervency of prayers, Theophilus would recover. All of Egypt prayed for his health. Cyril believed in miracles, but felt in his heart his uncle's time had come. The thought shook his body with grief tinged with fear and anticipation. He rose, twitched his woolen robes into order, and strode toward the door with renewed purpose.

The Patriarch's chief steward sat on a bench next to the bed. A dour, horse-faced man with an uncanny nose for corruption, Paulinus had been chosen with the approval of all the clergy thirteen years ago to "keep the ministry of God free from avarice." Theophilus had encouraged Cyril to be on friendly terms with the steward who oversaw every aspect of the church's financial activity. Paulinus received the congregation's tithes and offerings. His staff of treasurers and auditors provided the funds for the church-run poorhouses, hostels, hospitals, and homes for the elderly; drew up the list of subsidized poor and widows; and inventoried valuable consecrated vessels. Paulinus even provided the almoner who accompanied the Patriarch on visits and processions to give gifts to the poor.

"Chief Steward." Cyril bowed to the senior churchman.

"I want you to hear our discussions, Nephew," Theophilus wheezed from his bed. "When you are Patriarch, you should know these things."

Cyril didn't know whether it was the prospect of his succeeding his uncle or the sharing of privileged information with a junior church member that caused the chief steward to look like he'd sucked a bitter lemon. From his past dealings with the conservative steward, it was probably both. At least the man did not challenge his presence directly.

"I am at your disposal, Uncle." Cyril deliberately emphasized the relationship rather than his uncle's title.

Paulinus straightened, his face smoothing to a neutral mask as he consulted his notes. "This quarter's distributions include increasing amounts to the sick, poor, and elderly. With the influx of peasants to the city, their plights are most grave. As is customary, we've set aside funds to build temporary shelters for the homeless in the vicinity of the Caesarion during the cold season. We are also increasing our contributions to the Mariner's Guild."

"Why is that?" Cyril looked at Theophilus with a frown.

"The Mariners are taxed heavily by the Emperor. They are required to transport the grain tithe to Constantinople without recompense. We help ease that burden and gain their support in matters more important to our interests."

"We also have a list of nobles to whom we are repaying debts." Paulinus' mask cracked somewhat.

"Yes." Theophilus subsided into a fit of coughing. Paulinus and Cyril collided in their efforts to pour water for the stricken man. The steward backed off, allowing Cyril to minister to his uncle. The Patriarch took a few sips. "These nobles loaned the church money during the early days of my episcopate and I felt we should make good on our debts."

"Who are these nobles?" Cyril inquired.

Paulinus read off the short list. Cyril recognized four prominent men in current financial difficulty. If they survived, they would be in positions to further his claim to the episcopate.

Paulinus frowned. "Did not the Lord say 'A rich man had as much chance of attaining heaven as a camel passing through the eye of a needle?' Why not remind these good men of their obligations and keep the money?"

"My dear steward," Theophilus coughed. "These men helped me in the time of my most dire need. They suffer in their turn from financial hardship and it is in my power to help them." He waved Paulinus away. "Go now and execute your duties. I will see you tomorrow." He lay back wheezing on a pile of cushions.

"I have no record of these men loaning the church money." Paulinus continued stubbornly.

Cyril stared at the steward with half-lidded eyes. "My uncle says they loaned the church money. Those were riotous times and doubtless the records were lost or destroyed. Do you question the word of our Patriarch?"

"No." The chief steward bowed out the door. "I will execute the Patriarch's will."

Cyril approached his uncle with more water. The stricken man waved the cup away. "I have more to show you. Look below the bed."

Cyril dropped to his knees and pulled up the soft woolen blankets concealing the space under his uncle's bed. Three large chests, each made of mahogany and bound with brass, sat there. Two were of a size, but the third was smaller. He pulled each out and lined them against the wall.

"This is my personal fortune," Theophilus whispered from his reclining position. "I will leave ample provision for you and your sister. See that she marries well." Theophilus fumbled at his breast and extracted a chain with three keys. Cyril opened the chests and gasped at the treasure of gold and silver coins, jewelry encrusted with precious gems, and silver plate.

"I vowed you and your sister would never be threatened with the same troubles as I and your mother." Theophilus and his sister had been impoverished and orphaned in early childhood. A faithful family slave rescued them from a miserable fate by presenting the children to Patriarch Athanasius. The Patriarch raised the children, training Theophilus as his successor and marrying Cyril's mother to a godly man in Lower Egypt.

Theophilus loved his sister dearly and, when she and her husband died of a fever, he took in her son and daughter. The cycle repeated as Theophilus prepared his nephew to be the next Patriarch.

Cyril ran his hands through the pile of gold and silver coins. The slick texture of the precious metal against his skin felt almost sensuous. Being raised in the church, he felt no personal need of such wealth, but knew his uncle had his own reasons for amassing such a fortune. It would, indeed, provide a more than handsome dowry for his sister.

"There are also carpets, household goods, and clothes listed among my effects. You should use your portion to your advantage. I've prepared a list of nobles and councilors whom you need to support your claim to the bishop's chair." Theophilus waved vaguely toward a table that acted as a desk during his illness. "Make sure they receive substantial gifts. Have you contacted the desert monks?"

Cyril nodded. "They stand ready at my word to enter the city and express their wishes for the election." He frowned. "The suburban monasteries can be reached within a day, but it takes three to cross the Mareotis to Nitria and another three to come back."

"You must send word right away," the old man gasped.

"You have guided me well in all things, Uncle." Cyril bowed his head. "Do you not feel this may be premature? I've prayed for your recovery."

"I, too, have asked the Lord to let this cup pass me by. I would see you advance through the church offices and your sister happily settled, but I fear my time is coming fast." Theophilus lay back on his cushions and closed his eyes. "There is a man I've found most useful. A teacher by the name of Hierex. I've arranged for him to meet you on the morrow."

Cyril, a lump in his throat, clasped his uncle's hand. "Anything you wish, Uncle. I will see my sister well-cared for and carry out your wishes to the best of my ability." The ill man squeezed Cyril's fingers, then lapsed into a fitful sleep.

Cyril watched the shadows deepen on the old man's face and prayed for the strength to carry out his uncle's will. As a young man inexperienced in the church offices, he faced stiff opposition and sometimes wondered if his Uncle's plans in this regard were wrong-headed.

"IF I HAD KNOWN how much work a commission took, I would have enlisted as a simple soldier," Nicaeus complained to Selene on their way to her classes. Orestes had given his recommendation, then promptly left for a tour of

111

the province two months ago, leaving Nicaeus to the tender mercies of the bureaucrats.

He started with a simple document; ended with seven addenda and signatures from several clerks in the offices of the quartermaster general of the army, the accountant general, the minister of finance, paymaster-in-chief, recording secretary, and corresponding secretary. Nicaeus kept the bundle of documents in a leather pouch which flapped at his hip.

A sharp dawn breeze tugged at Selene's robes, causing her to clutch her rolls of drawings and wax tablets more tightly. She looked up at the brooding dawn sky, tinged bloody red. The fall stormy season approached.

"Have you learned any good cures for a sore ass?" Nicaeus continued. "If I have to sit on one more unpadded bench in another condescending petty clerk's office, I'll put my swordsmanship to better use than sticking some godless barbarian. Do you think the world would miss two dozen bureaucrats?"

"No one but their families and me." Selene laughed and leaned close. "I am grateful to them for keeping you here. I will miss you, Nicaeus."

"I know." He took her arm. "I've had time to think these past months. On some days, I regret my decision and think seriously about tearing up this cursed batch of papers." He slapped the leather pouch. "But most days I'm thrilled at the prospect of seeing another part of the world; showing Father I can make my own way. It's what keeps me going from one dusty office to another."

"We're almost at the hall." Selene kissed his cheek. "Thank you for the company." They had arrived early at her anatomy class. She was to give a presentation—her first—to her teacher and fellow students. Selene hadn't eaten breakfast for fear she wouldn't be able to keep it down. Talking with Nicaeus helped calm her nerves. "Leave me to the lions while you visit with Alexandria's finest. I look forward to hearing your scintillating stories of dense clerks and obstinate bureaucrats at dinner."

"You'll do fine, little sister." He kissed her lightly on the forehead. "If any of those boys disagree with you, let me know and," Nicaeus stepped back, drew an imaginary sword and brandished it. "I'll rid the world of a few stupid students as well as reduce the population of clerks."

Laughing helped settle the feeling of insects flitting in her stomach. Selene waved to her brother and entered the dim classroom. She wanted to get the feel of the place before it filled with distracting movements and the pungency of male bodies. She ran her fingers over the scarred walls and benches covered with generations of schoolboy scrawls. Her own father had probably left his mark somewhere in these rooms. The thought comforted Selene. She looked around and, seeing no one, quickly scratched her own name in the mortar behind a supporting column. That small act of desecration made her feel temporarily part of the larger student community. A feeling she relished and held fast as long as she could.

Selene desperately wanted to do well. Haroun had allowed her in his advanced class with the students already apprenticing. She was the youngest, as well as the only girl. At first, the older boys tried to shove her aside when crowding around the specimens, but, with her height and sharp elbows, Selene made a place for herself. Two young men quit, expressing publicly their disdain for a female in the class. Haroun called them fools for letting such a small obstacle deter them.

Today, Selene presented her theories on the structures in the eye. In lieu of forbidden human dissection, she had compared the eyes of apes, pigs, and dogs, attempting to draw conclusions from their similarities. Auxentius helped her find drawings of the human eye by ancient doctors. Haroun, pleased with her research, had asked her to explain her findings. She shuffled her notes and drawings nervously, wondering if she had missed something and would look a fool.

"Selene, are you ready?" Haroun asked behind her back.

She twitched, startled by his voice. Turning around, Selene took a deep breath. "Yes, Honored Teacher." Haroun presented a neutral face as the other students filed into the room, no evidence of encouragement or discouragement. She was on her own.

As the others settled onto their benches, Selene moved to the front. She started to lecture in a quivery voice, then dropped her drawings. Some students laughed. Others shifted in their seats or coughed behind their hands. Haroun gave them a sharp look and they quieted.

Selene became angry with herself. Why was she so timid? What did she care what these boys thought? In her calmer moments, she realized their regard meant little, but she came from a family where her accomplishments had always been praised. Her isolation and her fellow students' active disdain took its toll, shaking her confidence. She hesitated the few moments she needed to pull herself—as well as her drawings—together, and started again in a stronger voice.

Selene paused at the end, looking out over her fellow students. "Are there any questions?"

Pontine, a handsome, well-spoken young man and a charismatic leader of the philoponoi—zealous Christian students recruited from the upper classes—rose to speak. Selene's heart sank. Pontine made a point of belittling her at every opportunity and complaining of Haroun's paganism on the flimsiest of pretexts. She wondered why he bothered to attend the class, but the self-satisfied smile on his face gave her a clue.

"Do you expect us to believe the structures you identified at the back of the eye mysteriously provide pictures to the brain? What has the brain to do with this? Everyone knows the seat of consciousness is in the heart."

"Who is this mysterious everyone?" Selene's voice turned sharp. "Plato and Aristotle hypothesized the heart as the seat of consciousness, but on what evidence? Hippocrates drew different conclusions." She pointed to her head. "How else would you explain the nerve connecting the eye to the brain? There is no similar structure to the heart."

Haroun stood up. "Excellent work, Selene. You pulled together documentary and observational evidence to support your theories. However, I suggest you consult with Hypatia on your rhetorical skills." He turned to the youth. "Pontine, you might do well to observe more closely. Because something is written does not make it so."

A triumphant grin flashed across Pontine's face. "Do you not believe in the truth of the written Word of God?"

Selene now saw the trap Pontine set for Haroun, and her part in it. She prayed fervently that Haroun saw it as well.

"The Christian Bible is a sacred text. I speak of medical texts which claim to be the literal truth, but both contain much that is fantastical." Haroun fixed the youth with a stern eye. "I am encouraging you to believe the evidence of your own observations before what is written. This is a modern age. Test the words of the ancients and add to their knowledge."

"No one can test God's Word, nor should anyone compare God's Word to the works of man." Pontine jumped on Haroun's statements. "You should not be allowed to teach, Sir. I will see this class closed." Pontine gathered his wax slates and stalked to the front of the room. In the doorway, he looked back. "All who fear for their souls should join me."

Almost half the class gathered their things and streamed past Selene. Pontine pulled his mouth into a sneer, turned on his heel, and left.

"They are well gone." Haroun said in icy tones. "I will not have any in my class who do not, or will not, challenge writing with observations and experiment." He turned his glare on the remaining students. "For instance, one well-known text claims eating the herb dittany extracts arrows from a wound. Selene, perhaps you can explain to those who remain how to test the author's assertion?"

All eyes again turned to her. Selene gulped. "I believe it would be easy to test, Honored Teacher. A physician could treat a soldier with an arrow wound by having him eat dittany. If the arrow loosened and fell out, the premise would be proved. If not…" she shrugged her shoulders.

"Exactly!" Haroun pointed at the students. "You will make poor physicians if you persist in remedies that have no proven worth. I know not a single battlefield surgeon who treats arrow wounds with dittany. Why? Because they have seen what works and what doesn't. Dittany doesn't work. Now, are there any other questions for Selene?"

"I HEARD ABOUT THE CONFRONTATION in your anatomy class," Hypatia stated after their lesson on rhetoric.

"I'm sorry, Honored Teacher." Selene descended from the lectern. "Is Master Haroun in any trouble? Will his class be closed?"

"There's no need to apologize, child. Haroun is protected from such as Pontine. Haroun saved the life of a rich and powerful man when all others gave up hope. That noble pays his stipend."

Hypatia, who had been standing, settled on a bench and motioned Selene to join her. "Pontine is a bright, personable young man who influences many. He walks a different path and takes many with him." She looked around the classroom. "A generation ago I filled this space. Now I have but a handful of students."

Startled, Selene contemplated the empty room. She hadn't noticed the decline in students. Was that the reason they were willing to accept a girl? "Why are there fewer students, Lady?"

"It's my observation that men of talent are abandoning the Museum as a place of study and flocking to the Christian Church."

"I don't understand." Selene chewed her lower lip in concentration. "The Church offers no breadth of study. They read only the Bible; prepare only for church offices."

Hypatia smiled and patted her hand. "The innocence of youth is refreshing, but dangerous. You must look beyond the obvious. Human behavior is many-layered like the onion. The old gods were variable, cruel, and no One had ascendancy. They made no promises of redemption for a life lived in sin. Men of talent focused on the present life and tried their best to ignore their capricious gods. They studied a wide range of subjects, explored the world around them, and commented on what they learned. Modern men are told from birth to look forward to the next life. They have no need to explore this world, but spend their time debating the essence of God and what is to come."

Even more confused, Selene asked, "But, Lady, isn't that exactly what you do in philosophy?"

"Indeed, studying the nature of the soul is the heart of philosophy." Hypatia smiled, her gaze turned inward. "But to know God, you must know yourself and the world around you. Where do we fit in this grand scheme? Philosophy is a rigorous study and a way of life which few are able to master. Men of talent used to strive for that perfection, living a life of observation and rational thought. The Christian Church offers an easy way for many to succeed. 'Have faith! Obey!' It requires no thought, only belief, so everyone can partake. Where the masses go, power follows. Where there is power, there is influence."

"Power and influence attract men of talent and ability to positions of leadership. That is why they no longer continue at the Museum," Selene completed the argument. She sat quietly for a moment, thinking how to ask her next question, then put it baldly. "Lady, is that why you made room for me? Because there were no others?"

"No!" Hypatia looked grieved. "I would have made room for you if I had four times the students I have now. Selene, all your teachers agree you have a gift. In your first three months you have shown enthusiasm, intelligence, and innovation. Your talents might not lie in rhetoric, but you will bring light to the world in your own way. So forget about Pontine and his followers. Concentrate on your studies and you will be a superb physician."

The praise spread throughout her soul, warming all but the chilliest corners where Selene kept her severest criticisms and self-doubts.

CHAPTER 14

CYRIL ABSORBED THE VOICES praying by his uncle's bed. The soothing staccato rhythm washed through him, making him feel part of a greater whole. At his summons all of the church elders had gathered this morning before dawn to make their final peace with the Patriarch.

The pungency of incense, mixed with the sour scent of the sick room, tickled Cyril's nose. He stifled a sneeze. For the past two weeks he had rarely left this place, ministering to his uncle, sleeping on a pallet in the corner. He performed every office with love, even removing the soiled sheets and washing his uncle's wasted body.

Theophilus had spent what few private moments they had tutoring him in the politics of the church, giving him background on each of the numerous daily visitors, drilling him in the actions Cyril must take upon his uncle's demise. Cyril listened and questioned, coming early to understand the great burden his uncle bore. Doubts plagued him. Each night he prayed for the strength and wisdom to be a worthy successor. Last night, he dreamed:

He walked in the desert. His muscles aching with fatigue; his eyes gritty with dust; his body tortured by cold, thirst, and hunger. He cried out in fear, then saw a great light burning, as if the sun had come to rest on the earth. He stumbled toward the beacon on bloody feet and collapsed at the edge of a beautiful garden. Many-colored birds trilled in trees laden with heavy fruit. Flowers opened delicate petals to infuse the air with their sweet scent. He heard water splashing in the distance and, tormented by thirst, rose to follow a path of dewy moss that soothed his cut feet.

He came to a clearing where a rough rock thrust through soft grass. He sat a moment to ease his aches. From the surrounding trees, three women approached: the first dressed in humble peasant's robes, the second as a dutiful matron, and the third in resplendent court garb. Their faces exuded a blessed light that made it difficult to distinguish their features, but Cyril knew, in the way of dreams, they were the three Marys of Jesus' death and resurrection.

Mary Magdalene approached first, with a humble clay goblet and a loaf of bread. "Drink and eat, refresh your body, for your trials have ended." He drank deeply, letting the delicious coolness of water, sweeter than any wine, ease his parched throat. One bite of the bread filled his empty belly. Strength coursed through his blood.

The matronly Mary, mother of James, came forward, offering a wool robe rent in three pieces. Cyril recognized the sacred pallium of St. Mark of Alexandria. "Don this garment, but be aware that, while it is in parts, it offers little comfort." Cyril reached for the pieces. At his touch they knit together. He wrapped the garment around his chilled body, creating immediate warmth.

Finally, the Blessed Virgin Mary approached. He knelt before her glorious form. "Look up, my son. See that for which you strive." He raised his eyes and beheld a curiously wrought golden crown. It resembled the ancient double crowns of the Egyptian Pharaohs, but a cross replaced the rearing snake over the brow. The Mother of God set the crown upon his head. He rose. The rough stone transformed to a golden bishop's chair, shining with an inner brilliance. He took his place upon it. The first two women knelt before him while the Blessed Virgin took her place at his right shoulder.

Cyril awoke from that dream filled with certainty and light, all doubts banished. His uncle had declared him fit, and God had given His blessing. It would not be easy, but he must marshal his resources, unify the church, and take firm hold of his domain. His first goal would be to convince the men in this room of his right to the bishopric. Many had made clear their opposition during the past two weeks. Indeed, the Archdeacon's supporters occupied their own space in the room, clustering together at the foot of the bed. They were a smaller band than several weeks ago.

"Cyril?" Theophilus' cracked voice drew his nephew's immediate attention.

He reached for the skeletal hand resting on the sheets. It was cold and dry. "I am here."

The nearly translucent lids fluttered open. "I will soon join Our Father in Heaven." His eyes shut again for several fitful breaths, then reopened. The Patriarch frowned. "You know what you are to do?"

"Rest, Uncle. Do not fret. I will continue your work, never fear."

"My son," Theophilus whispered. Cyril felt the lightest pressure as his uncle squeezed his hand.

"All of you," the old man wheezed, slightly louder, "come near."

The men crowded around the bed, expectantly silent except for small rustlings of feet on carpet and the occasional rasp of indrawn breath.

"You all witness." Theophilus stopped to gather his strength. He propped himself up on one elbow and reached his other hand to rest on his nephew's head. "Cyril is my choice for Patriarch." His hand slipped back to the bed and he collapsed onto his cushions.

Cyril sat, tears streaming, holding his uncle's hand as the old man labored to breathe. Their gazes locked until Theophilus' eyes filmed and the old man gave a final gasp. Cyril thought his uncle's face looked more surprised than at peace. He gently closed the staring eyes.

A useless physician approached, held a silver mirror close to the Patriarch's face. When no mist formed on the cool metal, he declared the bishop dead.

Relief that his uncle's trial was over flooded Cyril's soul, while his stomach and throat twisted into hard, hurting knots of grief. He dashed the tears from his eyes. He must pull himself together, and quickly, if he were to put his plans in place. Cyril started a fervent prayer. The rest of the grieving men joined him.

When done, he looked around the room and declared. "You heard the Patriarch's wishes. I will stand for the bishopric. I ask that you confirm me now."

"That cannot be done, Reader Cyril." Paulinus smiled from the foot of the bed. "Your uncle's wishes are contrary to custom. Archdeacon Timothy is the logical successor."

Cyril, seething from the chief steward's reminder of his lowly church status, opened his mouth to reply, then shut it before he could utter harsh words. Taunts would do no good. He and his uncle had hoped the Patriarch's dying wish would carry the day, but planned for its failure. Cyril's back stiffened and his eyes narrowed. His dream had warned of trials.

Timothy hobbled forward on his withered leg. "I will also stand for the bishopric." He looked sorrowfully at the quiescent corpse. "But this is not the time or place for this discussion. Let us bury our friend and father, Theophilus, and take time to grieve. We can call the clergy together after the funeral to select our next Patriarch."

"I cannot allow my uncle to be buried until the succession is settled. It was his wish I take his place and I will fight for that right." He and his uncle had discussed the need for speed if Cyril's first bid for power failed. The people, unaware of the split among the churchmen, expected Timothy to succeed. If Cyril hesitated, this expectation would set like Roman concrete. Making his uncle's corpse hostage to the proceedings carried a risk, but the body would be a strong physical symbol of the Patriarch's last words.

Several men started talking at once, protesting and arguing.

"Enough!" Cyril's imposing voice cut across the din. "It is my choice to make. Let us repair to the meeting rooms." He indicated several deacons, the traditional messengers of the Patriarch. "Send word to all the presbyters and deacons. We will have a conclave and put the choice to the people as soon as possible."

To Cyril's annoyance, the deacons turned to Timothy for his approval. "He does have the right. Let the others know. Send messages to the Prefect and councilors as well. Post notices in the agora. We will convene at noon."

Everyone trooped out, some smiling at Cyril, others muttering.

"Master Cyril?" An old man who had served Theophilus for decades shuffled from the anteroom. Three other servants followed. "Would you like us to prepare the Patriarch for burial?"

"No. I wish to do this last service for my uncle. Stay in the next room. When I am done, I want you to sit with the body."

The servants bowed out. Alone, Cyril set about preparing his uncle's corpse. He lovingly washed the cooling flesh, anointing it with aromatic oil. He recalled more carefree days, as he combed the old man's hair and beard, when his uncle allowed the child Cyril to climb onto his lap and cry over a bruise or cut. Finally, he dressed the body in ceremonial robes and arranged the arms across the chest.

Cyril surveyed his handiwork and sighed. His uncle's soul had truly left this mortal husk. The waxy skin seemed translucent, the nails and lips pale in death. Already the face sagged, robbed of its animating spirit. Cyril prayed for his uncle's soul one last time then left candles burning at the foot and head of the body.

*****

CYRIL STOOD BEFORE a full-length window in his uncle's office, staring into the garden. It had been weeks since this room had seen sunlight. Now the golden rays chased each other across his face as clouds whipped across the sky. Rain would soon replace the sunshine. Mid-October weather varied wildly.

"Cyril? You should eat something before the conclave."

Cyril turned to see Teacher Hierex put a tray of cold mutton and bread on the table. Theophilus had arranged for them to meet several weeks before. Hierex, a nondescript little man of uncertain age, had the uncanny ability to disappear in crowds, become one with the shadows. With his brown hair, brown eyes, and common brown robes, he could be taken for a laborer except for one distinguishing feature: delicate hands. The long tapering fingers, nails pared short and buffed to a dull luster, were meant to hold precious things. Cyril visualized them wrapped around a crystal goblet, holding an orchid, or stroking a silk robe. He gave himself extra penance for the feelings such thoughts aroused.

Cyril indicated the platter. "Help yourself, if you wish."

"I know you grieve for your uncle, but you must keep up your strength." The little man picked over the meat until, finding a slice to his liking; he rolled it around a piece of bread and nibbled at one end.

"I will fast until my investiture." Cyril took a seat while Hierex ate. "I've been given a sign. I should neither eat nor drink until I sit in the Bishop's chair."

Hierex stopped chewing. "What sign?"

Cyril told him his dream.

"Truly you are chosen and blessed by God." Hierex' eyes gleamed. "The people must know of this. The monks of Nitria are already preaching in the streets on your behalf."

"Good. I've met with all the presbyters and deacons in the past weeks. Many are sympathetic with my plans for leadership. We need a dramatic show from the congregation on my behalf to sway the remainder."

Hierex smiled. "All is in place. I will see to it."

They both rose. Cyril clasped his friend's shoulder. "Thank you, Hierex. You've been a strength to me during this trying time."

PHILLIP ROARED AT THE COARSE JOKE one of his unkempt companions made at the serving girl's expense, while surreptitiously spilling some of his beer into the sand covering the earth floor. Since the Patriarch's death the day before, he had frequented the taverns, assessing the mood of the people; looking for any likely sources of riot. With Orestes still touring the provinces, Phillip reported his suspicions directly to the captain of the guard.

He enjoyed this game of cat and prey, stalking information while impersonating someone else, going places he normally wouldn't. In Constantinople he had frequented a disreputable inn favored by entertainers, laughed at their stories of riotous adventure and improbable sexual escapades, while feeling slightly envious. Now he was living his own adventures, all too aware of the danger. He shrugged off a momentary feeling of guilt that he should be taking on more responsibilities at home with the excuse that what he did was for the greater good.

This company of ruffians was well and truly drunk. They flashed more coin than a casual inspection of their ragged clothes and broken sandals would have promised.

"How does a good man come by some of that coin, John?" Phillip asked.

"A good man don't!" John doubled over, laughing at his own wit.

Waggling his eyebrows, Phillip leered. "Well, how does a bad man, then?"

"I can give you a name. Do ya wish t'join our little band?"

"If the pay is good." Phillip tossed back his remaining beer, wiped his mouth with his sleeve and shouted to the proprietor. "One more for my good friend John, here."

John reached for the new flagon, gulped deeply, then belched. "Ah! Good pay and the chance for a little plunder if you're not too greedy. The monks don't want too much larceny; just throw a little scare in 'em."

"In who?" Phillip sipped at his now empty cup.

"What we find on the streets. They don't want anybody but their own out 'n' about."

"The monks? Why would they want people to stay home?"

John had trouble focusing his eyes. One kept wondering off to the side giving him the look of a desert lizard. "I don't know. I just take their orders and their money." He smiled, showing several gaps among his discolored teeth. "Do ya want the name or no?"

"Sure." Phillip patted a flat purse. "I can always use a few more coins."

"Ammonius. A crazy desert monk named Ammonius is giving out the coin. You can find him in the Serapis district in the morn."

"Thanks, my friend." Phillip kept drinking from his empty cup.

The man on John's other side seemed to become more morose than boisterous with the drink. He sat quietly, downing cup after cup, rattling something in his hand.

John turned to him. "Gessius, what're ya hiding in your palm? Some gems from that old Jewish merchant?" He laughed and forced his friend's hand open. A small pile of hard black beans spilled to the table. "What in Christ's name are you doing with those?"

Gessius looked up with red rimmed eyes. "They're my protection. Didn't you know throwing beans into the eyes of evil spirits drives away the demons?"

John laughed at his friend. "The demons already got your soul." He turned back to Phillip. "The devil take us all, because God sure don't want our sorry asses!"

Phillip shivered, thinking of his family on the streets with these brigands. He would have to curb Selene's jaunts and arrange for male servants to take over Rebecca's shopping duties. Or he could accompany her himself. The thought warmed him, but he must be careful. He had fought long and hard to persuade his father to let Rebecca return to service. If Calistus suspected his sons' feelings for her, he might dismiss her again. A remarkable woman, Rebecca. She wasn't beautiful, but exuded a calmness and strength of spirit, like the eye of a storm in this chaotic time. She anchored him in a way he didn't understand.

Another burst of drunken laughter interrupted his musings. He put thoughts of Rebecca aside as he ordered another drink. This one he did not spill.

THE STORY OF CYRIL'S DREAM flashed through the collection of clergy like wildfire. Many took it as a sure sign of his fitness. Others labeled the dream "convenient" and his vow to fast until his uncle's interment "an extravagant show of grief." So the debate continued, picking over minute details of past behavior, ignoring the big question: who could unite the church and lead it to the power it should have in this city?

Cyril paced his uncle's office at the end of the second exhausting day of deliberations. Seven paces forward, seven paces back. He ignored the hunger in his belly, but thirst began to torment him; his voice harsh from overuse as well as lack of water. He had given a brilliant and stirring argument for his election that day. Timothy, more concerned with day-to-day administration in the church, could not match the biblical scholarship Cyril had gained in five years of study with the Nitrian monks, nor his fiery delivery.

Cyril stopped in front of the window and gazed into the dark, deserted courtyard. He silently prayed for the strength to carry out his uncle's mission. He felt a quickening; a centering that always followed his personal correspondence with his Maker. God gave strength to the righteous. Cyril would win this challenge because he was chosen.

"Cyril?" Hierex asked from the doorway.

"What news?" Cyril turned from the window. "Is our careful planting bearing fruit?"

"I delivered your gifts to the designated council members. The monks of Nitria preach in the streets on your behalf, your uncle's bodyguard talk in the taverns against Timothy, and the Mariners await your orders. When you are elected by the clergy, the populace will acclaim you without reservation." Hierex' smile faded. "We have one major obstacle."

"Orestes?"

"No. He is still fast approaching from his tour of the province, but in his absence, Abundantius declared for Timothy."

Cyril rubbed his bearded jaw. "The Egyptian dux is capable of sending in troops to enforce his wishes, but it would take a day to mobilize at Nicopolis. It is time to bring this wrangling to an end, before Abundantius can move. We must show the clergy a small portion of our power."

"Everyone is in place and awaits your word, Master."

"Do it."

CHAPTER 15

O N THE THIRD DAY of the conclave, Selene sensed a shift in the mood of the city from anticipation to frustration. She and Nicaeus had left before Phillip arose, to attend her anatomy class, but now Selene regretted her dedication. Threatening gray clouds and occasional showers kept many off the streets. Those who braved the elements met a more frightening storm of human passion. Hordes of desert monks thronged the streets, clamoring in favor of Cyril.

Selene and Nicaeus tried to navigate the agora. Her brother peered between the stoa columns into the central city forum. Selene took little hops, trying to see over his shoulder. She finally gave up. "What's happening? Can we get through?"

Nicaeus shook his head. "It looks like a riot ready to happen. We'll have to go around, toward the docks."

A sudden roar from the crowd drowned Nicaeus' next words. Selene saw the shifting bodies as a dull mosaic of browns, blacks, and grays. The roar resolved into a deep rhythmic chant: "Cyr-ril! Cyr-ril! Cyr-ril!" The booming noise rattled through her chest and pushed at her ears. She pulled her dark wool cloak over her head to muffle the sound.

They skirted the crowd, staying close to building facades. Selene had a flash of fear as part of the mob surged, pushing them against a wall. She looked at Nicaeus in near panic. In the cool morning air, sweat stood on his forehead. His eyes narrowed as his gaze swept the mob. Nicaeus grabbed her hand and shouted in her face, "This way!"

He pulled her toward a tall door at the end of the colonnade. It flashed bronze even in the dull light. The Merchant's Hall. They struggled toward it, Selene trying to hold on to her bag of waxed tablets and texts. Nicaeus tried the handle. Locked. He pounded on the ungiving metal, shouting, "Open! Open, for heaven's sake!" Selene added her fists to the efforts, but the door didn't budge.

"The Hall is closed!" she screamed to her brother. They looked around in desperation.

A horn sounded. The crowd suddenly stilled. Selene watched a wild dark figure in desert robes ascend a podium and raise his arms to lead a chant. The throng roared, "Cyr-ril! A true ascetic! Beloved of God. Give us Cyr-ril!" The crowd swarmed toward the podium, leaving a small corridor to their right.

"There!" Selene grabbed her brother's hand. They raced down the temporary opening. Selene stumbled on the hem of her long robes, falling to one knee. Nicaeus took her book bag and helped her to her feet. She gathered handfuls of damp cloth, hitched her garments above her ankles, and ran. They ducked down a narrow alley between buildings and came out on a large boulevard heading north, toward the harbor.

They traveled but half a block when a wave of men flowed onto the street and headed their way shouting. Most wore the short sun-faded tunics of seafarers and waved the hooks and staves of dockworkers as they poured through the broad avenue. Small knots of men broke off at corners and dispersed throughout the city, crying, "Cyr-ril. Give us Cyr-ril. We'll have no other Patriarch!"

Selene had never seen such a demonstration. Her breath quickened and heart pounded.

Nicaeus, eyes wild and mouth twisted, yanked her sleeve. "Back to the alley!"

They retreated to the narrow space between buildings and leaned against the wall to catch their breaths.

"We can't go back to the agora," Selene cried.

Nicaeus wiped sweat from his face. "The groups split off at main streets. They should pass us by."

They could hear the crowd roaring closer. The chants dissolved into riotous shouts with no rhythm, just the fearful pressure of a noisy mob. Nicaeus backed Selene against the wall, sheltering her with his body and outstretched arm. She saw the backs of the men's heads as they streamed past. She held her breath, trying to blend in with the shadows.

When the last of them straggled past, Selene wiped her brow. She looked up at Nicaeus; his face pale under his normal tan. "Thank you, brother." She leaned into his shoulder. "I'm glad I didn't have to face that alone."

"It's a good thing Father insisted on a chaperone. I don't think it's safe for you to be on the streets until the bishopric is decided."

"I agree." She sighed. "Let's go home."

They headed north, then west, dodging small groups of shouting mariners. Near their father's house, they came upon Phillip and Rebecca. Phillip wore neatly mended robes of the lower class and smelled of beer. Nicaeus gaped. "Why're you dressed like that?"

"I didn't want to seem out of place, escorting Rebecca to and from the market. Lucky thing, too. The market filled with monks chanting for Cyril and the guards shut it down."

Rebecca pointed to her sparsely filled basket. "I fear we'll be eating dried and preserved food for the next day or two, unless I can get beyond the walls to the vegetable merchants."

"Don't worry, Rebecca. We'll send male servants after greens and fruits tomorrow." Phillip flashed white teeth. "Now, both of you, to shelter. I don't want to see either of you out until this trouble is over."

"How soon will that be?" Selene asked.

"I don't know." Phillip shrugged. "I wish Orestes were here. Cyril's supporters are taking advantage of the Prefect's absence to foment this disorder. I doubt Orestes would have stood for it."

The mention of Orestes sent a thrill down Selene's spine. During his three months' absence, she had studiously avoided thinking about him. Her body's reaction at the mere mention of his name annoyed her. That, and the prospect of being confined to the house, put Selene in a foul mood.

LATER THAT EVENING, Hypatia studied a letter from Synesius, Bishop of Ptolemais. Beloved Synesius, one of her brightest students and the leader of a band of young men who had dedicated their lives to her—until marriage, parents' deaths, or church service took them away.

Hypatia found it ironic that so many congregations chose her bright young men as bishops. Her training prepared her students well for lives of service and contemplation. Scattered across the Empire, her protégés showed their brilliance, but were no longer young. Dear Synesius still wrote often to gossip about their wide-flung friends, ask her advice on his writings, or implore her to help a young country noble with her influence.

This letter worried Hypatia. Synesius sounded ill and unhappy. The last of his three boys had died recently and he grieved excessively. He complained of growing old alone, and reminisced about the "golden years" of his studies in Alexandria, almost twenty years earlier. It made Hypatia feel ancient, that her students aged. Her pen wasn't as steady as in the past. There were spots on the back of her hand. When had they appeared? It seemed such a short time ago that…

A knock at the door interrupted her thoughts. "Hypatia, may I attend you?"

Her initial annoyance at being interrupted dissipated as she recognized the voice. "Orestes, you're back!"

The Prefect opened the door, carrying a tray of spiced wine and sesame honey cakes. "I made the best time I could when I heard the news of Theophilus' decline." He set the tray on a low table. "I intercepted your servant." Orestes indicated the honey cakes. "I never suspected you favored such sweet treats."

Hypatia laughed and patted the couch next to her. "It's my one vice. I've purged my life of excess, but when I am troubled I crave sweets." She shrugged. "It gives me something to live for—correcting this last imperfection." She looked sharply at Orestes. He seemed worn and troubled, his clothes dusty from the journey. "You didn't come to hear an old woman prattle about honey cakes. From your appearance, you came here directly. Do you bring news?"

"Cyril is now Bishop of the See of Mark and Patriarch of Alexandria."

Hypatia folded her hands in her lap and sat still. "That means difficult times for you."

"Possibly." Orestes poured wine into two goblets and raised his own, drinking deeply. "Cyril is young for his post, but youth can be molded."

"Youth can be most passionate, stiff-necked, and jealous of its prerogatives, as well." She glanced at the letter in her hands. "I've had many years of experience with the young men who attend me."

Orestes chewed a honey cake absently. "What do you know of Cyril?"

"He never studied with me. His followers call for consolidating the Christians and ridding the city of its pagans and Jews. Cyril is in a precarious position, coming from such a contested election. He needs to heed his supporters and reward their loyalty. We will miss Theophilus."

"I'm puzzled by your regard for Theophilus. He was harsh and autocratic. I've heard him referred to as 'The Pharaoh of the Alexandrine Church.' He fomented riots, closed the pagan temples, and drove the pagan priests from the city. How could you stand aside and let that happen?"

"Theophilus brought peace after decades of troubles." Hypatia sipped her wine. "You've attended my lectures. I don't teach religion. I teach philosophy—a way of life, not a way of worship. I believe in one god, not the multitudinous personalities worshipped by the ancient Greeks, Romans, or Egyptians. I believe in the need to strive personally to know God, the same as the Christian church. After all, 'I am the Word'—God as Logos—is a Greek concept.

"Theophilus and I had many discussions on this point. We came from the same philosophical rootstock, but branched in different directions. I believe only a chosen few have the strength of character and intellectual capacity to know God. He believed all could know God through Christ's redemption, baptism, and faith. We respected each other's opinions. The priests of Serapis were dogmatists in their own right, refusing to acknowledge others' beliefs. Their polytheism and cultic practices were more inimical to my way of thinking than any Christian sect."

Orestes shook his head. "Does Cyril respect you and your choices? If he is intolerant, this city could erupt in violence. You might be in danger."

"Cyril is not his uncle. Some say he seeks power not for God's sake, but his own. He might complicate my life. However, I am a part of this city. I have wielded influence since before Cyril was born. Do not fear for me, my dear friend. Rather let us wait. The new Patriarch may yet prove amiable."

They lifted their goblets in a spontaneous toast. "To a better tomorrow!" Orestes proclaimed.

Hypatia smiled. Orestes had his own rigidities, but a hidden pool of passion lurked beneath his cool exterior, and a sharp intelligence informed his conversation. She gloried in his company. There were still a few bright young men in the city—and in her life.

IN THE CHAPEL at the Bishop's quarters, Cyril knelt in simple white robes to receive the sacrament that would make him priest, bishop, and Patriarch. It was fitting that the first food to pass his lips since his uncle's death was the body of Christ; the first drink, the blood of Christ.

The Archpresbyter intoned, "These are the things thou must hold and teach, for this is the Faith of the Catholic and Apostolic Church, to which all Orthodox Bishops throughout the West and East adhere. We believe in One God the Father Almighty, Maker of all things both visible and invisible; and in One Lord Jesus Christ, the Son of God, the Only-Begotten, begot of the Father, that is of the Essence of the Father, God of God, Light of Light, Very God of Very God, Begotten not made, consubstantial with the Father, through Whom all things were made, both that are in heaven and that are on earth, Who for us men and for our salvation came down and was made flesh and made man, suffered and rose on the third day, went up into the Heavens, cometh to judge quick and dead; and in the Holy Ghost."

The Archpresbyter continued in a like vein for nearly an hour. Cyril let the words roll through him, igniting his passion. He was acutely aware of the press of bodies, the sour smell of unwashed flesh mixed with perfumed candles, the feel of the rough cloth between his knees and the marble floor. Cyril looked to the altar, covered with embroidered silk showing the twelve apostles. Heavy gold candlesticks and an ancient scroll containing the new gospels rested beside the jewel-encrusted wineglass and gold platter holding the host.

When prompted, he raised his head and said huskily, "I believe with my whole heart that which the Church teaches, and as Bishop will defend it with my body, striking down blasphemers, and rooting out heresy wherever it may be found. I pledge myself, soul and body, heart and mind, to spread the Word of God and attest to its Truth. I will lead this flock in righteousness to prepare a heaven on earth for our Most Blessed Christ's return. In His Name, I will do these things. Amen."

Cyril rose. The Archpresbyter draped him with the purple robes of a Bishop, a gold embroidered chasuble, and the chain containing the key to the Church treasury. Next he handed Cyril a gold-headed staff, the Bishop's seal, and, finally, placed the heavy ceremonial Bishop's crown on the new Patriarch's head.

Cyril raised his head proudly. The ceremonial vestments felt comfortable— right. He led the mixed crowd of church leaders, and abbots from the desert monasteries, in prayers and songs. The new Patriarch looked over his flock with profound satisfaction. They were his to command and to care for. He would fulfill his promise to his uncle and make their church the most revered in all Christendom.

No imperial or religious authority could stop him.

CHAPTER 16

S ELENE PULLED THE DARK VEIL from her head and shook the rain from her cloak. The whole populace had processed past the city walls to accompany the Patriarch's body to its last resting-place, within the martyrium of St. Mark. The skies seemed to mourn the great man's passing. October storms pounded the coast with a vengeance, closing the harbor, drenching mourners with the tears of God.

Selene found it hard to believe he was gone. Patriarch Theophilus had been a force in the city since before her birth. She grew up listening to his sermons, hearing her father argue with council members about his policies. He *was* the church in Alexandria, the Patriarch who battled for the soul and well-being of his flock.

Rumors claimed the corpse remained uncorrupted, exuding the sweet smell of flowers even after lying three days in the meeting rooms where the clergy wrangled over the succession. One desert abbot touched the body and was instantly cured of a painful skin affliction. Selene wished she could examine such a marvel. In her experience, dead flesh rotted quickly unless preserved, and skin rashes took many days to heal—if they healed at all. Many laid claim to such miracles, but she had never seen one herself.

Nicaeus and Antonius came out of the rain into the foyer, water streaming from their dark hair. Phillip helped her father, who looked well today. Orestes trailed the sodden parade, accompanied by Antonius' father, Lysis. Servants took their cloaks and quickly mopped water from the heated tiles. The ingenious Roman hypocaust system of hot air pipes under the floor kept the house warm on those occasional cold wet days.

Selene took Calistus' arm to help him to the triclinium for the funeral banquet. As they moved through the corridors, Selene imagined Orestes' eyes following her every move. Her heart pounded. She turned her head when they reached the dining area and found not emerald eyes boring into hers, but the soft brown ones of Antonius. He blushed and looked away. Selene touched her hair and twitched at her robes, which clung damply to her body, hoping nothing was amiss. Perhaps she could get a glimpse of herself in a silver platter.

She didn't want to embarrass herself in front of her guests, and especially not Orestes. Her body, which usually felt so natural, betrayed her around the Prefect. She blushed, stammered, and felt at her most awkward. For his part, Orestes always acted correctly toward her and never encouraged her feelings. Selene cursed herself roundly for a fool and tried to keep her mind on the business at hand.

She settled her father on a comfortable couch and ordered the servants to bring food and drink. "My apologies for the fare, Prefect. It's simple, but there's plenty for all who wish it."

"I'm sure it will be most delicious, Lady Selene. How go your studies? It's been five months, has it not?"

To her profound annoyance, she blushed. Why did he still have such an effect on her? She looked up into his startling green eyes, lowered her lids, and said softly, "They go well. Thank you for your concern."

"I feel an obligation and would like to be informed of your progress."

"You don't want her talking about her studies during a meal," Nicaeus broke in. "Just thinking about what she keeps in those jars in her room is enough to put me off eating."

Orestes gave Selene an inquiring smile.

"Just a few specimens Master Haroun loaned me." She glanced at her father. "I'm studying the heart and have several examples from a number of animals."

Antonius joined the conversation. "In my experience, the human heart is rather fragile."

"Oh, not at all! The heart is a remarkable organ. Tough. Made up of muscles, like your arm or leg, with the most ingenious valves to let the blood flow, like the irrigation gates on canals…"

"I warned you not to get her started!" Nicaeus laughed. "Now we'll be subjected to gory stories all through dinner."

"Anatomy is not a suitable topic for dinner conversation, my dear," Calistus gently admonished his daughter. "Perhaps another time,"

"Of course, Father." Selene glared at Nicaeus, but he had already turned to talk to Antonius. Selene signaled the waiting servants to bring in the food. They filled wine goblets and passed among the reclining figures with platters which the guests picked over and transferred to plates. First they made the rounds with grapes, dates, figs, and black olives. Next, lamb and lentils, followed by cold pheasant stuffed with wild rice and redolent with garlic, then salads dressed with vinegar and oil. The meal finished with sharp goat cheese spread on thick brown bread, sesame cakes, and sweet red wine.

Selene watched carefully for the guests' reactions to the fare, anxious that they be satisfied. Except for Nicaeus, they seemed little interested in the feast, tucking away the food with hardly a glance or comment. Conversation drifted from Nicaeus' impending departure for the army, to tales of Orestes' travels in the hinterland, finally settling on the aftermath of the Patriarch's death.

"How are the people taking Cyril's election?" Orestes asked.

"The council supports Cyril," Calistus said, "but then he was most... helpful...to several key members."

Orestes raised an eyebrow. "How so?"

"A scurvy monk came by with a sack of coins, a 'gift' from Cyril." Calistus took a sip of wine. "I sent him packing, but I'm sure others were appreciative. 'Gift,' indeed!"

Lysis flushed and frowned into his cup before speaking up. "I believe the other Christian sects fear Cyril. He comes from the Nitrian tradition. They are notoriously intolerant of differences in doctrine. Some Origenist acquaintances of mine speak of leaving the city."

"The commons favor Cyril," Phillip chimed in. "During my, uh, business about the city, I've heard much talk about Cyril's piety and charity." Selene noticed a glance between Orestes and Phillip, and listened for what was not being said as much as what was. "Rough elements in the taverns support Cyril and seem prone to riot on his behalf."

Calistus glared over his cup. "You have time to frequent taverns, my son? Perhaps I should give you more responsibility at home."

Orestes interceded with a chuckle. "Let me beg your indulgence, Calistus. Phillip has been my eyes and ears in places I dare not be seen. He does significant service in making sure I know the mood of the people."

"Drinking in the service of the Empire." Calistus' eyes narrowed at his son. "Do you find it suitable work?"

"When I can drink our good Egyptian beer, it is not so onerous a chore." Phillip pursed his lips. "However, the vinegar they serve in the guards' taverns is vile."

"Why, the wine we serve our guardsmen is the nectar of the gods." Orestes laughed. "At least, that's what we tell them."

"If that's what the gods drank, no wonder they died out!"

Selene noted that Rebecca briefly hesitated when Phillip mentioned his exploits. Between her duties and his, Selene had seen little of her brother these past few months. Engrossed in her studies, Selene had not picked up on the plots and intrigues in her own household.

That would change.

Calistus daubed his mouth with a linen cloth. "The quality of tavern wine aside, the aftermath of the Bishop's election seems clear. With one or two notable exceptions, the whole city acclaimed Cyril's elevation to Patriarch."

"The Jewish students speak of blood in the streets." Nicaeus looked troubled. "They are preparing for attacks."

Selene threw a murderous glance at her brother. With such news, Father might restrict her to the house indefinitely.

"Such an outcome is for me to prevent," Orestes said. "Abundantius loaned me a troop of his soldiers until we can convince the desert monks to return to their homes." Orestes rose and gestured to a servant holding a washing bowl. "I must be on my way. There are many plans I have yet to put in place. Phillip, perhaps you could accompany me?"

"Of course." Phillip rose. "I'll roust your escort from the kitchen."

"Thank you, my friend." Orestes bowed over Selene's hand. "Thank you again, Lady Selene, for a pleasurable evening on short notice."

Selene murmured something polite. Her heart thumped so loud, she feared Orestes would hear.

AFTER OVERSEEING THE CLEANUP and her father's comfort, Selene retired to her room. Rebecca showed up shortly for the nightly ministrations. Her servant's brief absence made Rebecca all the more precious to Selene. She had little time for friends now that she studied at the Museum, and missed female companionship. After removing her cosmetics and changing into her sleeping robe, Selene relaxed while Rebecca combed her short hair. It was at that awkward stage of growth, too long to be fashionable for a man and too short to be adorned properly as a woman's.

"So what is between you and Phillip?" Selene asked casually.

Rebecca hesitated. "What makes you think anything is between us, Mistress?"

"Oh, Rebecca! You needn't keep secrets from me. If I asked, Phillip would tell me in an instant."

"Then ask him."

Selene turned to look directly at the older girl. "Rebecca. We have gone through much together. Please, I am deeply concerned for my brother."

"Your brother is a man grown. He can fend for himself. I might ask the same question of you."

"What question?"

"What is between you and Master Antonius?"

Selene laughed. "What makes you ask that? He is betrothed to Honoria. Antonius is like another brother to me. He even accompanies me from classes if Nicaeus is late."

"I saw how he watched you all evening. Hungry. He couldn't get enough of you. Sad, too. Like the sight hurt."

"You are mistaken, Rebecca. Antonius has been troubled lately, but it has nothing to do with me. I overheard Lysis ask my father a few weeks ago for a loan to pay his corn tax."

Rebecca put away the comb and picked up the discarded robes.

"You didn't answer my question," Selene accused. "What's going on with you and my brother? How does he know your family so well?"

Rebecca rolled her eyes. "He asked me for help in gathering information. I told him the best places to meet people in our neighborhood, and introduced him to my brothers when they came back from their voyage."

"Is he putting himself in any danger?"

"My brothers will vouch for him in our community." Rebecca patted her shoulder. "Believe me; he is as safe as I can make him."

Selene reached up to cover Rebecca's hand. "Thank you, for caring for us all. I don't know what I would do without you."

*****

Phillip and Orestes relaxed in the Prefect's private quarters, enjoying a warm cup of wine. Demetrius discreetly provided for his master and guest.

Orestes stared over his cup at Phillip. "I know you had to be circumspect in your father's house, but how goes your 'business' in the city?"

"It's troubling." Phillip frowned. "Have you heard of a monk called Ammonius? He hired ruffians to intimidate people during the three days before Cyril's election. I don't know if he's working alone or at someone's instigation."

"Others have brought me reports of Ammonius of Nitria. Let us hope he goes home, now that his objective is accomplished." Orestes rubbed his tired eyes. "These reports of gifts and intimidation trouble me. Cyril is willing to use less than honorable means to attain his ends."

"It is not uncommon among the church elders to scheme for power." Phillip laughed. "Many look forward to an election as a time of great generosity."

"It is not that much different at court. I and my patron passed out a few purses to get this appointment for me, but I did not have anyone beaten, nor did I threaten riot." Orestes frowned. "I had pinned my hopes on Timothy, a most amiable fellow. The church usurped many civic prerogatives during my predecessor's tenure which I intend to get back. I fear Cyril will jealously guard what his uncle won."

Phillip shook his head. "If Cyril takes too strong a stand, he will alienate all who might have more moderate opinions. And they are many."

"In his youth and inexperience he might overestimate his strength." Orestes gazed into the flickering coals, speaking in a troubled voice. "He might look to me as an elder. I have a small hope we can work together."

Phillip smiled and clasped his friend's forearm. "You will succeed, Orestes. You have many allies in this city, and Cyril has many enemies. He needs time to consolidate his position. During that time you can make Alexandria yours."

Orestes, recognizing the truth of his friend's words, returned the embrace.

Cyril and Hierex met in the Patriarch's sitting room, a comfortable place carpeted with thick rugs and warmed with braziers. Cyril sipped spiced wine, musing on his plans.

"You gave a brilliant funeral oration, Patriarch," Hierex said.

"There's no need for titles in private, my friend. I need your honest advice and counsel, not flattery." Cyril smiled to take any sting out the words. "The crowd did seem enthusiastic, even in the rain. Our, or should I say your, hard work succeeded."

"The people have accepted you fully. Now is the time to complete your uncle's vision and purge this city of the last of the pagans and Jews."

"Not yet, Hierex."

The little man's face fell.

"We must first knit up the rents in our own garment. There are still unorthodox churches and false presbyters about the city. We must bring them back to our fold before we can look outside." Cyril rested his forehead in his free hand. "Even within the Orthodox Church we must make changes. I've prepared a list of the presbyters who supported me. They will retain their parishes. Those that did not will be replaced. I will also review the Bishops throughout Egypt. Those who do not hew to the orthodox doctrine will be dismissed. I might take a page from our Prefect and make a procession through the land."

"It would be better to have the Bishops come to you."

"Excellent idea." Cyril sighed. "I have too much work to do here. Perhaps when the church is whole again, I can visit the rest of my kingdom." He narrowed his eyes and twirled his glass between thumb and finger. "What do you think of our Prefect? Will he support our efforts?"

"Ah, Orestes." Hierex stroked his beard. "He is an imperfect Christian, for all that he claims he was baptized in Constantinople. He attends lectures by that pagan woman philosopher and does not acknowledge that the rule of Caesar must give way to God's."

Cyril's face grew troubled. "Hypatia is indeed a powerful force. She might unduly influence Orestes, as she has others. I traveled by her home the other day, and saw rich and powerful men crowding her door. They fall away from Christian teaching and cleave to hers." Cyril laughed bitterly. "Those same men claim I am too young for the high post of Patriarch. They oppose the expansion of the church into city affairs because it threatens their hereditary power."

"The ordinary people of Alexandria will support you. Nobles' squabbles and Hypatia's philosophy mean nothing to them. The Lady Philosopher and her rich friends are distant, removed from common lives. The Church provides for the poor and friendless. They remember."

"Your words lighten my heart, Hierex, and give me hope. We have much work to do, but God is on our side, so we will prevail." Cyril rose. "Let us take a well-deserved rest. We'll meet in the morning to make further plans."

CHAPTER 17

THE CITY SETTLED into an uneasy peace during the week following Cyril's elevation to Patriarch. People kept to their houses as autumnal storms blew themselves out and soldiers herded desert monks outside the city walls. The Museum cancelled classes and lectures.

Selene took the opportunity to coddle her father, made sure he wore his warmest garments, and spiced his favorite dishes with herbs to strengthen the blood. They had gotten in the habit of reading aloud to each other before the main meal. This afternoon Calistus requested Homer. He enjoyed the stories of clever Odysseus and his cursed journey home from Troy. Selene thrilled to the adventure, but felt faithful Penelope had the harder task of ruling a kingdom and raising a son, while her husband fought monsters and sorceresses in faraway lands.

She sighed as she closed the book and looked out on the sodden courtyard. A weak ray of sunshine wavered through the clouds, making the sky seem grayer by contrast. The flickering light of oil lamps inside their sitting room made the Nile River wall mural seem eerie rather than cheerful.

"Do you grow weary of entertaining your old father?"

"Of course not." Selene looked up, startled out of her reverie. She smiled and saw the answering warmth in his eyes. "I grow weary of these walls, of reading about other's adventures."

A worried look came over her father's face. Selene rose, crossed the wool carpet, knelt by his chair, and placed her head in his lap. "The weather oppresses me. I am anxious to resume my studies, to have something occupy my mind other than household tasks and menus for meals."

Calistus stroked her short hair. "I too grow weary of rain. It's unusual to have so much so early in the season. I hope the estates are less drenched. Floods will delay the second planting and rot the current harvest."

Selene felt him shiver and rose to settle a woolen wrap about his shoulders. He chuckled and patted her hand. "It's good to have you here, daughter, but don't worry about me. The damp settles in my bones. When the sun comes out, I'll be my old self."

CALISTUS WAS AS GOOD as his word, gaining color and strength with the return of sunny days. Selene resumed her studies with Nicaeus, and occasionally, Antonius as an escort. Throughout the fall, Phillip seemed to be little about the house. He would show up suddenly, dirty and hungry, sometimes after several days. Selene suspected her father kept Phillip as busy as the Prefect did. Calistus wanted first hand reports on his country estates.

One day in January, Selene and Nicaeus returned from a natural history lecture by Hypatia. For once, Nicaeus had been more interested than Selene. Hypatia demonstrated how to build and use an astrolabe to navigate. Nicaeus, scheduled to leave for Constantinople and his army assignment in less than a month, showed an intense interest in all things having to do with his journey. He studied maps, read accounts by ancient travelers, talked to traders and sailors. Selene had never seen him so intent or happy.

They chatted easily about the best route to Constantinople as they entered a small square in front of a parish church. The name chiseled over the door marked it as Novatian. A vigorous young man stood on the steps, facing down an older man with stooped shoulders. A small crowd listened to the arguments, but didn't seem to take sides. Smoke rose from a bonfire in the middle of the square.

"Let's hear what they have to say." Selene tugged Nicaeus to the edge of the crowd. They were soon hemmed in as more people joined the throng.

The older man waved a piece of parchment. "In the name of Patriarch Cyril, I close this hotbed of Novatian heresy and confiscate the contents of this building. It will be rededicated to the True Orthodox Church under my leadership."

"I do not recognize Cyril's authority." The young Novatian priest stood his ground. "Only Bishop Theopemptus can command me." He folded his arms across his chest and sneered at the stoop-shouldered man. "Your church is tainted with those who renounced their faith in the face of adversity. It harbors the worldly and unworthy, and therefore your sacraments are not valid. Only the most holy and elect—we followers of Novatian—will attain heaven."

"You dare to impugn my faith?" The challenger's face turned bright red. "Come prove your superior holiness." He pointed to the bonfire, dying down to red glowing coals in the center of the square. "Let us both walk in the fire and see whose faith will protect them."

The crowd started to mutter and surge toward the Novatian. The young man's face paled as he held out his hands as if to stem the tide. "I have no need to prove my faith again. That was done during my baptism and initiation."

Two burly men in monks' robes grabbed the young priest and pinioned his arms to his sides. He made a valiant effort to free himself, kicking and twisting, but the mob demanded his trial by fire, and his captors deposited him in front of the glowing coals. Fire licked most intensely in the middle, where the coals heaped the highest.

"They are going to burn the Novatian!" Selene exclaimed in horror.

"Let us leave, Selene," Nicaeus hissed in her ear. "He will take no hurt if he walks quickly and keeps his robes from the coals."

"How so?" Selene looked at her brother in surprise.

"I don't know the way of it." He shrugged. "Anyone can move their hand through a flame without harm. The fire burns when the hand stops over the flame or a man stays in one place on the coals."

She nodded and they slipped from the restless crowd.

At the edge, Selene put a restraining hand on her brother's arm. "I want to see the presbyter walk the fire. If the Novatian is burned, perhaps I can help."

"What can you do? You're not an apprentice physician yet."

"I don't know, but I feel I should stay."

Nicaeus surveyed the throng, then conceded. "It seems safe enough, here on the fringe. If the crowd becomes rowdy, we can escape down the street."

The stoop-shouldered man stepped toward the fire, shed his sandals and long over-tunic. He raised his hands. The people quieted.

"I will prove my faith, by walking in the fire. God will protect me from all harm." He closed his eyes briefly, opened them, then stepped onto the coals with bare feet. The crowd gasped. He calmly walked across the bonfire, declaiming, "It matters not the holiness of he who administers the sacrament. A most vile murderer could put on the robes of a priest and, if the one receiving the Eucharist is pure of heart, he will be saved." He pointed to the captive Novatian. "That misguided man would have your ascendance to heaven depend on the purity of your presbyter, not the holiness of your own deeds or heart. Let him prove the worthiness of his beliefs in the fire."

The stoop-shouldered-man stepped off the coals. Those nearest him examined his feet and clothes. "It's true, he bears no harm. God protected him. Throw the other priest on the fire. See if his faith is as strong!"

The two burly captors picked up the Novatian priest and tossed him on the fire face first. Coals scattered. The wind whipped the flames briefly higher. The young man scrambled to his knees, screaming. Coals caught in his hair. The folds of his tunic started to smolder. He jumped to his feet, beating at the incipient flames with his hands. Ash blackened his face except for his two round staring eyes. He hopped from foot to foot, looking for a break in the wall of people surrounding the fire. He made a dash, but the crowd caught him and threw him back onto the coals. Flames licked up his tunic.

Selene took a deep breath and, in a voice that would have made Hypatia proud, cried out, "In the name of the merciful Jesus Christ, let that man go. Do not do murder in God's name."

The mob muttered angrily and turned in her direction. Nicaeus grabbed her arm, preparing to flee. That brief distraction allowed the young priest to jump off the fire. He threw himself to the ground and rolled out the flames. The rabble roared and converged on the singed priest to throw him back onto the fire, but the stoop-shouldered man intervened.

"Enough! His faith has proved worthless. Let him go."

The Novatian fled down the street, trailing smoke. A large part of the crowd followed, shouting taunts and pelting the priest with whatever was handy: vegetables, rocks, dung.

The stoop-shouldered man and the two burly men marched up to the church door, followed by the remainder of the crowd. They wrenched the door open and poured in.

Nicaeus said, mouth agape, "You saved that man's life."

"But will he thank me for it? He lost his church, his home, perhaps even his faith. He might have preferred to be consumed by the fire."

"He made his choice when he fled." Nicaeus laid a gentle hand on her shoulder. "You gave him the opportunity to make that choice. The outcome is on his head, not yours."

Selene couldn't shake the look of horror on the young priest's face. Was it fear of the crowd, or the realization he didn't have the faith to be a martyr for his beliefs?

Cyril listened to the litigants' arguments from his carved Bishop's chair. Several scribes wrote down his words and documented his decisions. Arbitrating disputes in the Christian community was one of his favorite new responsibilities. Some Bishops loathed the petty disputes between families and neighbors: arguments over inheritances, property encroachment, broken promises, unpaid loans. They claimed the duties previously done by city magistrates took time away from prayer, studies, and good works. Cyril delighted in seeing the moral path through the dangerous swamps of human perfidy. He gloried in the power of judgment. It made him feel closer to God, the Final Judge.

This case had the added complication of demonic intervention. A couple who had been married for seven years wished to separate, and argued over property held jointly since their marriage. There were no children, and the man claimed a curse had been put on his wife. He wished to set her aside and take another.

Cyril would normally urge them to stay together in a chaste marriage. But he had examined both parties separately and found the man's testimony compelling. The wife, a sweet-tempered girl, had become a different person upon the marriage; complaining of her husband's absences, dismissing his favorite servant girl. The wife had refused to allow her husband in her bed, pleading women's troubles. When he claimed his marriage rights, the wife consulted a sorceress. Obviously the husband acted in good faith against supernatural forces.

"I have reached a decision."

The litigants came forward; their families standing back a few steps. The man crossed thick arms over a barrel chest. The woman's pretty face marred by a lumpy nose and the look of fear as she flinched away from her husband.

"This marriage is ended. The husband may take the house, the leather shop, all its goods, and such money as he has accumulated during the seven years of marriage. The couple must post a notice of their intention to divorce and pay all debtors from the joint property. The husband is free to seek another wife."

The barrel-chested man broke into a broad grin and bowed low to the Patriarch. Cyril nodded his acknowledgement and continued. "The wife may take her dowry portion and no more. She is forbidden to take another husband until such time as her presbyter pronounces her free of demonic influence."

The wife trembled. Tears sprang to her eyes. Her father came forward, taking her arm and whispering in her ear. Cyril heard her reply, in a low voice, "No, it is enough that I am away from him." They both bowed and the parties withdrew.

The next case concerned one of the presbyters who had supported Timothy for the Bishopric. Along with three others, he had been replaced shortly after Cyril's investiture. Cyril frowned over the notes handed to him. These were serious charges. What he was about to do would be perceived by his enemies as persecution, but he had no choice.

"Arius, come forward."

A heavyset man with gray-tinged curls made his way through the crowd. He wore the simple robes of a presbyter.

Cyril leaned forward and said, sorrowfully, "I am told your son engages in lewd behavior on the Sabbath, consults magical books, and conducts auguries. These are sorcerous practices."

Arius stood straight, but sweat stood out on his forehead. "Those are false charges, Patriarch. My son is a student and mathematician. He has occasionally attended the theater, or prepared astrological charts for friends, but he conducts no magic, casts no spells."

"Theater going, and the practice of astrology, are forbidden to those in the church. You have failed to control your son and therefore have put him in danger." Cyril leaned back in his chair. "You must hand him over to me for judgment."

"But conviction of sorcery means death!" Arius paled. "I cannot turn over my son for execution."

"If what you say is true, he is in no danger." Cyril's voice grew hard. "The laws are clear. Until you produce your son, you are banned from all participation in the church. You cannot attend services, partake of the sacraments, or minister as a presbyter. You are cut off from the body of Christ and his holy community."

Arius clenched his jaws till the ample flesh trembled from the tension. He narrowed his eyes and ground out between his teeth, "As the Patriarch wills."

The scribes noted the outcome and prepared copies for all the deacons. Arius would not be able to enter any church until the Patriarch absolved him. Cyril turned back to his list of supplicants secure in his judgment.

*****

ORESTES WATCHED CYRIL JUDGE his last two cases: one a breach of contract between two merchants; the other determining a guardian for an orphan boy with a rich inheritance. Orestes felt the Patriarch rendered fair decisions based on the facts as presented. The previous Prefect had agreed to the church taking on magisterial duties as a way of reducing state costs and, consequently, making those funds available for his personal enjoyment. Orestes had to admit it reduced congestion in the courts, but he resented the easy assumption of power. The people, used to bringing their tales of woe to the church, increasingly accepted arbitration from the Bishops.

When the last supplicant had been ushered away by the Patriarch's attendants, Orestes made his presence known.

"Lord Prefect." Cyril stayed seated in his Bishop's chair. "I'm pleased you could attend me. I received your letter asking for an audience."

"Patriarch." Orestes was obliged to stand in the Patriarch's presence, unless bade to sit. Heat began to flush up Orestes' neck at the lack of an invitation to do so. "Perhaps we could conduct our business in a less public setting."

Cyril looked around as if noticing for the first time the dozens of clerks, deacons, and other attendants. "Of course." He rose from his chair. "Join me in my sitting room."

Orestes left his entourage of guards in the inner courtyard, but signaled Demetrius to attend him in the Patriarch's chambers. They left the vast receiving hall and climbed narrow steps to the Patriarch's private rooms. Cyril had removed the heavy draperies after Theophilus' death, but changed little else. The furniture, carpets, and appointments exuded lushness out of keeping with the austere demeanor of the Patriarch. In the privacy of this room, Cyril ushered Orestes to a chair and gestured to a servant for refreshments. Demetrius stood at his master's shoulder to serve him.

"How may I be of service, Lord Prefect?" Cyril sat, elbows on the chair arms, fingertips touching in a peak.

"It is a matter most urgent. The Origenists have already left the city. Bishop Theopemptus of the Novatians has appealed to me for protection. It seems that presbyters under your orders have seized his churches and looted the congregational plate. His sect follows a strict code of asceticism, not unlike the desert monasteries in which you studied. What possible objection do you have

144

to their existence?"

"'Looted' is a harsh word. A recent Imperial edict allows Bishops to take measures against schismatics, including confiscating buildings and their contents."

"That edict named sanctions against the Donatist sect," Orestes countered.

"Of course." Cyril smiled. "The Novatians persist in the Donatist error that the priest must be pure to administer the sacraments. My brother Augustine, Bishop of Hippo, demolished that philosophy in his most recent writings. Pope Innocent of Rome has started the purge of Novatians from his domain. I only follow in the Holy Father's footsteps."

Orestes knew defeat when confronted with it. It left a taste of ashes in his mouth which the dry red wine the servant brought could not remove. The Origenists and Novatians had sided with Archdeacon Timothy in the fight for the succession. Cyril was purging the city of his political enemies under the guise of consolidation and with the sanction of the Emperor and the Pope.

Orestes set the goblet of wine on a wooden stand. "Then we have nothing to speak of, Patriarch. I had hoped for a more charitable outcome."

"What could be more charitable than saving those poor people from the error of their ways?" Cyril looked genuinely surprised. "They will be welcomed in our churches. They lose nothing but the harsh requirements of their masters. Can you not see the hardship their Bishop's belief wreaked on his congregations? The potential for schism and recrimination?" Cyril shook his head vehemently. "That cannot be allowed."

Unconvinced of the purity of Cyril's motives, Orestes rose and bowed. "My mission here is finished. Good day to you, Patriarch."

"We still have much we can discuss, Prefect. Your attendance at church services, the abomination of the mimes and entertainers. These require your attention. Leave the internal affairs of the church to me and attend those in your domain."

Stung by Cyril's censuring tone, Orestes said, "I'll take it under advisement, Patriarch," spun on his heel, and left, Demetrius trailing.

In the street, Orestes said ruefully to Demetrius, "Cyril made sure I knew my place."

"The Patriarch was within his rights concerning the other churches."

"I know. I hoped to use his youth and inexperience to my advantage." Orestes shook his head. "I won't underestimate him again."

"His youth and inexperience prompted him to treat you in such a manner. Give him time to grow into his role." Demetrius opened the door to the street. "I'm sure you two will be able to work out an amicable relationship."

"I hope so, for Alexandria's sake."

CHAPTER 18

SELENE! WAIT FOR ME."

Selene looked around the crowd of students for the source of the familiar voice. She spotted Antonius weaving down the side of a colonnade, and waited for him.

"I see your father gave up on the chaperones." Antonius grinned at her. He topped her by a couple of inches, now that he had reached his full height.

"Never!" She laughed. "The Prefect has kept the peace the last few months so, after Nicaeus left for the army, Father agreed to let me take Rebecca. She goes to the market or visits her family while I go to classes."

"It's been a year since you proposed your crazy scheme. Are you happy, Selene?" He led her by the hand to a nook shaded by a large date tree, where they settled on a stone bench.

"More than I thought possible, Antonius. I am learning so much! Auxentius says I have learned all I can from the texts without experience. He recommends I start apprenticing. Haroun grumbles that I'm not ready, while arranging for me to assist the surgeons at the city charity ward. It's more than I ever dreamed." Selene's face settled into a radiant smile. "And you, my friend? Are you happy? You wed Honoria in two weeks. I know she is ecstatic."

"Honoria is a fine girl, but her major asset is the dowry she brings." Antonius' head drooped. He stared at his clenched fists resting in his lap. "Father is in dire straits and this is one way to stave off financial ruin—for a while."

"I'm so sorry." Selene clutched his arm. "Your father sponsored the new statue of the emperor. I thought his money troubles were over."

"He puts on a brave front. Many of the old families are in similar difficulties. Taxes go up, expectations for city improvements continue, while crops fail."

Selene nodded. "Father complains that many prosperous merchants are declining the honor of becoming a civitas. The obligations of city, church, and empire are too burdensome."

"Honoria's father is one of those shrewd enough to hold on to his wealth while marrying into nobility," Antonius said bitterly.

"But you're well educated and of an old family. Surely there will be a position for you. You don't have to marry Honoria if it makes you so unhappy."

"With my future father-in-law's money and influence, I can acquire a function in the city government. My father has his good name, but little else. Without a rich patron, my prospects are slim. Nicaeus once joked that I could join the army or the hermits. Neither appeals to me. I have no wish to travel beyond this city for either war or peace."

"My dear friend, I would give anything to make this right." Selene rested her head on his shoulder as she wrestled with divided loyalties. "Can't you learn to care for Honoria? She is sweet, loyal, and loves you very much."

"It's impossible," Antonius whispered.

Selene sighed. "Then I will speak to Phillip. He is much in Orestes' company. They can find a place for you. If not here, possibly in Constantinople."

Antonius' face lightened briefly as if considering the possibility; then his shoulders slumped. "I think not. My father needs this dowry and I have two other brothers who require places. At least this marriage allows me to stay here."

"Why is it so important to stay in Alexandria? Constantinople is a thriving city, with many opportunities for clever young men. You might make your fortune at court."

He lifted a lock of her shoulder-length hair and curled it around his finger. "Would you wait for me, Selene?"

"What do you mean?" She pulled away in confusion.

"I have long known you did not feel for me what I felt for you. We grew up together and you are all I've ever wanted. I love your courage, your wit, even your stubbornness. But you have only called me 'friend'." Antonius gripped her arms. "Last year, when my father revealed his plans for me to wed Honoria, I ranted, refused to consider it. I thought of asking you to run away with me."

His eyes searched her face. Seeing her frown of shock and surprise, Antonius dropped his grip and turned away, head in hands. "What kind of life would that be for you? You are so happy with your studies. I can offer you nothing, but I can do a great deal for my family."

She should have known. All the hints, the teasing, the warm looks. She was blind not to see. No, not blind. Selene hadn't wanted to see; hadn't wanted to act on her own feelings; the confused urgings that pulled her toward the warmth, caring, and safety of marriage—things she didn't want to want.

"Tell me, Selene, have you given your heart to another, while I hesitated?" Antonius raised his head, pain pinching his mouth. "I've seen how you moon about Orestes."

She babbled, giving herself time to make sense of his declaration and her reactions. "The only woman Orestes shows any interest in is Hypatia. There is a scandal rumored among the servants, though I think they are just great friends and she an able advisor." The lines of hurt deepened at the corners of his eyes. "Oh, Antonius, why didn't you say something sooner? Why now?"

"I saw you walking down the colonnade, looking so beautiful, and had to talk to you, tell you my feelings. I know this is selfish, but it might be my last chance."

Selene's heart pounded. She had tried so hard to put away love, ignore cravings for physical affection while pursuing her studies. Now those urges coursed through her as inexorably as the Nile floods, sweeping all her carefully built dikes before it. She lowered her gaze to her left hand clenching her linen tunic, and absently smoothed the wrinkles.

"Have no suitors approached your father?" Antonius asked.

Selene looked into his eyes and smiled. "My reputation for stubbornness precedes me." She turned solemn. "I fear my father is falling into similar straits as yours. He is unhappy for days after Phillip returns from the farms. I sometimes hear them arguing. The fact Father allows me to study a profession tells me he fears for the future." Selene gave Antonius a level stare. "With or without the prospect of a dowry, I've found no suitor for whom I would give up my aspirations."

"So you have given your heart." He barked a bitter laugh. "Just not to another man. My dreams of us together could never compete with your ambition to be a physician, as I never could compete with you in a race." He tipped her chin and looked deeply into her eyes. "Let me at least know what I'm missing."

He bent his head to hers, covering her mouth with a hard, insistent kiss, caressing her back. Warmth flashed from her groin, trembling along her nerves.

Her eyes flew wide then drooped in dreamy ecstasy. She leaned into his body, feeling the firm muscles of his chest against her breasts, smelling the musk of his sweat, kissing him back with a fierce intensity that surprised and confused her.

Antonius broke off the kiss with a gasp and cradled her tightly against his chest. "I never should have done that. How can I be happy with Honoria when I want only you?"

With a strangled sob, he rushed off before Selene could utter a protest.

She sat, sorting through her tangled feelings. The memory of his body pressed to hers sent another flood of warmth coursing through her. A hot flush spread across her face. She pressed her forehead to the marble of the nook, momentarily distracting herself with the silky feel of stone against flesh. What a Gordian knot!

Antonius loved her.

She repeated the phrase over and over in her mind, chasing it in circles, coming to no conclusions other than to wonder at the fact.

Antonius loved her.

How could he? He had seen her with skinned knees and dirt on her face. He accused her of smelling like a chariot horse and acting like a donkey. He laughed at her, challenged her, beat her at javelin throws, and been beaten by her in foot races. He kept her secrets and encouraged her dreams even when those dreams took her from him. Now it was too late. He would marry Honoria in two weeks.

Antonius loved her.

A deep sense of loss washed through her, making her breathing ragged with the effort not to cry. A dull pain spread from her chest to lodge in her throat. She dashed tears from her eyes and took a deep breath. Moments before, she had been blissfully unaware of her feelings, content with a scholar's life, planning her future as a physician. Now she cried like a silly twit of a girl who thinks life is over because she can't marry the boy of her choice. A fresh round of sobs racked her body.

"Selene? Is anything the matter, child?" She looked up to see Hypatia's worried face peeking around the screen of date leaves. "Are you ill? Are you having trouble with your studies?" Hypatia entered the alcove, seated herself beside Selene, and patted her awkwardly on the back.

Selene gulped her tears and fumbled for a cloth to wipe her nose. "It's nothing, Honored Teacher. Do not bother yourself."

"I beg to differ, my dear. You are the only girl currently taking public instruction at my sponsorship. If something is wrong, I should know." A twinkle came to her eyes. "Besides, I spend my entire professional life surrounded by men—academics, politicians, students. It's pleasant to have the company and conversation of an intelligent woman."

Selene, flattered at being accorded such familiarity with the famous philosopher, was almost giddy with the highs and lows of her emotions. But most of all, she longed for the benefit of an older woman's advice and sympathy. "Thank you, Lady. I'm afraid my distress is a matter of the heart."

Hypatia's gazed narrowed. "Young Antonius?"

"Yes! How did you know?"

"He quit this alcove with most unseemly haste. There are other signs for people with sharp eyes. He's betrothed to the corn factor Ision's daughter, is he not?"

"Honoria. Yes, she's a dear friend of mine and desperately in love with Antonius. He says he loves me, but must marry Honoria for his family's sake."

"And you, my dear? How do you feel about him?"

"I don't know. I want him to be happy. Of all the boys and men I've known, he is the only one I would consider marrying. If I asked, he would run away with me. But his family would be ruined and Honoria devastated." Selene hesitated, looking off into the distance. "And I want to be a physician. I know I can be a good one. What should I do?"

Hypatia patted her hand. "I'm a poor one to ask advice of in matters of the heart." She tapped her head. "I've lived primarily up here. As a young woman, I occasionally had physical urges, but suppressed them. Philosophy is my life and my love."

"You've had no one to love you?"

"I didn't say that. I've had the love of many—a pure spiritual love." Hypatia's eyes took on a dreamy look. "Only one had the audacity to express physical love—a young man when I was quite new to teaching."

"What happened?"

"I treated him rather badly. He stood up in one of my lectures and declared his feelings in front of all my students. He praised me lavishly for my beauty. Most women would have been flattered. I was furious."

Selene tried to imagine her teacher a young woman suffused with passion and anger. In the face of Hypatia's age and serenity, her imagination failed. "What did you do?"

The older woman blushed. "I removed the bloody rag I used for my monthly courses and said, 'Is this what you love? This physical body? If so, your love for me is false, for the flesh is but a thing of fleeting beauty.' " Hypatia looked at her age-spotted hands. "The young man left the city, never to return. I was right in my philosophy, but wrong in my actions."

Selene's eyes rounded with wonderment. For Hypatia to publicly engage in such a shocking act seemed overly dramatic. Maybe her teacher was telling her the passions and follies of youth could be weathered. "Do you miss not having a husband and children?"

"I've known many men over the years. None could convince me to leave my calling, although many tried. Children?" Hypatia smiled. "I've had hundreds— eager young minds waiting for me to mold them. I've taught two generations and my children now fill positions of power and influence throughout the region. But that recognition is not why I teach. Philosophy and teaching is not only what I do, but is my essence. Few are the people who rise each morning greeting the sun with prayers of thanks for their calling. Are you one of those, Selene?"

"I thought so. I'm not so sure now. I boasted about remaining husbandless and making my own way in the world. Now that perpetual maidenhood is likely, I feel lost and alone."

"A scholar's life is hard for a woman, but not all scholarly women are unmarried. Nor are all women physicians maidens. Pantheia made common cause with her physician husband Glycon, sharing a home and her life's work."

Selene looked up in surprise. Auxentius had told her about the Pergamon physician who died many years before Selene was born, but she had forgotten.

"I speak for myself and my choices." Hypatia continued. "You might make different ones. My best advice is to listen to both your head and your heart. In my experience they are frequently in more agreement than it seems at first."

"Thank you, Honored Teacher." Selene stood and took the older woman's hands in hers. "I'll remember your words." She glanced over her shoulder. "I need to find my servant. She has suffered much on my account already."

"Good day, Selene. I'm sure you will make the right decision for everyone."

SELENE LOOKED FOR REBECCA at their appointed meeting place, next to a public kitchen. The tantalizing scent of fresh bread led her to the spot as surely as her eyes noted the landmarks. She spied Rebecca laughing and warding off Phillip's attempts to pop a tidbit into her mouth. Selene stood, observing the light in Phillip's eyes, the saucy tilt of Rebecca's head.

A flood of jealousy flashed through her. How dare Rebecca act that way toward her beloved brother? She was a servant, and a Jewess! As quickly as it flowed, the acid torrent ebbed, leaving Selene shaken.

Rebecca turned and saw her in the crowd. Her smile faded to a look of concern. She hurried to Selene's side. "Are you feeling well, Selene? You're pale, as if you saw a spirit or felt faint."

Phillip arrived and took Selene's arm. Two hectic red spots appeared on her cheeks. "I think I suffer from the heat."

Phillip pointed down the street. "Let's repair to the Tychaion for a cooling drink." He ushered them into the former temple of the goddess of good fortune and seated them at a small corner table near a pillar. He sat with his back to the wall, Selene assumed so he could watch people coming and going.

Unlike other former temples which had been converted to churches, most of the Tychaion's statues and cult objects remained on display. Tyche herself presided over the room, clutching a rudder in one hand and a cornucopia in the other, a slight smile on her lips. An Egyptian modius—a basket for measuring grain—adorned her head. Selene's spirits lifted slightly. In spite of priestly disapproval, everyone she knew carried a good luck charm or whispered wards against evil. Tyche was a good omen. Maybe she would give them bounty and good fortune.

Phillip must have given a sign she missed; shortly after they all sat, a slatternly woman brought three goblets of watered wine. Selene found the vintage harsh. However, the coolness soothed her fevered brain. Rebecca clucked over her like a mother hen, adjusting her robes, smoothing her hair.

"What?" Selene pulled herself out of a fog when she realized Phillip had asked her a question.

His look of annoyance was quickly replaced by concern. "Should I hire a litter to take you home?"

"No!" Selene straightened her back and took a closer look around. She was rarely out of touch with her physical environment. She took comfort in the feel of the smooth wooden benches and the acrid odor of unwashed bodies packed in too small a space. "I'm fine. It's been an exhausting day. What brings you to the scholarly part of the city?"

Phillip smiled. "I attended a lecture."

"Whose? I didn't see you on the Museum grounds."

"I went to hear Teacher Hierex." Phillip casually drank his wine.

"Hierex! His students among the philoponoi cause much trouble. I told you about that odious Pontine and what he did during my anatomy presentation."

"It's good to know what others think." Phillip watched the crowd. "The philosophers at the Museum are out of touch with the common people. Hierex speaks to the masses and he has a dangerous message."

"Dangerous how?" Rebecca asked.

"He speaks against Orestes, accusing him of being under the influence of black sorcerers."

"How dare he?" Selene's eyes narrowed. "Why doesn't Orestes silence him?"

"Hierex is subtle. He doesn't accuse the Prefect of wrongdoing, but of being weak-minded. I doubt Orestes will take immediate action. People preach on every street corner. If he locked up all, there would be no room in the jails. He will have to wait until a more compelling case can be made against Hierex."

Rebecca asked softly, "What does Hierex say about the Jews?"

Anger suffused Phillip's skin under his dark tan. "I wished to spare you his venom, Rebecca."

"I have heard rumors. I would know the truth."

"Hierex preaches that the Jews should be made to convert or leave the city. He also says powerful Jewish leaders have undue influence with Orestes."

"Does he accuse the Jews of being the black sorcerers?" Selene gasped.

"No, but he urges good Christians to attack Jews and take their property." Phillip's hand covered Rebecca's.

"Do the people listen?"

"Enough to cause problems. I've sent word to your brothers."

"My people will take precautions." Rebecca sighed. "We have suffered this before and know how to defend ourselves."

"I'll tell Orestes. Things have been so peaceful since the Patriarch consolidated the Christians; I hate to see new disorders."

"Orestes needs to get Hierex off the streets," Selene muttered. She watched her brother and Rebecca through her lashes as she drank—the easiness of their conversation, the warm glances. A trickle of fear for her brother and Rebecca cut through her self-absorption. Selene thumped her empty flagon onto the table.

"Selene, are you ready to go?" Rebecca asked.

"Yes, I think I am quite recovered."

"Good." Phillip pushed back his bench. "Let's be off. Selene scandalizes the neighbors enough without rumors spreading that I brought her to a wine shop—and a pagan one at that!"

"HAVE YOU MISPLACED the good sense God gave you?" Selene rounded on her brother when they were alone after dinner.

"What are you blathering about, little sister?" Phillip examined his fingernails with a bored expression.

"I'm talking about spying for Orestes, roaming the streets in servant's garb, getting Rebecca involved." Selene crossed her arms and set her chin at a stubborn angle.

"You are not the only one in this family who can brave the streets of Alexandria in disguise." Phillip grinned.

Selene colored. "I did that only twice and you, or Antonius, escorted me most of the time. We aren't talking about me. I'm worried, Phillip. I need you here. Nicaeus is gone and Father isn't well. If something happened to you, it would kill him."

"I doubt it," Phillip muttered, then looked up at Selene with a wicked grin. "And you, little sister? Would you mourn me?"

She stomped her foot and struck a dramatic pose, nose in the air. "I would curse you for a fool and hate you forever for leaving me alone."

"With Nicaeus gone, father dead, and you cursing me, will there be no one in the house to remember me kindly?" Phillip pulled a mock-wistful face.

She looked at him from the corners of her eyes. "Rebecca might be foolish enough to mourn you, but not I." Relaxing, she turned serious again. "You do have feelings for her, don't you? You're not taking advantage because she's a servant?"

Phillip looked stricken. "How could you think such a thing of me, Selene?"

"I had hoped you had not changed, but we've had so little time together since your return. You're always out, or we have company. I'm not sure I know you anymore."

He held out his arms. She slipped into his embrace.

"I have changed." He spoke into her hair. "Though Father might deny it, I've grown up. My actions may be those of a carefree youth, but they are for a purpose. I know too much, and with knowledge comes the obligation to act."

Selene smiled. When had she last foregone action in favor of contemplation? She hugged her brother fiercely. "I know. But please, take care. I don't want to lose you." She pulled a little away and poked him in the ribs. "And don't break Rebecca's heart or I will break your head."

"I would cut off my right hand before I harmed Rebecca and I certainly have no intention of acquiring a broken head from the toughs in the street or from you." He pulled her closer again. "Trust me. Orestes can bring a new era of tolerance to Alexandria. I want to help."

"I don't see how you and Rebecca can be together even in this new age you speak of. Never mind that she is a servant." Selene settled onto his chest, listening to the double thump of his heart. "Both Jews and Christians forbid intermarriage without conversion, and the law forbids you to convert to Judaism. If Rebecca will not become Christian, what will you do? I would not see you shame her by keeping her as a concubine."

Phillip's voice became gruff. "We'll make it work—somehow."

CHAPTER 19

ORESTES AND HIS ESCORT made their way through the throngs toward the open-air theater in the eastern quarter.

"A rousing crowd tonight, eh, Orestes?" Jesep's elbow jostled his. Orestes tolerated the inappropriate familiarity. Jesep, along with several chief men among the Jews, had invited the Prefect to a play. The Patriarch pressed hard to ban such spectacles; the Jews lobbied equally hard to keep them. Orestes understood that this bitter public disagreement over entertainers masked deeper motives on the part of both parties, and tread lightly between the two. He came prepared to make conciliatory remarks, hoping to reconcile the feuding factions—at least on this dispute.

Orestes chatted with his companions as they entered the theater. It sat at the edge of the ruined palace district, nestled into a limestone ridge. The rows of seats marched in a semicircle up the slope, affording the audience a magnificent view of the grain fleet and the Pharos Lighthouse. Seven ships, their bright sails furled, sat low in the water, filled with sacks of grain. Over thirty ships a week during the next five months would make the round trip to Constantinople to deliver the precious golden cargo. Orestes saw the laden ships as a sign of his success.

The Master of Ceremonies announced Orestes' presence and bade him welcome. The crowd came to its feet, roaring. Orestes' chest expanded. These people approved of him; they wanted his presence. He was doing what he came here to do: keep the peace, expand prosperity, build his reputation.

Orestes strode into the arena, put out his hands and waved the crowd to silence. "Thank you, fellow citizens, for the warm welcome. I'm pleased to share this night's entertainment with you. Following the play, I'll speak, but for now—let the show begin!" The crowd gave one final roar before settling in their seats.

ORESTES CLAPPED ENTHUSIASTICALLY. The young men playing the Theban prince Theseus and his escort created a thrilling interpretation of Cretan bull dancing. Orestes found himself shouting with the crowd as the naked players grabbed the horns of an actor wearing a bull's head and somersaulted over the smoke-snorting Minotaur. They danced in, one after the other, to tease the monster, somersault over, poke the beast in the ribs, and vault back to their original spots.

As the players took their bows, a commotion broke out near the stage. A dozen or so men dressed as monks rushed into the arena and started beating the actors—most with their fists, but a few had cudgels. A larger contingent from among the audience rushed into the arena in defense of the players. Before the entire theater could empty onto the stage, Orestes stood and shouted, "Stay in your seats! I will deal with this disturbance." He turned to the captain of his escort. "Stop the melee and bring the churchmen to me."

Orestes clenched his fists, arms stiff at his sides. He thought he had come to an accommodation with Cyril concerning the parabolani. The force of five hundred was to be reduced to fifty, to guard Cyril's person, not patrol the streets. Abundantius had withdrawn a similar number of soldiers, so the streets of Alexandria were, Orestes thought, policed by the city guard.

His captain returned with a protesting monk. "This one claims to be their leader, sir."

"Who are you and why do you cause such riot?"

"I am Ammonius of Nitria," the monk said, face red, a line of spittle dressing his beard. "I came to do what you will not—close this den of unrighteousness."

"I have not yet ruled on the matter of entertainers," Orestes said in a deceptively mild voice. "It's my understanding the Patriarch protests lewd mimes, naked female players, and theater performed on the Sabbath. I witnessed none of those conditions."

"It's the Jewish Sabbath. By their own laws, these—people!—should be home or worshiping. Instead they fill their eyes with filth!"

158

"Silence!" Orestes raised his hand. "Who appointed you keeper of Jewish law?"

The monk's face set in a hard line. A fanatical gleam sparkled in his eyes. "God directs my actions."

Jesep stepped forward. "This smacks of a man's hand, not God's. A man named Hierex, an agent of the Patriarch."

"Hierex," people near enough to hear muttered.

"Hierex is Cyril's agent," several shouted. "Hierex speaks against us."

Orestes turned to Demetrius with a raised eyebrow. This confirmed reports from Phillip. His secretary leaned forward and spoke in low tones. "Hierex is a teacher known to be loyal to the Patriarch. He is well regarded in Christian circles."

"I've other reports of his actions. He seems to be at the root of much trouble." Orestes turned back to Jesep. "What proof have you that Hierex's will drives these men?"

"He spreads lies and builds outrage among the common people. He has also spoken against you, Lord Prefect. Saying you are no true Christian, in that you favor the company of pagans and Jews."

"Do not listen to them; they pour poison in your ears, Prefect!" Ammonius struggled in his captor's grip. "Jews are the agents of the devil."

Jesep turned red and stood toe-to-toe with the monk. "I protest the actions of this...Christian." He turned to Orestes, hands outstretched. "We've been here since Alexander the Great built this city, yet the Patriarch in his festal letter says we are 'filled with every type of impurity.' He denounces our beliefs and, though he has not urged violence, Hierex and his followers raid our neighborhoods and attack our people. I call on you, Augustal Prefect, to stop this heinous behavior and protect the Jewish citizens of Alexandria."

Orestes' anger neared the boiling point. The two factions could not have planned such a public confrontation if they tried. He could not maintain a façade of neutrality while the parabolani made free rein of the city. Orestes turned to the listening audience. "My fellow citizens, I came to your fair city to serve all Alexandrines. I am the representative of Imperial authority in Egypt and Alexandria. It is my duty to protect all citizens of the Empire and I will carry out that duty. Those who wish to foment unrest—be they Christian or Jew—will suffer the consequences."

Ragged shouts of approval went up in some quarters. Muttering rumbled in others. A dozen or so people rose and left the theater. He motioned one of his guards to follow. "I keep the peace in this city, not the parabolani. All who wish can freely travel and attend entertainments, as they will. I will not keep their consciences."

"Pagan! Jew lover!" Ammonius spat at Orestes.

"Guards, take this monk in for questioning. Pick up Hierex as well. I want to know what he is plotting and who controls him."

The guard saluted. "Yes, sir. I'll deliver them personally."

The soldiers removed the monk. Orestes turned to the subdued crowd. "We came here in good fellowship to enjoy an evening's entertainment. Let us put aside our rancor and ill-will in the common cause of peace in our city."

"Well said, Prefect. Our community needed to hear your support." Jesep bobbed his head. "Would you care to join me and some colleagues to discuss our concerns?"

Orestes sighed inwardly. "Certainly."

HIEREX STIFLED A MOAN as his torturer turned to heat the tongs in a brazier of blazing coals. His hands and feet were numb from the tight leather bands that held his naked form spread-eagled on an upright X-shaped rack. He wished the rest of his body exhibited a similar lack of feeling.

He couldn't see out his left eye. His tongue probed bloody holes where three of his teeth recently lodged. Burns blistered the skin inside his thighs and across his belly. "Good Lord Jesus, give me strength to endure these tortures in your name," he mumbled over and over.

The burly guard turned back to him with the glowing tongs. Hierex quickened his prayers.

"Tell me who is behind these attacks."

He said nothing.

"Come now, you need only give me a name. Any name."

The red glowing tongs came closer to his genitals. Hierex' mind raced like a dog chasing its tail as he sought a way to avoid the pain without betraying his Patriarch.

"Pentadius!" he cried out, mangling the name through swollen lips and broken teeth. "Pentadius asked that the parabolani assist in expelling the Jews."

"Liar. Tell me of the Patriarch."

The tongs burned the hair from his groin. Hierex contracted his belly muscles as far as he could, in a futile effort to avoid the searing pain. He screamed as blistering heat touched his scrotum. The sickening smell of his scorched flesh filled the room.

"Gallus, what's this?" A deep voice stopped the torturer's movements. "I asked you to question this man, not kill him."

Hierex tilted his head to see a blurry image of Orestes standing in the doorway. The Prefect looked angry, but not horrified, at the sight of his tortured body.

"Prefect, forgive me." Gallus spoke in stricken tones. "He refused to answer. This is standard procedure for questioning prisoners."

"I'm well aware of that." The chill in Orestes' voice seemed to lower the temperature in the dank dungeon. "This is a delicate matter. I expected a little less obvious physical damage." The Prefect sighed. "I should have overseen the questioning from the beginning." Orestes looked him over, a deep frown on his face. "Take him down and clean him up. I want him in my quarters in the morning."

"Yes, sir." Gallus bowed as Orestes left the room.

Hierex sent one venomous look at the Prefect's retreating back, then passed out in relief.

"THE PATRIARCH TO SEE YOU, SIR." Demetrius showed Cyril into Orestes' office. The bishop presented a calm face. Orestes hoped Cyril had come to disavow the rogue elements in the church.

"I understand you have detained a Nitrian monk and a member of my staff, Prefect. May I inquire as to their crimes?"

Orestes rose as the Patriarch entered the room and indicated a chair. "Disturbing the peace. Ammonius and several parabolani attacked a band of players. Hierex spreads sedition."

"Hierex spoke against the most Christian Emperor Theodosius? I find that hard to believe."

"Hierex incites Alexandrine citizens to riot."

"Surely not. Hierex is in training for the priesthood. He comes under my jurisdiction. I want him now."

Orestes sat behind his desk without asking Cyril's permission. "Hierex will be brought shortly. I have other matters to discuss with you, Patriarch. Ammonius led a band of armed monks. I thought we agreed the parabolani were to be disbanded."

"They have been, Prefect. I know nothing of this Ammonius."

"He is a monk, and claims allegiance to you."

"All monks in the city of Alexandria are under my protection. Give him over to me and he shall receive the punishment he deserves."

Orestes' hope faded fast. "Alexandria is a fragile city, Patriarch. Let us work together to make it stronger. I am attempting to keep the peace, but you must keep your people in line."

Cyril stared hard at Orestes, frowning. "Alexandria must be a Christian city, Prefect. God and the Emperor have decreed it. Help me in this endeavor or stand out of my way."

"The Emperor never decreed his citizens be attacked and their property confiscated."

"Christianity has been the state religion for over thirty years. The Imperial Senate and the Emperor himself have provided ample laws concerning the treatment of heretics. We cannot tolerate citizens who believe in anything other than the One True Church. I seek no more than what the Emperor wishes: a Christian community throughout the Roman Empire."

"God may whisper in your ear, Patriarch, but don't pretend to speak for the Emperor. I am his representative in Alexandria."

"The Emperor's representative? Or the Regent's?" Cyril's smile did not reach his eyes. "Things are changing at court. I understand the Emperor's sister Pulcheria—a most Christian lady—is taking an interest in running the Empire."

Orestes smoothed his face into a mask. He had hoped Cyril's sources wouldn't be as effective as they proved. "Until I hear differently, I am still the Imperial representative and Governor of Egypt." Orestes spread his hands in a supplicating gesture. "I do not wish to argue with you, Patriarch. No one benefits when a city goes up in flames. Your followers suffer as much as the non-believers."

"Speaking of my followers, I demand you turn Hierex and the monk over to me."

Orestes nodded to Demetrius who exited. He turned back to Cyril. "Cooperate with me. Together we can make this a great city—one of peace and learning."

"We can have peace when all have accepted the True Word of God. Learning is useless unless it reveals that Word."

Demetrius returned with the two men; Hierex supported by the limping monk.

Cyril turned to Orestes, rage pulsing through his voice. "How have you used my people?"

"They caused riot and would not answer my questions."

"These men are protected by the One True Church of Jesus Christ."

"Surely, you understand I cannot tolerate public disregard for the laws even by churchmen?"

Cyril pointed at Orestes and pronounced, "Let you not harm them again, or any others under my protection, or everlasting damnation will be your fate."

Orestes rose, a vein pulsing in his forehead. He pointed toward the door. "Out! The Emperor shall hear of the actions of his Patriarch in Alexandria."

Cyril looked up from shepherding the injured men. "And be assured, the Emperor—and his sister—will hear of the actions of his Prefect."

Orestes sat, jaw clenched.

Demetrius approached. "Master, may I speak freely?"

"What?"

Demetrius looked down, hands behind his back. "Master, that was not well handled."

Orestes' mouth dropped at the slave's audacity. His immediate reaction was to whip the man, but he was too honest not to acknowledge the truth of the matter. "The Patriarch will not listen to reason. The arrogance of youth and position puts iron in his neck. What am I to do with him?"

"Perhaps if you gave him a more public show of support, he could be more lenient, call off his dogs. You have…sometimes…through your attentions to Hypatia and Jesep, given the impression you favor them over the Patriarch. You could be more conciliatory, allow him to show his supporters he has access to you, that he has other ways to attain his ends than through violence."

"My experience says that to show weakness invites attack." Orestes squared his shoulders. "I will not offer support to Cyril while he orchestrates these riots. He is still accountable to his congregation. I will try to build a coalition of older nobles and counselors to advise the Patriarch. Maybe he will be guided by other, cooler heads."

Demetrius bowed. "You know best, Master. Shall I bring in the next visitor?"

Orestes eyed the piles of scrolls. "Yes. Though for once I would rather deal with paper than with people and their obstinacies."

Cyril sat at his desk, reviewing his intentions. The leaders of the Jewish community would arrive shortly. He needed to project a strong presence. He heard a knock at his door and rose to open it.

"Hierex, my friend, what are you doing out of bed?" The man still limped from the torture ten days past; his face was mottled yellow and green from fading bruises.

"I need to be here. I want to look on the faces of those who caused me such harm." Hierex hobbled into the room.

"You need to go back to bed. Let me handle the Jews." Cyril tried to steer his friend back through the door.

Blood suffused the injured man's face. A mad look came into his eyes. "No. I will confront them myself."

"Hot tempers will not serve our purposes. Save your rage for later. We need to present a calm, reasonable face. The Jews must feel shame for their intemperate actions and our moderate response."

"They will not be punished for their crimes?" Hierex spluttered.

"Of course." Cyril put a calming hand on his friend's shoulder. "But it must not look as if we orchestrated it. Many powerful men watch us closely. We cannot afford to lose their support. Soon, my friend, we will be rid of the Jews, and without them at his back Orestes will bend to our will. Now, off to bed."

Cyril called a servant to assist Hierex. He limped away, giving his master one last imploring look.

Cyril returned to his desk, but couldn't concentrate on the papers in front of him. The Jews had the Prefect's ear. He couldn't even have a reasonable conversation with the man. Cyril snapped the reed pen he held. The water clock sounded the hour with hollow bongs.

Time.

He smiled.

All would come about as he wanted, given God's good grace and time.

CHAPTER 20

S ELENE WOVE THROUGH THE CROWDS in the market, looking for a special wedding gift for Honoria and Antonius. Bright swirls of color chased each other as women trailing servants picked over piles of goods. The duller grays and browns of pilgrims, going to or coming from holy sites, punctuated the vivid mosaic.

A large contingent of beggars worked the crowd. Selene hesitated over giving a bronze coin to a small girl missing a leg, knowing she would be besieged within minutes. She gave it anyway, and let Rebecca shoo off the dozen urchins who immediately converged on them clamoring for alms.

After dealing with the children, Rebecca pointed to a frantic merchant in desert-colored robes. "Mistress, how about a carpet?" He saw them considering and spoke louder, extolling the colors and softness of his wares.

Selene shook her head. "Something more personal."

"Perhaps a book?"

"No. Honoria can barely read." Selene surveyed the available stalls. "Maybe glassware or embroidery."

The glaziers occupied the next quarter. Selene could tell they were close by the occasional whiff of noxious fumes that made her eyes water. At the first shop, a young man, on hearing of a wedding, offered them a tour of the premises. "We make the finest glassware in all of Egypt, ladies. Come see our wares. We will make to your order. Vases, plates, perfume bottles, beads. Any color you wish." He ushered them into a small courtyard surrounded by fourteen small workshops, none more than six strides across or deep.

All the workers to the right made platters of various sizes. Some tended furnaces, melting the sand, lead, and minerals to make the liquid glass. The men tending the furnaces glistened with sweat and charcoal dust. Some wore cloths over their mouths and noses, but frequent wracking coughs indicated weakness of the lungs. Other workers poured the glowing liquid into granite molds or polished the final products with grit-embedded cloth. The plates, a deep blue, reminded Selene of the color of the western desert sky after sunset.

On the left, workers made more delicate objects. Selene admired a set of goblets to match the plates, and a flawless perfume bottle of rose pink. She and Rebecca watched a roomful of little girls threading beads into intricate necklaces and bracelets. The dim light made them hunch and squint.

"Is there much illness among your workers?" Selene asked the glass merchant.

"No more than most." The man shrugged. "They are a lazy lot of slaves. If they complain too much, I sell them to the porphyry mines. That keeps them in line."

"Even the children?"

"No, Lady, not the children. They come from an orphanage. I teach them a trade in exchange for a small fee." He took Selene's elbow. "Perhaps, Lady, you would like a glass of wine in my office while we talk of your new glassware. How many sets will you need for your household?"

"You mistook me, Sir." Selene shuddered at his touch. "The wedding's a friend's, not mine."

His face stiffened in disappointment at the loss of a large contract, but he recovered quickly. "Surely you saw a suitable gift among my fine wares?"

"Perhaps, but I wish to look further. Thank you for your time." Selene turned to leave.

The merchant followed her to the street. "You'll find none finer for a better price in all of Alexandria," he shouted after them.

"Did nothing suit you?" Rebecca asked as they walked back toward the market. "I thought he had fine wares."

"He did not suit me. I found him repulsive."

Rebecca laughed. "You did not have to buy him—only his glass!"

"I wish I could buy him, and show him the same misery he shows his workers. Did you see those little girls? Their eyesight will be ruined before they are adults. If they live that long. They were all thin, and most coughed as often as the furnace tenders."

"You can't save everyone in Alexandria, Selene." Rebecca rested her hand gently on Selene's arm.

"Beautiful lady, look at my fine bronze ware. It comes from all the corners of the Empire and beyond. Elephants from India, torques from Britannia, urns from Germania."

Selene turned to the smoothly chanting voice and looked over the pieces displayed on a white linen cloth. There were many fine bracelets, earrings, and a delightful statue of a many-armed woman dancing on a snake.

"You like the Kali, Mistress? I have statues I show to special customers. Come with me to the back." He covered the wares on the table with a green silk cloth and held a striped hanging back from the doorframe, indicating they should precede him into the dim interior.

Rebecca whispered into Selene's ear, "I don't believe you should go into the shop with that man. Have him bring his wares out."

Selene, depressed over the child glass workers, compounded by her failure to find a suitable gift, replied irritably, "Oh, Rebecca, don't be such a stick. What could happen in the middle of the market? Besides, you'll be with me." She shoved her servant toward the opening.

They edged around the table and into the dim light of the shop. Selene blinked as her eyes adjusted, and stumbled over something small but heavy, banging her shin. She hopped, rubbing her leg.

"This way, ladies." The bronze merchant waved them to the back, where he uncovered a knee-high statue.

Selene saw arms, legs, heads, and torsos contorted in impossible positions. When she realized it was a man mounting a woman, she gasped. She was aware of male anatomy, but doubted two human bodies could twist that way. As her sight improved, she saw many such statues, in various sizes and positions; as well as a number of miniature figures of men with large erect penises and women with voluptuous breasts and buttocks.

"Oh my! Rebecca, I think we should leave. Thank you, sir, for the viewing, but we must go."

"But, Lady, surely there is something here to your taste? I've supplied bronze art to the best households in the city." He reached out to touch Selene's sleeve.

"Thank you, sir, but not at this time." Selene and Rebecca fled the shop.

Rebecca giggled, her eyes sparkling. "Well, that would make a fine wedding present. Maybe Antonius would thank you for providing Honoria with some instruction. You can always send someone to purchase it later."

The thought of being in such a position with Antonius brought a flood of warmth to Selene's body, and color to her cheeks. Honoria's face intruded on her torrid thoughts and turned her excitement to guilt and shame. "I don't think so, Rebecca. I'm tired. We can search again tomorrow."

THE STATUE HAUNTED SELENE all day. While Rebecca helped prepare her for bed, she suddenly blurted, "Have you and Phillip made love?"

Rebecca stopped brushing Selene's hair, her mouth pursed in a small frown.

"Forgive me for a blunt fool, Rebecca. I have no one to talk to about these things and I thought, uh, after seeing the statue…" She turned to Rebecca with pleading eyes. "You are older."

"I see." Rebecca continued brushing. "We should have discussed this earlier. Among my people, the older women pass on their knowledge when girls have their first courses. You had no one to mark your passing into womanhood. What are your questions?"

"I know what men are like. I've seen animals mating. I want to know, does it hurt?" Selene looked up down with curiosity and shame.

"I've heard it sometimes hurts the first time, like when you've tried a new exercise and your muscles are sore. It can also hurt if the man is careless or the woman unprepared. Two people who love each other should take their time and make sure each is ready."

Selene turned pale. "I've heard women bleed the first time."

"Sometimes, when the girl is quite young or the man is rough. It's not unusual for healthy a young woman not to bleed. But many men believe blood is a sign the woman is a virgin." Rebecca added with a knowing smile, "A smart bride brings a small bag of chicken blood to stain the sheets on the wedding night."

Selene giggled. "The life of a chicken is a small sacrifice for peace in the family."

"When you wish, I can take you to meet my mother, perhaps. She has much more experience than I, and can better answer your questions."

Rebecca turned to tidy the cosmetics table. Selene snagged her hand. "Thank you, Rebecca."

*****

ON THE MORNING OF THE WEDDING, Selene woke feeling crampy. A trickle of blood stained her thighs. "Mother of Jesus, save me. Why did I have to get my courses now?" She washed with water from the night pitcher and rummaged in her chest for clean linen cloths cut from her outworn robes.

Rebecca entered to help dress her in a dark green gown, fix her shoulder-length hair and apply cosmetics. Selene felt the dark ring of kohl around her eyes and the pale powder made her look haunted and tired, but she didn't much care. She would have avoided this ceremony if she could, but her absence would have been made the subject of gossip.

She joined her father and Phillip in the vestibule. The ceremony would be a simple one, at the bride's home, for family and close friends. A priest that Ision housed as a favor to the church would officiate, but the important parts had been handled weeks before, when the bride and groom's fathers signed the papers, transferred the dowry, and entered the transaction in the city and church records.

Selene trudged to the house, feeling hot and drained. The sheltering coolness of Ision's vestibule revived her somewhat. Soon Honoria's younger sisters, fluttering and cooing like a bevy of quail, surrounded and led her away to a side room. She briefly glimpsed the men congregating under the colonnade by the interior garden. Antonius looked trapped as several friends boisterously clapped him on the shoulder and back. She had heard most of the tired jokes, and didn't envy him the role of eager groom.

Honoria was the center of a similar, but more subdued, coterie. Her mother Arete presided, so ribald remarks stayed at a whispered minimum, but sly glances and giggles abounded. Honoria turned when Selene entered the room. She looked stately in her pale umber dalmatica stitched with gold over a white tunic. The traditional orange veil draped a nearby chair, fluttered in the slight breeze, showing the fineness of the silk weave. Today, Honoria, who had never been accounted pretty, looked beautiful. Happiness and excitement beamed from her face. For her, at least, this was a love match. A rare thing in their circle.

She bounced toward Selene, took both hands in hers. They brushed cheeks and parted. "My dear friend! I told Mother we couldn't start without you. Help me finish preparing." Honoria turned again as her mother approached with the veil and a circlet of flowers to hold it in place. Selene murmured something polite and helped the older woman arrange the veil in flowing folds down her friend's back.

Arete stepped back and smiled. "My daughter, you look beautiful."

"Do I?" Honoria fussed with her robes, tweaking them one way, then another, jangling various gold bracelets and necklaces. "I so want Antonius to like me. I do want to be beautiful for him. What do you think, Selene? Father paid a fortune for this material. Does it suit me?"

Selene broke into her first smile of the day. "Yes. It suits you, my friend. The color is perfect for your skin, and your eyes out-sparkle your jewels. Antonius will have no complaints."

Honoria gave her a quick hug, then turned to her mother. "I'm ready now." They pulled the veil over her face and the women trickled out toward the courtyard.

The garden's air was thick with the fragrance of hundreds of roses set in vases, twisted in lavish arrangements, scattered in pools and fountains. It gave Selene a headache and made her nose itch. Leave it to Arete to go to extremes for a simple ceremony. The wedding feast was likely to be equally lavish. At the thought of exotic food, Selene's stomach rebelled.

Honoria's father came forward to claim his daughter. He was a short, pear-shaped man, with a stubborn set to his jaw, and the hawk nose of his Syrian ancestors. Ision took Honoria's arm and tucked it under his own, leading her to the center of the garden, in front of a splashing fountain. Antonius and his father waited there. Misty drops sparkled in Antonius' dark curls. He looked as pale and drawn as Selene felt. His glance crossed hers and held for a brief moment. The hint of a smile warmed his face before he turned his gaze to his bride.

The priest came forward, a gaunt black crow among the plump many-colored plovers of Ision's family. He joined the bride and groom's hands and launched into a homily on the sacred nature of marriage.

Selene bitterly contemplated the unlikelihood she would ever make a match; her emotional pain was mirrored by the cramping in her womb. Nausea gripped her stomach. Her courses rarely caused her so much trouble. Panic rose at the thought that she might disgrace herself by vomiting in the bushes or fainting from the smell of the roses. She calmed herself with deep breaths, trying to focus on the priest's final words.

"The purpose of marriage is to honor the One True God, to mirror in the union of a man and a woman the love Jesus has for us. May the Lord Jesus

Christ look favorably on this marriage and give Antonius and Honoria peace, prosperity, and happiness. May Holy Mary, Mother of God, bless this union with many children. Let us pray."

Selene spread her arms and bowed her head, blinking back tears. At the end, she raised her head to see Antonius' despairing glance.

Ision turned to the company. "Good friends, esteemed guests, please join me in honoring the bride and groom at the wedding feast." A cheer went up from the small throng, subsiding into loud murmurs as family and guests wandered toward the triclinium.

Calistus took Selene's arm. "Care to escort an old man to the feast, my dear?"

Selene smiled up at her father. "There's no one I would rather accompany."

They strolled through the garden in companionable silence until her father stumbled against her with a gasp.

"Father, is something wrong?"

"A shortness of br..." He collapsed, pulling Selene to her knees.

Women shrieked and male bodies bullied close. Selene poked a sharp elbow into a soft belly, shouting, "Stay back! Give me room!" She knelt next to her father and felt for a pulse in his neck. It was fast and irregular. His breath came in great ragged gasps; his face pale and sweaty; his left arm drawn up across his chest. She knew it must be a weakness in his heart. There was nothing she could do but make him comfortable.

"Father?" she asked as his eyelids fluttered. "Can you hear me?"

"Pain...in my chest." He gripped her arm with his right hand. It was surprisingly strong. "Phillip. Must get Phil..."

"Yes, Father, I'm here." Selene's brother knelt on the other side of Calistus. "I've sent for a physician and a litter. We'll take you home." Phillip pushed disheveled hair from his father's forehead as the older man slipped into unconsciousness. Selene saw her brother's ravaged face as he tried to control his fear.

"Selene, is there anything we can do for him?"

She mutely shook her head.

Ision loudly ordered everyone to the banquet room, then instructed the servants to place Calistus on a litter. Selene, dimly aware of Phillip making their apologies, stood, turned around, and walked into Antonius. "I'm so sorry, Antonius," she said as she burst into tears.

He clutched her tightly to his chest, stroked her hair, and mumbled soothingly. She sobbed, then struggled away, leaving a black smudge of kohl and a wet spot on his white tunic. In panic she searched for Honoria, expecting her friend's face to reflect rage or pain. It showed sorrow.

Honoria approached and enveloped Selene in a hug. "Oh, my friend, take heart. Your father is yet alive. Maybe God will have mercy and let him abide awhile yet with his earthly family."

Selene disentangled herself. "This was to be a day of happiness for you. I'm sorry we spoiled your wedding, but we must go."

Honoria took her friend's arm and escorted her in the wake of the litter. "Of course. We'll all pray for your father. If there is anything I, or Antonius can do, please send word."

CHAPTER 21

SELENE WATCHED CLOSELY as Urbib sniffed her father's breath, lifted his
eyelids, and laid an ear to his chest. Although a Jew, the physician cared
for many of the Christian elite.

In consultation with Auxentius, Selene had been dosing her father's bedtime
wine with tincture of nightshade. She knew there was little medicine could do
once the heart reached an advanced state of decline, but she had felt she had to
try. Now she worried about her presumptuous actions. What if her meddling
had made things worse?

She chewed her fingernail, lost in guilt, until the pain of a ripped and
bleeding cuticle brought her back to the present. Haroun had warned Selene
about doing surgery with cuts on her hands. He claimed the miasma of illness
could enter a healthy body through openings and cause wounds to fester. She
had nearly broken her habit of biting her nails during the last year.

"What do you think, Honored Doctor?" Phillip asked.

Selene looked up with hope.

"His humors don't sound good." Urbib harrumphed, pulled at his curly
beard, and turned to Phillip. "I don't think he will live much longer. At fifty-
and-two years, he is older than most of my patients. I feel it is time the family
said good-bye."

"No!" Selene cried. "There must be something else we can do."

He looked down his long nose at her, paused for a breath, and addressed
her sternly, as he would an errant child. "I am aware you have been dabbling in
medical studies. A practice, of which, I am in strong opposition." He addressed

his next remarks to Phillip, dismissing Selene. "I've delivered my diagnosis and learned opinion. I will send a tincture of poppy to ease his pain. Give him three drops in a cup of warm wine every four hours. Do you have any other questions?"

Phillip's gaze tracked from his sister's angry red face to the physician's disdainful one. "No, sir. We appreciate your prompt attendance." He escorted Urbib to the door, talking low, and handed over a laden purse.

Selene pulled a three-legged stool to her father's bedside and held his hand. Tears trickled down her cheeks. She feared her father would leave her soon and she wasn't ready.

She winced from a sharp cramp roiling her womb, followed by heaviness in her groin, and sticky wetness between her thighs. Curses! She was bleeding through her cloths.

"Mistress?" Rebecca softly touched her shoulder. "You should get food and rest."

Phillip returned in time to catch the last remark. "Yes, Selene. Get something to eat. I'll watch father for a while. If anything changes, I'll send for you."

Selene followed Rebecca out of her father's room. "I feel so helpless," she wailed to her servant and confidante.

Rebecca put an arm around Selene's shoulders and led her upstairs. She helped Selene clean up and left to tend her father. Selene sat on her bed, plucking at a nub in the fabric of her coverlet. She reviewed the remedies she had learned, rejecting one after the other. In the end, she was left with prayer, which did not come naturally to her.

Since God had seen fit to ignore her childish pleas to spare her mother, Selene had lost faith in the power of prayer to heal. Instead she relied on human knowledge and the study of medicine. She recognized now how woefully she had ignored her spiritual life. She had little faith to sustain her in her fear and confusion.

She smelled the concoction before Rebecca came into the room: mint with honey to take away the bitterness of the healing herb. Rebecca placed the tray on a stand next to the bed. Selene picked up the cup and absently sipped the steaming liquid. The mint soothed her upset stomach and the medicine eased her cramps. She concentrated on the flavors; a smoky aftertaste she couldn't quite place.

"Rebecca, where do you get this mixture? No one I know makes this infusion."

Rebecca turned to her in surprise. "An old Egyptian woman who lives on the border between the Jewish and Rhakotis quarters. She supplies medicines and charms to servants and slaves for small coins or in kind."

"Does she specialize in herbs?"

"She is quite renowned for her healing arts and spells."

"What kinds of ailments do people take to her?"

"All kinds. Barrenness, wounds, weakness of the lungs, fevers."

"Weakness of the heart?" Selene put her cup down with a thud.

"I imagine so."

Selene jumped to her feet and grabbed Rebecca's arm. "Can you take me to her?"

Rebecca pulled back. "You can't go to that quarter, Selene. Your father would—"

"My father needs me to do this. Will you help me, or do I have to ask one of the kitchen staff?"

"At least let me fetch Phillip to accompany us."

"No. Someone has to stay with Father."

Rebecca frowned as she looked Selene over from head to toe. "We'll need to find something suitable for you to wear. You can't go traipsing about in your best finery; you'll attract every thief and murderer for miles."

SELENE DRESSED IN THE WORN SERVANT'S ROBES Rebecca provided for her: rough brown cloth with many patches and a wine stain on the left breast. At least it's clean, she thought. She pulled a beige shawl over her head and stepped into much-patched sandals. Rebecca had already combed out her hair and dressed it in a simple braid.

They took the back ways through the private rooms to the servants' quarters, out the kitchen, to the alley. They joined throngs of servants headed for the marketplace, then worked their way through the Jewish quarter to Rhakotis, site of the original Egyptian village on top of which Alexander built his city.

Selene momentarily forgot her father's illness at the alien sights and sounds. She remembered the smell of garlic and fried fish wafting from the public kitchens from her visit over a year ago. Gangs of small children still roamed the streets kicking balls, hauling baskets or minding even smaller children. But there seemed to be a tension in the air.

Rebecca called to people she knew. They looked at Selene, exploring her face, noting her clothes, and passing judgment on her fitness to be there. None barred her way, but she felt sharp eyes bore into her back. They wended their way down a narrow side road to a hut tucked behind a public kitchen on a back alley.

Rebecca entered the hut first, calling, "Mother Nut?"

Selene followed, stepping over piles of discarded clothes and heaps of bones. A cracked voice called out from a corner. "You've come to see Mother Nut, little ones? Come closer."

Selene sidled across the floor, trying not to touch the odorous piles. As she approached the dark corner a slightly larger heap began to move. In the dim light she could just make out matted gray hair and a dark face with skin like cracked leather. A claw-like hand grabbed Selene's arm. The old woman sniffed at her. "Come for my wonder potion for women's difficulties?"

"How did you know about my problems?"

"Women in their courses smell different." The old woman chuckled and pointed at her ear. "You are not what you seem. My ears are as good as my nose, and your accent is not of this quarter. Who brought you here? Why does a lady visit my hut?"

"I brought her, Mother Nut. This is my mistress, Lady Selene."

The old woman squinted at Rebecca. "Miriam's daughter, aren't you? Rebecca?"

"Yes. I've bought remedies from you before."

"I've been told you deal in special charms and herbs that heal," Selene said. "My father is gravely ill with a weakness of the heart. His physician has given up hope, but I haven't. I've been dosing him with nightshade for several months. Do you have anything else that would be of help?"

"Do you know herbs, child?" Mother Nut cackled, gusting breath so laden with garlic Selene stepped back.

"Some. I've been studying medicine at the Museum for more than a year."

The old woman snorted. "You can't learn medicine from dusty books, girl. You need to get out among the sick." She turned to a shelf and rummaged. "I think I have something that might help your father."

"I have coins." Selene started to dig into her pouch.

Mother Nut pulled two items from the shelf, turned, and stared at Selene. "That's too easy, child. How much do you want to help your father?"

"I'll pay anything, do anything!"

"Anything?" The old woman rubbed a whiskered chin. "What do you know of healing?"

"Herb lore." Selene saw the old woman frown and continued quickly, "I've studied anatomy, surgery, and dentistry."

"Midwifery?"

"No, Mother."

"Then what use are you?" Mother Nut stamped a foot. "You can't cure people with book knowledge and a knife."

"What has that got to do with payment for your herbs?" Selene asked impatiently.

"I need a girl to learn my trade from me. I am old and my people will need another to take over their care." She looked at Selene from head to foot, as if measuring her worth and finding her wanting. "I had thought of asking you to apprentice, but such a fancy one as you would be no use to my people."

An apprenticeship? With this old witch? Selene hesitated. Both her teachers had recommended she apprentice, but she doubted they had Mother Nut in mind. However, Urbib's disdainful reaction was typical of the physicians she met at the hospitals. Alexandrine doctors, renowned throughout the Empire, kept their numbers small. The best took one or two students sponsored by powerful patrons, and the students paid handsomely for the privilege. Why would any physician take on a woman apprentice, and one uncertain to pay at that? She could spend the rest of her life changing bandages and cleaning beds in the charity hospitals, or she could learn as much as she could from those willing to teach her.

"Mother, if I offered my help, what might I learn?"

The old woman looked at her through matted hair. "Humility to start. Death is inevitable. Healers can only postpone it for a while." She smiled a gap-toothed grin. "And I have secrets. No one knows herbs and minerals as I do. My magic comes from the god Imhotep himself. You are Christos, are you not?"

Selene nodded.

"A weak god."

"Christ was a great healer," Selene huffed. "He made the lame walk and the blind see."

"Miracles!" The old woman's eyes disappeared in a mass of wrinkles as she laughed. "I see such miracles every day as the beggars return home, take off their bandages, and remove their sores. Yes, child, you could learn much from me!"

Selene's breathing quickened, which she regretted when she caught another whiff of garlic. The thought of returning to this dreadful hovel was almost more than she could bear, but Mother Nut held a compelling spell over her. Obviously the old woman had some success or she would not have such a reputation as a healer among the poor. The crone, after all, might be able to teach her something.

"If your cure works on my father, I will gladly apprentice with you."

"Whether it works has little to do with you or me, and everything to do with your father and his strength of spirit." The old woman handed Selene two objects: a packet of medicine and a small statue. "Come back, or not, as you wish."

Rebecca asked. "How are we to use these, Mother?"

"Make the herb into an infusion. Give a cupful at sunrise, noon, sunset, and midnight for two full days and the heart should strengthen, if it is not too late. After that, give him a cup once a day before he breaks his daily fast. The second thing you must do is put the charm under his bed. I've already laid a healing spell on it."

"Thank you, Mother Nut. I'll be back as soon as Father can spare me."

"We'll see," the crone muttered.

Selene bowed to the old woman. "If your medicine is as good as you claim, I will want to know your secrets. If my father survives, I will return to serve you as you wish. Come, Rebecca."

They escaped the hut. Selene held the charm to the light. It was a small clay-fired statue of a mother suckling a child. "The Virgin Mary and Baby Jesus!" she murmured.

"May I see?" Rebecca held out her hand for the brightly painted statue. She turned it over, squinting at the details. "I don't think so. See the headdress? This is the Egyptian goddess Isis and her son Horus. They're protective deities."

She handed the charm back to Selene who put it in her pouch.

"I am constantly amazed at how little difference there is between religions." Selene sighed. "The arguments are always over the details. Mary or Isis, Jesus or Horus. Maybe Hypatia is right and names don't matter, just the search for godliness in the life we live."

She looked up at the lowering sun. "Let's get back quickly, Rebecca. I want to try Mother Nut's remedy."

They hurried the way they had come, but Selene sensed a disturbance in the crowds as they passed. The earlier tensions strengthened to dark foreboding. A dancing girl packed up her coins; women and children disappeared from the street. Young men congregated on corners, muttering among themselves.

Rebecca, her forehead creased in a frown said, "I don't like the looks of this." She craned her head to spot someone she knew. "Rachel," she shouted at an older woman herding several toddlers toward a rundown building.

Rachel turned at the sound of her name. "Rebecca? Get off the streets, child. The parabolani are headed this way. The young men intend to fight back." She turned back to her charges, shooing them inside the welcoming shelter of an open door.

"What did she mean?" Selene asked.

"Since the Prefect had the Patriarch's henchman arrested, the parabolani have been even more active." Rebecca laughed bitterly. "Cyril means to have a Christian town one way or the other. He organizes food for the hungry with one hand, and sends militant monks to destroy our homes and livelihoods with the other. Our people won't stand idly by and let that happen." Rebecca looked around at the fast emptying streets. "We must get out of here." She grabbed Selene's hand and ran down a side alley.

Selene heard faint shouts. She looked back to see a small mob of men with knives, sticks, and one pitchfork, pass the entrance to the alley; their faces grim.

"Where are we going?"

Rebecca peeked around a corner, then waved her forward. "I know a way to avoid the main streets, but we'll have to climb."

Selene covered her concern with a grin.

They reached the corner of a two-story building. Rebecca pulled a ladder from a lean-to and Selene helped her push it in place. They pulled their robes between their knees and tucked the hems into their belts, making pantaloons of their tunics and freeing their legs to scramble up the ladder. Potsherds littered the flat roof.

"This way." Rebecca led off. Selene followed closely, wondering what childish escapades provided Rebecca with knowledge of these rooftops. They crossed several buildings, some of which, had people on top watching the streets. Boys piled stones at the edge of the roofs. Older people, seeing they were young women, turned back to the street. At one point Selene smelled smoke. Rebecca sniffed the air, judged the direction of the passing breeze from flapping laundry, and led off in another direction.

After several minutes, they approached a high wall enclosing a private compound. Rebecca looked over the side of the roof. "I think it's safe to come down here. The main road to the market is two buildings over." A twisted willow tree grew close to the wall. Rebecca leaned out and grasped a thin branch with both hands. She turned to Selene. "This is something my brothers taught me, but I haven't done it in years. The branch is too thin to hold my weight, but should lower me close enough to the ground to drop without injury. Stand back. When I release it, the branch will whip up. When I reach the ground, I'll get a ladder."

"Nonsense. If you can do it, so can I."

"Selene, this once will you do as you're told? You're heavier than I am. The branch might break."

Selene reluctantly agreed to wait.

Rebecca jumped away from the roof, the branch flinging her out and down. As Selene heard an ominous crack, Rebecca let go and dropped several feet to land awkwardly. She let out a hiss of pain and limped to another of the ubiquitous lean-tos to look for a ladder. The branch hung down, attached by a thin skin of bark.

Rebecca found a ladder and leaned it against the side of the building. Selene scrambled down. "Are you all right?"

"I think it's sprained." Rebecca rubbed her ankle. "It twisted under me when I dropped."

"Let me look at it."

Rebecca sat on a rock under the tree while Selene rotated her foot. "Does this hurt?"

Rebecca flinched. "Yes, that hurts! What are you doing?"

"Checking for broken bones. I didn't feel any scraping. Let me wrap it so we can get home." Selene ripped rags from the old shawl around her shoulders, and tightly wrapped the rapidly swelling ankle. "That ought to hold us until we can get cold cloths on it. Let me help you up."

Selene put her shoulder under the shorter woman's arm and helped her to her feet. Rebecca grunted with pain. "I'm not sure I can make it."

"You need only get to the market. I can hire a litter there." She patted her pouch. "Remember? I came prepared to pay a price. I didn't think it would be service to an Egyptian witch or a run for my life across the rooftops of Alexandria."

*****

SELENE UNWRAPPED THE BANDAGES and poked gently at the purpling ankle. Rebecca winced. "Put your foot in this water. The coolness should ease the swelling." Rebecca, sitting on the edge of Selene's bed, slid her foot into a bucket of cold water. She sighed in relief.

Selene propped her servant up with cushions and went for a cup of wine with a drop of poppy tincture. When she came back she quietly observed Rebecca's drawn face, pale and pinched with pain. Selene realized how much she regarded the young woman who had cared for her these last several years. Rebecca filled an empty space in Selene's soul, the place reserved for sister and friend.

"Here, this should ease your pain." She held the cup to Rebecca's lips and let her take small sips.

"You should go back to your father, Mistress." Rebecca pushed the cup away. "I can sit here for a while, then go to my quarters."

"His body servant tends him. I expect Mother Nut's remedy to take time to work." Selene extended the cup again. "And there's no need to call me 'Mistress' in private, Rebecca. You've been a better friend than most of the girls my father sees fit to have me associate with, although I haven't been a good friend to you." She shook her head. "Getting you in trouble with my father, putting us in danger. I would like to do something for you. What would you wish of me? Name it."

"I wish you to remain as you are. Warm hearted and clear-eyed."

"That's a wish for me, not for you. I could give you money, help your family. Why ask for so little?"

"I have learned to keep my hopes small so they will more likely come true." Rebecca patted Selene's cheek. "In this case, your determination to apprentice with Mother Nut will do more for me than a pile of coins. My religion teaches a life well lived is one spent in service, caring for one's family, engaging in acts of kindness toward the poor, and studying the wisdom of God."

"That is little different from Christian teachings."

"Jesus was a Jew, was he not?" Rebecca smiled at Selene's stunned expression. "He was a great teacher, a most learned rabbi. Isn't it fitting the religion carrying his name be based on our best traditions? Besides, money is fleeting, and God's judgment cannot be bought."

"But with more coin, you could better care for your family, or give it away to those poorer." Selene grinned at having caught Rebecca in a philosophical dilemma.

"True, but if you discharged your debt with money, what would be our relationship? Mistress and servant." Rebecca smiled gently. "You called me 'friend.' The obligations of mutual regard bind us close. Accepting money for acts of service or friendship breaks those bonds of affection."

"I would far rather call you 'friend' than 'servant'," Selene said. "Consider my offer in that light. Call upon me at any time for any service."

Rebecca looked up through pain-filled eyes. "Given the times I see ahead, I might redeem your pledge, but not today." She put a hand to her mouth to stifle a yawn, and promptly fell asleep.

Selene lifted her friend's foot from the water, dried it, and covered her with a blanket. Rebecca's face relaxed in sleep, the pain smoothed from her brow.

Selene gathered bedding to make a pallet and trudged to her father's room. Phillip sat in a chair by the bed, an account book lying open in his lap. As she entered the room he observed her servant's garb and shook his head. Selene had forgotten to change and blushed to her roots.

"I don't even want to know." He rose, stretched and yawned. "At least, not tonight."

"I'll stay with Father." She arranged her bedding on the floor. "You get some sleep."

Phillip hugged her on his way out and whispered hoarsely, "Call me if anything changes. I'll post a servant outside the door."

Selene sat for several moments, holding her father's hand. Calistus' unconscious face twitched and flickered with pain. Selene, unaccustomed to personal prayer, bowed her head and bargained with God for the life of her father.

Chapter 22

"PREFECT, THANK YOU for your invitation, but we feel no more can be accomplished while armed monks roam the streets." Jesep and the small Jewish contingent rose to leave the conference. "We've suffered their incursions for three months. Until the Patriarch sends them out of the city, or you lock them up, we will continue to defend ourselves."

Cyril sat at the table looking like the proverbial Nile crocodile.

Orestes stood as well. "Please reconsider. Both sides must talk, or we can reach no resolution."

"We've enough of talk. We want action." Jesep's face hardened. He pointed to the Patriarch. "Stop him or there will be blood in the streets."

Cyril rose. "Be warned. If you harm any Christians, I will not be able to control my people. They are already incensed over the treatment of Teacher Hierex, which they attribute to false Jewish accusations."

Orestes stepped between the two men. "If the city guards find armed citizens on either side, they will be banished from the city. Do you both understand? I will tolerate this situation no longer. Disarm your people and return to your churches and temples."

"Understood, Lord Prefect, but we will not tolerate the loss of Jewish life or property. If you cannot control these people, we will." The Jews bowed and left.

Orestes turned to the young Patriarch. "I thought you agreed with the nobles of this city to keep the peace." He reached for a paper on his desk and read. "The Jews of this day are worse than their fathers. Through their rejection of Christ, the Jews have shown themselves the most deranged of all men, senseless, blind, uncomprehending, demented, foolish God haters, killers of the Lord, unbelievers, and irreligious…Their synagogue is a leprous house which perpetuates their monstrous impiety."

Orestes slammed the paper on his desk. "This festal letter hardly supports amicable relations between the Christian and Jewish communities."

"The nobles did urge me to less inflammatory remarks. I could not, in good conscience, oblige them. The Jews are an abomination and must be removed from our city."

"Jews are Roman citizens, protected by imperial edicts." Orestes held his voice even with difficulty. "Their religion and Patriarch in Jerusalem are recognized by the Emperor."

"Imperial edicts change monthly. A new one concerning the Jews—or the appointment of a new Prefect—could be speeding its way as we speak." Cyril gathered his papers. "I heard from friends at court that the Emperor's sister, the Lady Pulcheria, is to be declared Regent and Augusta. Have you heard any such rumor?"

Orestes turned a neutral face to the Bishop. "Indeed. The public announcement will be made shortly, when her commemorative statue arrives from Constantinople."

"Most interesting. She is young for the post of Regent. Fifteen, isn't she? But the church could not ask for a more passionate adherent. I look forward to her inaugural." Cyril packed his papers in a leather pouch and paused at the door. "Good day, Prefect."

"Good day, Patriarch."

After Cyril left, Orestes slumped in his chair.

Demetrius detached himself from the shadows. "Another impasse, Master?"

"Yes. The nobles have failed in their efforts to sway Cyril. The Jews will stay armed as long as the parabolani roam the streets. The parabolani claim they are protecting Christians from Jewish attacks. Putting guards in the middle might calm things for a space, but the cause of violence and mistrust is obdurate leadership. Only an act of God will change either side, and I do not believe in political miracles."

Demetrius poured his master wine. "The Lady Pulcheria's ascension to Augusta complicates things considerably."

Orestes took a sip. "My patron Anthemius is dismissed as Regent and Pulcheria will take the post herself. She's vowed to remain a virgin and dedicate her life to caring for her brother's empire. She surrounds herself with priests and seeks their advice on all matters." Orestes smiled. "I have heard the Patriarch of Constantinople does not see eye-to-eye with our own dear Bishop. In the long view, this shift in power might not be as much to Cyril's favor as he would like to believe." His smile deserted him. "But we might not have time for the long view."

"You could abandon the Jews and side with Cyril. At your command, they could be expelled from the city, peace restored."

"I've considered that course." Orestes ran his hand through his short-cropped hair. "The Jews hold positions of power in city government and mercantile interests, as well as providing skilled labor. They are a political balance to Cyril. Without the Jews, the Patriarch will run this city. I can't allow that."

"Surely, Augusta Pulcheria will not tolerate disruption, due to riot and destruction, to the flow of grain that feeds Constantinople?"

"I don't know." Orestes tucked his fist under his chin. "If Cyril is any example, she might be so blind as to starve her people for her faith. I hope her transition to power takes long enough for me to bring order out of this chaos. Once the city is stabilized, I doubt the Augusta will interfere directly." Orestes looked out the window at the bright sunshine. "I believe I'll get out of these stuffy rooms and see for myself the mood of the city."

"I'll get your cloak." Demetrius bowed. "Might I be so bold as to suggest a visit to Lady Hypatia? She might be of assistance in sorting out these difficulties."

"An excellent suggestion, Demetrius. Cancel my appointments for the afternoon. I will eat my evening meal out. I'm not sure when I'll be back."

"Should you take a larger escort, Master?"

"No more than my customary. The pot is only simmering. It needs a specific incident to start boiling over. Let's deploy the guards before that happens."

"How does your father, my child?" Mother Nut asked Selene as she ducked through the door.

"Much better, Mother. He sits up in the solarium and feeds himself." Selene hung her shawl over the back of a sturdy wood chair and surveyed the tidy hut with satisfaction. One of the first things she and Rebecca did on returning, was to thoroughly clean the place. If the Romans had contributed one good quality to civilization it was an appreciation, bordering on obsession, with hygiene—both public and private.

"Good!" the old woman lisped through sparse teeth. "In a few weeks he'll be walking. Don't let him do too much. Make him listen to his body. It will tell him when to rest."

"What have we today, Mother?" Selene enjoyed her thrice weekly visits with the old woman. Between nursing her father and continuing her studies at the Museum, she had had little time at first, but soon made more. Mother Nut's tutelage seemed every bit as valuable as, and imminently more practical than, her formal studies. Selene brought a skill in simple surgeries to Nut's patients, and in return, learned far more about plants, minerals, and midwifery than she thought possible. Most of the herbals at the Museum told only what sickness a plant could be used to treat. Mother Nut showed her which part of the plant to use, how to prepare it, and in what proportions to administer the remedy.

"I want to make up medicine for the sweating sickness. The season is near and we must be ready. Then we will visit families who have asked me to come by."

Selene perused a shelf with dozens of neatly labeled bottles and packets. It had taken her weeks to match Mother Nut's colloquial names with the Latin names of the herbs in Auxentius' books. "What will you need, Mother, and how much?"

"Manroot and treewort. Bring what you find on the shelf. You have them so well organized, I can't find anything."

Selene brought the ingredients to the table. Mother Nut frowned at the small quantities. "Well, there's nothing for it. We'll make up what we can and get more later. Grind these together, three portions to one." The old woman handed Selene a stone bowl and pestle. "Be sure to use only the best."

Selene carefully inspected and discarded any herbs with spots on the leaves or other sign of malformation, then ground the medicine. "How fine do you want the grind, Mother?"

"It must dissolve in wine or water without silting the bottom of the cup."

They worked in silence for several minutes until Selene had filled one third of a stone jar.

"Now divide the powder so." Mother Nut used a knife to separate a pile of powder the size of the end of her smallest finger out of the larger portion, scraped it onto a piece of paper, folded, and twisted it into a single dose packet. She watched Selene deftly add to the growing pile of twisted packets and nodded. "Good. We'll need five times that for the season." She looked at Selene slyly. "Can you obtain more supplies, my child?"

Selene smiled to herself. Mother Nut did not demand gold for her tutelage, but she did not hesitate to have Selene supply herbs and minerals. "Yes, Mother. I'll buy it in the market tomorrow and bring it day after next."

Nut patted Selene's cheek with an arthritic claw. "Good girl. You will save many lives. May your Christian God bless you." The old woman looked over her pharmacopoeia, then packed a small pouch with herbs and trinkets. "Come. Let's see how our patients are doing."

Selene shouldered a heavy bag of surgical instruments and took the older woman's arm to offer support. Half a block down, they entered a tall dwelling, and ascended to the top floor where the poorest families lived, frequently several to a room. The building smelled of rancid fat, unwashed bodies, and urine.

Mother Nut pushed back a ragged blanket that served as a door. A woman, with a baby in a sling, bathed the face of a man moaning on a thin pallet in the corner. A crone tended a small brazier. Several children of various ages and stages of undress screeched as they chased one another around the room.

The woman with the baby looked up as the tenor of the children's screams changed in response to Selene and Mother Nut's presence. "Thank Isis you're here. Poimen is worse." She turned back to the moaning man. Selene noticed the sickly sweet smell of rotting flesh as they approached. The man seemed fairly young but his face and neck swelled grotesquely on the left side. He tossed and mumbled in delirium.

Both Mother Nut and Selene examined the man. Selene noted a blackened tooth, foul breath, and swollen tissues around the tooth. Red and yellow streaks ran down the side of his neck.

"What do you recommend?" Mother Nut asked.

"Pull the tooth, drain the abscess, and pack the wound with feverfew." Selene privately did not give Poimen much chance for recovery. Tooth wear and loss were common among the poor, due to the wretched quality of the bread distributed on the dole. Fine sand adulterated the flour during the grinding process, which over time wore down teeth and allowed abscesses.

Mother Nut nodded in agreement. "He is far gone. You must do the pulling, child. I'll heat the needle to lance the abscess."

Selene turned to Poimen's wife. Though only a few years older than Selene, wrinkles creased her dark face; her sagging belly and breasts indicated repeated childbearing. Selene unpacked her instruments, selected a pair of pliers, and turned to the woman. "Hold him while I pull the tooth."

The woman shifted the baby sling to her back and leaned across Poimen, pinning his shoulders to the ground. Selene gripped the blackened tooth with her tool and pulled with all her might. It loosened, but did not come out. Poimen moaned and thrashed about. His wife muttered soothingly. Selene pulled again. This time she rocked back on her heels with a grunt when the tooth came out. The man screamed and fainted. A terrible stench filled the immediate area as yellow pus and blood oozed from the wound. Selene put the rotten tooth aside, wiped her instrument with a soft cloth, and packed it away.

Mother Nut approached, holding a needle that glowed red from the fire. "I see my needle is not necessary. The ill humor is already escaping. You," she told the wife, "get me hot water." The old woman cleaned the man's mouth with wads of wool. When the hot water arrived, she added herbs, dipped in fresh wads, and packed them into the gaping hole.

"Change the wool in his mouth every day before you sleep. Get him to eat broth with this in it." Nut gave the woman three packets of willow bark and poppy. "One packet per meal. It should ease his pain and fever. Put this under his pallet." Mother Nut gave the woman a fired clay trinket in the shape of a tooth. "And don't forget your prayers."

"Thank you, Mother Nut, but I have nothing. Since Poimen can't work, and I have to nurse him, we have only what the older children beg or steal." Poimen's wife lowered her head and sobbed. The baby woke and started to mewl. The woman unselfconsciously bared a breast and put the child to suck what poor substance it could from the starving woman's breast.

Mother Nut patted the wife's shoulder. "When you have something extra, give it to someone in need in my name." She looked around the room at the children tumbling like puppies. "If you wish not to be with child in the future, come to me. I can help."

The woman looked up at Selene. "And thank you, Lady, for your help."

Selene slipped her a silver coin. "For the children."

Selene took Mother Nut's arm and they descended the stairs.

They attended several families that afternoon: a boy with a belly swollen from hunger, a woman with childbed fever, a quarry worker with the coughing sickness, young men with various wounds—one in a coma from a cracked head.

A few gave the old woman a bronze coin or food. Most had nothing to give. Selene gave the poorer families a coin or two.

As shadows lengthened, the two women worked their way back to the hut. Mother Nut leaned harder on Selene than at the beginning of their afternoon. When they reached the hovel, Selene settled the old woman in a chair, then laid out the fish and over-cooked vegetables she had bought at a public kitchen. Selene sat, head in hands, listening to her mentor chew.

"What's going to happen to them, Mother?" Selene looked at the old woman. The ancient face, softened by the shadows, seemed more wise than weathered.

"To whom, my child?"

"Poimen's wife and children, the starving boy, the angry young men. What will happen to them?"

"They will die, as will we all. Some sooner than others. Some with more pain than others." Mother Nut soaked bread in the fish sauce and popped it into her mouth.

"Do we do any good? It seems so hopeless sometimes."

"We do what we can. The gods do the rest."

"I'm not sure I can believe in any god that allows such misery," Selene whispered.

"Don't blame the gods for man's foolishness. If men could live in peace, there'd be plenty for all. Come, my child, don't fret over this. You can help only one person at a time. Do your best with that person and you will fulfill your destiny." Mother Nut squinted at the shadows gathering at her door. "Time you went home. It's almost dark."

Selene looked up in alarm. She pulled her shawl over her hair and kissed Mother Nut on the cheek. "Good night, Mother. I'll be back day after next with the herbs."

"Good night, my child. May the gods deliver you safe to your home."

Selene ducked out the doorway, continued down the alley toward the better-lit street, passing several burned buildings from the riots of months past. Although her height, bearing, and healthy good looks marked her in a neighborhood of undernourished people, Selene had felt no animosity since her first visit. The people had become used to seeing her with Mother Nut. The word spread about her medical work, allowing Selene to feel safe in a quarter known for its violence. Still, when she noticed the lengthening shadows, Selene picked up her pace. She didn't want to worry her father.

As Selene passed a darkened alley, a man jerked her off her feet, clamped a dirty hand over her mouth, and hissed, "Be quiet, Christos lady, and you won't be hurt."

CHAPTER 23

S ELENE WENT LIMP as she gathered her wits. The grimy man pushed her against the wall, fumbling with the cord around her waist. She nearly gagged from the stench of his breath as he clamped his mouth over hers—a mixture of cheap beer and shallots. Selene jerked her head away and pushed against his chest.

He pinned his forearm across her throat, slowly cutting off her breath. "What's the matter, Christos lady? You too good for the likes of me?" Her attacker ground his hips into hers, ripping at her tunic with his free hand. He hissed into her ear through broken teeth. "Your men come here all the time and take what they want. This time, I do the takin'!"

Before her gaze completely darkened, and with her last strength, Selene jabbed a sharp knee into his groin. The man howled and doubled over. She gasped for breath then hit him over the head with her bag of instruments.

Her attacker fell to his knees, gagging, but grabbed Selene's ankle as she turned to run. She landed on the stones like a felled tree, sharp pain flashing through her left hip and elbow. Instruments scattered from her bag.

Still hissing with pain, the man pulled her toward him by the leg. Selene kicked her free foot at his face. The man blocked her, grabbed both legs, and sat on her ankles. Hitching his way up her legs, he pinned her hips beneath his weight. Her attacker reached down, grabbed her tunic, pulled her body to a sitting position, and slapped her hard across the face. "Try another trick and I'll kill you, bitch."

Selene sagged from the blow. No one had ever struck her in anger. Pain and shock warred with rage.

He leered, showing stained broken teeth. "That's better. Lay quiet and pray like a good little Christos girl." He began working her tunic up around her hips.

A glint of iron caught the corner of her eye. Selene slid her right hand toward her bag of instruments.

The man was intent on pulling up his own ragged tunic.

Her fingertips grazed cool metal. She strained a bit and grasped a pair of forceps. Light weight and dull of end, they would have to do.

She froze at the feel of his flesh against hers, then screamed, "No!" striking at his eyes with the forceps and bucking her hips.

The man rolled off her body, but not before she scratched across the left side of his face.

"My eye!" he howled, covering it with both hands. "Christos bitch, you'll die for that!" Blinded by the blood pouring down his face, he lunged toward her on his knees.

Selene scrambled to her feet, kicked him in the head, and fled down the alley, scooping up her bag, leaving a few scattered instruments.

She stumbled from the alley, blood pounding in her ears, bag clutched with white-knuckled fists. People on the street, instead of starved and pathetic, looked feral and cruel, promising more danger than succor. She ran as she hadn't run in months. Faces turned to her in a blur as she fled. Pain lanced up her side. Her breathing grew ragged.

Near the market she slowed, found a quiet corner and doubled over. Shudders racked her body; nausea twisted her stomach. She vomited against a wall, shakily wiped her mouth, and looked around for the thin bearded face she knew would haunt her waking and asleep. People politely ignored her. She straightened, went to the nearest public fountain and rinsed her mouth.

Her father, Phillip, Antonius—they had been right. It wasn't safe out here for a woman alone. She put her hands to her head and squeezed as if the physical pressure would push out the jumbled scenes of the attack her mind insisted on reliving over and over.

A shift in the mood of the crowd cut through her panic. She looked up to see Hypatia with Orestes in her chariot, cutting through the throng.

Selene pushed toward the horses, bared her head, and screamed, "Hypatia! Lady! Please stop!"

Orestes turned, caught sight of her, and said something to Hypatia, who pulled the horses to a halt.

Selene struggled through the crowd. After an eternity she came up to the wheel.

Orestes helped her onto the chariot. "Great heavens, girl. What are you doing out here alone?"

Selene collapsed trembling against him, grateful for his strength. The horses pushed onward, while Selene caught her breath and steadied her nerves. She pulled away from Orestes. Why, whenever she met him, did she look like something a cat dragged in? She rearranged her shawl to cover her dirty robes.

"I'm sorry. I was tending the sick in Rhakotis when…" She stopped; suddenly unsure she wanted to admit what had happened.

"When what, my child?" Hypatia looked over her shoulder.

"When I, uh, noticed it getting dark and realized I wouldn't make it home in time to oversee dinner." Selene brushed at the stains on her clothes. "I ran and stupidly fell. Could you take me to my father's house and spare me the humiliation of being late again?"

Hypatia arched an elegant eyebrow. Selene blushed at being caught in her lie, but defiantly lifted her chin, daring the older woman to contradict her. Her teacher's face settled into a neutral mask, but a final sharp look promised a more private discussion later.

Orestes seemed oblivious. "Of course, we can take you home, can't we, Hypatia? I haven't offered my regards to your father since his illness. How does he, Selene? Is he receiving visitors?"

Selene pushed her lingering fear and panic to a dark corner of her mind, chatting innocuously till they reached her father's house. After showing her visitors in, she escaped to the bath to scrub the stain from her body.

AFTER A NEAR SLEEPLESS NIGHT, Selene sought Phillip. She had a vague notion of asking him to accompany her on her visits, but that would be a tremendous burden on his time. She wasn't sure what she wanted from him, but she knew she didn't want to be alone.

She found her brother looking over reports in her father's study, his face creased in a worried frown. She hesitated. Maybe this was not a good time to approach him.

"Come in, Selene." He smiled, wearily. "Since when has my little sister been afraid to say her piece? Believe me, you are a welcome distraction." She came forward and kissed his cheek. "Oh, ho! You have a favor to ask of me."

"I do not!" Selene flung herself onto a bench, looked at Phillip, and grinned. "Well, I do. But cannot a sister give her brother a kiss without him thinking it a bribe?"

"Of course." He waited expectantly.

Selene rubbed her fingertips over the embroidery on her robe, took a deep breath, and plunged in. "Since Nicaeus left for the army, I've had no real escort when I visit Mother Nut. The streets are beginning to feel dangerous."

"You've been going there alone?" Phillip eyed her sharply. "I thought you took servants."

"Sometimes Rebecca accompanies me, but I am gone so much, she runs the household in my stead and I..."

Phillip blanched then turned brick red. "You have both been wandering the streets without a male escort? How could you be so foolish? The parabolani are targeting Jews. There are reports of Jews attacking Christians." He pounded the table. "I forbid either of you to go anywhere near that part of town!"

Selene's intemperate retort was stayed by the memory of her attacker's rancid breath, the flood of fear that paralyzed her limbs, the angry voice. What was she thinking, wandering dangerous neighborhoods without a care? She trembled, tears spilling over her cheeks.

Phillip rushed to her side and hugged her close. "Selene, my dear, what's wrong? I didn't mean to be so harsh, but surely you see the wisdom in my commands? It would kill Father if anything happened to you. Give up this foolishness of becoming a physician. Stay home where you are safe and I can take care of you."

Hearing her own thoughts echoed by her brother, Selene stiffened, but the tears still came. Give up her calling? She considered life as a wife—the constant round of household duties and childbearing. No. She had chosen her path two years ago and would stay the course.

But she couldn't go back to Rhakotis. Not yet.

She blinked the tears from her eyes and hugged Phillip back. "I do see the wisdom in your words, dear brother, but cannot give up my chosen work. I don't know what to do."

He patted her back. "When things have settled, maybe you can resume your apprenticeship. We'll see."

Selene was content to let Phillip make decisions for her—for now.

As the sun lowered the next day, Selene relaxed in the solarium, reading a medical text. Rebecca entered looking wildly about. "Where is Phillip? I have news that must get to the Prefect."

"Phillip left several hours ago to deliver herbs to Mother Nut." Selene sat up. "What news?"

"The young men are planning a trap."

"Which young men?"

"My people." Rebecca wrung her hands. "My oldest brother sent word to stay inside tonight, that there would be an attack. The Prefect must send guards or there will surely be many deaths."

"Where?" Selene stood and grabbed Rebecca's arms. "When? How much time do we have?"

"I don't know. We must warn Phillip."

Nausea cramped Selene's stomach at the thought of leaving the safety of her home. "We can't go to Rhakotis."

Rebecca's eye's widened with fear. "But we must find him. He could be in great danger."

"Of course." Selene dropped her grip, fighting down her own panic. "We must send word to the Prefect as well. I'll write a note. Get one of the slaves to take it directly to Orestes or the captain of his guard. Come, we must be quick."

The shadows of dusk crept out of dark corners to claim more territory. Selene pulled her courage together and strode down the dim street. Rebecca huffed to keep up. Outside Ision's home, Selene stopped so abruptly Rebecca nearly collided with her.

"Antonius!" Selene mumbled.

"What? We can't stop now." Rebecca plucked at Selene's sleeve.

"Antonius may help us. The more of us there are, the more likely we can find Phillip."

She marched to the entrance and rapped on the door. A servant promptly inquired as to her needs. "Tell Master Antonius that Mistress Selene begs his assistance on a matter most urgent. We will wait here for his answer."

Within moments, both Antonius and Honoria, rounder than normal with her first pregnancy, came to the foyer. Honoria waddled forward. "Why, Selene, I hope all is well with your father?"

"My father is recovering quite well, thank you, Honoria. However, we have reason to believe Phillip is in danger. I wish Antonius to accompany us while we seek him out."

"Of course Antonius will help, won't you, dear?" Honoria turned to her husband with a timorous smile.

His grim face belied his words. "Nothing would give me more pleasure." He pointed to a servant lurking in the background. "Get my cloak and short sword."

Honoria's eyes rounded. "Surely you will not need your sword?"

"If there is danger, it is better that I have it. Don't worry. I'll take care of myself as well as these ladies." Antonius leaned down to his plump wife and said quietly, "You should rest. Don't wait up for me."

"Of course." She rose on tiptoe to kiss his cheek. "Selene, don't let him do anything rash." Honoria waved to them from the doorway as if they were going on a long journey.

Selene told Antonius what she knew about the situation as they hurried down the street.

"Selene, how could you contemplate going there alone?"

Growing impatient with the constant reminder she frequently acted without caution, Selene snapped back, "That's why we asked your help."

Antonius stopped and grabbed Selene by the arm. "I should send you both back and continue on myself."

She snorted. "How would you know we had gone home? We could as easily continue after you had turned your back. We do this together, Antonius." She shook off his hand and met his eyes. "Are you coming?"

He said in a voice pitched to her ears only, "I love you, Selene, but those very qualities I love make my heart most sore. Please go back."

She desperately wanted to do as he asked, but if she returned home, she might never leave again. "I can't. I must do this for myself as well as Phillip."

Antonius nodded in defeat, took her arm, and hurried her on, Rebecca trailing.

Small knots of people crossed their path, some armed, others not. Everyone converged on the neighborhood between the forum and Rhakotis.

"Fire! Fire at St. Alexander's!"

A jolt of fear seared through Selene. One of the oldest and most beloved Christian churches in Alexandria, St. Alexander's destruction would cause much sorrow and anger in the Christian community.

A young monk ran toward them with a torch, knocking on all the doors as he passed. "Help! Fire at St. Alexander's!"

People poured out carrying buckets, pots, anything that could hold water. Men and even a few women joined the stream of people heading to save their beloved church.

Antonius grabbed Selene's hand. "Keep close." She in turn grabbed Rebecca's hand as they followed the crowd.

The mob picked up speed as they neared the square in front of the church. People shouted angrily. Antonius tried to keep on the edges, but a torrent of bodies pushed them directly into the center of the throng.

Selene lost Antonius' hand as the crowd eddied in different directions. She held tightly to Rebecca's, struggling against the press to keep up with Antonius.

"Selene!" he shouted, trying to push back. He reached his hand over several heads. She reached toward him, fingers straining.

"Antonius! Wait for us!" she screamed as the mob whirled him away.

Rebecca pressed tight to her side and shouted in her ear. "There's no smoke!"

Selene sniffed the air. Rebecca was right. There was no smell of smoke or sign of flame. She and Rebecca were caught in the trap they had come to warn Phillip about, and Antonius was lost to them.

CHAPTER 24

THE CROWD SURGED toward St. Alexander's, shouting, "Save the church! Don't let the dirty Jews burn it!" From the direction of the church, others pushed back.

"Murder!"

People screamed in pain. "The Jews are killing everyone!"

Those in the middle shouted angrily, struggling within the press.

Selene pulled Rebecca tight and tried worming her way out of the mob. Her heart raced; time seemed to slow. Torchlight flickered across faces contorted with rage and fear. Selene shrank back, but there was no space, only bodies pressing closer and closer. She tried taking a deep breath to calm herself, but the air seemed to be sucked from the square.

With a shout, the crowd stampeded right, forcing Selene and Rebecca to run. Several people fell. The mob poured over them. Selene tried to avoid the twitching bodies, but it was impossible.

Rebecca stumbled. Selene jerked her to her feet, fear adding strength to the pull. Her friend grimaced in pain, but Selene had no time to ask why.

They ran for an eternity down a long straight street, until the mob slowed. Selene maneuvered toward a thinning area. Rebecca's arm hung limp, her face drawn with pain.

They had barely reached the wall of a private residence when Selene felt a rhythmic thump through the soles of her sandals. She looked up. A mounted troop pressed down the street. In front of the horses, a line of guards with shields linked pushed everyone before them.

The crowd reversed toward the church square.

Selene shouted, "On my shoulders. Jump for the top!"

"I can't!" Tears coursed down Rebecca's face. "My arm won't hold me. You go." Selene grabbed Rebecca, rotated her arm and pushed on her shoulder. It popped back into the socket with an audible snap. Rebecca screamed then sobbed.

"Get on my shoulders, before we get swept back up into that mob!" Selene squatted, forming a stirrup with her hands. Rebecca stepped into it and up to Selene's shoulders. Selene straightened, leaning against the wall.

Rebecca grabbed the top with her good arm, using her toes and injured arm to boost herself the final distance. She unwound her cloak and let it down. Selene grabbed the end. Rebecca leaned back, pulling with one arm. Before Selene could start climbing, the edge of the mob swept her away in a crush of bodies.

"Selene!" The cloak torn from her hands, Rebecca tottered on the wall.

"Stay there!" Selene's shout disappeared in the roar.

Gauging the movement of the mob, Selene worked her way slowly but steadily forward. Others, who had not lost their heads in panic, also sought a way out. Ahead, she spied an alley she had missed the first time they ran past. It led behind the private residences fronting on the main road.

Selene angled across the front of the mob, trying to reach the opening before the crush carried her past. She reached the alley at the head of a splinter group also escaping. With an open path ahead, she hitched her robes and ran as fast as she could, leaving all but a few to stagger behind.

After several blocks, hearing nothing but her own ragged gasps, Selene stopped. She leaned against a wall to catch her breath, then sat, head and arms cradled on her knees. Her heart slowed. The sweat dried on her grimy face.

She tried to make sense of what happened, but failed. She had never seen people act that mindlessly. The relief she felt at having escaped quickly soured with fear.

Selene heard footsteps. Two men, one propping up the other, headed toward her. She was alone—again—in a dangerous situation, but nearly too emotionally spent to care. She peered down the dim alley. More people headed her way.

With her last bit of will, Selene rose and walked on nerveless legs to the next street. She circled back toward St. Alexander's, knowing that she must find Rebecca, Antonius, and perhaps—if she were very lucky—Phillip.

Selene knew she was in the guard's wake when she narrowly avoided stepping in a pungent pile of horse droppings. She continued down the street, searching for the wall where she had left Rebecca. All along the route, people descended from walls and trees, hurrying off as fast as they could.

She finally found Rebecca, slumped, legs dangling, hair unraveling in ragged clumps. Selene, limping with exhaustion, shouted hoarsely. "Rebecca! Come down. It's safe now."

Relief lit Rebecca's tired eyes. Selene placed herself against the wall. Rebecca dropped to her friend's shoulders, then jumped to the ground.

Rebecca turned and hugged Selene with one arm. "I thought I would never see you again!" She pulled away. "Are you hurt?"

"Nothing a good soak in the hot baths won't take care of."

Rebecca touched her sore shoulder. "Why is it I always come home injured from our little adventures?"

"Not always." Selene giggled on the edge of hysteria. "Only when we get caught in riots."

They hugged again. Rebecca pointed toward the church square with her uninjured arm. "We must find Antonius and Phillip."

They headed toward St. Alexander's. Guards blocked the street opening to the square, allowing a few people out at a time, but none in.

Selene approached a guard writing on a slate. "May we go in?"

He looked up in annoyance. "No, Lady. It's dangerous. Go home."

"We're looking for a friend, Antonius, son of Lysis, a City Councilor. We were separated in the rush. How might we get word of him?"

"Unarmed citizens are passed through; armed persons detained. The wounded are being cared for in the church; the dead laid out in the square."

Selene looked at Rebecca. She nodded, clutching her arm, pain etched on her face.

"Sir, I'm Selene, daughter of Councilor Calistus. My servant is injured. I'm a healer. If we could go to the church, I will tend her and any others who need such service."

The guard examined the fine cut of Selene's torn cloak, the quality of the embroidery on her dirty dalmatica. He peered closely at Rebecca's pale face and bruised eyes, then called to a young recruit. "Escort this healer and her servant to the church."

The recruit gathered two comrades and herded Selene and Rebecca past the roadblock. Torches and lamps lit the scene almost as bright as day. People huddled, propping each other up. Some sat on the ground, heads in their hands. Those faces Selene could see reflected exhaustion and shock. No one had escaped without a bruise or rent clothing. Occasionally someone wandered by crying a name, peering into slack faces.

Selene pulled on the recruit's sleeve. "Please, might we view the dead on our way to the church? We are looking for a friend."

He scratched his head under his helmet. "I guess it'll do no harm," he answered in heavily accented Greek.

Two dozen bodies lay in front of the church. Holding her breath, Selene looked closely. A few, badly trampled, would not be taken for human except for their clothing. Others lay with limbs in grotesque angles to their bodies. Two looked as if they slept with no visible wound or injury.

Selene slowly let out her breath and turned to the recruit. "Thank you. He is not among the dead."

"I'm glad, Lady. This was a bad night. Shouldn't no one been dead. This way." Inside the church, he handed them over to a harried looking middle-aged woman in penitent's robes, her gray-shot hair cut even shorter than Selene had dared.

The woman looked up from bandaging a ragged cut on a young man's face. "I'm Sister Martha. Have you come to give or receive aid?"

"Both." Selene saw over fifty moaning injured lying on pallets hastily manufactured of blankets and straw. "I'm Selene. My servant needs attention. Then I can set bones, dress wounds, and do minor surgeries. What equipment do we have?"

"The guard surgeon has the usual kit. There are a few needles and flax thread. We're working mostly with hot water, cloths, and our hands. Over there." She pointed her chin to a young woman ripping fabric into strips and stirring a pot over a brazier. "Take care of your servant then do what you can."

"Where's the surgeon?"

A piercing scream echoed from the next room. Sister Martha nodded in that direction.

Selene and Rebecca appropriated bandages, which Selene used to fashion a sling for Rebecca's arm. That done, Selene surveyed the still and moaning bodies. "We were lucky. I pray to God, we never get caught in such again." She looked at Rebecca. "Rest. I'll see if the surgeon needs assistance."

"I can help a little," Rebecca protested.

"Maybe later. Rest now." Selene helped her friend find a free corner and headed for the surgeon's room. Long before reaching the door, she smelled fresh blood and spilled intestines. The surgeon, a short man with the arms and chest of a blacksmith, worked with two assistants. Wearing gore-spattered leather aprons, they operated on an unconscious man with a belly wound. Scalpels lay in their open wooden carry case on a nearby bench. Selene watched the trio quickly pull the guts from the body cavity and examine them.

"Lucky man." The surgeon pointed to a spot. "The cut is in the large intestine. I could do nothing with a wound in the small bowel." He took needle and thread and sewed the cut. The assistants washed the intestines in wine and packed them back into the body. The surgeon then sewed up the wound. The whole operation took only a few minutes. The assistants applied a linen bandage and tightly bound the sutures.

Selene approached the surgeon. "Sir, I have some small skill in surgery. Perhaps I can be of assistance?"

The surgeon looked her over, washing blood from his hands in a copper bowl. "I'll handle the most serious cases. You don't look strong enough to set bones. Can you sew? Clean and dress a wound without fainting?"

"Yes, sir." Selene nodded, mildly prickled at the surgeon's off-hand appraisal. "I've had much practice lately."

"Then you may attend those." He indicated a row of people sitting and, sometimes, lying along a bench.

Selene worked steadily. Most wounds she washed with water. The shallow ones she bandaged with linen, the deeper ones she stitched muscles and skin. There was nothing for the pain except wine.

Selene came to a frail old man lying down with a purpling bump on his temple. He moaned and panted, his shallow breath barely raising his frail chest. She pulled up an eyelid, noted the dilated pupil and called the surgeon over. "Could you trephine the skull to relieve the pressure?"

"Such an old one would never survive the surgery." He felt the patient's pulse and smelled his breath. "Make him as comfortable as possible. There's nothing I can do for him."

Selene propped the old man up and gave him wine.

"The church," he whispered. "Is the church safe?"

"Yes, grandfather, you saved the church. You're in St. Alexander's now."

Selene applied a cold compress to his brow.

"Thank the Good Lord. He gave us the strength to save His house." The old man's eyes rolled up and he lapsed into unconsciousness. Selene sat silently as his breathing slowed and finally stopped. She wanted to cry, but felt only a bone-deep weariness.

Rebecca touched her shoulder. "You've done all you can. Let's go home."

Selene looked around. The surgeon packed his instruments. Assistants gathered bloody bandages. Sister Martha and the young woman wandered among the moaning wounded, providing water or prayer as the patient needed.

"Yes, it's time to go." Selene released the old man's still-warm hand.

At the church door, Selene looked up at the star-studded sky in shock. She had thought it well past dawn. They faced a long trek home in the dark without benefit of male escort.

The number of bodies stretched out before the church had grown, but the number of survivors had shrunk considerably. Two groups, a few dozen each, sat on the ground as guards questioned individuals closely about their whereabouts during the riots and their purposes in being there. Weapons—mostly swords, a few knives and cudgels—lay tumbled in a wagon.

Selene's sluggish brain stirred. Weapons. Swords. Of course. "Rebecca, we must speak to those guards. Antonius was armed. Maybe he is being detained."

They approached the guards, quickly scanning the prisoners' faces. One man in familiar clothes sat with his face resting in cupped hands. "Antonius!" she cried. The man did not look up, but a guard approached, looking weary from a lost night's sleep.

"What's your business here, Lady?"

"I seek Antonius, son of Lysis, the Councilor. He escorted me last night and came armed to protect me. He might be mistakenly detained."

"A councilor's son, eh?" The guard scratched his neck. "Come with me." He led them to a centurion questioning a sullen young man. "I think you should speak to this lady, sir."

Selene repeated her story, adding that she had been helping with the wounded. The centurion listened closely. "I would like to help, Lady, but we've detained no one by that name."

Selene bit her lip in frustration. "I thought I saw him among the prisoners. Please, sir, may I look closer?"

The centurion looked over the cowed prisoners and motioned to the guard.

"Take her, but be quick about it."

Selene went to the man she had spotted earlier. He had a form similar to Antonius', but when he raised a scarred face to the light, Selene's shoulders slumped.

She heard a scuffling to her right and turned. A seated figure rose from the shadows. She pulled the cloak from her hair. The man stumbled forward, enveloping her in a crushing embrace.

"Thank God you are safe! I don't know how I could have lived with myself if you had been hurt," Antonius whispered into her ear.

"Leave the lady alone, you." Rough hands separated them. Her guard escort faced off with an angry Antonius.

Selene put her hands on the guard's arm. "Please, sir. This is the man I sought." Her eyes pleaded with Antonius to keep his temper. "Can he come with me?"

The guard looked skeptically at Antonius' bruised, dirty face. "He gave his name as Leiksos, Lady."

Antonius waved his hand dismissively. "I didn't want to embarrass my father."

The guard snorted. "He'll have to be questioned by the centurion before we release him." He motioned to Antonius. "You, come with me and behave toward the lady." The guard escorted them back to the centurion, muttering about spoiled sons of rich men.

Selene noticed a stir in the crowd. The guards walked with more energy and stood taller. She looked up to see Orestes on his horse and—thank the Lord!—Phillip standing by his foot, conversing with the Prefect. Relieved, she ran forward, shouting.

Phillip looked up in surprise, which turned to consternation.

"Good God, child!" Orestes exclaimed. "What are you doing here?"

"Rebecca and I came..."

"Rebecca's here?" Phillip frantically searched faces.

"She's safe with the centurion. Antonius..."

Phillip grabbed her tightly by the arms. "He's here as well? Why?"

Selene sighed in exasperation. "If you stop interrupting, I'll tell you."

He relaxed his grip. Selene rubbed her arms. "We came to find you. Rebecca heard the Jews were setting a trap and we came to warn you. But," she motioned around her, "we were caught in the riot. Rebecca and I helped with the wounded afterward."

Orestes nodded. "Your sister had the good sense to send me a warning. The carnage might have been much worse."

Selene turned to Orestes. "Prefect, might I ask a favor? Our friend Antonius escorted us here, but is being detained because he was armed. He carried a sword to protect us. Could you release him?"

"Of course. But you must make me a promise."

"Anything!"

He looked at her sternly. "The next time you hear of a riot, stay away."

"You have my most solemn promise, sir. I never want to see again what I saw tonight." She shivered. Phillip put his arm around her protectively.

"Good. I'll see to young Antonius." Orestes descended from his horse and strode toward the centurion, returning shortly with Antonius, Rebecca, and two guards in tow. "Phillip, see your party home. These men will provide escort."

"Thanks, Orestes." The two clasped forearms. "If you need my help, send word."

"You and Selene have already helped immensely. Go home and rest."

Selene, leaning heavily on Phillip, didn't even thrill to Orestes' compliment.

CHAPTER 25

ORESTES EYED THE CREEPING DAWN, put his hands to his lower back and stretched. He had done all he could. The wounded had been dispersed to their homes or hospitals, the unclaimed dead taken to the mortuary. The centurion concluded his interrogations and made his report. Now Orestes had to make sense of it. He gave Demetrius final instructions and headed home with an escort.

Hypatia waited for him in his private quarters. "My dear Lady, I'm delighted to see you, but what brings you out at such an early hour?" He snapped his fingers at his servants, who rushed to fetch food and drink.

Hypatia rose. Dark circles shadowed her eyes. "I am always up before dawn. It's good discipline. This morning my servants brought news of riot in the city. Is it true?"

Orestes sighed, shedding his cloak and taking a comfortable seat. His servants arrived with warm bread, cheese, cold roast lamb, and spiced wine. The smell reminded him he had eaten no dinner. He indicated the tray laid for two. "Care to join me?"

Hypatia poured a goblet of wine and spread a piece of bread with runny cheese. She settled on a couch opposite Orestes and watched him eat. Finally, Orestes asked, "What do you hear from your servants?"

"Only that all the churches burn, Jews and Christians fight in the streets, and the dead number in the thousands." Hypatia put down her bread, untouched.

Orestes choked briefly and sipped. "That's all?"

"It's a fair estimation of the stories racing through the city." Hypatia asked gravely, "I surmise the truth is somewhat short of the rumors?"

"I asked Demetrius to post notices and have proclamations read from the street corners. I suppose word hasn't spread far enough." He scrubbed his face with his hands and looked at Hypatia with haggard eyes. "Apparently, young Jewish hotheads decided to take revenge for the attacks in their neighborhoods. They raised an alarm that St. Alexander's was on fire. When the congregation came to save their church, the Jews attacked and killed many. More died in the rioting that followed."

"The young fools! They've played right into Cyril's hands. What do the Jewish elders say?"

"They're defiant, saying they did not plan this but it was inevitable. They claim now that the Christians have seen their strength, the parabolani will stop their attacks."

"I thought better of Jesep and his faction." Hypatia shook her head. "Violence begets more violence in this city. The Christians rarely practice turning the other cheek, as their messiah counseled. What are you going to do?"

"I have asked both sides to meet with me this morning."

"I doubt either party will come." Hypatia leaned back on her couch, frowning. "The Jews feel they have made their point. Cyril will trumpet his moral right and retaliate shortly."

"If so, we are at a significant disadvantage. I've appealed to Abundantius for troops but it will be at least one day before they arrive. I've built a coalition of nobles who seek to advise Cyril. Maybe they can put pressure on him to allow heads to cool."

"Many of the city fathers are unhappy at the high-handed way Cyril has managed his Bishopric. Opposition is building, even among those who supported Cyril. Let me make a few visits." Hypatia rose, rearranging her wraps. "I'll start with Calistus. I want to see if Selene has recovered from her fright."

Orestes started. "How did you know she had been caught in the riots? She seemed tired, but well enough when Phillip took her home."

"Selene? In the riots? What are we going to do with that girl? I had thought she learned her lesson."

Orestes looked puzzled. "What are you talking about?"

"The day before yesterday, when we picked her up in the marketplace. She had obviously been frightened and, from the look of her clothes, possibly attacked. Whatever would have possessed her to venture out at night into a riot?"

"She said she had to warn her brother."

"And she had to do it herself." Hypatia smiled sadly. "Ever listening to the heart before the head; the impulsiveness of youth. I sometimes despair of Selene ever becoming a scholar."

Orestes rose and took her hand. "She will never be the famous Lady Philosopher of Alexandria. There is only one." His eyes took on a faraway look. "We can guide Selene only when she lets us."

"You must think me a foolish old woman, trying to relive my youth through another."

"No. I think you are quite wise and a good friend. You are the most remarkable person I have ever known. I don't know what I—or this city—would do without you." Orestes encased her hand in both of his. "What you despair of in Selene are the traits I admire in you: independence, the need to make things better, and a stubborn belief that you can." He released her hand. "Go, my friend. We'll see what we can do to calm the city. Between us maybe we can stop this course of destruction."

HYPATIA PREDICTED TRULY. Both parties refused to meet with Orestes.

Shortly after the noon meal, Demetrius came to his office, looking shaken. "The Patriarch is on the march. He and thousands more head for the Jewish quarter."

"Damn! He didn't give us time. We have only the guards and they will not be enough." He leapt up. "Get my horse. Call my escort. I'm going to meet him."

"It's too late, Master. He will have reached it by now. The guards are unhappy about defending Jews. Your escort might not be reliable."

Orestes donned his cloak. "I can't sit here doing nothing. Do as I say, damn you, or I'll have you whipped!"

Demetrius bowed.

ORESTES RACED DOWN THE STEPS to his waiting mount and vaulted into the saddle. He urged his horse to a ground-eating canter and headed out the gate. His escort scrambled to catch up. They dodged through the streets toward the Jewish quarter in the eastern part of the city.

As they approached, Orestes had to slow his horse to navigate the carnage. Thousands of people clogged the avenues, systematically breaking in doors and herding occupants into the street. Some refugees carried bundles, but most fled before the onslaught with little more than the clothes on their backs. Women cried desperately for children, neighbors hauled the sick on pallets; men from the workshops struggled to find their families.

Behind the first wave of Christians, a second looted the buildings, throwing such poor possessions as could be found into heaps. Anything of value—a cooking pot, a spindle—disappeared. The rest, broken, littered the street. This section of the quarter offered little loot, so the first wave moved quickly toward the shops and merchants' homes. The very wealthy lived beyond the walls in a suburb established after the last expulsion. The mob might not go there and, if they did, the staff of the walled estates might resist.

Orestes drove his horse forward. "Make way!" His crop struck right and left to clear a path. His escort strung out behind him. He broke through the crowd into the square in front of the main synagogue.

Many young Jews lay quiet and grotesque where they had fallen, swords and clubs still clutched in their hands. The Patriarch stood in the middle of the square, pouring oil over sacred objects from the temple: scrolls, chalices, and prayer shawls. Armed monks held several bruised and bleeding Jewish priests.

"The torch!" Cyril cried.

"Stop!" Orestes pulled his horse to a prancing halt on the other side of the oil-soaked pile. His mount smelled blood and rolled its eyes. "Patriarch, you have no right."

"I have every right! These people slaughtered Christians. They must be made to pay!"

The crowd let out a deafening roar.

Orestes' horse reared. Several of his escort trailed into the square and took up positions on his flank.

"These people!" Orestes bellowed in his parade ground voice. "Do you mean that child? Or that old man?" The crowd quieted slightly. "You punish the many for the sins of a few. Send your people home. I will bring the real culprits to justice."

"Never! The murderers will not be caught. These people protect their own. They must be made to leave Alexandria!" Cyril threw the torch onto the pyre.

Flames leapt high, sending Orestes' horse skittering backwards.

"No!" One of the priests broke loose. "Not the sacred Torah!" He threw himself on the blaze, trying to beat out the flames with his hands. His clothes and beard caught fire. His screams echoed around the suddenly quiet square. Orestes watched in horror as the human torch stumbled around the pyre and fell twitching to the ground, ashes from the sacred texts floating into the air.

A bestial howl rose from the mob. Those Jews remaining streamed for the gates out of the city. Orestes pulled his horse close to Cyril and screamed, "What is it you want, Cyril?"

The Patriarch looked up with hard flat eyes. "God's will."

Orestes' gut turned ice cold, even as a white-hot rage fixed his face in a ferocious snarl. He raised his whip as if to strike Cyril.

His horse skittered as a young guard muscled his mount between Orestes and the Patriarch. "Sir! We must leave."

"I won't go."

"You must, sir. We can't protect you. Several of the escort have already turned back. If we stay, we die."

Orestes looked at the frightened young man fighting his nervous horse and surveyed the chaos. The madness he saw on faces boded ill for anyone in their way. His temper cooled. He turned back to the young Patriarch, standing defiant. "I won't forget this. The Emperor will hear of this calumny."

Cyril smiled. "I'm sure he and his sister will be most pleased by this day's work."

Orestes jerked his horse around and rode with the young soldier through the smoke to the forum. He didn't look back.

Orestes returned to his private quarters grimy and exhausted.

Demetrius met him at the top of the stairs. "How goes it, Master?"

"Cyril expelled the Jews." Orestes' shoulders slumped. "I fear for Hypatia, out in this madness. Any word?"

"None, Master." The two continued to the Prefect's rooms. "The runners report Abundantius will be here with the troops by sunset tomorrow."

"Too late." Orestes ran a hand through his hair, releasing a shower of ashes. "Are guards posted where I ordered?"

"Yes. We should be able to contain the damage to the Jewish quarter."

"I'll set up a command post here. Have the runners report to me for orders."

"Should I bring food? Wine?"

"Both. And make sure the wine is unwatered."

His secretary spoke quietly to a servant, then followed Orestes to the offices.

Orestes scrubbed his tired eyes and said, "I fear I've met my match. Cyril's rage blows a bitter wind through this city that I cannot turn aside."

"It is surely a dark day, Master. Can you come to an accommodation with the Patriarch that will end this impasse?"

"The lines are clearly drawn. Only the Emperor, or possibly the city fathers, can rein him in." Orestes strode into his office. "I must write my report to the Emperor and make my needs clear."

"Selene, wake up."

She moaned and rolled over.

"I need your help. Please!"

Someone shook her shoulder. She put a name to the voice and opened one eye. Rebecca. Selene shot up, suddenly awake. "What?"

Tears streamed down Rebecca's face. "The Patriarch is expelling the Jews from Alexandria. My brother Aaron is in the kitchen."

Selene grabbed a robe and followed her friend. Aaron sat at the kitchen table with a bloody bandage on his arm and bruises around his neck. Although he had matured to a slightly built youth with the downy beginnings of a beard in the past two years, Selene knew his mind was still that of a child.

Rebecca placed her hands on her brother's shoulders. "Tell Mistress Selene your story, Aaron."

He relaxed slightly at Selene's encouraging smile. "I was home alone with Momma 'cause our brothers..." His eyes shifted quickly to Rebecca and back.

"Yes," Selene prompted.

"Cause our brothers didn't come home last night. Anyway, I was home with Momma, when they broke in."

"Who broke in?"

"Them. They hit Momma. That wasn't right, was it? They shouldn't of done that!" The boy looked up with pleading eyes.

Selene patted his hand. "No, Aaron. That wasn't right. They are bad men. What happened then?"

"I tried to protect Momma, but a bad man put his hands around my throat and squeezed. It got dark." He touched the bruises and shuddered. "I don't like the dark."

Rebecca put her arms around the boy and rocked him. "You were brave to fight the bad man, Aaron. Tell Mistress Selene the rest of your story."

The boy took a deep breath and continued, shakily, "When I woke up, Momma was gone. I hid until it was real dark, then I sneaked here like Becca said to do if there was trouble. It's scary in the dark without Momma." Tears traced muddy runnels down his dirty cheek. "Where's Momma?"

Rebecca patted his back. "You did well, Aaron. You tried to help Mother and you found your way here all by yourself, like I taught you. Come. You can sleep on my pallet tonight."

"What about Momma?" the boy pleaded.

Rebecca hugged his frail body. "I don't know, duckling, but you'll be safe here." She led him to the servants' quarters and returned shortly to sit opposite Selene at the table. Rebecca hung her head in her hands.

"What can I do?" Selene asked.

"Keep Aaron safe. I have to look for my mother. It's all over town. Jews are being beaten, killed, forced out of the city. The richer ones are trying to sell their businesses and possessions before moving on. The poorer ones have already lost everything. They're camping in the Boukolia."

Selene shuddered. The Boukolia, pasture lands of sparse shrubs and wild cattle, also boasted a fair number of brigands. The soldiers of Nicopolis kept order among the rough inhabitants, who were known to assault travelers, murder one another and break into open rebellion, but it was uncertain the troops could or would protect thousands of fleeing Jews.

"What about you?" Selene grasped Rebecca's hands. "I don't want you to go, but I've said many times I will help any way I can. Ask anything of me."

"I must try to find my family."

"But your shoulder! The Boukolia is not safe even if you were uninjured."

"I may not have to go to the camps, but if I do, I'll be in better shape than most." She glanced at the dark archway leading to the servant's quarters. "Please care for Aaron until I get back. He'll be frightened when he wakes up in a strange place." She shook herself and rose. "I hope to be back by dark tomorrow. If I'm not, wait another day before doing anything."

Selene rose and hugged her friend. "What should I tell Phillip?"

"Nothing! He must not follow me to the camps! It would be his death if they discovered he was Christian. If I don't come back, maybe Lady Hypatia or Mother Nut knows someone who can help, but please keep Phillip here."

"I'll do what I can, but Phillip is a man grown. I have little influence in such matters." Selene's mouth quirked in a lopsided smile. "After all, he is my brother."

"He is, indeed." Rebecca glanced despairingly at the empty doorway. "Do what you can...for his sake and mine."

Selene captured Rebecca's hand. "Be well, my friend, and stay safe."

CHAPTER 26

SELENE WAITED ANXIOUSLY FOR REBECCA throughout the next day. She set Aaron some small tasks to keep him busy. When the sun lowered, she had to calm his fears as well as hers. Luckily, Phillip was out of the house, and she did not have to apprise him of Rebecca's absence.

On the second morning, Hypatia came to visit. Selene greeted her in the vestibule and conducted her to the solarium. "Honored Teacher, I'm so glad you're here. I missed your visit to my father two days past."

"I'm afraid that visit bore little fruit." Hypatia looked grim. "Your father was receptive, but we didn't have time to stop the Patriarch. Perhaps now that he has achieved his ends, Cyril will be more accommodating." She shook her head and smiled. "I've come on a more personal errand, to assure the health and good countenance of my favorite female student."

Selene snorted. "Lady, I'm your only female student. My health is good and—I'm told—my countenance fair, but my heart is troubled."

"How may I help?"

Selene told Hypatia about Rebecca and her fears.

"This is a delicate matter." Hypatia said. "Abundantius has arrived with his troops and is restoring order, but it is still dangerous." She looked sharply at Selene. "I highly recommend you do not rush off to the camps."

"I don't intend to." Selene blushed, then paled. "But I have to do something!"

"I am not without resources, but in these times it is difficult to get reliable information. I'll send word as soon as I can."

"Thank you, Lady. It is more than I hoped."

"More than you hoped?" Hypatia raised an eyebrow. "Do you feel I hold you in such low esteem that I would be unwilling to help?"

"No, Honored Teacher! Only that, with so many demands on your time, the troubles of a Jewish servant might not be worth your attention." Selene lowered her head.

"Ordinarily, the troubles of a Jewish servant would not be worth my attention," Hypatia answered dryly. "But these are not ordinary times and you are no ordinary student." She put her hand under Selene's chin and tilted her face. "When you see something wrong, your first impulse is to fix it, to be the strong one. You sometimes forget others can help. You needn't go through life keeping secrets and fighting all your battles alone, Selene. It sometimes helps to talk."

Tears tickled the back of her throat and blurred her eyes. Selene took several deep breaths to calm herself. As she looked into Hypatia's concerned face, a dam seemed to burst in Selene's chest. Tears welled; she shook with deep, bone-wracking sobs. Hypatia gathered Selene to her breast and rocked her with soothing nonsense words, until she quieted.

Selene pulled away, wiping at her eyes. "Thank you, Honored Teacher. I'm better."

"I had hoped by now you would regard me as more than your teacher," Hypatia said with a touch of sorrow. "You once asked me if I missed having children and I said I've had hundreds. But they are all sons. You are my only daughter."

Selene acknowledged Hypatia's affection with a bowed head and a simple, "I'm honored." Still shaking from her emotional outburst, Selene told Hypatia of the last several days: the terror, anger, and shame of near-rape; the horror and exhaustion of riots and death; her fear for Rebecca and Phillip; her self-doubts. Hypatia said little during Selene's recitation, encouraging her with nods and murmured syllables. Stumbling to a hiccuppy close, Selene felt drained.

"Much has been asked of you these past few days." Hypatia patted her hand. "More may yet be required."

"How so?" Selene inwardly cringed.

"You've admitted your fears and now must find the courage to carry on despite them."

"But I've nearly been killed—twice!" Selene frowned. "And it's not just me. I've put my friends in danger. Some would consider me supremely unlucky."

"We make our own luck, child." Hypatia gripped Selene's shoulder, looking deep into her eyes. "You wear your soul on your face. It is your nature to move, act, change. You could no more ignore those suffering people in Rhakotis or leave your brother to his fate than a flower could turn from the sun. You must not deny your nature or cripple your soul out of fear. That path leads to bitterness and a wasted life. Many obstacles littered my path. Each one I overcame made me stronger and surer. You have set yourself on a similar road, Selene. Do not turn aside. However," Hypatia's eyes sparkled, "you might give a thought to safer ways to pursue your course."

"I will." Calmness settled over Selene after the storm of her emotions. "I didn't know who to talk to. Thank you."

A warm smile brightened Hypatia's face as she pushed a strand of hair out of Selene's face. "The most important lessons in life are not learned in the classroom, my child. Come to me anytime your mind or heart is troubled." Hypatia gathered her robes and rose. "Now I must be on my way. I'll send word of my researches."

Selene saw her out and collapsed on a bench by the entrance. She knew Hypatia spoke wisely and out of love, but Selene trembled at the thought of taking up her previous course. She needed time.

REBECCA HAD NOT COME HOME by sundown that evening, but Phillip did. He looked around expectantly as Selene greeted him. "How's father? Where's Rebecca?"

"Father is fine." Selene sat on a bench and patted a spot beside her. "Sit with me a moment, brother."

He sat, a worried frown marring his handsome face. Selene told him of Aaron and Rebecca.

Phillip's face paled. "Rebecca left? I never thought she would go with the others." He jumped to his feet. "I've got to talk to her."

Selene grabbed her brother's arm. "Rebecca didn't want you to follow her. You can't help her by going to the camps and getting killed. Hypatia promised to find out what she can. Go to Orestes. Surely he has people who can help. Promise you won't go into the camps after her."

"That's a promise I can't make." He shook off her hand and crossed his arms.

She crossed her own and barred his way to the door. "If you go to the camps, I'll have to follow, so we might as well go together." She gathered her loose hair at the nape of her neck. "What do you think? Will I be safer going as a boy?"

"You aren't going!" Phillip shouted, turning dusky red. "I'll tie you to your bed, if that's what it takes."

"I have many friends among the servants. I'll not long stay confined." She shook her head. "I am better suited to go to the camps and come back unharmed. The soldiers will pass a woman healer through and many will trust me. As a man, you will be suspect."

His face sagged. "I won't allow you to go to the camps in my stead."

"I'm only asking that you not go until we have more information; till we have a plan." She put her hand on his arm. "Rebecca said she would try to get us word. She wouldn't abandon Aaron. Think, brother, and promise me you won't be foolish."

"I'll see Orestes, but if we've heard nothing in two days' time I'm going after her myself."

"If we have heard nothing in two days' time, we both go."

Phillip's jaw tightened but he nodded.

SELENE AND PHILLIP EXITED the servant's quarters and proceeded to the east gate. They traversed streets filled with soldiers, but few civilians. A vegetable merchant waved as they hurried past. Few patrons meant spoiled goods, but at least his family could eat the wares. The purveyor of used clothes they passed, and his family, could not dine on cloth.

At the gates, Phillip showed the guards a pass from Orestes. Beyond the city walls, they crossed a canal and onto the road to the Boukolia. The sun grew hot in the sky as they passed the empty cattle market defining the boundary between the suburbs of Alexandria and wild pastureland. A troop of soldiers, stationed here, checked people in and out of the camps.

Refugees trickled onto the road, heading east to Judea. Selene watched them trudge past, despair stamped on their faces. A few drove scrawny donkeys or goat-drawn carts, but most traveled with what few possessions they had piled on their backs. Mothers with babies slung on their chests bowed under the burden of a pack; young men pulled bundles tied to poles; old ones and toddlers carried their own water. Selene looked at the worn, exhausted people and lost all fear.

Abandoned objects littered the road. Something sparkled under a shrub. While Phillip talked to the soldiers, Selene walked over and retrieved a small wooden doll with painted face and hair, glass eyes, and jointed limbs. A child was either dead or carrying something more useful to her survival. Selene tucked the doll into her medical bag.

Phillip waved to her from the checkpoint. "The soldiers say the camps are quiet now, but be careful not to start trouble. They suggest we start asking at the well. It's this way."

"Is there a hospital?"

Phillip shook his head. "Just a dispensary where a couple of holy women minister to the sick."

They headed to the well, passing refugees sheltering from the sun under woven mats or cloaks strung between shrubs. Some crouched by dung fires, protecting their meager food. The stench of unwashed bodies and human waste overpowered Selene's senses.

"Why haven't the soldiers dug latrine trenches?" Selene asked as they held folds of their cloaks over their noses. "If a plague starts here, it could spread to the city."

"They don't want permanent camps." Phillip shrugged. "With primitive conditions, people will more likely move on than stay hoping to go back to the city."

At the well, a long line of people—mostly women and children—stood with pots and bowls. More joined the end every moment.

"You ask the new arrivals," Selene suggested. "I'll go to the well and work my way back."

She went to the head of the line and helped an old woman lift the bucket. "Grandmother, do you know of a young woman named Rebecca, daughter of Miriam? Her mother was injured in the riots. She may be caring for her."

"Why do you want her? Has she done something to you?"

"No, Grandmother. She's a friend and I fear harm may have come to her. I've come to help if I can."

The old woman shook her head. "I know several Rebeccas, but none such as you describe. Many are missing." A tear tracked down the old woman's face. "My only grandson hasn't been seen since before the Patriarch forced us out." She spat on the ground. "May Cyril be plagued with boils, and maggots eat his living flesh."

By noon they had no news and the crowds had thinned. They found a rock to sit on—all the shady spots taken by refugees—and shared bread, cheese, and fruit. Selene noticed new lines etched at the corners of Phillip's eyes and across his forehead.

"We'll find her." She patted his knee. "Or she'll find us. We'll talk to every person in the camp, one at a time if we have to."

"One brother is dead, another in the dungeons, but Judah, the oldest, is still free. What if he took Rebecca and her mother away? What if they are already in another city?"

"And leave Aaron? Rebecca would never allow that."

Phillip dropped his head into his hands. They sat quietly until distracted by a rustle.

A little girl, of not more than five, peered at them. "Sir? Ma'am? Are you the ones lookin' for Rebecca?"

"Yes!" They jumped up and answered as one.

"Do you know of her?" Selene asked.

"There's a lady named Rebecca over by my gran'ma." The child jerked her head vaguely over her shoulder. "She's a nice lady. She helped Gran and me, but she's awful sick."

"Take us to her, please?" Phillip asked.

"This way." The child skipped ahead, while they scrambled around rocks and between squatters. After several minutes, the little girl stopped by a substantial woman dressed in black. "Here's Gran."

"Where you been, Sarah?" The big woman picked up the girl and hugged her tight. "I told you not to go a wanderin'."

The woman seemed familiar to Selene, especially in the way she treated her granddaughter with rough affection. "Are you Rachel?"

The woman looked her up and down. "Who're you?"

"Selene. Rebecca introduced us once. This is my brother, Phillip. We've come to find Rebecca."

Rachel put one hand on her hip and cocked her head to the side. Finally she smiled. "I remember. Mother Nut's apprentice, aren't you?" Her face turned serious. "Rebecca could use a healer. Over here."

Rachel pulled a cloak away from a shrub to reveal Rebecca's form shivering under a blanket. "She's got a fever. It came on her sudden. She can't keep anything down and she's got runny stools. I've tried to help, but," indicating the little girl, "I've my own to care for."

Rebecca looked shrunken, her blankets soiled, and stinking. Selene knelt by her side, Phillip peering over her shoulder. "Oh, my friend, what's happened to you?" She felt Rebecca's forehead, pushing lank hair from her face. Rebecca moaned; her eyelids fluttered but didn't quite open. "Help me lift her," Selene said to her brother as she raised Rebecca's shoulders and started to remove the soiled bedding. Rebecca shivered, teeth chattering.

"Your cloak!" Selene barked. Phillip handed over his thin servant's garment. Selene took off her own warmer cloak and covered Rebecca with both.

"Can you help?" Phillip held Rebecca's frail, dry hand.

"I don't know. I can give her something for the fever and we must make sure she drinks, but beyond that..." Selene shook her head. "This sickness either kills or it doesn't."

"You have to do something for her!"

"The young and the strong have a better chance. If anyone can survive, Rebecca can."

"I want to take her home." Phillip reached as if to pick Rebecca up.

"I'll do what I can." Selene restrained him. "It's dangerous to move her. Besides, the guards would never allow us to carry a sick woman into the city. Rumors of plague spread faster than riots."

Phillip stood, hands dangling at his side, looking around helplessly. Purpose firmed his stance. "She needs clean blankets and water. I'll see what I can get from the guards." He headed toward the checkpoint.

Selene shouted to his retreating back, "Send word to Honoria. She promised to care for Father." She turned to Rachel. "How long has she been like this?"

"Since last evening." The big woman scratched her nose. "Her mother died yesterday morn. Worn out from days of nursing, Rebecca lay down and went to sleep. When she woke, she raved with fever."

Selene rummaged in her bag for feverfew. "Have any others come down with this illness?"

"Many are sick." Rachel's eyes grew round. "Is it the plague?"

"This illness strikes swiftly and kills many. We must get word to bring the sick to the dispensary." Selene balled up the soiled bedding. "Burn these."

"We've got to get away." Rachel backed from the odorous pile. "I got to stay alive for my granddaughter. We're all that's left of our family."

"I understand." Selene reached into her bag, took out the doll and a few coins. "Give this to Sarah and use the coins to get on the road."

Rachel gave the doll to the child and hid the coins in her voluminous robe. She bundled their meager possessions, snatched her granddaughter's hand, and headed for the road, saying, over her shoulder, "May God be with you."

CYRIL LABORED OVER HIS REPORT to the Emperor. Normally words—written or spoken—came easily to him. He needed to craft this letter in the best possible light to justify his actions.

He had not been surprised when several city nobles told him of their intent to submit protests to Constantinople. He suspected Orestes' or Hypatia's influence at work.

Cyril crossed out his last two sentences, breaking the nub on his reed pen.

Hierex entered the room. "Forgive the intrusion, Patriarch. A visitor from Constantinople wishes to see you. He said to give you this." Hierex held out a signet ring—gold, inset with a porphyry seal. It showed a two-headed eagle, the sign of the Imperial family.

"Show him in." Cyril put away his writing instruments and signaled his servants to bring refreshments.

Hierex led in a short robust man in sturdy travel clothes. The man bowed low to Cyril, sweeping back his cloak. "Patriarch, I'm honored. The Augusta Pulcheria particularly recommended you. My name is Thomas."

Cyril kept his face neutral, but his heart beat faster at the mention of the Emperor's sister. His sources at court said she held the reins of power at present and was quite religious. If she supported his actions, Orestes would have to come around to his way of thinking.

"Welcome to Alexandria, my son." Cyril indicated a chair. "What news do you bring us of the capital? I hope the Emperor and his sister are in good health."

Thomas seated himself. "The Emperor and the Augusta Pulcheria enjoyed good health when I saw them last, several weeks ago."

"You see them often?"

"When I am at court, I frequently dine in private with the Augusta." Thomas presented a bland face to the Patriarch. "She is interested in my travels and observations. She particularly wanted me to visit this fair city, as it is vital to her plans for the Empire."

"You are most welcome in Alexandria." Cyril allowed a warm smile to lighten his face. "Please let me offer accommodations. You will find our guest rooms quite comfortable."

Cyril had dispatched his most trusted deacon to Constantinople upon his investiture, but the man had been unable to penetrate the thick wall of local priests and clergy already established around the Augusta Pulcheria. Cyril could make good use of a personal emissary from the court.

"Thank you, Patriarch. I have taken rooms with a dear friend." Thomas spread his fingers in a deprecating manner. "I must report to the Augusta, but am at a loss to describe the current state of affairs. There seem to be significant disruptions in city life. Since this is the main staging area for grain to the capital and the frontiers, I hope I will be able to report that all is well?" Thomas examined his fingernails while Cyril pondered a reply.

"It is my understanding the Augusta Pulcheria is a most devout lady," Cyril stated in a ringing voice. "I'm sure she would approve of the latest developments in Alexandria. The Jews attacked and murdered a number of Christians. We rose up in righteous wrath and expelled them from the city. As a result, Alexandria may be counted among the foremost of the devout."

"That is all well and good, Patriarch, and I am sure the Augusta Pulcheria will applaud your efforts. But it has come to my attention that you and the Egyptian Prefect have a less than amicable relationship. His job is to insure peace in this region and deliver the grain to Constantinople. The Emperor and his sister would be most pleased if you worked more closely with their chosen representative to attain that end."

Cyril stiffly bowed his head. "I will do God's will and, as it coincides with the Emperor's, I will do his as well."

"I see." Thomas nodded, eyes glittering. "I'm sure you perceive how God's will and the Emperor's conjoin in this matter. Our own devout grow fractious when deprived of daily bread. Our soldiers' loyalty wavers on empty stomachs. It would serve neither the Emperor's nor the Catholic Church's interest for the Arian Goths to invade the Eastern Empire as they did Rome. They wait on our borders, looking for weakness. If a boy emperor cannot control riots in the cities or feed his army, the heretic barbarians may feel the time is right. We must deny them that opportunity. Do I make the situation perfectly clear, Patriarch?"

"Yes." Bile rose in Cyril's throat. So close to his vision; and to be checked in this manner! "I will do what I can."

"That is all the Emperor asks of the Lord's servants." Thomas rose and bowed.

"I will take my leave, Patriarch, and after meeting with the Prefect and Egyptian dux will continue on my journey to the capital."

"Please convey my felicitations and my assurances to the Augusta that I will act in the best interest of God and the Empire."

When the door closed, Cyril snatched the paper on which he had been writing, crumpled it into a ball and threw it into a corner. He rose and paced the office, stopping in front of a window. The sun streamed in, touching everything with a golden light. He stood there, eyes closed and head bowed, for several moments.

A smile slowly grew across his face.

CHAPTER 27

PHILLIP RETURNED WITH CLEAN BLANKETS, wood, and fresh water. A bundle of stinking rags marked the furthest boundary of the campsite. He would burn them as soon as he could, to spare Rebecca, always fastidious about her person, the indignity of seeing or smelling them.

Rebecca.

His breath caught as he looked at her wasted form. Phillip knelt and took her hand, the skin dry and brittle. "What more can I do, Selene?"

"Stay with her. Talk. I've seen many respond to the voices of loved ones."

Phillip hoped his blush went unnoticed, then upbraided himself for a fool. Selene gave voice to what he knew, but left unsaid. Over the past two years, Rebecca had entangled his heart. He loved the way her hair and skin smelled of soap and roses, how she modestly denied his praise, how she passionately cared for those she loved.

"Rachel said she came down with the fever yesterday evening. This disease usually kills within a day." Selene put her hands on his shoulders. "She's still alive. That gives me hope. I'll build a fire and make some decoctions. Until they're ready, try this." She thrust a pouch of watered wine at him.

Phillip tried dribbling the wine into Rebecca's mouth. More spilled into her hair than between her lips. He sat back on his heels, fists clenched in frustration. The distant bleats of a goat sparked a dim memory. He had raised an orphaned kid when little more than a toddler. His mother had showed him how to feed the baby animal.

Phillip unsheathed a knife, cut off a piece of blanket, and soaked it with the wine. He then put an end in Rebecca's mouth. She sucked reflexively. Phillip smiled briefly and remoistened the cloth. He had used nearly all the watered wine when Selene approached with her medicines.

She looked on approvingly. "Let's see if she will take the cup."

Phillip propped Rebecca up while Selene held a chipped cup to her mouth. Rebecca opened her eyes. "Mother?" she croaked through parched lips.

"No, it's Selene. Drink this." Rebecca took ragged gulps, draining the cup. "I'll get you more."

Rebecca closed her eyes, her breast barely rising with each breath. Phillip tightened his grip, as Rebecca's head lolled off his shoulder. His voice edged with panic, "Selene, she's dying!"

His sister rushed to his side, listened to Rebecca's breathing, and smiled. "She's sleeping. Much better than delirium." Selene gently shook her friend and pressed a second cup to her lips. "You must drink. It will cool the fever and replenish your body."

Rebecca raised a hand a few inches either to take the cup or ward it off. "I'm so tired," she whimpered.

"Don't try to do anything. We'll take care of you. Drink." Rebecca managed to drain another cup and part of a third, before again falling asleep. Selene laid a hand on her forehead. "She's cooler."

"Thank God." Phillip lowered Rebecca to her pallet as if she might shatter.

"She may yet succumb." Selene gripped his arm; the bruising strength of her grasp matched the depth of his own feelings. "It's important to keep her warm and make her drink. It will be many days before she fully recovers, but we might move her to a more convenient place to convalesce tomorrow."

Phillip squatted beside Rebecca, stroking her hair. His mouth twisted in a bitter line. "She will live, sister, if I have to move heaven and earth to make it so. When she is well, we will be married."

"Brother." Selene put a hand on his shoulder. "Rebecca may recover, but we know not what she will wish to do."

He set his chin in a stubborn line.

"All this," Selene indicated the camps, "might change her affection towards us. I also love Rebecca and would welcome her as a sister, but would Father accept a servant as a daughter? Would the church sanctify your marriage? There are many obstacles."

Phillip scrubbed his face with both hands. "If Rebecca returns my affection, we'll make it work."

He and Selene took turns sitting with Rebecca through the night, pouring wine and medicine down her throat whenever possible. In the morning, Rebecca awoke alert but enervated. Her body looked visibly plumper. Phillip fussed over her, feeding her clear broth and gently berating her for running off to the camps and getting sick.

"What else was I to do?" Rebecca whispered, eyes clouding with pain. "Leave my mother to the jackals?"

Phillip, stricken, clasped her hands in his. "No, no, my love. I'm selfish, thinking of my own pain at almost losing you. Rachel told us about your mother."

"I think she died of a broken heart." Rebecca shuddered. "Her sons dead or missing. Turned out of her home. All she worked for since Father's death, gone to dust. The mob did not kill her with blows to her body." She withdrew her hands from his. "Once she knew Aaron was safe, she gave up her life, as if it were too heavy a burden." A single tear trickled down her cheek. She turned her face away. "Why did she have to die like that? Why do you hate us so?"

Phillip sat in stunned silence, Rebecca's words slicing his heart. He finally spoke. "I love you, Rebecca. Those men who did this are no part of me." Phillip put his arms around her and rocked her gently. "Let me protect you. No one could ever do this to you again, if you married me."

Her eyes flew wide. She shook her head and opened her mouth.

Phillip put a finger to her lips. "Shush. Don't answer now. We can talk later, when you're stronger." Before she could protest, he picked up the cup. "Drink this."

Rebecca drank the concoction and made a face. "Tell Selene I'd rather have the wine. Her bitter medicines have done their work." She lay back on her bedding and yawned. "I'm still so tired."

"Go back to sleep, my love. I'll watch over you."

When Rebecca slept, he moved to the small charcoal fire Selene tended. He watched her preparing the medicine, marveling at how the gawky girl had become a beautiful and clever woman, skilled in a profession. Selene had turned her stubborn independence from detriment to desirable trait - at least in his eyes.

She looked up from the fire, searched his face and smiled. "She's better?"

He sniffed the acrid odor from the small pot hanging from a tripod. "Enough to ask relief from your witch's brew."

"If she can complain, she's getting better." Selene's forehead creased in a small frown. "We must get her out of here soon. Now that her fever has broken, the guards might let us pass into the city. Tomorrow we'll move her to the infirmary. In a day or two, you can hire a litter or cart to carry her home. I'll go to the infirmary and see what accommodations they have."

Phillip looked around. The camp was emptying. Soldiers patrolled the perimeter. He nodded. "Don't be long."

SELENE STRODE PAST THE CHECKPOINT, down the road toward the cattle market. It felt good to stretch her muscles after a night on rocky ground. Rising dust marked the passage of a small knot of people coming from the city. Selene squinted through the pall. A short man with a pronounced limp led a procession of half a dozen people. Selene hurried forward. "Archdeacon Timothy! What are you doing here?"

The archdeacon, eyes twinkling, said in a voice loud enough to be heard by the guards. "My child, I've come with these other good Christians to minister to the sick as our merciful Lord commanded." He hooked his arm in hers and said lower, "I heard rumors of plague. It is better to contain it. If it spreads to the city, the mob might burn the camps."

"Surely these people have suffered enough?"

"The Prefect has things under control for now, but our zealous Patriarch might seize this excuse to complete a task, if he feels it undone. Perhaps we can forestall more tragedy."

The infirmary was a makeshift affair of tents and converted cattle stalls. A steady trickle of people carried in the sick. A soldier helped a young man, who'd collapsed by the side of the road, to his feet and into the first tent. They followed. Selene caught a now familiar whiff of vomit and human waste and involuntarily held her breath.

Row after row of pallets lay on the floor, occupied by bodies ranging from comatose to delirious. Selene's stomach sank. She had had no idea of the extent of the illness. Only three women cared for the hundreds of ill. Timothy's six would not stem this tide of need.

"Holy Mother of God have mercy." Timothy's face settled into a grim mask as he surveyed the scene. He turned to a woman dressed in rough gray robes. With a gentle smile, he placed a hand on her shoulder. "Sister, we have come to help in the Lord's name. You look exhausted. Get some food and rest while we take over your labors."

The woman fell to her knees and kissed Timothy's fingers. "Bless you, Archdeacon, but the children need me. I will stay with them."

Selene helped the woman to her feet. "I have medicines for the fever. Show me the children. I'll help you tend them."

"I put my faith in prayer." The woman looked through careworn eyes. "But maybe you're God's answer. Bring your medicines to the next tent." As she followed the woman, Selene heard Timothy deploy the others.

They entered another tent where over a hundred children lay two or three to a pallet. Those in the early stages showed yellowish skin and sweated profusely. Many had fouled their bedding with watery bowel movements. Those closer to death lay quietly, eyes shut, barely breathing through cracked lips.

Selene's gut twisted.

She had enough medicine for a dozen doses. Her heart cried out to give succor to the sickest, but the medicine would be wasted on those at death's door. She quickly used up her small store of medicines on the strongest children.

With no other recourse, Selene washed ravished bodies, comforted weak whimpers as best she could, and covered more still forms than she wanted to remember. She worked steadily, taking time only to eat a couple of dried figs and drink stale water from a pail.

Late in the day, Selene tended a small girl who put out her hand, groping, crying piteously. Selene searched the area and found a wooden doll with a painted head and moveable joints. Selene stared in dull horror. She hadn't recognized the sprightly girl who took her to Rebecca. In all that misery, no child had a past or personality, just a needy body.

Selene tucked the doll into the girl's arms and looked around. Rachel must be sick or dead. The child sighed, then stopped breathing. Selene sat stunned at the suddenness of the death. The lady in gray put her hands on Selene's shoulders. "There are live ones that need your attention."

"What?"

"This child needs you no longer. Others do." The woman closed the girl's eyes, wrapped her in a blanket and picked her up.

Selene took up the doll, which had fallen from the child's limp arms. She followed the woman outside. A burly monk transferred bodies from an ever-growing stack to a raging fire. Oily smoke rose from the pyre. Jackals crept close on the other side, attracted by the smell of roasting meat.

Slow tears coursed down Selene's cheeks. "How do you stand it?" she asked the woman.

"God sets me many tests and trials, but never more than I can bear." The woman laid her pitiful burden on the stack.

Selene noticed the orange quality of the light. Sunset. Phillip would be frantic. She stared at the stack of small bodies, torn between conflicting duties.

"You have done enough here, my child." Archdeacon Timothy put a kind hand on her shoulder. "Go home and tend your father."

"There is so much more to do!"

"Leave the rest to those of us who have pledged our lives to do the Lord's work."

"Is this the Lord's work?" Selene asked bitterly. "Dead and dying children?"

"No, my child, this is Satan's work." Timothy clasped her shoulders with steady strength. "You, me, these others ministering to the sick. We are God's work."

Selene slumped in his grasp. Exhausted from days of worry, labor, and little sleep, she gave up. "I'll be back tomorrow with more medicine."

"Go with God, my child."

Selene threw the doll on the pyre and turned her back to the light. She picked her way back to the campsite as fast as she could.

Phillip met her, face red. "Where in the name of all that's holy have you been?" he shouted.

Fresh tears welled. She wanted to be held tightly and told all this would go away, not scolded. Resentment added a bitter edge to her voice. "We can't take Rebecca to the infirmary. Death infests the air there."

"What's wrong?" The color drained from Phillip's face. "Why were you so long?"

She told him of her day's labors. He held her while she cried over Rachel's granddaughter. Selene dried her tears on her sleeve.

"We're going home." Phillip hugged her close. "In the morning we'll move Rebecca to the checkpoint and I'll go to the city for a litter."

*****

AT THE CITY GATE, Selene listened inside the litter as Phillip argued with the guards. The litter bearers conferred over whether they were likely to get their fee if the guards turned them back. She and Rebecca held a hasty conference. Rebecca pulled a cloak over her hair, leaned back against the seat and feigned sleep.

A scarred brown hand pulled back the curtains. The guard frowned as his eyes searched the dim interior.

"Is there a problem?" Selene asked. "If not, I would like to get to my father's home. He is a city councilor and expects us shortly." She regarded the soldier with a cold eye.

He appeared unimpressed, scrutinizing Selene's well-worn clothing and Rebecca's even shabbier appearance. He sniffed and pointed toward Rebecca. "Who's she?"

"My nurse. My family bought her before I was born." Selene turned a warm smile toward her companion. "She's old and falls asleep with the swaying of the litter. My father promised to retire her when I marry, but she claims she wants to raise my children, too."

Rebecca let out a soft snore.

The guard snorted. "Old'uns do like to sleep." He dropped the curtain back in place. Selene heard a brief exchange between the guard and her brother. The litter lurched forward.

Well away from the gate, Selene giggled. Rebecca opened her eyes and smiled ruefully. "Do I look so bad I pass as your old nurse?"

Selene patted her friend's knee. "You'll look better in a few days, after you've rested and eaten." Selene giggled again and leaned against the seat, light-headed.

At last they reached her father's house. Phillip lifted Rebecca from the stuffy litter and carried her into the cool vestibule. Selene followed, giving directions to scandalized servants that Rebecca be taken upstairs to the family quarters.

As they approached the rooms, Selene was gripped with intense cramps. She barely made it to the toilets, where her bowels let go a stream of watery stools. Her cramps eased briefly, but a wave of nausea over took her. Afterward, Selene wiped her mouth and shook with fear.

She stumbled back to where Phillip helped Rebecca settle in a guestroom. He looked at Selene in alarm.

"Get me to my room, brother, I'm not well."

He reached for her as she collapsed against the cool wall. She whispered, "Get Mother Nut," before passing out.

SELENE AWOKE, aching in every fiber of her body. She licked a leathery tongue across cracked lips, and croaked, "Water."

She felt as if she had been left in the sun to dry like a hide. Confused images blurred in her mind; something about Rebecca and a little girl. She tried to shake her head, but it felt too heavy.

"Drink this." A familiar face hovered over her bed, exhaling the unmistakable stench of garlic. A wiry arm propped her head, and a cup of bitter-smelling brew appeared at her lips. Selene drank greedily, ignoring the taste, glorying in the moisture that soothed her mouth and throat.

"More," she rasped. She drank a second cup of bitter herbs and a third, before sinking back into an exhausted sleep.

On the edge of her consciousness she heard low worried voices.

CHAPTER 28

CYRIL SURVEYED THE COUNCIL DELEGATION from behind a screen, surprised to see Calistus, hands trembling on a walking stick. The Councilor had not been seen in public for several weeks. Calistus' presence gave Cyril pause. The councilor must feel deeply about his mission, to risk his health. But Calistus did not know God's will. Cyril did.

The clergy, students, mariners, and merchants continued their vocal support, but the nobles and councilors pretended horror at his most recent actions. They came to urge the Patriarch to an accommodation with the Prefect. Cyril clenched his fists. Orestes had set himself on the side of the pagans and Jews. There could be no accommodation unless the Prefect admitted the error of his ways.

Hierex touched his sleeve. "Are you ready, Patriarch?"

"Yes." He patted his robes and smoothed his beard. "Let's set them on the right path."

As he entered, all stood and bowed. Cyril stopped in front of Calistus. "Councilor. I'm honored by your attendance, but shouldn't you be in bed or overseeing the progress of your daughter's illness? I heard she risked her own life to nurse the sick. Be assured our prayers are with her."

"Thank you, Patriarch, for your blessings. Your prayers will surely help." Calistus bowed low. "But we have come on a matter most urgent."

"Please be seated." Cyril took an imposing Bishop's chair, while the rest settled on benches and stools. "My companion is Hierex, a teacher and my secretary. How may I be of service?"

Calistus spoke for the delegation. "As the leaders of our city, we have come to beseech you to desist in your actions and seek accord with the Augustal Prefect."

Cyril raised his right hand to his chest. "What actions do you speak of?"

"The slaughter and expulsion of our Jewish citizens."

A low mutter of assent followed Calistus' words.

"The Jewish community conspired to murder our fellow Christians. Do you defend their acts?"

"Only a few hotheaded youths devised that plan. You are a young man without the experience of our grayer heads. We feel you were wrong to lead a mob against old people, women and children who had nothing to do with that conspiracy."

Cyril swallowed his anger at the rebuke. He needed the support of these men. He motioned, palms down, fingers spread wide as if in supplication. "I welcome your advice, but fail to see my error. I could not allow such a heinous crime to go unpunished."

Calistus' eyes held a haunted look. "The Prefect is responsible for maintaining the peace. You had no right to lead armed men against Alexandrian citizens."

"The Prefect failed to protect innocent Christians." Cyril raked the gathering with fiery eyes. After assessing their unyielding faces, he sat back, sighing sorrowfully. "You should be pleased that my actions resulted in a large number of conversions. Those Jews are saved."

"And those expelled from the city?"

"The nonbelievers may return to their homeland." Cyril flicked his fingers in a dismissive gesture. "After all, those 'citizens' live in a Christian Empire. If they do not convert, they are welcome to relocate beyond our borders."

Another councilor stood, in the back. "Our workshops are empty of skilled workers. Shipping is disrupted. We cannot fulfill our contracts for goods. When our businesses fail, we cannot do our duty to city and church."

"Thousands move to the city every week looking for work." Cyril shrugged. "You will soon fill your workshops."

"Illiterate Egyptian peasants!" the councilor sputtered. "I'm talking about the loss of skilled artisans: potters, weavers, dyers, bricklayers. The farmers who come here to escape the land taxes are a drain on our resources, not an asset."

Calistus interrupted his colleague with soothing tones. "We realize the fate of our Jewish citizens is past remedy, but the intolerable situation between you and the Prefect still remains. We ask you to take the first step in mending the breach with Orestes. Patriarch, show the city leadership reflective of the New Testament. Do not the texts say 'Blessed are the peacemakers'?"

Cyril nodded. "A most noble proposal. This rift is not of my making or inclination. I would be most happy to approach the Augustal Prefect, if he is willing to receive me." Cyril steepled his hands and touched fingertips to bottom lip. This could work to his benefit.

"We ask only that you both meet in good faith to reconcile your differences." Calistus' face lightened with honest relief.

"I agree nothing good can come of this continuing discord between us." The Patriarch widened his eyes and addressed the whole room. "The city needs unity. With the Jews no longer whispering in Orestes' ear, I'm sure we can come to an agreement." The Patriarch bowed his head to simulate penitence. "It was never my intent to cause misery. I am aware of the difficulties presented to innocent Christians through disrupted trade and the threat of plague. Even as we speak, our brothers and sisters minister to those outside our gates. As to the Prefect, I will wait on him shortly to discuss our mutual interests."

Calistus beamed. "We will be happy to work on your behalf. Orestes is a reasonable man. I'm sure you'll reach an accord."

"Of course." Cyril addressed the gathering. "I will again offer my support and guidance to the Prefect."

The delegation rose, bowed to the Patriarch, and made small talk as they left.

"A most satisfactory outcome, don't you think?" Cyril smiled at Hierex. "Those same parties that urge me to accommodation also approach Orestes. His coalition is falling apart. We have stripped him of the Jews; the nobles and councilors take a neutral stance. Now is the time to approach him."

"There is still one powerful obstacle." Hierex added slyly. "Hypatia still stands at the Prefect's side, poisoning him with her pagan philosophy. He no longer attends Christian services. Many others listen to her as well."

"I have seen the crowds around her door, waiting for her to speak." A slow red flush suffused Cyril's face. "Yes, she is a fierce lion in our path. My Uncle Theophilus admired her and suffered her to teach, but these are different times." He tapped his teeth with a fingernail. "We must be clever in how we wean our Prefect away from her unwholesome advice. She is a venerable woman, almost an icon in the city."

"But not invulnerable." Hierex frowned. "Everyone has a weakness. I will find hers."

SELENE WOKE TO THE SILENCE of late night. An oil lamp burned on her stand. She rolled onto her side; the effort made her pant. Why was she so weak and desperately thirsty?

A shadow detached itself from the wall and hobbled toward her. Selene's heart thudded painfully until the shadow resolved into an ancient woman.

"Mother Nut," she whispered. "What are you doing here?"

"Drink this." She held a cup to Selene's lips. It was a cooling mint drink with an undertone of anise. Selene collapsed to her back. Mother Nut poured another cup. "Drink as much as you can, child."

Selene raised her head for the second cup. Memories flooded back. She grabbed Mother Nut's hands. "Rebecca? My family?"

"All are well. Rebecca is recovering nicely. I let no one near you and ordered all to drink only unwatered wine or beer. Meat or fowl only, no food from the sea. The gods have seen fit to spare your household."

Selene sighed in relief and thought more closely about what her mentor had told her. She didn't recall any such remedies in her textbooks. Selene's professional curiosity piqued. "How does the drinking of wine and eating of meat help prevent the plague?"

"It's not what is eaten, but what is not." Mother Nut shrugged. "The gods require a sacrifice. Sometimes, when people give up water and what comes from water, the gods' anger passes them by." She grinned broadly, showing a clove of garlic stuck on one of her few remaining teeth.

Selene smiled weakly in return. "And garlic helps ward off evil." She plucked at her bed covering and peeked at the old woman between crusted lashes. "How soon can I be out of bed?"

"We barely snatched you from Anubis' jaws, child." Mother Nut frowned and clucked. "Stay in bed for a week and we'll see."

"A week!" Selene squealed. "But I promised Archdeacon Timothy." An overwhelming lethargy crept up her limbs. Her eyes grew heavy and she yawned. "Well, maybe," she mumbled, and drifted off.

*****

AFTER THREE DAYS' CONVALESCENCE, Mother Nut allowed Calistus to visit Selene. He looked frail, but had put on weight, and his color was much improved. He attributed this to a special diet of garlic and lentils and a daily walk Mother Nut had recommended.

"A remarkable old witch," he laughed. "She gets me to do things no one else could. If I didn't know better, I would say she cast a spell on this household. The servants walk in fear of her, but every one of them follows her orders and no one is sick."

Selene's nose twitched at the thought of the servants' precautions. "And after a while, you don't notice the reek of garlic, I suppose."

"No, I don't."

"Has the plague reached the city?"

Calistus shook his head. "It seems confined to the camps. They're nearly empty now. Most of the poor souls have either moved on or died." His face settled into a pained expression.

Selene squeezed his hand. "What is it, Father?"

"Archdeacon Timothy…"

An icy lump formed around Selene's heart. "Is he dead?"

Her father nodded.

"And the others with him? Did God see fit to spare any of those kind souls?"

"Only one." He sighed. "There's a strange story about a woman they called the Gray Lady. She cared for the children until the last died, then walked into the Boukolia with no food or water. No one has seen her since. Some say she was the Blessed Mother Mary come to care for the children and see they made it safely to heaven."

"The Virgin Mary helped, even though they were Jews?" Selene frowned. The woman helping in the children's ward had seemed flesh and blood to her.

"A monk baptized them as they were brought in."

Of course! Baptism cleansed the soul of all former sin. Many, including the Emperor Constantine, put off baptism till their deaths to insure they went directly to heaven. The unfairness of redemption for a life lived deliberately in sin pricked Selene's sense of justice. Sometimes the paradoxes of religion made her head ache. She longed for happy news. "Is Honoria well?"

"The babe grows great and Lysis claims Ision daily regales him with predictions of a strapping grandson."

"Have they been here?"

"Antonius comes by daily to inquire about your health on Honoria's behalf. Lysis accompanied me in a delegation to meet with the Patriarch." Calistus snorted. "Ision did not attend. He's in favor of Cyril's actions and stands to improve his profits greatly by buying Jewish businesses for far less than they are worth. I would have thought Ision had gold enough, and would turn his thoughts and energy to more gentlemanly pursuits."

She thought of Antonius, sadness swelling her throat. "Does Lysis regret the match?"

"No. Antonius seems happy enough, and Honoria is a loving daughter-in-law." Calistus sighed. "Lysis and I had once talked of marriage between you and Antonius, but he cooled on the idea when Ision approached him. I'm sure the boy is better off with a biddable wife. You can be more than a handful, traipsing off to do your own will." Calistus looked at her lovingly. "I'm grateful you are alive. Mother Nut is a most remarkable healer for an unschooled Egyptian."

"Why did you send for her?"

"You cried out for her when you collapsed." He flushed slightly. "I wanted Urbib, but he disappeared during the troubles. He recently returned as a Christian convert, but Mother Nut had already worked her miracle on you. Rebecca made quite a persuasive case on her behalf." Calistus chuckled. "The old crone would only come if I provided a litter 'like a real lady'."

"And why shouldn't I be treated like a real lady when I come to such a great house as this?" Mother Nut cackled from the door. "Now you, sir, be gone. My dumpling needs her rest."

Calistus bowed deeply to the old woman. "As the Lady commands." He turned to Selene and lightly kissed her cheek. "I'll be back tomorrow."

Selene started to protest, took one look at Mother Nut's face and subsided into silence. Her questions would wait.

"PATRIARCH CYRIL." Demetrius bowed as he opened the door.

Orestes had anxiously awaited this meeting. His friends on the council had told him Cyril would privately apologize for his unwarranted actions and had agreed to cooperate in restoring the peace. Orestes prepared to be gracious in accepting the apology, but firm about the Patriarch's future role. He hoped Cyril would be satisfied with his victories, or at least take time to savor them. Orestes needed to realign his political support.

The Patriarch entered carrying a sumptuously wrapped bundle. A dozen church officials crowded into the sitting room after Cyril. Among them, Orestes recognized Hierex glaring balefully at him. Orestes held his dismay in check. He had planned a private meeting, where he and the Patriarch could work out their differences. He deliberately kept his contingent intimate—just Demetrius—to minimize the Patriarch's embarrassment.

"Demetrius, more chairs for the Patriarch's entourage." Orestes rose. "Welcome, and please be seated. Would you care for refreshment?"

"No, Prefect. We've come to speak of matters of the soul, not the body. I offer you the opportunity to follow Christ's word." Cyril slowly unwrapped the bundle, revealing a New Testament; its cover worked in red leather, the letters picked out in gold. "Jesus taught we should forgive our enemies. I have publicly stated that I forgive you your sins and misguided actions in defending the Jews."

Orestes kept his temper with difficulty. "Do you consider me your enemy?"

"On the contrary, I have requested the populace to pray for your soul and personally ask for divine guidance in helping you lead this city." Cyril bowed slightly. "And I would be more than pleased to oversee your religious instruction myself. It would give us the opportunity to be in daily contact. You might find my advice useful in your decisions concerning the health and welfare of our fair city."

Orestes felt his battle heat rising. Cyril offered no apology, only more interference. If Orestes accepted the Patriarch's offer, he gave Cyril and his minions admittance to his administration and tacit approval of past and future actions. If he refused, the Patriarch could accuse him of obstinacy and sit back in righteous innocence as the city fathers pressured Orestes for an accommodation. He could live with only one choice. "Patriarch, thank you for your more than generous offer. As I have told you, I completed my catechism in Constantinople and was baptized there."

Cyril smiled gently, speaking as if to an errant child. "You've claimed that in the past, but your actions and attitude toward the pagans and Jews belies that teaching."

Smiling as sweetly, Orestes shot back, "The Bible teaches us that God created the earth, the plants, and all the animals, does it not, Patriarch?"

"Indeed."

"It also teaches us God made man in his image."

Cyril answered more slowly this time. "Those are the earliest teachings. It is

238

clear you have some knowledge of the Bible."

"I believe the God who made us did not intend for us to loathe his creations. I believe the Emperor does not intend for his loyal citizens to be hounded from their homes, their businesses ruined, and their families destroyed."

Cyril met Orestes' eyes. "A pretty speech. Do those beliefs truly come from your heart, or from your thwarted ambition and desire for personal acclaim?"

The corners of Orestes' mouth twitched. The Patriarch's verbal arrows hit close to the mark. The riots reflected on his ability to govern, and touched his pride. He sympathized with anyone in pain or unjustly treated, but, in war, the innocent were often hurt.

Orestes tried one last ploy. "There remains Jesus' admonition to render unto God what is God's and unto Caesar what is Caesar's."

"When Our Dear Lord spoke those words, Caesar was a pagan." Cyril fairly beamed benevolence. "Our Most Esteemed Emperor and his sister Augusta Pulcheria have pledged to establish God's kingdom on earth. What was Caesar's is now God's. Acknowledge that fact publicly and let us work together for this city's future."

Orestes cleared his throat, "I most humbly beg to differ with your understanding of that passage. My patrons in the Imperial Court gave me a clear mandate for administering Egypt, and put the resources of the city at my disposal." In a low voice, directed to Cyril, "I suggest, Patriarch, that you retire to your Bishop's chair. If you persist in making it difficult for me to fulfill my duties, I will recommend the Emperor remove you from your See."

The blood drained from Cyril's face, then flushed back, bright red. "Even the Emperor has a Patriarch at his right hand, advising him in all matters. You might do well to emulate him."

Orestes leaned forward. "The Emperor is a boy of fourteen; his sister, the Regent, a girl of sixteen. In their youth, they need many kinds of advice. I don't."

Cyril straightened his shoulders and spoke to his contingent. "It is obvious our services are not wanted here, and our mission at reconciliation failed."

They filed out the door. Hierex' lips twitched, as if trying to suppress a smile.

The Patriarch turned as the last official left the room. "You aren't the only one with influence at court, Prefect."

As the door shut, Orestes collapsed into his chair, head in hands. He foresaw another round of written recriminations on his and Cyril's part, another smirch on his reputation.

Demetrius brought him wine. He drank, gagging on the sweet honeyed taste, then pushed it away, longing for the harsh vinegary stuff they served to the troops. After a moment's reflection, he realized what he truly longed for were those simpler times when he could fight his enemy directly, not through others' wiles and machinations.

Demetrius cleared his throat.

Orestes pondered his slave's careful mask. "Out with it."

"I can't help feeling, Master, that you might have chosen to accept the Patriarch's offer."

"I strongly considered it, but I can't abide the man."

"Could you not have feigned interest? If the Patriarch felt his voice heard, he might be more flexible. By keeping him close, you would have more knowledge of his actions and intentions. It would be easier to understand and counter him."

"You are a wise man, Demetrius." Orestes sighed. "But I cannot have him here. To do so would say to all that I found him right in his actions."

"I understand, Master." The stiffness of Demetrius' demeanor expressed his disappointment.

Orestes left, slamming the door.

CYRIL REVERENTLY REPLACED the New Testament on its stand in his chapel. "That was not the outcome I had hoped for."

"But not an unexpected one." Hierex spoke soothingly. "The Prefect will see the error in his judgment. We have sheared away his support, piece by piece. The masses are desperate for someone on whom to blame their misery. It will take little to turn them against Orestes."

"We cannot move directly against the Prefect." Cyril stared at a flickering lamp. "The Augusta Pulcheria has made her position clear. She is sympathetic, but will not abide disruption in the flow of grain. If our actions endanger her position as Regent, we lose her support."

"The legacy of Rome—bread and circuses." Hierex snorted. "The Lord Jesus might return to us any day and what will he find? Sodom and Gomorra."

"Not in Alexandria. We will have a fully Christian city." Cyril clapped Hierex' shoulder. "But we must work quietly for a while: redouble our efforts among the poor, distribute gifts to councilors who suffered losses in the riots, allow the city to recover. As he realizes his isolation, Orestes will be more reasonable."

"What if he asks Abundantius to support him with troops?"

"That action would prove his ineffectualness." Cyril stroked his beard. "My fear is that Hypatia wields enough influence with the city fathers to win them back for the Prefect."

"The Lady Philosopher has little influence with the lower orders."

"As you discovered, that is her weakness." Cyril smiled. "We must think on that."

CHAPTER 29

"M ISTRESS, WAKE UP!"
Selene groaned and rolled away from the finger poking her in the
shoulder.

Over the past three months, she had recovered from her illness and attacked her apprenticeship with a vengeance, trying to make up for lost time. Between that and her household responsibilities, it seemed she never got a full night's sleep.

The finger kept poking and the voice took on a decided whine. "Please, Mistress Selene. The Lady Honoria sent a servant to fetch you. She's in labor."

"Go away!" Selene mumbled into her covers.

"What should I tell him, Mistress?" The voice turned pitiful.

"Tell who, what, you silly goose?" Muzziness lifted from Selene's brain. She sat up. Anicia bobbed from foot to foot. Selene rubbed her eyes and glared at the girl, then sighed. "I'm awake now. What needs my attention?"

"The Lady Honoria sent a litter, Mistress. She's in labor and wishes your attendance."

"The baby's coming? Why didn't you say so?" Selene threw the covers off her bed, pulled her night tunic over her head and rummaged in her trunk for a serviceable robe. She chose one of her student garments, already besmirched with stains. "Don't stand there, Anicia, tell the Lady Honoria's servant I will be down shortly."

The girl bowed and ran down the hall.

Selene washed her face and pulled on her clothes. She was hastily combing and braiding her hair when Rebecca entered with a tray. "You always know what I need without my asking! How's Anicia? Did I scare her silly?"

"That would take little effort. The girl has goose feathers in her head. Let me finish that." Rebecca set the tray on Selene's cosmetics table so she could eat while Rebecca finished braiding and pinning her hair. "Do you want me to come with you?"

Selene slowly chewed a chunk of warm bread with melted cheese and mumbled, "I don't think so. If there is one thing I've learned from Mother Nut, it's that first labors are usually long."

She stiffened. "Oh! I was supposed to visit Mother Nut today. Could you take this food and these medicines I bought for her?" Selene reached for a pouch on the floor beside her table and handed it to Rebecca. "Give her my regrets. I'll send word if I need anything else."

Selene rose, shaking crumbs off her garment onto the floor. She rummaged for her surgical bag, slung it over her shoulder, and left Rebecca with a wave.

Honoria's servant lounged in the vestibule. He frowned at her well-worn clothes. Selene followed him out and reluctantly entered the stuffy litter. She would rather have walked the short distance to her friend's house in the fresh air, but the sky was still that deep purple just before the gray dawn. She didn't wish to scandalize Ision's servants more than they already were.

Minutes later, the litter lurched to a stop and settled to the ground. Selene steeled herself to see Antonius. She had consciously avoided him since the riots, visiting Honoria when she knew he worked. Antonius had ended his studies and reluctantly thrown himself into the mercantile life.

The servant parted the curtain and offered a hand to pull Selene up from her seat.

In the entrance hall, one of Honoria's sisters waited to escort her to the women's quarters. The horde of women in attendance impressed Selene with their quiet but purposeful air. Servants bustled back and forth with hot water, clean cloths, and food for the guests. Several older women quietly prayed at a household shrine.

Selene entered a small room lit by two stone lamps. The air smelled sour with vomit and sweat. Honoria sat on a bed, supported by cushions, while servants washed her face and changed her soiled clothes. Her face contorted and she leaned forward to retch in a copper bowl held by another servant.

Honoria's mother Arete approached Selene with raised eyebrows, eyeing her clothing. "My dear, would you care to join the ladies' prayers?"

Taken aback, Selene said, "I will gladly pray for Honoria's safe delivery, but I thought she wished me to attend her. I've assisted many births in my apprenticeship."

"I'm sure you have, child, but we have a skilled midwife and no need of your, uh, services." Arete smiled thinly. "All is progressing normally. Come greet Honoria. Your presence will cheer her." She led the way to the small crowd surrounding the laboring woman. Selene followed, covering her embarrassment over the misunderstanding with the knowledge that no one here would pay any attention to her. All focused on Honoria, who leaned back on the cushions, enjoying a brief respite from the pain.

Selene approached, took her friend's hand and spoke in low tones. "How does it go?"

"As the church fathers told us, women are cursed to bring forth young with pain and tears. I did not know I also had to give up my dinner." Honoria smiled wanly.

"It sometimes happens. I have herbs which might settle your stomach. Shall I make a decoction?"

"Please! I am so thirsty. The wretched midwife will not allow me to drink anything, because I keep bringing it back up."

A middle-aged woman, with the short hair and dark robes of a Christian penitent, frowned at Selene. "Who might you be, girl?"

"Selene. I'm a friend of Honoria's. I've been studying medicine at the Museum and apprenticing with an Egyptian medica. And you, Lady?"

The older woman took in Selene's serviceable clothing and youth and smiled. "Melania." She had no need to state her credentials, given her reputation as midwife to the wives and daughters of the elite. Honoria was indeed in good hands.

"May I stay, Midwife? I'm sure I could learn much from you." Selene did not want to be relegated to the prayer circle when she could observe a respected colleague.

Melania nodded. "I can always use a pair of skilled hands. Do what I say, when I say it."

"If you two are through chatting, do you think you might help me?" Honoria interrupted petulantly. "I feel another pain coming on." Her grip tightened on Selene's hand and her face contorted.

"Don't hold your breath, child. Breathe swiftly, like a panting dog. Ride the pain, don't let it ride you." Melania chanted in a low soothing tone, "Relax. Don't fight the pain. Let it roll through your body." She massaged Honoria's neck and shoulders.

"How long has she been in labor?" Selene asked.

"The hard pains started shortly after midnight. God willing, we should have a baby by noon."

Melania and Selene spent the next several hours taking turns helping Honoria through her pains and taking brief rests on a hard bench outside the room. By sundown, Melania confided her concerns to Selene. "Honoria is bleeding. She's getting weaker, and the baby's breech. I've tried to turn it through massage, but it stubbornly insists on being born backwards. I may have to ask Urbib to attend."

Selene nodded. Urbib had resurfaced to take up his old practice. As a physician he could perform an embryotomy, the dissection in utero of a fetus which cannot be delivered. The mother frequently died during this rare and dangerous procedure. Without it, the mother always died. Midwives were not allowed to perform such surgery.

"Surely we needn't resort to that yet."

"We'll see how she does in the next hour." Melania sighed. "I can't let her go beyond that or we lose both mother and child. I'll have Arete send word to Urbib now. Why don't you go in to comfort her?"

Selene returned to the birthing room. It seemed more stifling than before. Honoria lay moaning weakly, her huge belly rippling with contractions visible through her soaked linen gown. Selene dipped a cloth in cool water and wiped the sweat from her friend's face.

After another half-hour of agonizing labor, Honoria gripped Selene's hand. "What's wrong? Why does it hurt so? Why won't it stop?" Her hand lost its grip and flopped to her side. Honoria's pale face had dark smudges under glazed eyes. Her hair lay lank with sweat.

"Honoria, stay with me. Don't give up." Selene clapped her friend's hand between both of hers, rubbing briskly. "Work just a little harder and we can get this baby out. Your baby, Honoria. Try harder for the child!"

"I want to sleep, Selene. Please make the pain go so I can sleep." Honoria turned on to her side and cried.

Selene held her face, looking into her eyes. "A little more. Do you feel you have to push yet?"

"No. The pains keep coming without stopping." Her eyes widened with fear. "Am I going to die, Selene? I don't want to die! I want to give Antonius his son." As she spoke, a shadow came over her face.

Selene shouted. "Someone bring Antonius! Call Melania. Lady Honoria is fading." She heard a flurry of footsteps behind her, and worried voices. She turned back to Honoria, climbed onto the bed, propped her friend up from behind, and held her tight. "Stay with us, Honoria. Don't die." The pregnant woman's breath came in catching gasps.

Selene heard Antonius at the door, arguing with Honoria's mother.

"Antonius, in here, quickly!"

Antonius pushed past the wall of women and rushed to the bedside. He knelt on the floor beside the spasming body of his wife and pushed her hair from her face. "Honoria? What I have I done to you?" Tears started down his cheeks.

"Antonius?" Honoria's wandering gaze searched for her husband's face. "I'm so sor...oh!" She gasped again. A gout of blood stained the sheets between her legs.

Melania came up behind Antonius, sending a sorrowful glance to Selene. Honoria's body went slack. Her breathing stopped. Melania closed Honoria's staring eyes and touched the shocked man's shoulder. "There's nothing more we can do. God has called them to heaven."

Selene, still holding the body, felt Honoria's belly give another shudder. "The baby! We might be able to save it."

Melania looked at her in horror. "Are you mad? The woman is dead. It's God's will."

"It's not mine." She dropped Honoria's shoulders, climbed out of the bed and searched frantically for her surgical bag. She pulled out a sharp scalpel and a wad of clean cloths.

Melania grabbed her shoulder in a vise-like grip. "What do you think you're doing?"

Selene shook her off and addressed Antonius. "A Cesarean. Urbib would do it, but he isn't here. It's our only chance to save the baby. Every moment counts."

Melania half turned toward Antonius, her jaw set in a stubborn line. "I don't recommend this. Let the lady rest in peace."

Honoria's mother wailed in the hallway.

Antonius looked at Selene with questioning eyes.

She raised her chin. "It's the only chance for the baby."

He nodded. "Stand aside. Let Selene try."

Selene turned back to the bedside, pushing her own feelings of grief and inadequacy aside. She looked at the body clinically, as if in anatomy class. She pulled the robe up over the belly and made a swift incision laterally from side to side through skin and underlying fat. The next cut, through abdominal muscle, exposed the womb.

No movement.

She carefully cut through the uterine wall, so as not to damage the child, and worked the baby out head and shoulders first. The infant boy was blue and still.

Selene laid the small body face down on her lap and gently thumped on his back to expel fluid.

Still no response.

She glanced up to meet Antonius' despairing gaze.

Selene remembered a trick Mother Nut had tried on a normally born infant that did not breathe. She flipped the baby over, gently opened its tiny mouth and, covering it with her own, sucked out the fluid, spitting it to the side and gently puffing air into the fragile body.

She heard the servants' low murmurs at the edge of her consciousness, but Urbib's horrified tones cut through her concentration. "What, by all that's holy, is she doing?"

Antonius' voice floated back, soothing the offended physician.

After several puffs, she turned the baby onto its stomach and thumped its back again. The baby coughed, twitched, coughed again. It gave a lusty yell. Its blue color faded to angry red. It screwed up its tiny face and opened its mouth in a sustained cry.

Selene righted the infant, held it to her chest so it could hear her heartbeat, and covered it in a clean cloth.

Urbib examined Honoria's body, muttering.

"Well done, Selene. I didn't believe it possible to save the child." Melania took the baby and looked it over critically. "A strapping boy. The Lord was with you today." She handed the baby back to Selene. "I'll cut the cord."

After Melania tied off the birth cord, Selene washed the blood off the wiggling body and wrapped it in a swaddling cloth. She turned to find Antonius shifting from foot to foot, rubbing his palms on his tunic.

"Would you like to hold him?" She gently laid the baby in his arms. "You have a fine son."

He held the bundle awkwardly. The baby opened its eyes, looking vaguely at its father. Antonius' face broke into a broad smile. "I'll name him Honorius Posthumous, after his mother. How can I thank you, Selene?"

She laid a hand on his arm. "I did what I could." Tears choked her throat. "I wish it could've been more."

"You did quite enough to the poor girl." Urbib's sanctimonious voice cut through their conversation. "I looked at the body. Butchery, sheer butchery! Had I been called sooner, I could have saved both mother and child."

"I doubt it," Selene fired back. "The placenta was misplaced and caused hemorrhaging. Nothing you could have done would have saved her, and an embryotomy would have destroyed the child."

"Insolence!" Urbib turned to Antonius. "This from a chit of a girl whose father shouldn't have allowed her to leave the house, much less study medicine. Sir, would you take her word over that of a well-respected physician? Dismiss this female abomination at once."

Antonius' face turned red. He clutched his son tighter. "Leave this house. I would not have you insult the woman who saved my son's life. I trust her abilities any day over yours."

Urbib drew himself to his considerable height and looked down on both of them. "You, boy, are a fool. And you," he pointed a finger at Selene, "will be held accountable for your incompetence." He turned on his heel and stalked from the room.

Tears welled in Selene's eyes as exhaustion and grief caught up with her. Her limbs shook; she felt lightheaded. She reached for the support of a wall and slid down to a stone bench. Antonius hastily passed the baby to a servant and put his arms around her. She trembled against him, letting the tears fall silently. Melania brought her a drink and cloth to wash her face. Selene hiccupped then took a sip.

"Don't worry about Urbib." Melania soothed. "He does not credit women with the same abilities as men. It offends him that you, not he, saved the baby. His pride will recover."

Selene looked at the determined crowd of women. The praying ladies consoled Honoria's wailing mother with stories of their own losses. The servants equally divided between caring for Honoria's poor battered body, comforting the infant, and cleaning up the bloody room.

"I've done all I can. I want to go home and sleep for a week." Selene looked around the floor. "Where's my bag?"

"Here." Antonius knelt and helped her pack the instruments. They finished the task in silence. "I'll see you safely home."

She looked into his face, feeling lethargy so profound she thought she might fall asleep on her feet. "Thanks." She pushed a curling tendril of hair out of her face. "I could use the company."

"Would you like to walk, or should I ask for the litter?"

"I need fresh air. Would you walk me home?"

"Anything you ask." Antonius took the heavy bag of instruments from Selene.

They walked to the door in silence, and exited onto the broad avenue. Selene breathed deeply of the evening air, trying to purge the stink of blood and death from her lungs. Antonius took her hand. She had a vague notion this was unseemly, but was too tired to protest.

As they approached her father's home, Antonius' grip tightened. "I never loved Honoria, but I had no wish for her death."

"I know." Selene squeezed back. "She was a good friend to me and loved you very much. She did everything in her power to make you happy."

"She tried, but there was one thing she couldn't do for me." He stopped in the shadow of the portico, cupped his hand under her chin, and whispered, "She could never be you."

He bent to kiss her lips, but she turned her face so he brushed her cheek instead. "We shouldn't be doing this. Honoria isn't cold, much less decently buried and mourned. Antonius, I can't talk to you now. I'm so tired, I don't know how I feel."

"When can we talk?" he asked bitterly. "At the funeral? At the christening? Family and friends always surround us. We never have a moment alone." His jaw firmed. "I gave you up once; I won't again."

"What has changed since we last talked of this?" Selene looked into his haunted eyes. "Honoria's dowry will go to her son. Your father and mine struggle to meet the taxes and keep their councilor obligations. We are a year older and not much wiser."

He pulled her closer. "We can find a way, Selene. I swear it."

She shook her head. "Not tonight. Let this tragedy play out. We'll talk again."

He opened his mouth to protest.

She put a finger to his lips. "Soon. I promise. But you have a wife to bury and a newborn son to care for."

He let her go, trailing his fingers down her arm as she turned to enter the house. "I love you," he whispered.

"I know," she whispered, closing the door.

CHAPTER 30

ELENE TOLD THE SERVANTS not to disturb her, and went to her room. She barely had energy to strip off her soiled clothes and unpin her hair before dropping into an exhausted, nightmare-ridden slumber. Just after dawn, she woke, unable to go back to sleep. Her mind kept reviewing the events of the day before. At the thought of Honoria, her throat constricted and tears threatened. Before she gave way to another round of weeping, Selene swung her legs over the side of the bed, intending to throw herself into the day.

She heard a soft knocking at the bottom of her door. "Enter."

Rebecca shoved the door aside with her hip, her arms laden with a tray of food and a pot of hot water for washing.

"Rebecca, you're an all-seeing oracle! Were you waiting outside my door?"

"Not me." Rebecca smiled. "But I did tell Anicia to let me know as soon as you stirred. I didn't expect you up quite so early."

Selene ran a hand through her tangled hair. "It's not my choice. My body's schedule doesn't seem to include sleep." She yawned. "I need to go to Mother Nut today. We have many patients…" her voice trailed off at Rebecca's concerned face.

"Is that wise? You've just recovered from the plague, and Honoria's death must be quite a blow to you."

Selene's shoulders slumped and she bowed her head. Rebecca put down the tray and sat next to her on the bed. "I'm sure you did everything you could."

"I did. Even Melania couldn't save her." Selene choked back a sob. "I'm sure the Good Lord has his reasons for whom He chooses to take, but they aren't clear to me."

Rebecca sat, arm around her shuddering shoulders until Selene's stomach growled. "That is perfectly clear. If I know you, you haven't eaten in two days." She rose briskly. "I brought your favorite sharp cheese, figs, and pomegranates. Food in the stomach has a way of soothing the heart."

During the leisurely breakfast, Rebecca convinced Selene to stay home and rest. "Check up on the household, read to your father, take a nap," she advised.

Afterwards, Rebecca helped her dress. Then Selene wandered to her father's study, still immersed in her pain. He was already up and studying correspondence.

"Father, what are you doing up so early? You need your rest."

"I could say the same for you, child. You look worn to the bone. You try to do too much."

"Much needs doing. If I don't take care of it, who will?"

"Rebecca is a sensible young woman. Phillip was right in convincing me to take her back. You could leave more of the household duties to her."

"I already do, Father. She's my secret." Selene smiled. "I rarely make any decisions about the household. She stands in my stead, so I can keep up with my studies, do my apprenticeship, and nurse you."

"I don't need that much nursing anymore." Calistus harrumphed and eyed her speculatively. "I've had plenty of opportunity to think lately. I've been a selfish old man, keeping you at my side. It's more than time you married and started a family of your own."

"I was under the impression there were few suitors knocking on your door." Selene laughed softly. "I've been told on good authority that my unorthodox education and proclivity for waywardness make me a most unsuitable match."

Calistus' face flushed. "Who dares say such things to my daughter?"

"Calm yourself, Father!" She poured him a glass of watered wine. "The mothers of most of my friends have made no bones about their distaste. That I work at a profession makes me an outcast in my circle. Have you noticed I am rarely invited to other girls' homes? Their mothers don't want me infecting their daughters with wild notions." Tears came unbidden to her eyes. "Honoria was one of the few friends who never changed. She loved hearing about my 'adventures,' as she called them, and never tired of giving me advice on attracting a husband."

"I know you will miss her." Calistus patted her hand. "You have given unsparingly. Now is the time to think of yourself. You are a beautiful girl and

I'm not without influence. We can find you a suitable match. With a husband and children of your own, those peahens won't dare snub you."

Selene thought of Antonius. Would his father require a large dowry from his next bride? "Father, I do not want you to bankrupt the family for my dowry. I know we are doing poorly and have been for the past few years." This time her father turned pale. "It doesn't matter. I chose this life and I'm grateful to you for allowing my choice."

"But I feel I've failed you." Calistus bowed his head into his hands and mumbled, "What kind of man can't provide for his family or arrange for a suitable husband for his daughter?"

Selene moved behind his chair, reached down, and hugged his thin shoulders. "You are a kind, loving man who has provided quite well for me and my brothers. Many Christian women give their portions to the church and devote their lives to contemplation and good works. I'm no worse off than they; in many ways, much better."

"Fatherless widows!" he snorted. "If they had a man to look out for them, they wouldn't be reduced to such circumstances."

"Father, those women have a true calling, as I do. Besides, there are a few virgins among the penitent—if they have their father's approval. Please don't regret your decision to let me study medicine. I certainly don't." She kissed his cheek. "You should be more worried about marrying off Phillip. Has he said anything to you about a prospective match? We could use children around here to liven up the place."

Before he could retort, a male servant entered with a message. Calistus unfolded the missive and read. "It's from Antonius. Honoria's funeral is in two days."

Selene's sorrow settled like a shroud on her soul. "Of course. I'll send word of our appearance."

SELENE PREPARED FOR THE FUNERAL with listless attention. Rebecca picked out her clothes and jewelry; dressed her hair in the tiny rows of curls and braids that were the current fashion. Selene's thoughts were colored by guilt and despair; her emotions a downward spiral.

She regretted letting Rebecca talk her into staying at home. It gave her too much time to think and feel. The last two days had been as emotionally exhausting as the previous two had been physically. Antonius' last kiss seemed to burn her cheek, and his dark sorrowful eyes haunted her asleep and awake. When Selene thought of his hands on her, her breath quickened and a wonderful tingling throbbed from deep in her groin. How could she feel this way, with Honoria lying cold in her sarcophagus?

Did she mean what she had told her father? Did she really want to spend the rest of her life a virgin, in service to medicine? Most girls her age were safely espoused, many with child.

Even if she wanted to marry Antonius, could she? Their families were no better off than before. She had little she could expect as a dowry. Selene chewed her lower lip. She could live with Antonius as his concubine. Some girls of respectable families with no dowries resorted to that, but the church frowned on it. She knew how to keep from getting pregnant, so no children would suffer her shame.

She shook her head. She couldn't do that to her father.

"Selene! Will you keep still? How am I to finish your hair if you're bobbing like a duck?"

"I'm sorry. I can't seem to concentrate on anything." She looked at Rebecca in the mirror. "Will you marry Phillip?"

The brushing hesitated. "No. I cannot marry your brother."

"Do you love him?"

"I do, but love is not enough."

Selene's shoulders slumped. "I had hoped you and my brother, at least, could manage happiness." She grabbed Rebecca's hand and pulled it against her cheek. "I think of you as a sister. You know that, don't you?"

"I do." Rebecca's eyes filled with tears. "In a different time or another place, it might be possible, but not now, not here."

"Why?"

"I will not convert to the religion that persecuted my family, and this city will not tolerate a councilor's son with a Jewess for a wife, much less a former servant, a penniless dependent. Phillip would be shamed and shunned, unable to take his rightful place in society."

"There might be a way. Orestes is his patron. Phillip could have an imperial appointment if he gave up his intrigues and settled down to a real occupation."

Rebecca smiled.

Selene realized the incongruity of her talking about Phillip's wild ways and blushed. "What I say is true. There's no reason for you not to marry Phillip if you truly want that grinning monkey."

"It's not that simple." Rebecca shook her head. "I feel unsafe in this city. Every time I go into the street, I feel eyes on me; hate dogs my steps. What I saw in the camps haunts my sleep. If I had any other recourse, I would pack up Aaron and leave for Judea. Only you and Phillip keep me here."

Selene rose and hugged her friend. "I didn't know. But surely, as Phillip's wife...?"

"No. I've already refused Phillip." Rebecca dashed tears from her eyes. "He left this morning to visit your father's outlying farms. He said when he returns in a fortnight he will ask me again to marry him. I won't accept. He needs to look elsewhere for a wife. On his betrothal day, I will ask you for money to travel to Jerusalem."

Selene suppressed a flicker of bitterness at the prospect of desertion by yet another friend. Rebecca deserved her affection, not recrimination. Besides, she had a fortnight to change Rebecca's mind.

SELENE ENTERED ISION'S HOUSE with trepidation. After Antonius' kiss, she felt unready to deal with him or Honoria's family. She stumbled on the low step from the peristyle to the garden. Her father put out his own unsteady hand to lend her support. Selene met his soft brown eyes and her own welled with tears, which she let trickle down her face. A servant led them to the viewing room.

Honoria lay in a splendid marble sarcophagus. The lid standing on end next to the coffin was covered with Christian symbols—an ankh, a lamb in a meadow—mixed with traditional Egyptian death scenes. The Sky Goddess spread her wings over the world in protection while an ibis speared fish in the Mother Nile.

Arete stood weeping beside the casket. Ision greeted the guests. A troop of professional mourners wailed softly in the background. They would ululate more passionately during the procession to the necropolis.

Selene approached the casket with her father and looked in. Honoria was smaller in death than in life, her body tightly wound in linen smelling of cloves and camphor to mask the scent of decaying flesh. A lapis-lazuli encrusted necklace rested on her chest, matching earrings adorned her ears, and an elaborate black wig covered her own hair. The mortician had been clever with the cosmetics. Her normally ruddy skin seemed the complexion of white peaches, her lips and cheeks rouged the palest red, as if she would at any moment open those lips and breathe.

Selene searched the face for a sign of the friend who had stood by her through all her wild escapades. Nothing. No hint of past laughter. No portent of future bliss. The presbyter would tell them Honoria went to a better, more perfect world; they should not mourn her passing, but rejoice in her salvation. Those thoughts didn't fill the emptiness in Selene's soul or soothe the bitterness of her failure to save her friend's life.

A touch on her shoulder brought her head up. "Selene, thank you for coming." Antonius stood so near she could smell the cedar fumes on his best clothes.

She stepped back and offered her hand. "I'm so sorry. I wish I could have done more."

His eyes begged for a response beyond the mundane, ordinary utterances of neighbors and friends. She averted her gaze, unprepared to give him what he most wanted.

"Murder was not enough?" Arete hissed, eyes blazing. "If not for you, my daughter would be alive, suckling her babe."

Antonius grabbed his mother-in-law's upper arm in a vise-like grip, spinning her to face him. He said, in low angry tones, "Enough. If not for Selene we would have lost the babe too, and you would be without a grandson as well as a daughter. I won't have you speak so to the woman I...the woman who saved my son!"

Arete jerked free with a startled glance. She searched Antonius' face. Her mouth twisted into a bitter smile. "So that's the way of it. Out of respect for my daughter, I say no more today. But keep this, this—butcher!—out of my sight."

Selene retreated to her father's side in shock. He put his arm around her shoulders. Arete had been there. She had seen the lengths to which Selene had gone to save the baby. Had not Melania explained what had gone wrong? Selene whispered to her father, "We should go. Lady Arete is distraught and seems to believe me culpable in Honoria's death."

Antonius turned and addressed her father. "You must ignore Lady Arete. Honoria's unexpected death came as a shock. When she has had time to mourn, she will come to her senses. To leave now would give credence to her wild accusations."

256

He put his hand under Calistus' elbow and ushered them from the room. "Come have refreshment." Antonius escorted them to a table laden with food and wine, where mourners mingled and chatted in low tones appropriate to the occasion. "I must attend the other guests, but will be back shortly."

Selene, alarmed at the prospect, detained him with a hand on his arm. "We will be fine, Antonius. It is not seemly that you escort us. This day you should be with your family and Honoria's."

A hurt look flickered over his face, quickly replaced with a stoic smile. "Of course."

Within an hour the last of the guests arrived and the crowd assembled for the funeral procession. Two burly servants covered the sarcophagus with the heavy lid, and eight more lifted it on poles. At the head of the procession, Ision's resident monk chanted a dirge and carried a palm leaf. One of Honoria's younger sisters carried a basket of flowers, strewing petals in the path. The scent of crushed roses wafted to Selene's nostrils, reminding her of Honoria's wedding. Had it been only a year ago?

Antonius, Arete, and Ision walked after the casket. Ision supported his wife, who wailed incessantly, sometimes drowning out the professionals. Honoria's sisters, Antonius' brothers, more distant family and, finally, friends and neighbors followed. Only royalty could be buried within the city walls, so the procession took a straight path down the broad avenues toward the western necropolis. People stopped in the street and bowed their heads in respect.

Ision had bought into a particularly fine crypt, built before the Christian era. The procession stopped at the underground entrance, which resembled a miniature Greek temple. The bearers lowered the sarcophagus by ropes down a deep well encircled by a spiral staircase. The mourners descended the steep stairs through flickering torchlight into a vestibule flanked with two semi-circular niches, each containing a stone bench. The niche ceiling was carved to resemble a shell. Selene and Calistus rested on the benches while he caught his breath.

Selene shuddered at the weight of earth and stone above her. Her breath came quick. Cool sweat broke out on her skin. She recalled herself following her mother's sarcophagus into a dark room; feeling lost and trapped forever underground. She took several deep breaths to steady her heart.

"Come, Father, let us pay our last respects." Selene stood and held out a hand. Calistus rose with a grunt and took her arm. They moved into a central rotunda covered by a domed kiosk and supported by eight pillars. Rooms containing burial chambers radiated behind the pillars. Selene smelled food from the banqueting hall on the left, and spied another staircase, decorated with the shell motif, leading to an upper story and more burial chambers.

They made their way past Honoria's resting-place, a niche cut deep into the living rock, big enough for the sarcophagus. A stone carved with her name, dates of birth and death and the epitaph "Beloved daughter, loving wife and mother. Go with God" stood to one side, ready to seal the opening. Hundreds of sealed niches, stacked ten or more high, stretched into the gloom. Selene ran her fingers over names and dates, wiping dust onto her dark blue robe. Most that lived beyond childhood had died in their thirties and forties. Only a few had more years than her father.

She clutched his arm tighter. "Let's leave this place."

They left the burial chamber and entered a chapel. Relief carvings on either side of the door showed bearded serpents next to the staff of Hermes and the pinecone of Dionysius. Inside, Christianity held sway. The monk presided at an altar adorned with a beautiful embroidered silk cloth. A wooden cross hung on the wall. The floor mosaics of an intricate geometric design sported no mythological characters to compete with Christ and his Holy Mother.

Selene's father spied Lysis standing next to the monk. They approached and Calistus clasped his old friend by the arm.

Lysis smiled. "It's good to see you both looking so well." Selene accepted the polite lie, thinking Lysis looked particularly hale.

"We are sorry for your loss." Calistus looked sober. "You spoke well of Honoria as a daughter. I'm sure you will miss her."

"She was a good girl and I'm sure she has gone to a just reward." Lysis sighed. "Will you join us at the banquet after the services?"

The idea of enduring several more hours in this place of death tightened a band around Selene's heart. She spoke quickly. "I fear not, sir. My father still needs his rest and it's been a tiring day."

Calistus turned to protest, saw the pleading look on his daughter's face and subsided. He patted her hand in understanding. "Yes, my friend. We cannot stay more than a few minutes. I have strict orders to nap every afternoon, and it is time I attend to my physician's wishes." They clasped forearms in a farewell grip and Selene escorted her father out of the chapel.

"Thank you, Father. I could not take much more public mourning."

"That's what fathers are for, my dear, to rescue their daughters, if only from unwanted social obligations."

She squeezed his arm. "You do so much more for me, Father. This loss helped me realize how truly blessed I am with my family."

Calistus smiled gently as they ascended the steps in easy stages. He fell asleep in the litter home.

SELENE RESUMED HER APPRENTICESHIP with Mother Nut, throwing herself into the work during the next week. She gradually let go her feeling of having failed Honoria; and comforted herself with the knowledge she had saved Honoria's son.

This particularly long day she came home exhausted and filthy. She gave her cloak to a servant and went immediately to the bathing room. She stood stripped, ready to enter the hot water, when Rebecca arrived.

"Your father wants to see you right away."

Selene looked longingly at the bath and jar of massage oil. "Can't it wait till after my soak? I stink of onions and smoke."

"He said it was very important and I should fetch you to his office as soon as you arrived home." Rebecca smiled. "Though I'm sure he will wait while you dress."

Selene sighed while Rebecca helped her back into her filthy tunic and robes. "Keep the water hot for me," she said to the waiting servant.

They traversed the warren of private quarters down the stairs to the public rooms. Rebecca denied knowing what was so important. Selene entered her father's study almost breathless. He sat at his desk, holding a piece of paper, looking inordinately pale.

"Father, what is wrong? It's not Phillip? Nicaeus has not been harmed?"

"No, my child, your brothers are fine." He handed the paper to her. The Augustal Prefect's seal adorned the outside.

Selene read the note and collapsed onto a bench.

CHAPTER 31

CALISTUS PICKED UP THE NOTE:

Selene, daughter of Calistus, is hereby summoned to give testimony concerning her role in the death of one Honoria, wife of Antonius, at the behest of Ision, Honoria's father, in the offices of the Augustal Prefect.

She was to appear the next day at mid-morning.

Calistus' hands trembled. "What is this about, Selene?"

"I don't know, Father. You saw Lady Arete's grief at Honoria's funeral. Perhaps she wishes someone to blame for Honoria's death."

"Or perhaps Ision has some twisted scheme in mind. The man has gotten entirely above himself. How dare he drag my daughter down to the Prefect's office like a common criminal?"

"Not so common, Father, if the Prefect conducts the inquest. If not for your position, I might already be condemned before a magistrate."

"Ision has no right to accuse you of anything other than saving his grandson."

Selene absently fingered the broken wax seal as her father vented his anger. Had she contributed to her friend's death? Had her feelings for Antonius influenced her actions?

No. Melania had not faulted her.

When her father took a breath, Selene rose from the bench with renewed determination.

"I'll send someone to help you to the solarium, Father, and will join you there for dinner." She indicated her filthy robes. "After I'm bathed and more suitably attired." Selene kissed him lightly on his bald spot. "Don't worry. Orestes is a fair man. This is a misunderstanding."

REBECCA HELPED HER DRESS in sober clothes for the inquest: a dark blue dalmatica, with rich but subdued embroidery, over a long-sleeved tunic. No belt showed off her womanly attributes, but a voluminous wrap of snowy white doubled as a head covering. She chose small gold earrings, shaped like lucky scarabs, and a matching bracelet from her mother's jewelry. Rebecca applied subtle cosmetics to enhance her pallor and draw attention to her eyes, but not so obvious she could be accused of vanity.

In the silver mirror, Selene looked older than her almost seventeen. Rebecca studied her critically, twitched a piece of the wrap into a more appealing drape, and pronounced her ready. Then she pulled Selene into a fierce hug, undoing all her careful arrangements, and whispered, "This is all a mistake. You'll be back safe this afternoon. We're all praying for you."

Selene mumbled thanks and fled to the vestibule. Her father sat on a bench by the door, dressed in his best robes, bedecked with the honors of his office. He looked so frail. Selene wished to spare her father the ordeal of this day. If only Phillip, or even Nicaeus, were here. But Phillip couldn't be reached for several days and it would take as many to return. In his last letter, Nicaeus had told of being posted to the Thracian border. She said a silent prayer for the safety of both her wandering brothers.

Calistus used a walking stick to rise. His steely eyes reminded her he was a man of substance in this city and not just her beloved father. "Come, Daughter. It's a father's duty to protect his family. Let's sort out this affair and restore my good name."

"Of course, Father."

She offered her arm and they exited to the street. A litter took them to the central government building, a massive but elegant pile of marble-faced limestone, located on the agora. The tops of the Greek columns, carved with Egyptian plants and animals, towered four stories above Selene's head. She had walked by the building many times, but never had occasion to enter the imposing legal center of the province.

She felt dwarfed.

They entered a cavernous waiting hall with benches pushed against the wall. Small groups of people milled about, talking to their advocates or awaiting the opportunity to speak to a magistrate. Clerks carrying messages and books scurried purposefully from one room to the next.

Calistus indicated a side corridor. "The Prefect's offices are this way."

They moved leisurely, to accommodate the ailing man, and entered a smaller, much better appointed anteroom. There were carved benches with cushions, elaborate floor murals of Poseidon and his sea creatures, and stucco walls decorated with beautiful paintings of Nile scenes. In one corner, atop a wooden chest delicately inlaid with ivory, was a silver tray holding dates, figs, and a glazed pitcher with matching goblets.

Ision, Arete, Urbib, and several servants took up one side of the room. Ision was deep in conversation with a small man in monk's robes. Antonius and his father Lysis stood by the chest drinking wine. Seeing them enter, Lysis strode over, clasped Calistus' forearm, murmured, and led him to a bench. Urbib pointedly ignored Selene's brief bow in their direction, but Arete glared with the baleful gaze of a wild dog protecting its kill.

Antonius approached, face haggard, shadows around his eyes and bitter lines at the corners of his mouth.

"Antonius," Selene spoke in low tones, "I wish we met under happier circumstances. How fares your son?"

Antonius reached toward Selene, then vaguely waved his hand in the air instead. "Despite the terrors of his birth, the child thrives. The wet nurse tells me he has a lusty appetite."

"I'm pleased." Selene's smile turned anxious. "Antonius, what do Honoria's parents accuse me of? Why are you here?"

"I am implicated as well."

"Implicated in what?"

Antonius took a deep breath. "Ision was waiting when I returned from escorting you home that night. Urbib convinced him he could have saved Honoria's life, and you were incompetent or possibly had criminal motives. I explained how you saved the baby when Arete stormed in, clothes in disarray, streaming tears. She screamed at me not to defend you, using names I would not repeat to your face. I left her to Ision to control.

"All seemed well the next morning, so I put it down to Arete's grief. The day after Honoria's funeral, Ision asked me to leave his house and wouldn't let me take the child." His mouth quirked upward. "Knowing how shrewd Ision is, I suspect him of taking advantage of Urbib's professional jealousy and his wife's grief to take control of the baby, and through him Honoria's dowry."

"Surely not!" Selene's hands flew to her face. "How could a man use his family so?"

Antonius' smile faded. "He sold his daughter for my family connections. I've worked with the man for the past year. He uses anything and anyone to get what he wants. I don't inherit Honoria's money, her child does, but as his father, I control it. To take the baby, he has to discredit me. I'm afraid you're caught up in his schemes." Antonius looked grief-stricken. "I'm sorry, Selene. I would give anything to spare you this."

"I know," she replied softly. "Orestes is a fair man. He will recognize the truth when he hears it." She refrained from touching his arm, from offering a small token of comfort.

Selene turned back toward her father as a door in the far wall opened. A well-groomed man in the Prefect's livery stepped inside. "I'm Demetrius, the Prefect's secretary. I'll record the proceedings. Are all the parties represented?" Heads nodded. Demetrius held the door open and motioned into the next room. "Please proceed."

Being closer to the door, Ision's party filed into the chambers first, followed by the others.

Orestes sat at a massive table completely cleared of all papers, which were piled haphazardly on a second, narrower table behind the Prefect's chair. Ision, Arete, Urbib, and the monk took chairs in front and to the right of the table. The servants stood at the back of the room.

Selene hesitated as she entered. Orestes looked intimidating in his official robes. He looked in her direction, giving no hint of past association. Selene shivered at the lack of acknowledgement and sat to the left of her father. Demetrius came in last, closing the door and proceeding to a chair behind and to the left of Orestes. He took out a lap desk, paper, ink, and pen.

Orestes cleared his throat. The soft rustlings of people settling themselves stopped.

"Good morning, citizens. Given the parties involved, I will function as magistrate in this inquest into the death of Honoria, wife of Antonius, daughter of Ision. If I determine the death was in any way unnatural, formal charges will be brought against appropriate parties. I'll ask you to present your information one at a time, and I will ask the questions. Each of you will be given opportunity to speak. Do not interrupt while others are talking. Citizen Ision, you consider yourself the aggrieved party in this affair. Come forward and state your position."

Ision approached the table. "Thank you, Prefect, for hearing our tragic story." He bowed to Orestes. "Ten days ago, my much beloved oldest daughter went into labor with her first child. Shortly after sunset we called in Mistress Melania, a well-respected midwife, to attend her. The midwife pronounced that all was as it should be and the birth progressed normally. After several hours, Antonius, my daughter's husband, came to visit her. He entered the room against my wife's wishes and talked briefly with my daughter."

Orestes addressed Arete. "Why was this against your wishes, Lady?"

"It is unseemly for a husband to be present in the birthing room," Arete answered from her seat. "That is a place for women."

"I see. Please continue, Ision."

"The slaves attending my daughter at the time overheard Antonius suggesting that Selene, daughter of Calistus and friend to Honoria, be summoned."

"I did no such thing!" Antonius jumped from his seat.

"Quiet!" Orestes thundered in a parade ground voice. Selene flinched at the harsh tone, clasping her father's hand. Orestes continued, in a stern voice, "If you interrupt the proceedings again, I will have you removed."

Antonius sat down.

Orestes addressed Ision. "The hearsay of slaves is not compelling. Did you or your wife overhear this conversation directly?"

Ision shook his head. "No, but shortly after his visit my daughter insisted her friend be present. My wife saw no need for help, but Honoria became quite irrational. Arete, seeing no harm, agreed—much to our later sorrow."

"Your wife seems to have strong feelings about men in the birthing room. Were you present for these conversations?"

"No, sir. My wife relayed this information to me later."

"Then I wish to hear directly from Lady Arete." He motioned to her. "Would you please tell me what happened when Lady Selene was summoned?"

Arete stiffly approached the table. "I sent a servant and litter to Calistus' house to collect that woman—" She shot a venomous glance at Selene.

"Lady Selene?" Orestes inquired.

"I mean Selene, daughter of Calistus," she spat. "I would not give my daughter's murderer the title of Lady."

Selene gasped, hand to chest. Murder? Not medical misconduct?

"No one has proved murder, Lady Arete," Orestes said flatly. "Please proceed in a more tempered tone."

"She arrived attired in butcher's clothes, worn and stained with the blood of other victims," Arete continued coldly. "She refused to pray. Shortly after she arrived, the pains became harder, Honoria bled heavily, and the labor did not progress. Melania suggested we have Urbib attend."

"This took place in the middle of the night. Did Urbib arrive by daybreak?"

Arete shuffled slightly. "No. Physician Urbib did not arrive until evening that day."

Orestes frowned. "Was he delayed?"

"No. Melania did not make the suggestion until then."

"A skilled midwife let your daughter bleed heavily for all those hours?" Orestes frowned. "That seems negligent on her part."

"The bleeding didn't start until late afternoon," Arete mumbled.

"I see. Your sense of 'shortly afterward' is somewhat different from my own." Orestes brought the tips of his fingers together in a wedge. "What happened then?"

Arete blushed furiously. "By the time the good physician arrived, it was too late." She burst into tears. "That demon spawn cut my daughter open, murdering her before my eyes. I tried to stop her, but Antonius held me back. I couldn't save my child from the two of them!" Arete collapsed, sobbing, into her husband's arms.

Selene gripped her father's hand until he winced. Did Arete truly believe Selene capable of such a horrendous act? Antonius stared at his in-laws in horror, the blood draining from his face.

"We'll give Lady Arete a few moments to compose herself." When the sobbing subsided, Orestes continued sympathetically. "I understand your loss, Lady, but I must ask you a few more questions. Do you think you can go on?"

Arete straightened, dabbing at her eyes with a linen cloth. "Yes, Prefect."

"Good. When did Antonius make his second appearance in the birthing room?"

Arete frowned in concentration. "I was praying in the chapel when I heard shouts. Melania appeared and said I should come at once. When I got to the birthing room, she," Arete pointed at Selene, "was in the bed with my daughter, shaking her. Antonius ordered the servants and Melania out of the room. Melania argued, then stepped back when Antonius threatened her. That's when that woman took out a knife, cut open my daughter, and pulled the baby from her womb. When she found it stillborn, she performed an unholy ritual, compelling its innocent soul back into its body."

"Was your daughter dead when Lady Selene performed this operation?"

"I don't kn—. I don't think so." Arete cast a swift glance at her husband.

"You were not in the room when your daughter died?"

"No, I was in the doorway. He wouldn't let me pass." She reserved a venomous look for Antonius.

"And Lady Selene delivered to you a live healthy infant?"

Arete's gaze softened with a brief smile. "Yes, we now have a grandson."

"Can either of you tell me why Lady Selene would have murdered your daughter in front of a room full of witnesses?"

"I don't believe she acted alone." Ision paused for effect. "I believe she and my son-in-law, conspired to make Honoria's death appear as a natural consequence of the birth."

Selene closed her eyes. She couldn't breathe the air; it was so thick with malice.

"Why do you believe that?" Orestes asked.

"My daughter Honoria loved Antonius, but the boy was reluctant. To spare her feelings and make her happy, I pledged a substantial dowry to Lysis to make the match, thinking the boy would settle down after marriage and do right by my daughter. But I kept a close watch on him. It soon came to my attention, through a trustworthy slave, that Antonius was unhappy with the union and had wished for another."

"How had this slave reached this conclusion?"

"He attended Antonius and his friend Nicaeus in the baths, and overheard a conversation touching on Antonius' affection for Nicaeus' sister Selene." Ision pointed at Antonius. "He proposed to abandon his wife and persuade Selene to run away with him. The girl is prone to wayward behavior and might have agreed."

Selene's chest constricted and hands trembled. How much was truth, how much did Ision fabricate for his own ends?

"I have no doubt Antonius would have followed through had not Honoria announced her pregnancy soon after." Ision turned back to Orestes. "The opportunity of staging a seemingly natural death in childbirth was too good to pass up. Antonius engaged the help of his lover and murdered my child!"

Her father started to rise. Selene tugged his hand, shaking her head. Calistus settled back, his dark expression boding ill for Ision. Over his shoulder she saw Antonius' stricken face and Lysis' barely contained fury.

"You offer nothing but your own suppositions, Ision. Refrain from using the term 'murder' until such time as wrongful death has been established." Orestes frowned. "I will not allow the testimony of slaves. Nicaeus is not available to give evidence. Have you or your wife observed anything directly?"

"Yes!" Ision threw back his shoulders. "On the night of my daughter's death, Antonius took that woman into his arms and comforted her under my own roof. He then accompanied her to her father's house. My suspicions aroused by my servant's reports, and Urbib's words, I followed them. I couldn't hear what they said, but they held hands during the walk, and at her home they embraced." Ision's rotund form seemed to swell as he raised his voice. "Antonius kissed that woman, with my daughter not yet dead an hour!"

An angry murmur swept the room. Orestes' cool gaze quelled it. "So you believe Antonius and Selene conspired to kill your daughter for love of one another. Why would Selene try so hard to save the baby? Would not an infant be an impediment?"

Ision's voice rang with triumph. "They planned this not just for love, but for greed. If Honoria died without issue, her dowry would come back to me. Antonius needed that baby alive to keep control of Honoria's wealth!"

CHAPTER 32

CALISTUS AND LYSIS both rose, shouting. The red spots on her father's cheeks boded ill for his weak heart.

"Father, be seated." Selene rose to calm him. "For my sake, if not your own."

"Enough!" It took Orestes a moment to bring the room under control. He stood, raking Ision, Calistus and Lysis with his gaze. "All of you, conduct yourselves with the gravity this inquest merits. This is my last warning." Lysis, Calistus, and Selene took their seats. Orestes waited for total silence, sat, then turned to Ision. "Conspiring to commit murder is a grave charge. Both Antonius and Selene come from old, well-established families. Why would they do such a horrible deed for money?"

The merchant turned a scornful gaze on his social betters. "Lysis and Calistus have suffered financially in recent years due to the shortfall in crops. Both children might look upon this as an opportunity to help their families."

"You've described considerable suspicious behavior." Orestes sat back, both hands on the table. "But I haven't heard proof that Honoria died in any way other than a tragic childbirth."

Urbib stood up. "Sir, that is why I am in attendance."

Orestes nodded to Ision and Arete. "You may sit down." He motioned for the physician to come forward. "Who are you, and what light can you shed on this dark story?"

"I am Urbib, physician to many of the most prominent citizens in Alexandria." He bowed. "I don't believe I've had the pleasure of attending you, Prefect."

"I've had the fortune of good health during my tenure." Orestes' mouth turned up at one corner. "Your reputation is known to me."

Urbib crossed his arms, hands to opposite shoulders, and gave a deep bow. "I am here to give my professional opinion about this unfortunate matter. I have no knowledge of motive, but I do have prior experience with the so-called medica Selene. She attended the odd class or two on philosophy, and apprenticed herself to a notorious Egyptian witch, who claims to heal with herbs and charms. Selene isn't qualified to be a midwife, much less a surgeon. She had no business attending Lady Honoria."

"And yet she performed successful surgery, saving the baby's life."

"At the expense of the mother's. There was no need for such drastic measures. Had I been in attendance, I would have repositioned the fetus in utero, allowing the child to be born naturally. My examination of the body revealed significant blood loss. I believe Honoria was still alive when Selene cut her open to retrieve the child. The shock of the wound and loss of blood killed her."

"Were you present at the moment of Honoria's death?"

"No. I draw my conclusions from the condition of the body and profuse amount of blood on the bed." The physician curled his upper lip into a sneer and glanced at Selene. She met his gaze, eyes steady, but gut knotted. "A wound made after death does not bleed as a wound made in life. The bed was soaked in blood from the incision Selene inflicted on Lady Honoria, causing her death."

"Thank you for your learned opinion. Be seated. I will hear from Antonius now."

Antonius approached the table. "What would you know of me?" He bowed to Orestes.

"You've heard the accusations made against you. State your side of the tale."

"I do not dispute most of the facts as laid out by Ision. I did agree to the match reluctantly, but Honoria was a good woman and I did my duty as a husband, forsaking all others. When she became pregnant, I was happy, and honored her before God as the mother of my children. I never conspired with Nicaeus to abandon my wife or persuade Selene to run away with me."

Antonius took a deep breath. "The night Honoria went into labor, she sent a servant to fetch me. Lady Arete did, indeed, try to keep me away, but I honored my wife's wishes. Honoria asked for Selene. She wished her friend to be present and trusted Selene's medical skills, as well. I opposed the idea."

"You opposed Lady Selene attending your wife?" Orestes looked startled. "Why?"

"Selene and I have been friends since childhood. At one time I believed I was in love with her and proposed marriage. She refused me, and I felt the rejection deeply." Antonius lifted his chin. "My love for her passed, but the sight of her pricks my pride and reminds me of my failure. That night, Honoria insisted on Selene's presence. I finally acquiesced, leaving the room before she arrived."

A lump of unshed tears choked Selene's throat. Antonius' lies protected her, but they made it impossible to ever be together.

"The next evening, a slave came to me in frantic haste, saying I was to attend my wife immediately. When I arrived, Honoria was hemorrhaging. Blood soaked the bed. I held her hand as she breathed her last. After Melania closed my dead wife's eyes, Selene proposed saving the child. I agreed to let her try. The baby was delivered blue and still. Selene acted quickly and revived it. Afterwards, we comforted each other, but not in secret, behind closed doors as guilty lovers or conspirators. Selene was devastated by the loss of her friend. I mourned my wife. We openly showed our grief in the company of Honoria's family. I escorted Selene home and, in our mutual sorrow, we did embrace one final time. I kissed her on the cheek, as I would a sister, and went home to my son.

"Prefect, I swear to you before Almighty God that neither I nor Selene had any malice toward Honoria. Her death is a tragedy for us all. Out of that tragedy, Selene saved my son. I will be eternally grateful to her. Her courage and action should be the subject of praise, not condemnation."

Ision muttered to the monk. Arete hissed. Orestes directed sharp glances at them, then returned to Antonius. "A pretty speech, my lad, but, as Ision pointed out, you have much to gain by my believing your story. What proof do you offer?"

"No more than Ision. My word should be as good as the testimony of slaves in my father-in-law's service," Antonius stated bitterly. "As he has accused me of greed, so could he be accused. By asking for my son, he gains back the considerable sum he bestowed on his daughter for her dowry."

Ision stood and ground out, in low tones, "I'm protecting the sole male heir of my family from his treacherous father!"

"Sir, be seated!" Orestes snapped. Ision glared at the Prefect as he sat. Orestes turned back to Antonius. "Have you anything to add?" Antonius shook his head.

"I believe Lady Selene hasn't had an opportunity to speak. Please come forward."

Selene gathered her robes and approached the table, avoiding Antonius' gaze as he passed her. "I have little to add, sir. I did indeed attend Honoria, as did midwife Melania. We were unable to save her although, through the grace of God, I was able to safely deliver her son."

Orestes nodded. "The main point of disagreement is when Honoria actually died. Physician Urbib says that the profusion of blood could only have come from the wound of a living body. Antonius claims his wife died before your surgery."

"Urbib is correct; the dead do not bleed in the same way as the living." Selene took a deep breath. "I discovered after delivering the baby, the afterbirth partially blocked the birth canal. The birth process caused excessive bleeding. Honoria experienced a massive hemorrhage before she died. The blood on the bed was from that, not the incision I made to deliver the baby."

"Why did you try to save the child?"

"As I held Honoria's body in my arms, I felt the baby move. I had no choice." Selene clasped her hands and lowered her head. "I had seen enough death."

"Lady Arete claims you refused to pray for Honoria, and used an unholy ritual to force the baby's soul back into its body."

Selene's head snapped up. "It's true I did not join the ladies in the chapel, but I prayed to God every minute to spare my friend and allow her child to be born healthy. The 'unholy ritual' referred to is a simple technique I learned in my apprenticeship. I have assisted in many births. In a few the babies are stillborn. The medica I study with has saved a handful by blowing into their mouths. It doesn't always work."

"What of you and young Antonius conspiring to wed after Honoria's death?"

"Antonius is a dear childhood friend. He has been like an older brother to me. Had my father proposed the match three years ago, I would have accepted. But I have chosen a different path, with my father's blessing." Selene lifted her chin. "I will never marry."

Orestes tapped his teeth with a fingernail. "I admit I'm in a bit of a quandary. Both stories have merit and no one here is without motive."

"There was one other person present at Honoria's death, Melania, the midwife," Selene offered. "She can attest to the truth in this matter. She is a penitent in the church and has nothing to gain in either material wealth or reputation."

"Why was she not included on the list of witnesses?" Orestes glared at Ision.

"I believed the word of a physician to carry more weight than that of a mere midwife," Ision said. "Urbib has nothing to gain in this matter."

"Is that so?" The merchant returned the Prefect's stern look, blandly. Orestes turned to Demetrius. "Summon the midwife."

The monk stood up. "Prefect, Penitent Melania has been sent to a cloister of holy women in the desert to serve God. She is not available to attest to these facts."

"Hierex, what interest does the Patriarch have in this case?" Orestes asked.

Selene started. What possible connection could the teacher she had heard so much about have with this matter?

"Why, none, sir." Hierex held his hands palm up in a gesture of openness and trust. "I am here as friend and spiritual counselor to Ision and his family. I happened to know the whereabouts of Melania and volunteered the information."

"That seems rather convenient."

Hierex shrugged.

"In the absence of any concrete proof of wrongdoing, I allow both Antonius and Selene to return to their families; however, Selene will refrain from practicing her profession. The child, Honorius Posthumous, will remain with Ision and his family until final disposition of this case. I ask that neither of the accused parties leave Alexandria. Their fathers will hold surety for their presence." Orestes rose from his desk. "You will be summoned when I have obtained the person of, or a sworn statement from, midwife Melania. Until such time, this inquiry remains open."

Demetrius went to the door and opened it. The families filed out in carefully spaced clumps. Selene, supporting her father, left last. She glanced over her shoulder to see Orestes frowning over his notes.

Selene could not count on her family's relationship with the Prefect. Her fate rested on the word of one woman.

ORESTES LOOKED UP when Demetrius returned. "That hearing turned into a viper's nest. Who do you believe?"

"They all have motives." Demetrius shrugged. "The curial class has been hit hard by the local cycle of draughts. The grain taxes do not abate because of poor crops. The two young people could have conspired to gain control of Honoria's dowry. On the other hand, Ision is tight with his money and might bring a specious charge to get the dowry back."

"I agree. This case has too many opinions and too little evidence. Discounting slaves and servants, there were three witnesses to the death, and two of those are under suspicion. Urbib's testimony was most damning, but he examined the body after the surgery."

"The man is a prominent physician, but well known for his political astuteness. He personally approached the Patriarch and begged to be converted from Judaism to Christianity immediately after the riots," Demetrius quietly observed. "And it is well known Urbib has taken a personal dislike to Selene since he declared her father as good as dead, and she nursed him back to health. Calistus' very presence is a rebuke to his professional competence. Selene saved the child and again put doubts in people's minds as to his value. His testimony is not without its own taint."

"Yes." Orestes stroked his chin. "If it were anyone other than Selene, I might rule in Ision's favor. The circumstances are most suspicious." He shook his head. "I can't imagine Selene at the center of such a cold-hearted plan. I know her family and I know her. She's bold and impulsive, but a murderer? No."

Again Demetrius shrugged. "Who knows the heart of a young woman? Many crimes have been committed in the name of passion. Maybe it wasn't planned. Perhaps she saw an opportunity to rid herself of a rival and took it."

Orestes stood, leaving the notes for Demetrius to order and put away. "I don't believe that, either. There is opportunism at work here, but it is not Selene's. We must talk to the midwife Melania." He paused, leaning on the table. "Another question: Why was Hierex here? I confess I see no advantage to Cyril with either outcome."

"That is a cunning puzzle. Perhaps we look too deeply. Possibly Hierex is a friend of the family and spiritual advisor."

"It is too much a coincidence that Melania is affiliated with the church and conveniently out of the way for this hearing." Orestes snorted. "There is a deeper game here. I intend to find out what. I need someone I can trust to find Midwife Melania." He looked directly at his slave. "Will you undertake the commission, Demetrius?"

"Of course, Master." Demetrius bowed and began tidying the room.

Orestes started for the door, then turned back. "Take an escort and leave first thing in the morning."

CHAPTER 33

I T HAD BEEN MANY YEARS since Demetrius ventured outside the city walls and many more since he'd ridden a horse. His duties and inclinations kept him firmly in government buildings. Regular exercise kept him trim, but riding strained muscles rarely used, and chafed areas he didn't know could be chafed.

Within an hour, his thighs burned and cramped. He suffered the rough humor of the two guards who served as his escort as he squirmed in his saddle and tried to ride with one leg, then the other, crossed in front. When they reached the solid walls of the Convent of Isaiah rising out of the rocky desert, Demetrius sent a prayer heavenward for his deliverance. The stone walls were blank, except for one high arch indicating the position of a small door—the only entrance he could discern. He dismounted and collapsed against his horse. The blasted animal skittered away as the guards grinned at his discomfort.

Demetrius limped to the door and pulled a rope hanging nearby. A sweet bell chimed in a small parapet above the entrance. A head sporting an excessive beard and bald pate poked out of the parapet window, then disappeared. Demetrius heard the unmistakable sounds of the gate being unbarred. The door swung open.

The gatekeeper looked with pity as Demetrius limped inside. "Good sir, did you come to commission healing prayers for your affliction?"

Demetrius' mouth pursed as if sucking a lemon. "No, I've come seeking a penitent woman, one Melania, most recently a midwife in Alexandria. I was told she came to this convent. It is most urgent that I speak with her."

The gatekeeper sucked his teeth and shook his head. "I will see what I can do. Please come to our guesthouse for refreshment."

Demetrius motioned to the two guards, who dismounted with practiced ease and led the horses inside to a low shed containing feed and water. On the way to the guesthouse, Demetrius noted with surprise that men and women worked an olive press, baked bread at a communal oven, and tended palm trees and gardens. In addition to the expected churches, refectory, and sleeping cells, Demetrius spied a granary and a mill. The monks and sisters likely produced other necessities, such as cloth and paper. A drawbridge from the parapet on the wall led to a keep; a final retreat if enemies attacked. It made sense that the inhabitants should do as much for themselves as possible. The next town was hours away, and the villagers surely could not support the growing population of the monasteries.

At the guesthouse, the gatekeeper settled them in a cool, comfortable room, provided them with water, left, and soon returned with a middle-aged woman in black robes. "This is Helaine. She is in charge of the sisters." The lady's face was saved from plainness by striking blue eyes that sparkled with kindness and good humor.

The gatekeeper returned to his duties.

"Mistress Helaine, I am Demetrius, a personal agent of the Augustal Prefect. I've come to find and question the midwife Melania about a matter most grave. Can you assist me in my mission?"

"I'm afraid I have bad news for you, good sir. Mistress Melania left here after a few days. She said Patriarch Cyril had asked her to visit the desert convents and attend to the health of the cloistered sisters. She traveled on when all who required her services had been tended."

Demetrius tried to keep disappointment from his face. This mission was becoming more than a simple interview. "Dear Lady, have you any notion of Melania's destination?"

Helaine shrugged. "The next monastery is but a few hours' ride. You can reach it by nightfall." A series of bells sounded outside the guesthouse. She glanced out the door, then back to Demetrius. "You and your escort are welcome to join us for noon meal. It is simple fare, naught but water, bread, and onions, preceded, of course, by the nourishing words of God."

Demetrius saw grimaces cross the faces of his escort and briefly entertained the notion of staying. Instead, he rose to take his leave. The movement sent a shooting pain from his buttocks down the back of his legs. He drew a sharp breath and grabbed the back of his chair.

One of the guards caught his elbow to steady him and said, in a kinder voice than Demetrius expected, "Perhaps we should stay and let you recover from your journey."

"No. Being still stiffens me. I'll recover once we're moving." Demetrius turned to Helaine. "Thank you for your offer of hospitality, but the sooner we move, the sooner we find Melania and complete our mission."

They both bowed. Demetrius and his escort headed for the gate. They gnawed hard journey bread on the way to the next monastery, and arrived shortly before sunset.

Melania was not there.

Orestes arrived at Hypatia's public lecture in time to hear an angry man protest, "God created the earth and set the sun and moon orbiting about it in the sky. Who is this pagan Aristarchos who says differently?"

"A learned Alexandrine mathematician and astronomer who lived over 600 years ago," Hypatia replied. "The Bible tells us that God created the heavens and earth. It doesn't tell us in what configuration He arranged them. God could have as easily set the earth to spin around the sun."

Angry mutters broke out in the crowd. Orestes admitted sympathy with the dissenters. It comforted him to think the sun, moon, and stars revolved around the earth; that God set the heavens in motion and kept them firmly in place.

"My father Theon came across Aristarchos' work and made confirming observations. The calculations are quite compelling. I think the prevailing belief has more to do with politics than science. The vain human desire to believe ourselves the center of the universe clouds the truth." Hypatia concluded, "I will entertain discussion on this topic at my home Tuesday next."

Men clustered, arguing vigorously about the merits of the hypothesis. Those with more mathematical training shouted to Hypatia for sources as she left the lectern.

"If you wish to see the original treatise, it is in the Library. My father Theon also published commentaries on the mathematics."

Thinking about the earth spinning through a vast empty space around the sun, Orestes experienced a sense of vertigo. He looked at his feet. The ground felt unmoving.

Orestes shook himself free of the reverie and moved through the crowd. Men bowed and gave way. He acknowledged several city officials and councilors as he approached Hypatia. "Lady, I need your advice on a less celestial matter."

"My pleasure." She bowed gravely to Orestes, then dismissed the others crowding about her. Hypatia linked arms with him. "Shall we retire to my rooms, or stroll the gardens?"

"Fresh air suits my needs admirably." He smiled. "Do you actually believe the earth and other planets race around the sun?"

"My observations of the heavens are consistent with Aristarchos' theories, though few here will concur." Weariness settled on her face. "Sometimes I feel the great scientific thinkers are all in our past."

Orestes indicated the vast complex of buildings and grounds of the Caesarion. "It takes patronage to maintain such an institution. The Ptolemaic Pharaohs built this for their own aggrandizement."

"But they did the world an incalculable service in collecting the Great Library and sponsoring so many scholars. Now the Church sponsors the scholarship. I'm one of the last non-Christians with a public chair." Hypatia learned on Orestes' arm. "I can't help thinking I live in the twilight of this great age of learning."

They walked past meticulously maintained hedges and beds of both native and exotic flowers, to a shady retreat under two massive date palms overlooking the harbor. Hypatia sat on a stone bench. Orestes sprawled at her feet, hands behind his head, looking up at the azure sky through the palm leaves. He laughed. "My staff would be most surprised to see me like this. They think I eat spikes for breakfast and spit them at clerks for exercise."

"Perhaps you are too hard on them?"

"I don't ask them to do anything I don't ask of myself. I live and breathe my office. They, at least, go home to families and entertain friends. I have many allies who will make common cause with me, but few approach me with a true face and open heart. I count my friends on one hand, and you are first among them."

"I'm honored by your trust, and hope my advice serves you well."

Orestes rolled onto his stomach and looked up Hypatia. "How fares your student Selene? I cannot inquire directly of her family without it seeming prejudicial to my neutrality."

"Are you neutral in this case?" Hypatia asked with a raised eyebrow.

"I believe I can make a fair judgment on the evidence."

"I visited Selene two days ago." Hypatia gazed out at the boats in the harbor and sighed. "She seemed worn and distracted. She has worked herself too hard since her illness, and I fear a relapse."

"Could guilt be contributing to her decline?" Orestes asked coolly. "Do you feel there is any merit to the charges?"

"At the risk of disturbing your neutrality, I will say with the utmost conviction that Selene is incapable of such a heinous deed." Hypatia smiled gently. "I've known her father since his youth, and Selene for three years as my student. I've looked into the girl's soul."

"Given the opportunity to save her father through the death of a friend, would she take it?"

"Never." Hypatia's voice rang with conviction. "She would consider such a deed the ultimate betrayal of her family."

"She has grown from the naive girl I first met at her father's house into a remarkable young woman." Orestes paused. "But this midwife must corroborate her story or I will be forced to bring charges and hold her, and possibly Antonius, for a capital judgment."

"But conviction of capital crimes means death!"

"The mildest punishment would be to sew both conspirators into a sack, weight it with lead and throw them into the river to drown." The lines on Orestes' face deepened. "Given the nature of Honoria's death, Ision would likely demand they be disemboweled alive and their entrails burnt."

Hypatia's eyes went round with shock. "You are the Prefect. Can you not do something?"

"I can recommend clemency in sentencing, but I cannot pardon the crime without undermining all I've worked for."

"I had not realized the case was so damning." Hypatia slumped on the bench. "What can we do?"

"Very little."

DEMETRIUS RANG THE BELL at the Convent of Macarius, a community established by a fellow Alexandrine. From outside, it was little different from the seven others he had visited. Some had men only, others women only, some mixed communities swore celibacy, but all practiced a form of asceticism designed to prove the superiority of the spirit over the flesh. Many holy ones refused to bathe or comb their hair.

The thought reminded Demetrius how desperately he wanted a bath. His own stench combined with his physical discomfort sparked a flash of bitter resentment. He toyed with the idea of escaping to freedom, living out what remained of his life on a small plot of date trees. The vision of a comely wife and a flock of children at his knee faded as someone unbarred the gate. Demetrius shook his head to rid himself of the last vestiges of impossible visions. He had duties to perform.

A tall woman, with the sun-brown complexion of native Egypt, swung the gate wide and asked his business. Demetrius stated his mission in well-rehearsed words and braced for rejection. The woman smiled, showing many gaps in her teeth. "Midwife Melania has been with us a few days. We had an illness and she graciously stayed to help nurse the unfortunate ones."

"Could I see her?" Demetrius leaned forward in his eagerness to enter the compound and complete his mission.

The woman stepped back. "This way. I'll let Melania know you're here." She escorted the small contingent to the guesthouse and set out water and dates. "We haven't much. With the sickness and all, we've not ground grain, much less baked bread in days."

"Perhaps we could repay your hospitality by doing work in the compound. We would gladly be of service."

The Egyptian woman eyed them speculatively. "We'll see."

In the guesthouse, Demetrius unpacked paper, ink, and reed pens, grateful at last to be doing his job. The guards squatted in a corner and began dicing. Their money had changed hands many times on the journey. Demetrius considered lecturing them on the evils of gaming in holy places, but after the first day they had been pleasant if crude company. They had given him salve to ease his pains and make the journey bearable.

It was the better part of two hours before the dark woman returned with a sister wearing the short hair and rough robes of a penitent. The new woman was in her middle years, with lines deepening around dark eyes and a generous mouth.

Demetrius bowed. "Are you the midwife Melania?"

She looked him over with curiosity. "Yes."

"I am Demetrius, personal agent to the Augustal Prefect. I've come to take a sworn statement from you concerning the events surrounding the death of one Honoria, wife to Antonius, daughter to Ision."

She looked troubled. "Am I under suspicion of wrong doing? Does the Patriarch know of this interview?"

"This is an inquest. No charges are levied against you. We want nothing more than your honest recollections of the events. The Patriarch was informed of my mission. If you wish to have another present, that is permissible. Otherwise, my escort will serve as sworn witnesses."

Melania slipped her hands up the voluminous sleeves of her robe and gripped her elbows. "It is not necessary to bother the other sisters. Childbirth is a chancy thing. The best midwives lose patients, but Honoria's death was unexpected and particularly horrifying. I will gladly answer your questions."

"Will you have a seat?" He ushered her to a chair and placed his portable lap desk on his knees. "Let's start with your assessment of Honoria's condition when you first were called to her bedside."

CHAPTER 34

SELENE TRIED NOT TO FIDGET as the families reconvened in the Prefect's audience chambers. Weeks of confinement, following the first inquest, left her edgy and depressed. She worried about Mother Nut. Rebecca had found her hut empty, and no one knew where she'd gone. Selene submerged her anxieties in exhausting physical labor. The house had not been so clean since her mother's death.

Everyone settled on the benches. Hierex and Urbib flanked Ision and his wife. Honoria's sisters sat in a knot behind them. Lysis, Antonius, his two brothers, and a family retainer versed in the law occupied most of the remaining places.

Lacking family, friends and clients, save for Calistus' comforting presence, Selene felt vulnerable. She missed her brothers. Maintaining a brave face for her frail father taxed her reserves.

If Phillip were here, with his ready smile and strong arms, or Nicaeus with an outrageous story to occupy her mind. But Nicaeus would only now be receiving her letter somewhere on the border, and they had received word yesterday that Phillip was ill with fever and could not travel. Fear for her brother's health upset Selene's fragile balance.

She searched Orestes' face for a sign of her fate. He did not look at her, but maintained a neutral mask. Selene tried to still her racing heart. She clutched her father's hand. Orestes looked up from a sheet of paper and cleared his throat.

The room quieted.

"My apologies to all parties for the lengthy wait between inquests. Midwife

Melania proved more difficult to locate than anticipated." Orestes nodded toward his secretary, several shades darker and considerably thinner. "I have a sworn statement from Melania describing the events as she saw them before and after Lady Honoria's death."

Orestes' eyes tracked the writing on the paper.

Selene held her breath.

"Among other details, Melania claims Lady Honoria died of excessive bleeding due to a misplaced placenta and no external or internal manipulation of the fetus could have saved the mother's life. She further states Lady Selene delivered the child after the mother's death using a known surgical procedure. She further testifies that Selene revived the child using a technique unknown to her. Midwife Melania believes Lady Honoria's death to be an act of God, not the deliberate mischief of man or woman."

Selene let out her breath in an explosive puff, her knotted stomach unclenching. Calistus' hand trembled in hers.

Orestes continued. "Based on this sworn testimony by a neutral witness corroborating the statements made by Lady Selene, I see no purposeful wrongdoing or accidental misadventure in the death of Honoria, wife of Antonius. The Prefect's office declines to bring any charges against Antonius, son of Lysis, or Selene, daughter of Calistus. In addition, the child known as Honorius Posthumous shall be given over to his father Antonius, who will make all decisions concerning his upbringing, education, and inheritance."

Selene felt as if a smothering blanket had been removed from her head. She wanted to laugh hysterically in relief, but suppressed the urge.

Arete sobbed. Ision stood, fists clenched, face turning purple. "You can't give my only grandson to that man!"

"It is not for this office to come between a man and his offspring. Children belong to their fathers." Orestes' gaze sharpened. "You, sir, will hand over the child to his father by the end of the day or face the displeasure of this office."

Hierex stood. His nasal tones cut through the initial hubbub. "Prefect, I understand your office is relinquishing jurisdiction in this matter?"

"No. We have found no grounds for prosecution. If additional evidence comes to light, we will entertain it at a later time."

"New evidence of a serious nature has come to light. The Patriarch asked me to take Lady Selene into custody to be examined by the Church in connection with witchcraft. She used an unholy method to return the child's soul to its body."

Selene collapsed against Calistus. His arms circled her protectively. Witchcraft! She glanced quickly at Antonius, who sat in stunned silence, blood draining from his face.

Orestes flushed, a vein throbbing visibly in his temple as he rose to his full commanding height.

"By what right does Patriarch Cyril interfere in this matter?"

Hierex bowed slightly to the Prefect, then pulled his lips into a sly smile. "You are quite aware that Emperor Theodosius chartered each of his Bishops with the spiritual health of his people. That includes investigating charges of heresy, witchcraft, and sorcery, and the disposition of people found guilty of such crimes. Whether or not you decided to prosecute, the Patriarch would be obligated to look into this matter."

"What evidence do you have of such conduct by my daughter?" Calistus' voice quavered.

Hierex turned to Calistus. "All in good time, sir. We need a private interview with Lady Selene. Will you kindly deliver your daughter to the Patriarch's offices after the noon meal?"

Calistus moved between the Patriarch's minion and his daughter. "I will do no such thing unless I am assured of Selene's safety and good health."

"Her immortal soul is in perilous danger. Only the Church can save her from the influence of malignant people or demonic spirits." Hierex' eyes hardened. "I strongly recommend you have her there at the appointed time." He turned back to Orestes. "Good day to you, Prefect."

Hierex made his way to the closed door of the chambers. A servant let him out. Ision gathered his entourage and followed the monk, pausing briefly to send a triumphant look toward Calistus.

Orestes left the protection of his table and approached the two remaining families. He extended his hand and Calistus clasped his forearm. "I'm sorry, councilor. This did not turn out as I wished." He bowed to Selene. "There is nothing I can officially do in this matter. Cyril has full jurisdiction."

"Why is the Patriarch doing this?" Selene asked. "I attend services regularly; do good deeds among the poor. What harm have I caused?" She trembled as much with anger as with fear.

"I have a theory about why." Orestes' face hardened. "I believe you are not the target of Cyril's interest, Selene." He took her right hand in both of his. "I will be present at this inquiry. I may not be able to do anything officially, but you will have my full support." He smiled, and the cares of his years and office seemed to drop from his face. "And my personal resources are considerable."

Selene smiled back, struck as she had been three years ago by the cool power of his emerald eyes. His tenure as Prefect had added lines to his face. Gray threaded the auburn hair of his temples, but he still carried his height with the grace of an athlete. His bureaucratic duties had not added an ounce of fat to his lean frame, or bowed his soldiers' stance. He radiated confidence.

Selene murmured thanks.

She looked up in time to catch the despair, rage, and guilt that flashed across Antonius' face. He approached and ushered her to a quiet corner while Orestes consulted with her father and Lysis. "I feel so helpless, Selene. This is my fault. If I hadn't agreed to marry Honoria, if I had followed my heart instead…"

She put a finger to his lips. "You made the best choice you could at the time. What's done is done."

Antonius lightly kissed her fingertips. She jerked them away, looking about to see if any had observed his rash action. He recaptured her hand and asked, in a low voice, "Did you mean what you said at the inquest?"

Looking into his bruised eyes, Selene's feelings crystallized. She had told the truth. She loved Antonius, but as a friend and brother. That would never be enough for him. He was obsessed with her, but blind to her needs and feelings. He wanted sympathy and absolution when she needed strength and assurance.

"Yes. I meant what I said at the hearing." She withdrew her hand. "Our chance at happiness together is past. Lavish your love on your child. Your love for me can only do harm."

Antonius' spoke through clenched teeth. "It's Orestes, isn't it? I saw how he looked at you."

"Orestes is a good friend to our family." Anger suddenly blazed through her. "Had you told the truth at the hearing and trusted Orestes to be fair, you could be more help to me now. Instead you lied, and any action you take on my behalf will be interpreted as proof of that lie."

Antonius' face blanched, leaving a greenish tinge to his dusky complexion. He dropped his head. "Of course. I handled this whole matter badly. I hope you can find it in yourself to forgive me, Selene."

Before Selene could take back her angry words, he turned away, collected his father and brothers, and left the room. What passion she had felt for him blew to ashes in the cold wind of her pity. He still thought only of himself.

Selene and Calistus left shortly after. She leaned heavily on her father's arm and was, for once, grateful for the stuffy litter which took her home. Calistus remained quiet while she gazed between the curtains. She felt like a piece of laundry battered on rocks, prodded with wooden poles, and finally twisted tight to remove the water.

Selene put her hand to her forehead and closed her eyes. She dampened her anger and tried desperately to stifle the fear that crept out of the dark places in her soul. Her eyes snapped wide, the whites showing around the deep brown irises. The litter seemed to close in around her. She wanted to leap into the crowd and run as she had never run before. Her body tensed for flight as her father spoke.

"Selene, my child, I will let nothing harm you." Calistus gathered her in his arms and stroked her hair. "No doubt this is all a mistake. I will speak to Cyril. If he does not listen to reason, I will marshal the council."

Selene trembled in the illusory safety of her father's arms, willing herself to believe he could put the pieces of her shattered life back together.

HIEREX ESCORTED SELENE into the Patriarch's presence. Her father and Rebecca remained in a sitting room, separated from her by two beefy parabolani guarding the door with cudgels.

Orestes had not appeared.

Selene hid her shaking hands in the long sleeves of her dalmatica and tried to present a calm face. After all, she kept telling herself, she had done nothing wrong.

Cyril sat at a dark desk on a low platform flanked by an elderly monk and an empty chair. Oil lamps, hung in an overhead chandelier, banished the shadows into the corners. He scanned papers and jotted notes with a quick hand. Selene approached, stopped five paces from the desk, and bowed. Cyril continued writing. Hierex took the empty chair.

Quiet moments stretched to minutes, disturbed only by the scratching of the reed on paper. Selene silently repeated a round of prayers. The old monk's head nodded as he slipped into a doze.

Just as Selene felt she couldn't take any more silence, Cyril pushed the documents away and looked down at her. His expressive brows came together over his nose in a frown, shadowing his eyes. He cleared his throat.

The old monk jerked awake, gazing vaguely around. A rude noise erupted and a sulfurous stench pervaded the room. Cyril wrinkled his nose and muttered to the old man about his diet of lentils and onions.

Selene hid a smile behind another bow. "I am at your service, Patriarch. What would you know of me?"

"Ah, yes, Lady Selene." Cyril regained his composure. "Serious charges have come to our attention. We have many questions for you."

"What charges, Holy Father, and from whom?"

"You have been accused of sorcerous acts. Your accusers need not be revealed. It is enough that the evidence presented to the Church substantiates the charges. This interview is to see if you are irredeemably damned, or if we can save your immortal soul."

Selene rocked back on her heels. She had been accused, judged, and condemned behind these walls without any defense. Her blood raged at the injustice, but she felt an outburst would hurt her cause.

Selene lowered her gaze and said, in a low clear voice, "I ask that you allow my father to examine the evidence against me and speak to you on my behalf. I swear before God, Jesus, and the Virgin Mary that I am a good Christian."

Hierex looked at her with ill-concealed malice. "Do you deny worshipping other gods, participating in pagan rituals, and holding souls in thrall by means of a pact with a demon?"

"I do." Selene's eyes grew wide. "I have never engaged in witchcraft. Who says differently? What is the evidence?"

Hierex' thin lips turned up slightly, as he consulted his notes. "Lady Selene, it has come to our attention that you frequently attend the sick in the poorer neighborhoods. Is that correct?"

"Yes. The Patriarch urges us to do good deeds in the way of Christ."

"Why do you choose to minister to the pagan Egyptians and Jews?"

"What better way to show the charitable nature of our Lord Jesus?"

"Do you proselytize to the pagans?"

"No. I minister to their bodies, not their souls."

Hierex pursed his lips. "A pretty and benevolent picture, my dear, but a fiction to cover your real activities. It is well known that you consort with a notorious pagan woman, commonly called Nut after the Egyptian sky goddess. Even her name is an abomination. Witnesses say the two of you cast spells, using prayers to demons and profane objects to affect your poor victims."

"That's not true! Mother Nut is a healer and I'm her apprentice. We've never consorted with demons. Ask any of our patients."

Hierex' smile grew broader. "Ah, but we have. Many have described the rituals the two of you perform and have provided these." He tossed a handful of fired clay objects on the table.

Mother Nut's charms of teeth, blank-faced heads, and small votive statues rattled to stillness.

Selene's breath hissed as she drew it in.

"Do you deny you pray to a pagan statue?"

Selene lifted her chin. "Of course I do. I was raised a Christian. I do not pray to foreign idols."

"Then explain the presence of this in your room."

Hierex pulled out the small statue of Isis and baby Horus that Mother Nut had given her for her father.

A chill gripped Selene's bowels as she recognized the trap and realized her inability to avoid it. She had no one to shield her. Nothing on her side but her pride and the truth. It wouldn't be enough.

"Mother Nut gave it to me as a gift. I do not worship it."

Her denial seemed to inflame the monk. "How do you account for your survival of the plague? All who attended the unfortunate heathens died. Why did you survive, unless you sold your soul to the devil?"

"Another lived. A woman dressed in gray who tended the children."

"Yes, the Blessed Mother of God." Hierex settled back on his seat, a smug smile blooming on his face. "All know She came to take all the deserving souls to heaven. Obviously she found yours unworthy."

"You twist the truth. Mother Nut attended me. With her skills, and the grace of God, I survived the plague."

"Your own father called the woman a witch, and claimed she held his servants under a spell, while she tended you during your illness."

"You cannot condemn me on the hearsay of servants." Selene straightened her back. "I am a councilor's daughter."

"Quite right." Hierex smiled. "Do you deny casting a malignant spell over Lady Honoria, causing her death, and clearing the way for your marriage to her husband Antonius?"

"That was settled at the inquest. You were there and heard the testimony,"

Selene said, aghast at the renewed accusation. "I cast no spell. Honoria was my friend!"

"Do you deny using a demonic ritual to compel the soul of the infant Honorius Posthumous back into its dead body?" he thundered.

"Yes, I deny it." Tears came to Selene's eyes, but her voice was steady. "I used a medical technique to save the baby's life."

Cyril held up his hand for attention and leaned forward. "Lady Selene, given your youth, and the impressionability of the female nature, we realize that you might have been led astray, overly influenced by evil personalities. This Egyptian woman has already confessed her demonic connections and died unrepentant."

His words stunned Selene. A knot of raw grief closed her throat. She croaked, "Mother Nut is dead?"

Cyril waved his hand as if removing an annoying insect. "The witch was but a small piece of the puzzle. We want to get at the heart of this conspiracy against the Church. It is my understanding you take classes at the Museum with the pagan woman Hypatia. Is it true you two are intimates, and she sponsored your admittance as a student?"

She looked Cyril directly in the eyes, puzzled by this sudden turn in questioning.

"Hypatia did, indeed, sponsor my studies. I attended classes on natural history taught by her as part of my medical studies. I also attend private lectures at her home on philosophy and astronomy."

Hierex stroked his chin. "Yes, it is well known that her father tried to fathom the influence of the stars. Hypatia follows in his footsteps in such sorcerous behavior. She is known to be devoted to astrolabes and other magical equipment. Did she ever include you in demonic rituals?"

Selene shook her head at her own stupidity. It should have been obvious to her by now that everything she said would be twisted to evil purposes.

"I have nothing to say about Lady Hypatia other than to praise her intelligence, compassion, and ethical behavior."

Cyril looked at her as would a loving and disappointed father. "I'm sorry, my dear, but the evidence against you is overwhelming. Unless you repent of your sins, and provide us with mitigating circumstances, we must consider you a danger to this Christian community. You will stay in our custody for the next several days and be examined again. Perhaps, if you reflect on your situation, you will discover your own salvation."

Despair curdled Selene's soul. Cyril had as much as promised her release in exchange for testimony against Hypatia. Something she could never do.

Cyril nudged the dozing monk awake. "Father Paul, our duties are concluded here. Hierex, please escort Lady Selene to her new quarters."

The old monk exited through a curtained alcove. Hierex came from behind the desk to take Selene's arm. She refused his grasp. A loud rapping came from the door, then abruptly broke off. Selene heard raised voices and a deep grunt.

Hierex pushed her through a side door before she could see who breached the Patriarch's sanctuary.

ORESTES STEPPED OVER one of the parabolani lying in the doorway and entered the room. He straightened his slightly mussed soldier's cape, ran a hand through his hair, and strode to the front of the desk.

"Patriarch, please pardon my lateness. The streets seemed unaccountably clogged with monks this afternoon. I had to abandon my chariot and come on foot." Orestes looked around, a carefully schooled look of surprise on his face. "Have you already released Lady Selene?"

Cyril coolly surveyed Orestes. Even at the Patriarch's elevation, they looked eye to eye. "I thought you had no more interest in this case."

"I am here as a friend to the family. Given her father's frail health, and her brothers' absence, I felt it appropriate Lady Selene have a man to advise her during this inquiry."

"Your services are not needed. Selene has been condemned as a witch. I cannot allow that young woman to corrupt the body of our church."

"Even the Patriarch cannot condemn someone without justification." Orestes crossed his arms. "Where is your evidence? Who are your sources?"

Cyril pointed to Mother Nut's trinkets.

"You are going to convict her on that?" Orestes laughed. "Nearly everyone in the city has bought a charm against evil, or a love philter, at some time in their life. What's the difference between that and keeping a dead martyr's bones in a fancy box to be worshipped?"

"We do not worship the holy ones' bones!" Cyril shouted; then, more moderately, "We merely ask that they intercede for us in heaven."

"I fail to the see the difference."

"That is why I have on many occasions offered to instruct you, my son," Cyril said with obvious relish. "Besides, many have seen Selene engage in unholy practices." Cyril recounted the previous testimony.

"Ridiculous!" Orestes' icy tones echoed in the chamber. "You present the gossip of servants and the lower classes as truth, and ignore the testimony of Selene's peers."

"We have the sworn testimony of an eminent physician."

"Urbib? The testimony of a man who would give up the religion of his fathers to further his career is impeached." Orestes stepped forward and leaned close to Cyril. "I have heard no overwhelming evidence in this case, Cyril. I'm asking you not to punish this innocent woman in pursuit of your own aims. What is it you want?"

"I want you to stop meddling in internal church affairs. The girl is mine to dispose of as I chose."

"We'll see." Orestes ground clenched teeth, turned on his heel and left.

CHAPTER 35

SELENE WALKED QUIETLY with Hierex through the labyrinth of church offices. Her skin twitched at sudden noises, her eyes roamed the walls noting details of color and design, mentally storing clues to her route. She breathed slowly, not wanting to appear weak or nervous in Hierex' company. She wondered if he felt ill at ease in hers. After all, if Selene were a powerful witch, couldn't she harm him?

He seemed confident of his safety.

Hierex spoke only to guide her steps: left, down, through this arch. After several minutes, he stopped at a heavy wooden door, bound in brass, and took a large ring of over a dozen keys from a hook on the wall. He chose one and unlocked the door. They descended two flights of stairs. From the cool damp air, Selene surmised they were underground.

She shivered.

The bottom of the stairs opened on a long corridor lit intermittently by flickering torches.

An old woman sat on a low stool. She rose and bowed to Hierex. He nodded. "Lady Selene will be our guest, Didyme. Show her to her quarters."

The woman looked at Selene with pity. "Come, child, to the third room." She hobbled forward on a clubfoot. The Church had probably cared for Didyme from birth, since parents frequently abandoned deformed children. Selene hoped the church fathers would show her a similar measure of mercy.

Didyme stood at the third entrance, fumbling with her own ring of keys. She finally found the correct one and opened the door. Selene crossed the threshold and eyed her new home with trepidation. She wouldn't dignify the space with the appellation "room." She could stand straight, but the rough stone ceiling loomed inches above her head. A thin layer of moldering rushes covered the floor.

She hadn't expected the comforts of home, but given her father's station Selene had anticipated accommodations more appropriate to her class. She turned to protest, but stifled it when she saw the satisfied look on Hierex' face.

"We leave you alone to reflect upon your actions. I advise using this time to pray; ask the Good Lord to bring your dark soul into the light. The law deals harshly with witches." Hierex' face took on an earnest look. "But you are young, and can still be saved, if you confess your sins and give up associations with the evil people who led you astray."

"I will think on what you have said." Selene bowed her head as the door eased shut on well-oiled hinges. Light trickled through a hole, barely a hand's breadth high or wide, set in the portal.

Didyme's creaky voice came from the other side. "There'll be food and water in a bit, dearie. If you need any supplies of a female nature, let me know. I'll be down the hall, on my stool."

"Thank you, Mistress Didyme. Is it possible to get a lamp and something to read?"

"I'm afraid not, dearie." The old woman clucked softly. "Nothin' more'n what I said. Food and water once a day."

Selene heard Didyme shuffle down the corridor, leaving her alone with her thoughts. She sat on the floor and bowed her head onto her knees. The room seemed smaller, crushing the breath from her. She started up and took a swift stride, bumping her forehead on the wall. The pain focused her. She paced off the cell, three strides from front to back, two from side to side.

Mother Nut had probably breathed her last in a cell like this. Selene sniffed for any lingering traces of garlic, but the waste pot in a corner overwhelmed any other smell.

No fresh air. No light. No one to talk to.

Selene felt as helpless as when Honoria had died in her arms. But then she had taken action. Now her fate rested in other's hands.

Unless—Selene slumped against the wall—she did as the Patriarch asked.

*****

"I NEVER THOUGHT CYRIL would go so far!"

Orestes had never seen Hypatia so agitated. Two spots of color danced on her cheeks as she paced her office, flinging her arms in dramatic arcs. Anger blazed from her eyes, crackled in her voice.

Orestes, with the distance of hours since his confrontation with Cyril, more calmly assessed the situation. "He has been clever, turning this unfortunate incident to his advantage. I can do nothing officially except protest. The Imperial laws give him every right to suppress heretical Christian sects, and deal with sorcerers and witches as he chooses."

A strand of smooth dark hair escaped from Hypatia's chignon. She impatiently tucked it behind her ear, eyes lighting on her desk. She strode to it, seating herself. "The Patriarch is young and not a favorite among his peers. I'll write to every one of my former students and clients installed in Bishoprics throughout the Empire, urging them to rein in Cyril's excesses." She muttered, "And they are legion," as she started a letter.

"Write to Aurelian, as well. I don't know the new Praetorian Prefect, but he was your student. I'll also send an official protest to court." Orestes rubbed his clean-shaven jaw. "Unfortunately, I don't think our efforts will bear fruit in time to save Selene. Cyril moves more rapidly than the post."

"Surely Cyril would not harm her?" Hypatia put down her pen. "The church has forbidden torture. Memories of their own martyrs are too fresh."

"She is but a means to an end for the Patriarch." Orestes shook his head. "He has already condemned her for witchcraft. If Selene, through pressure or trickery, implicates you, he eliminates your public influence. Cyril effectively severs us. You might even be in physical danger."

"Clever man." Hypatia rose and paced, hands clasped behind her back. "If Selene doesn't confess, she stays imprisoned. At the worst, Cyril gains Ision's considerable financial support and throws the fear of God into any of the curial class who oppose him."

Her face settled into lines of pain. Orestes sorrowed to see Hypatia look every one of her almost sixty years.

"Write your letters, Hypatia. Officially, we continue our efforts to persuade Cyril to reverse his judgment." Orestes rose to his full commanding height. "Unofficially, I have a considerable network of agents at my disposal."

"You can get Selene out of the Patriarch's basilica?"

"I must." Orestes said grimly. "For our sakes, as well as hers."

*****

Hierex came to fetch her on the fourth day, hours after the single daily meal of one hard biscuit and a crumb of sharp cheese. Selene had tried to keep herself presentable by combing out her hair with her fingers and braiding it down her back after each meal. She had lost the ability to smell herself, but still spared a few precious drops of water to scrub her face. At the sound of the key, Selene brushed at her filthy, rush-covered garments, adjusting her few pieces of jewelry.

As she emerged, Hierex wrinkled his nose. "I hope you have employed yourself usefully. The Patriarch wishes to meet with you."

"I would not offend the Patriarch with my presence. Could you provide me with a bath, clothes, and servant to help make me more presentable?"

"That is just a woman's vanity." Hierex' mouth quirked at one corner. "The Patriarch understands the body is the temporary repository of the soul, an envelope of clay to be sloughed off when we move to the next world."

They passed the stick-like young woman who alternated with Didyme in caring for the "guests" of the Patriarch. She was either mute or had taken a vow of silence. Selene suspected few other women shared her imprisonment. No one had answered her determined whispers when the torches went out, except Didyme, who threatened to decrease her already meager water ration.

When Selene stepped into the outer hall, light from a dozen oil lamps struck her eyes, stinging them to tears. She put out a hand to steady herself against the wall and wiped the moisture from her face with her other sleeve. She was surprised she had any tears. Her body felt as desiccated as leather, as in the throes of the plague.

The thought of becoming sick in this place sent a chill down her spine. Only Mother Nut's medical skills and her own youthful constitution had saved her before. Now, weak from hunger and thirst, she had no reserves to fight off illness, no tender care from family or friends. She straightened, but refused Hierex' proffered arm. Through blurry eyes she made out his scowl.

He grabbed her wrist. "This way."

She stumbled, then regained her feet. It felt good to move. She gained confidence as her muscles limbered, and matched Hierex' quick strides. By the time they reached the Patriarch's quarters she quite enjoyed this respite from her dark cell.

Hierex led her to an austere room beyond the formal offices. Late afternoon sunlight streamed through windows looking onto a garden. The Patriarch sat at a table laden with his dinner. Selene smelled spiced duck, saw crisp greens. Her stomach clenched. She felt vaguely nauseated.

Cyril turned at her entrance and presented her with a cut glass goblet filled with a blood red wine. "My child, would you have refreshment?"

She drank thirstily. The wine exploded in her stomach like Greek fire. Her senses spun. She looked at the Patriarch with suspicion. Would God's appointed shepherd poison one of his flock?

"Patriarch, could I have water? The wine seems not to agree with me."

Cyril nodded in sympathy, but made no move to provide water. "Yes, it does affect some that way when they have been fasting."

Selene swayed slightly, but he offered no chair. How would the Patriarch react if she fainted? Probably have her dragged back to her cell.

Selene needed to keep her wits about her, but she was so thirsty! She sipped at the wine and felt her stomach settle, but her head grew fuzzier.

"Thank you." She held out the half full goblet to Cyril. "I've had enough."

He took the glass and smiled gently at her. "So, my daughter, are you ready to cast out the demons that torment your soul? Confess to us who initiated you in pagan rites."

Selene lowered her head and said, in a clear, steady voice, "My soul is stained with imperfections, my life fraught with human frailties, but I have always strove to be a dutiful daughter to my father and my church. I am innocent of the charge of witchcraft. I have never engaged in sorcery, just sound medical practices."

Cyril looked sorrowful. "I see the devil still has his claws in your soul." He sighed. "I have unhappy news for you, my dear. Your father has been taken gravely ill. He is a most worthy man. I had hoped you would repent and be restored to him in these, his final hours."

The blood drained from Selene's face.

Cyril flicked his fingers in a dismissive gesture. "Hierex, take her back. We will give her more time to meditate on her condition."

She turned to leave.

"Selene."

She looked over her shoulder. Cyril's eyes bored into hers. "I caution you not to wait long."

Hierex escorted her back through the warren. As they approached the dark corridor he said. "If at any time you wish to speak to me, let the matron know. I will come day or night to take your confession."

Selene stumbled into her cell, numbed by the wine and the news. First Mother Nut, and now her father.

She didn't know if Cyril lied to pressure her or if her father had indeed relapsed. She didn't know if Phillip had survived his fever. Orestes had failed to save her.

Selene had never felt so bereft.

She threw herself on the filthy rushes and cried tears she could ill afford to spare.

CHAPTER 36

CRYING CLEANSED SELENE'S SOUL and exhausted her body, loosening the knot of grief in her chest. Quiet sobs eventually turned to peals of laughter. She clasped her hands over her mouth at the raucous sound. Was she drunk or mad?

Since childhood she had raced through life, meeting every challenge without thinking about the consequences. God made her this way. Was she to blame?

A stubborn core of anger strengthened her spirit. Selene had no regrets; would have done nothing different. The good that came of her actions always outweighed the bad.

Maybe that was God's lesson in this muddle: to look for the greater good. If so, it was a hard one. She would live with the consequences—this non-life— awaiting the Patriarch's punishment for being herself.

Was her soul forfeit in defying the Patriarch? The Church taught that communion administered by a corrupt presbyter did not negate the relationship between worshiper and God. Presbyters, bishops, and patriarchs were but men. Cyril may claim to know God's will, but Selene had lost faith in his sincerity.

She had been taught the Patriarch was the father of the church, a holy man doing God's work. Selene didn't believe God wanted her to falsely confess to witchcraft or cravenly betray her teacher. She had to hold to that one certainty through whatever trials came her way.

She giggled, having made a peace—of sorts—between herself and God.

Selene stared at the thin shaft of light coming through the tiny window, diverted by the dust motes. She had found it harder and harder to concentrate as the days wore on. She had heard that fasting purged the body and clarified the mind, but it seemed to make her weak and distracted.

The light disappeared with a suddenness that made Selene catch her breath. She sighed, lay back on the moldering rushes, and tried to sleep. Memories of the Patriarch's laden table tortured her thoughts. The mute woman brought no food or water.

Selene slipped into dreams of God as a spouting fountain in which she danced naked. The cool water rinsed the filth from her skin and the worries from her mind.

THE SLIGHT CLICK OF A KEY in the lock awakened Selene. Torchlight flickered through a gradually widening crack as her door opened. She sat up and blinked. The mute woman motioned for Selene to follow. When Selene started to speak, the woman put a finger to her lips, warning silence.

Selene scrambled out of the cell. The woman handed over a torch and keys, mimed ascending the stairs and running away. Selene hesitated, wanting to believe, suspecting a trap. What if Cyril provided this opportunity only to prove her deceit?

Plots and hidden motives. Trusting no one. Selene shook her head. That way was madness.

She mouthed to the mute, "What about you?"

The woman gave her strips torn from the hem of her robe. Selene tied the woman's hands tightly behind her back. She hoped it wasn't too uncomfortable.

At the top of the stairs, Selene unlocked the door and looked out. Silence smothered the corridor. Thinking she would fare better in darkness, Selene doused the torch in a bucket of sand by the opening.

She took a dozen steps before bumping into a solid body. A large, soft hand covered Selene's mouth, stifling her cry. An arm crushed her against coarse robes draping a stringy chest and sagging belly, while a voice hissed in her ear. "A friend sent me. I'm going to remove my hand. Stay quiet."

The man dropped his hand from her mouth, grasped her wrist and led her into the dim light of another corridor. Selene's savior was one of the ubiquitous lay clerks the Bishopric required to keep up with paperwork. Short, with the ink-stained fingers common to his profession and the red nose common to those with an excessive love of wine. Selene believed him the most beautiful man on earth.

He thrust a voluminous robe at her. She pulled it over her head to effectively hide her filthy clothes. She draped a fold over her hair to shadow her face. They moved down the hall through several levels, passing a male servant tending the lamps and a woman carrying a tray.

The woman looked at them curiously. "The latrines are this way, Brother Samuel," the clerk said in low, but distinct, tones as they passed her. "I hope your trip back to Cyrene tomorrow is a pleasant one."

They turned a corner and passed out of the building into a moonlit garden surrounded by a stone wall. The clerk inspected the garden for late night visitors, then hurried her to a low door shadowed by vines. "Someone will meet you on the other side."

Selene grabbed his hands. "I don't know how to thank you. I don't even know your name!"

"It's better you not know, Mistress, and no need to thank me." He patted a small purse hanging from his belt. "I've been thanked already."

"May God be with you." Selene ducked through the door.

Her new contact, dressed as a parabolani and carrying a cudgel, materialized from the shadows. "This way, Lady."

He looked at the three-quarter's moon approaching its zenith and frowned.

They walked abreast for several blocks. At the corners, she stood in shadows, while he looked down the cross streets. Selene, alert to any sound, started when she heard voices. At the next corner a patrol of parabolani caroused past them. They seemed drunk. Her escort flattened Selene against the wall with an outstretched arm. Her heart rose to her throat as one of the men broke off from the pack and headed in their direction.

"Where you going, Menas?" one of his fellows shouted after him.

"I gotta piss." Menas wobbled toward the wall and relieved himself, sighing with pleasure. Something in the shadows—a flutter of robe, a glint of light—caught his wandering attention. He quickly covered himself and strode toward them crying out, "Who goes there?"

Her escort whispered, "Forgive me, Lady," and enveloped her in a passionate embrace. His stubbled chin scraped Selene's face and his breath smelled of onions, but she returned the kiss with all the art she could muster.

Menas grasped her escort and spun him around. "I said who goes there?"

"A fellow parabolani, minding his own business. Why don't you mind yours?"

Four of Menas' companions ambled over. "What's you got, Menas?" When they saw Selene tucked close to her escort's side, they hooted, "Rousting lovers, now?" Then, to her escort, "Looks dangerous. Do you need any help?"

He gave them a broad wink. "Thanks for the offer, but I can handle this duty myself." He gave Selene another sloppy kiss, much to the delight of their audience.

"Sure you don't need help? How about sharing the duty?"

"Goodnight, boys!" He put his arm about Selene's trembling shoulders and escorted her in the opposite direction. Around the corner, Selene's knees gave way. He lowered her against a rough plastered wall.

"I'm sorry about the kisses, Lady."

"We do what we have to." Selene croaked. "Could I have water?"

"Only a little farther and you'll have all you can drink."

Selene rose and they continued another two blocks to a small limestone kiosk decorated with murals depicting water carriers. Her escort opened a door in the kiosk and entered. Selene ducked after him. The air was cool and heavy with moisture. She heard water lapping on stone. They followed a spiral staircase down to a cavern with a vaulted ceiling supported by pillars. Water filled the cavern within inches of a platform where the stairs ended. A small boat was tethered to a ring sunk into the wall. There was one torch, and the water stretched beyond the light.

"What is this place?" Her voice echoed from the dank shadows.

"The cisterns. Alexander had the city honeycombed with them, in case of siege. They provide water to most of the private homes."

"I thought we got our water from the lake. How big is this place?" Selene asked.

"This is one of the smaller ones. They're all connected by underground canals and pipes." He set aside his cudgel and reached for the rope to pull the boat closer.

Selene knelt on the mossy stone and scooped water into her mouth. The cool liquid coursed down her throat. After she had her fill, she scrubbed her face with a wet hem. She didn't feel clean, and her skin itched with insect bites, but she felt more like herself. She looked up to see her escort sitting patiently in the boat, oars in one hand, torch in another.

"I'm sorry to keep you waiting." Selene settled herself in the bow, facing the man. "Where are we going?"

He handed her the torch and grinned, showing a gold tooth. "To a friend's."

Up to now, she had avoided thinking about the agent of her escape. Had her father arranged this? Was Phillip back? She supposed she would find out soon. In exhaustion, Selene closed her eyes and listened to the water. The sound soothed her raw nerves.

They continued to a conduit wide enough to accommodate the boat, but had to duck for safe passage. After several minutes they entered yet another enormous reservoir divided by stone columns, like a drowned temple.

The man seemed certain of his destination, so Selene did not burden him with her doubts. At one point, she nearly dozed off and dropped the torch into the water. Her companion's sharp cry saved them from plunging into darkness.

"I'm so sorry!" Fear coursed along her nerves, banishing sleep. "That won't happen again."

"If it does, don't worry." He grinned. "I know these cisterns better'n my mother's face. I can find my way in light or dark."

Selene was not inclined to test her guide's prowess.

"We're nearly there, Lady, just beyond that pillar."

She looked over her shoulder. Another platform materialized out of the dark. He guided the boat to the dock. Selene stepped out. He tied the boat to another ring, took the torch and led her up stairs carved in the side of the wall. They came up in another kiosk at the bottom of a substantial hill crowned by the Prefect's residence. Selene filled her lungs with the smell of sweet honeysuckle and the briny tang of the sea.

Demetrius waited for them. He gave the man a purse and her escort disappeared into the watery underground with a quick bow.

"This way, Lady." Demetrius pointed up the hill to the Prefect's compound. Selene tripped on her long robe. He put a steadying hand under her elbow. "Are you well?"

Selene nearly sobbed, "I am now. Do you know of my father and brother?"

Demetrius shook his head. "No word of your brother, but I did hear your father is doing poorly. I'm sorry, Lady."

Her heart sank. She had hoped Cyril's information had been a ruse.

"Do you know who is attending him?"

"Thales. He has a good reputation."

"Yes, he is a good physician, but I would care for Father myself."

"I understand, Lady, but that won't be possible. Master will explain all when you've bathed and rested."

Selene arched a weary eyebrow. "I actually get to make myself presentable for the Prefect? Every time he sees me, I look worse than a street urchin. Why should this interview be any different?"

"Because my master wishes you to receive every comfort while you are his guest."

She chuckled derisively. "The Prefect's hospitality will surely be more gracious than the Patriarch's."

"You may judge for yourself, Lady." Demetrius ushered her into a suite of rooms that glistened in soft lamp light. Selene absently noted the magnificent floor mosaics and delicate murals, but what drew her attention was steam coming from a marble tub flanked by a tray of food and wine.

"I'm afraid there are no servants to care for you. Master wished to keep your presence a secret." He bowed. "There are clean clothes on the bed. I will return shortly to see to any other needs."

"Of course. Thank you, Demetrius, for all you've done."

"It has been my will as well as my duty, Lady." He bowed again and left.

Selene couldn't decide whether to start with the food or the bath, so she did both at once. After a hot soak, and a meal of fruit and cold pigeon, she donned a light robe and fell asleep, exhausted, on the soft bed.

She didn't hear Demetrius arrive to remove her tray.

SELENE AWOKE WITH A STARTLED CRY, thrashing in the bed linens. She sat up, took in her surroundings, and lay back on the cushions with a sigh of relief. A delicious feeling of security swept through her body, lulling her senses. She fell back to sleep.

The second time she awoke to the warble of a water clock announcing late morning. Selene got out of bed. Her filthy clothes had been removed, and clean—if exotic—robes laid out. She found her jewelry on an intricately carved dresser with a pink marble top, along with the various implements of a lady's toilet. She explored the jars and boxes, discovering a full array of cosmetics, lotions, and perfumes, as well as ivory-backed brushes and tortoise shell combs. A large silver mirror adorned the wall over the dresser.

She sat on a silk-cushioned stool at the toiletry table and examined her face in the mirror. Sleep and food had gone a long way to repairing the ravages of her confinement. She opened a jar and sniffed. Oil of Lilies! Wildly expensive; it took a thousand Madonna lilies to make a single batch. Selene smoothed the ointment over her face and arms, glorying in the delicate perfume.

Selene wandered about the room. It had a distinctly feminine feel, from the pinks and corals of the mosaics to the flowers displayed in frothy sprays in enameled Indian vases. She heard no servants or street noises; saw no one in the small formal garden outside her window. The clothes she discovered in chests were the bright colors and sheer fabrics of an actress or courtesan. And the statuary had a distinctly erotic style, not as blatant as the Indian brass dealer's wares, but an old-fashioned style depicting nude youths and maidens in romantic scenes.

Orestes had refused to ally himself with any local family through marriage, but seemed not to have lacked feminine companionship. A wave of jealousy surprised Selene. In the absence of any encouragement, she had put aside her feelings for Orestes. Now they came thundering back, confused with her gratitude for her release. Perhaps Orestes did take a personal interest in her. Maybe Antonius, in his jealousy, saw something she hadn't.

Selene ruefully shook her head. That was impossible. Orestes must have gone to such lengths to free her for her father's sake—or her brother's.

That conclusion left her feeling bereft.

She moved to the full-length window, arms outstretched, lifted her head to the sun, and closed her eyes, drinking in the warmth, trying to fill the empty spaces in her soul.

ORESTES STRODE DOWN THE HALL ahead of Demetrius, who carried a heavy tray. He knocked softly at the door with his foot, but heard no voice or motion. He feared she still slept but he needed to speak to her now, before his duties took him out for the afternoon. He opened the door. The anteroom stood empty. He proceeded to the bedroom and stopped in the doorway, transfixed.

Selene stood in the sunlight, head and arms uplifted, as if poised for flight. The sun sifted through her linen shift, sharply outlining her youthful body. Her muscles played under the fabric, rippling as she strained toward the healing sun, lean angles rounded at hip and breast. Her dark curly hair cascaded down her back, her face and throat bathed in golden light. Looking closely, Orestes saw traces of her ordeal: dark bruises around the eyes, a hollowness to the cheeks.

Selene reminded him of another girl, long ago, with red hair and blue eyes. His heart ached at the memory, the pain quickly replaced with anger at Cyril for wantonly trying to destroy such beauty, and regret for his own part in it.

Demetrius stopped behind him, rattling the tray. Selene glanced over her shoulder, her mouth forming a small "o."

Orestes bowed and pointed to a side door. "I'm pleased to see you up, Lady Selene. I will await your pleasure in the next room." He pulled his eyes away and proceeded to a private dining room. Demetrius set up a substantial meal of roasted lamb, greens in vinegar and oil, and sliced melon on trays, next to two couches; then poured wine that matched the buttery color of the sun into crystal glasses.

Orestes paced for the few minutes it took Selene to prepare herself and join them. In her haste, she had eschewed cosmetics and let her hair fall free. Her natural beauty more than made up for her lack of sophisticated artistry. She wore a richly embroidered turquoise tunic over a long-sleeved shift of cream-colored linen, one of the more conservative gowns available to her.

He took both her hands in his. "Welcome, my dear. I only wish you could have visited under more propitious circumstances. Come sit and share a meal with me." He put a hand to the small of her back to usher her toward the couches.

She looked up into his face, a smile trembling at the corners of her mouth. "I don't know how to thank you for all you've done, Prefect. I believe I owe you my life."

"The first thing you can do is call me Orestes. The second is to enjoy this humble meal." He seated her on a couch and took the one opposite. "You don't know how much I regret arriving too late at the Patriarch's to give you reassurances. Did Cyril mistreat you?"

Demetrius provided discreet service while Selene ate heartily and filled in the details of her confinement. Orestes noted that her hands shook as she described her meetings with Cyril. Orestes ate little, and drank more than he should, during the narrative. The girl had suffered much, and for what? A man's vanity and voracity for power.

Selene looked up from the remnants of the meal and asked quietly, "Demetrius told me of my father. Have you any word from Phillip?"

"I received a message this morning. He is recovering from his fever, but more slowly than he would like. When he received word of your troubles, he started back to Alexandria and fell ill again on the road. I sent a note ordering him to stay until he was well." Orestes smiled gently. "I assured him, as a friend, I would stand in his stead as your kinsman. He should be back in the city within a few days."

"When did my father take ill?"

"Calistus collapsed the day after you were taken into custody. He was lucid for a while, but two days ago lapsed into the deep sleep that precedes death. Thales does not know how long he will live, but there is no hope he will recover."

Selene leaped to her feet. "I must go to him."

Orestes rose at the same time. He grabbed her wrists and pulled her to face him. "You can't, Selene. Cyril has announced your escape. You are a condemned sorceress. Parabolani already watch your father's house. I doubt I could get you out a second time."

"I can't sit here, eating and drinking in safety, while my father dies in the company of strangers." She pulled her hands free.

"Do you think your father would want you to die trying to get to him?" Orestes asked softly. "He would want you safe. I visited myself. Your personal servant is taking most solicitous care of him."

"Rebecca. Of course she would look after him in my stead." Selene ran both hands through her hair. "I'll go in disguise."

"Cyril's men search all the women coming and going from the house."

"Then I'll go as a man." Her jaw set in a stubborn line. "I've done it before. Give me shears and men's clothes."

He grabbed her by the shoulders. "Selene, it is too dangerous." Her determined eyes alarmed him. Orestes loathed the idea of forcibly detaining her, yet he could not let her go. Not the least reason being she stirred long forgotten, dangerous feelings in him. Maybe if she knew the truth.

"You are just a move in Cyril's game."

"I know."

He stared at her.

"At first, I thought the Patriarch was using me to get to my father. He led the opposition to Cyril in the council." Selene clasped her hands in front. "When he pressed me about Hypatia, I realized he cast his net much wider."

"It doesn't stop with Hypatia." Orestes suppressed a wince as he watched comprehension dawn on Selene's face. Disappointment warred with bitterness, robbing her of her innocence.

"I can't stay here." She spread her arms wide, indicating her opulent surroundings; a blush crept up her neck to tint her face.

"I agree." Orestes would never shame Selene. He took a deep breath. "Cyril surely has informants among my serving staff. The longer you stay, the more likely someone will discover you."

Selene's arms dropped to her sides. Her shoulders slumped. She looked so bereft; Orestes stepped close and gently tilted her head. Unshed tears glistened in her eyes. His breath caught.

"I have a plan of sorts. Listen carefully, then decide." He escorted her back to one the couches and sat at her side, holding her hands in his. "You are not safe in Alexandria. I propose we smuggle you out of Cyril's jurisdiction; possibly to Constantinople. Or, if you wish, to one of the desert convents. They ask no questions."

Selene shuddered. "I'd rather die."

"I was hoping to spare you that fate."

A grim smile stretched Selene's lips, but it didn't reach her eyes. "That's the answer. I'll die!"

Orestes' bowels clenched.

CHAPTER 37

SELENE, THERE'S NO NEED—"

"I'll only appear to die." She jumped up and paced the room, excitement gripping her. "The guards can find wreckage on the shore with my jewelry and scraps of my clothes. Cyril won't hound a dead woman. He'll soon forget about me, and I can return to a semblance of a life close to my family."

"It'll take more than a bracelet and cape to convince Cyril."

Selene stopped pacing, her enthusiasm doused by Orestes' caviling.

"It might work if we find an appropriate unclaimed body and your brother identifies it as yours," Orestes mused. "The Patriarch, deprived of his target, would then move on to other plots. But, my dear, think on this carefully. You'll be dead not only to Cyril, but to the whole city. You couldn't live at home or go back to classes at the Museum."

"But I could take over Mother Nut's practice, do some good, and see my brother occasionally."

"Possibly." Orestes shook his head. "But it is still dangerous. You will have to live in hiding. Cyril has agents everywhere. Even if he thought you dead, the arrival of a young woman of your description in Mother Nut's precincts would arouse his suspicion. You would be better off starting your life over in another part of the Empire. Wars with Persia, Goths raiding Italy, all have created a tide of refugees in Constantinople. You can live more openly, study, and practice medicine there."

The thought of leaving her birth city frightened Selene. Could she abandon her family and teachers; live a life in the shadows? Did she have a choice? Her shoulders slumped. "I'll go."

"Then I will arrange your 'death'."

"How soon?"

"I'll have my agents scour the mortuaries. It might take a few days." Orestes rubbed his jaw, looking her up and down. "In the meantime, you must stay confined to these rooms."

Her mouth twisted in a bitter smile. "At least this prison is more comfortable than the one I left. Can I send a note to Rebecca?"

"Nothing written." Orestes shook his head. "But you can send her a verbal message. I or Hypatia will deliver it." He rose and motioned to Demetrius. "I must go now, but will return this evening."

Demetrius preceded him with the tray. Orestes hesitated at the door and strode back into the room. He took her hands in his, raised them to his lips and said, in a voice rough with emotion, "I am truly sorry this happened, my dear. I would have given my right hand to spare you and your family this terrible sacrifice."

Selene smiled up at him and said, in an unconscious echo of Demetrius, "It is my will as well as my duty. God will be the final judge of our wisdom or folly."

He bowed his head, kissed her fingertips, and rushed out of the room.

Selene stared after him in astonishment.

CYRIL LOOKED UP from his stack of paperwork as Hierex entered. "Any word?"

"No. I've interviewed everyone in that wing last night. No one saw anything suspicious. Rumor has it that the girl cast a glamour over herself and escaped invisibly. Others say a demon whisked her away in a cloud of black smoke."

Cyril snorted. "Why would a demon bother tying up the mute?" He steepled his hands. "No, she has shown herself an intelligent, resourceful young woman. She likely tricked the matron into opening the door and overpowered her. We should have warned the women of her wiles. Selene's meek demeanor lulled me into thinking her more compliant."

"Might she have had human help?"

"It's possible. As I have eyes in his household, Orestes could have agents in mine." Cyril nodded. "Interrogate everyone again. See if the mute can write or communicate another way. If Selene had help, I want to know who. Have all

Calistus' servants followed. Talk with anyone they talk to."

"It will be done." Hierex bowed.

"Pity. A few more days and we might have weakened Hypatia's reputation. Evidence of sorcery from one of the upper class would have shaken her friends in high places." Cyril shook three letters. "I've already received protests from the nearest Bishoprics. No doubt the pagan witch wrote to all her contacts."

"My alternative plan moves apace," Hierex said. "The parabolani speak against Hypatia in the taverns and gathering places of the poor. They accuse her of unholy influence with Orestes. That has the added effect of showing him a weak leader."

"Good. Keep the mobs roiled but do not let them boil over. I want the threat of violence, not the real thing, or we lose the support of the Imperial court. The new Praetorian Prefect, Aurelian, is a staunch supporter of the church. He recently stripped the Jewish Patriarch in Judea of his judicial powers."

"Excellent!" Hierex smiled. "That should allay any lingering criticism of your actions against the Jews."

"Yes. If we pry Hypatia from Orestes' side, this city will be ours—and God's."

His secretary turned to leave, but Cyril stopped him with a final comment. "Hierex, when we catch that girl, I need her confession."

"Understood."

SELENE SAT LOOKING out at the garden, desperately wanting to walk among the flowers. It was dark; surely no one would see. She breathed the sweet scent of pomegranates mixed with the citrus tang of lemon through the open window. She rose, turning her back on temptation. She had removed the heavy embroidered tunic from this morning and walked about the room clad in a thin linen shift.

She had spent the last several hours trying to regain the peace she thought she had attained the night before in her cell. One by one, she had taken out her hopes and desires and set them free on the breeze, like doves. She had examined all her loves, said goodbye in her heart, and buried the bright memories in her mind, like treasure. Orestes' confession came too late for any sanctioned relationship. Her tears washed away the bitterness and anger, except for a tiny kernel she harbored toward the Patriarch. A clean bright flame remained.

Possibilities.

Shorn of all entanglements, her own and others' expectations, she felt light and…free. This was a heady brew. Eventually she would take on new responsibilities—for her own livelihood, if not for others—but for now she was completely unencumbered. Dead, her life and soul were her own, to remake as she wished. Unfettered by class or position, the possibilities were endless.

Wildness born of freedom coursed through her veins. Dead, she wanted to taste life, to run across the desert. Her body vibrated with the need to move, to feel.

Selene danced.

She whirled, bare feet thudding on the marble floor to the rhythm in her blood, her head thrown back, hair whipping her shoulders. She danced a paean to passion, a hymn to hubris. Fire burned along her limbs, and in her breath, as she leaped and twirled. Barely keeping in mind the need for quiet, she stifled a wild ululation, letting out a low moan instead.

Selene lost all track of time.

As the wild flame burned higher, she spied Orestes staring open-mouthed from the doorway. She whirled to a stop in front of him, tossing back her hair in final flourish.

He grabbed her shoulders. "Selene, are you mad?"

All her feelings for Orestes crested. Selene wanted this tall, mysterious man. She wanted to burn away the failure that showed in his face whenever he looked at her. She wanted to feel his arms wrap around her body, his lips crush hers. She wanted to rekindle his confidence, make him a hero. Selene wanted him to quench the fire—the need—in her body.

She reached up, devouring his face with her eyes, and pulled his lips down to hers for a deep kiss. His arms tightened around her. He lifted her off her feet as his mouth explored hers with unexpected deftness.

He suddenly broke off the embrace, holding her at arms' length, heaving in ragged gasps. "You might not be mad, but I surely am."

"We are neither mad. I want you." Selene looked up with the soft glow of her passion. "Do you not want me?"

"Do I not want you?" He tightened his grip, hurting her shoulders, but she didn't wince. "I've marveled at your bravery, applauded your wits, and right now I want to gentle you as I would a wild mare, but I can't have what I want."

Selene loosened his hands, moving them to her waist as she stepped closer. "Why not?"

He looked into her eyes. "I can't have you, Selene, because I can't keep you." Bitterness edged his voice. "No one can. That way lays pain. I can't love you and see you go out into the world, lost to me."

"Selene is dead. She's a ghost, a memory." Her rising passion fed her fire. "Tonight, you can have me, a real live woman who wants to love you and feel you love her back." She pulled his head down next to hers and whispered, "Please."

"But tomorrow..."

She put her lips close to his. "...is tomorrow. Who knows what the dawn will bring?"

He swept her up. "Are you sure this is what you want?"

"Yes."

He carried her to the bed and laid her down gently. After all her bravado, Selene was suddenly unsure of herself. She had never done this before; her body didn't have a rhythm, a map. What if Orestes found her wanting?

His mouth on hers banished all doubts. Selene again surrendered to her senses. Orestes eased her diaphanous gown over her shoulders, then her hips. He nibbled his way down her neck and gently sucked on her breasts. Her nipples, already hard, sent ripples of sensation down to her groin. Selene shuddered with pleasure and arched her back, asking for more.

Orestes sat up, pulled his tunic over his head, and tossed it aside. Selene reached for him, tracing his muscles with a light finger, skipping over the ridges of old scars. She glanced down at his erect penis and had a second failure of confidence.

Orestes leaned across her, captured both slender wrists in one hand and pulled them above her head. He covered her face with kisses. His other hand reached down where her legs fell open. He teased her to distraction with light touches, then slowly inserted a finger, then two, rubbing an exquisite spot with his thumb. Selene writhed, moaning in sweet agony. He kissed her deeply, his tongue exploring every facet of her mouth, relaxing his grip on her wrists, hand moving from groin to breasts.

She freed her arms and wrapped them around his back, straining him to her. Orestes rolled onto his back, taking her with him, and gently guided her over his erect penis. "Go as slow as you want, my love," he said. "If it hurts, stop."

Selene settled her hips slowly, feeling him fill her up. As she slid over him, she gasped and contracted her belly muscles. She pulled away, then slid down again, riding him as she would a horse. He rotated his hips to meet hers. They settled into a rhythm Selene felt her body knew from the beginning of time. Sensation coursed through her, peaked in a burst of sweet pain, ebbed, and built again.

Orestes moaned and shuddered. He grew soft inside her, but she rode for a few more strokes, coaxing that last burst. Giving a final gasp of pleasure, she collapsed to his chest. He held her tight, breathing raggedly in her ear.

She moved and his flaccid penis slipped out. A thin trickle smeared her thighs. She slipped to his side, nestling under his arm. He stroked her hair and back as their breathing returned to normal.

Selene was stunned. Nothing in the hasty whisperings of girls or ribald remarks of boys had prepared her for the wild and satisfying act of making physical love.

She looked up at Orestes through half-closed lashes. He smiled gently. Selene's nerves still tingled. She felt every stroke of his hand, as if she had no skin. Gradually the fire banked and Selene relaxed into his arms. As Orestes' eyes drooped with sleep, Selene reached down to stroke his penis. It stirred and stiffened.

He laughed and nuzzled her ear, whispering, "Maybe Cyril is right. You do seem to have magical powers."

She pulled his face around for another deep kiss.

CHAPTER 38

MORNING BROUGHT GRAY CLOUDS, the threat of storm, and Demetrius with a breakfast tray. Disappointment, followed by embarrassment, washed through Selene as she reached across an empty bed. Orestes probably thought her no better than the women he regularly entertained in these rooms. Her body flushed with warmth. Maybe she wasn't.

Selene stretched and winced, profoundly sore.

Demetrius set up the tray by the bed, studiously ignoring her nakedness and the stained bedding. Selene, ravenously hungry, wrapped herself in a sheet and swung her legs over the edge of the bed.

"Demetrius, where is your master this morning?" she mumbled through a mouth full of bread and cheese.

"At the baths. He bid me tell you his plan is moving apace, and he will join you for evening meal."

A whole day stuck in these rooms. So much for the heady feeling of freedom that infected her last night. "Could I have a hot bath and a book or two? History or verses, if available."

"I'll draw the bath now, Lady, and have a selection of books for you when you are finished."

Selene watched Demetrius efficiently set about his tasks, noting the gray in his hair and beginning stoop to his shoulders. "Demetrius, how old are you?"

"I have forty-two years, Mistress."

"How did you come to servitude?"

Demetrius recounted his tale of a drunken father and slavery.

Selene set down her food. "Over twenty-five years a slave? That's outrageous! Why has no one given you your manumission?"

Demetrius shrugged. "One's service must be valued to earn freedom."

"I see." The basic injustice of such long servitude stung Selene. She should speak to Orestes. Yet, by what right did she interfere? She was not the mistress of the house and never could be. The privileges of her birth disappeared with her death.

Still, she thought as she watched the faithful servant clear away the dishes, it would hurt no one to bring up the topic.

As ORESTES AND HIS GUARD of four men approached the agora, he heard shouting. "The Prefect! The Prefect approaches!" The crowd thickened.

A young guard turned to Orestes and indicated an alley. "This way, sir. You will be safer going in the side entrance."

"Nonsense. I will not be seen skulking into my offices." Orestes surveyed the crowd. The majority wore bright colors and rich embroidery. This was no mob to be feared, although several monks in the ragged robes of the desert monasteries mixed with the citizens. Orestes looked up as the sky darkened. A cold wind kicked up leaves and dust. A storm would dissipate the throng.

"Speak, Prefect! Answer our questions!"

Orestes pointed to the steps of the massive municipal building. "I'll speak there." He and his guard pushed through the crowd and ascended the steps halfway. Orestes held out his arms for silence. "Good citizens. What do you seek of me?"

"Relief from the city tax!"

An assenting murmur rippled through the crowd.

"Bring back the mimes!"

Laughs and louder affirmations.

"Cease your pagan ways!" shouted an angry monk with a familiar matted beard and flashing black eyes. The crowd subsided into confusion.

"Who accuses me of paganism?" Orestes crossed his arms.

"Ammonius. We monks of Nitria demand you rid yourself of pagan influences and return to the Holy Church."

"The monks of Nitria should go back to their desert and leave Alexandria to the Alexandrines," someone shouted from the back of the crowd.

Ammonius. Orestes searched his memory, mentally shaking his head. He met so many people. The hatred stamped on the monk's face reminded Orestes of...

"Outsiders, go home!"

"Don't talk to the holy fathers so!"

"Good citizens, I will answer your questions." Orestes again stretched out his hands. "But there must be peace or you won't hear me." A ripple of laughter ran through the crowd. "I have sent reports of our hardship to the Emperor. He understands the burden he asks of Alexandria and begs his loyal citizens to bear it a while longer. Heretical Arian Christians mass on the Empire's borders, threatening Constantinople, as they threatened and overran Rome not four years ago. Only the armies keep the Goths from the city gates." Orestes paused then shouted, "Do you wish to serve a barbarian prince?"

"NO!"

"We drove the heretical Arians from our city before!"

"We won't bow to godless Goths!"

The monks filtered to the front of the excited crowd, massing on Orestes' left. Ammonius stepped forward. "You hide behind false regard for the Church, but by your own actions you are a pagan."

Orestes glared at the monk. "I am a Christian, baptized by Atticus, Patriarch of Constantinople."

"You don't go to church." Ammonius accused. "A black sorceress has seduced you from the holy path. Give her up!"

A rock struck Orestes' shoulder, stinging through the woolen mantle. A hail of pebbles rained about him. One of his guards yelped. The crowd surged forward.

"Stop!" he cried in his battlefield voice. Lightning crackled above, leaving the scent of ozone in the air.

Orestes' guard deserted his side. He started to order them back, but an agonizing blow behind his left ear sent him to his knees, gasping in pain. His hands came away from the wound covered in blood.

"Death to the Pagan Prefect!" Ammonius shouted.

Orestes lurched as a second rock struck him in the temple.

"Get him!" echoed through the crowd.

Before blessed darkness wiped out the pain, Orestes remembered Ammonius, blood pouring down his face after being tortured for disrupting the theater.

ON THE THIRD DAY with no word from Orestes, Selene grew angry. Demetrius avoided her questions, putting her off with suggestions of rest and reading. She determined to leave. How dare Orestes treat her as a plaything he could dismiss when he grew bored? If he couldn't be bothered with her, she would not impose on him further.

When Demetrius brought dinner, she confronted him. "I would like different clothes. Servant's garb, perhaps, so I may freely leave the mansion." She stripped off a gold bracelet. "Could you sell this for me and bring me the coin? I'll need it to rent a room."

Demetrius declined the bracelet. "Lady Selene, you cannot leave now. The guards and the monks of Nitria battle in the streets. My master..." He looked at the door with a worried frown. "My master would not wish it."

Orestes had another crisis on his hands. Foolish girl, to think he could take the time to attend to her problems. Her shoulders slumped. "If I stay here much longer, I'll go mad. Have arrangements for my death been completed?"

"We located a possible body today. I'll know by morning if we can implement the plan."

A chill ran up Selene's spine. She knew the ruse depended on someone dying, but had not followed the thought to its logical conclusion. An abandoned girl's life ended, and she benefited. Queasy, Selene said in a low voice, "I wish to leave as soon as possible."

"I will do what I can, Mistress." Demetrius looked pale. "Please be patient."

SELENE SPENT THE NEXT MORNING pacing and cursing herself for a fool. She alternated between anger at Orestes or Demetrius or whoever kept her from knowing what was going on in the world, and fear of knowing. How fared her father? Had Phillip recovered and returned to the city? And Orestes. His abandonment hurt more than she liked to admit.

Demetrius arrived with the noon meal. Orestes hobbled behind with a cane. Selene's anger drained. Bandages covered half his head. Purple and green bruises spotted his limbs.

Orestes approached Selene, took her right hand and kissed the palm. "I'm terribly sorry to neglect you these past few days, my dear, but I've been indisposed."

316

She moved closer, fearing to touch him. "How did you come to be so?"

He ushered her to a couch. As Demetrius laid out a light meal, Orestes told Selene of the monks' attack. He spoke emotionlessly, as if narrating someone else's exploits and pain, but his eyes flashed with anger.

"Where was your guard?" she asked.

"My escort scattered, thinking I was dead and they would be next."

"Cowards!" Selene spat out the word, as she would bitter wine. "I can't believe the Nitrian monks would be so bold as to attack the Augustal Prefect. They go too far!"

"Evidently the citizens felt so. They chased the monks and caught Ammonius. If not for them, I would have died on the street." He picked up his wine with a steady hand and drank.

"And what of this heinous monk?"

"He's dead."

Orestes' flat tone alarmed Selene. "How?"

"The punishment for attacking an Imperial Officer is death. The details are not an appropriate topic for a lady. Of course, our Good Patriarch is publicly castigating me. Ammonius' body resides in the church. Cyril has renamed him 'Thautmasios' and enrolled him among the martyrs venerated by the faithful."

" 'Admirable' is hardly a name I would give an assassin."

"Cyril has overplayed his hand." Orestes' smile chilled Selene. "He eulogized the monk, praising his magnanimity and bravery in defending the faith. I've heard more sober-minded Alexandrines circulated a statement saying Ammonius suffered the punishment due his rashness. Perhaps this will clip our ambitious Patriarch's wings."

Selene lightly touched the bandages. "And your wounds? How bad are they? Who's been caring for you?"

"The guard surgeon tended me." Orestes' face softened with a rueful grin. "My head isn't as hard as I thought. The rock cracked my skull. The surgeon feared brain swelling, but I recovered and came here as soon as I was able to walk."

Selene put her hands on her hips in exasperation. "You were gravely ill and didn't send word? If you had died, would I have had to wait until the new Prefect moved in to learn your fate?" She rounded on Demetrius. "Why did you keep this from me?"

"I forbade him to tell you." Orestes laughed. "You would have been in my rooms before the surgeon could open his bag. Word of your presence would have reached Cyril."

"Credit me with a little sense in approaching you."

"Better you not come at all." He took both her hands in his. "Demetrius tells me we can complete our plan. Cyril's on the defensive. He has more to think about than an escaped girl. When you are found dead, he will stop his hunt and you will be free." He stood, pulling her into his arms. "When that time comes, I hope you will consider staying."

"But I..."

He put a finger to her lips. "Don't answer now. Think on it. We have a few days." He kissed her softly but longingly. "I must make my reports to the Emperor. Tomorrow I'll let you know our progress."

CYRIL FIDGETED WITH HIS REED PEN, recognized the nervous reaction and put it down. Thomas, Augusta Pulcheria's agent, lounged in a chair across from Cyril's desk, legs crossed, eyes steady.

"The Emperor and the Augusta will be much concerned over this attack on their Prefect by a monk. Orestes took appropriate action in executing him. You must stop propagandizing the affair, Patriarch."

"I can see how their Majesties might be concerned, but they are unaware of the provocative actions of their Prefect. He is a lapsed Christian. Since his arrival in Alexandria, he has been under the influence of a pagan woman. He has stopped attending Christian services and publicly attends lectures by this infamous lady. His active disregard has inflamed the religious community, especially the desert fathers."

"The desert fathers are holy but exceedingly ignorant." Thomas' eyes grew steely. "You and I are sophisticated men, more aware of the larger issues at stake. The Lady Philosopher Hypatia, it is she of whom you speak?" Cyril nodded stiffly. "Lady Hypatia has long and ably advised the governors of this land. If important men prefer her advice to yours, you might consider looking to the content of your words or the manner in which you deliver them. I myself have attended her lectures." Cyril sat straighter, trying to stem the hot flow of blood this confession inspired. "She speaks persuasively, making her arguments and leaving men to decide their own course of thought or action. You, my dear Patriarch, have a—shall we say—less flexible style?"

"That does not exempt Orestes from proper public display of reverence for the Church," Cyril ground out.

"I agree." Thomas examined his fingernails. "It is your personal responsibility to counsel and bring him back to the fold. Clouting the Prefect on the head with a rock is not an effective way to bring him to your side."

"Do you think I'd urge the monks to murder an Imperial officer? They came into the city on their own." Cyril's lips twisted. "I can't be responsible for every member of my flock, especially when Orestes is so blatant in his contempt for the Church."

Thomas uncrossed his legs, put both feet on the floor and leaned forward. "You can stop inciting the ignorant fools. There is more at stake here than your pride or the justice of the sentence on that monk. Get your house in order, Patriarch, or the Emperor and the Augusta might find you incapable of leading such an important See. Do you understand?"

"Perfectly. Have we any other business?"

"None. I look forward to my next visit to your fair city." Thomas rose. "I can see myself out." The agent bowed and left the room, door open.

Hierex poked his head around the corner. "May I enter?" At Cyril's nod, he moved diffidently before Cyril's table.

"Out with it, man," Cyril commanded.

"I have distressing news."

CHAPTER 39

CYRIL KNEW GOD TESTED HIS LOYAL SERVANTS, but he wished this cup would pass him by. He silently asked forgiveness for his blasphemous thoughts. "Distressing news can't be any worse than what I just heard."

"The shore patrol found a battered body—a woman's—with the remnants of a boat on the beach. Evidently she capsized and drowned in the storm a few days ago. Calistus' son Phillip identified her as his sister Selene. It seems God exacted His own punishment."

"Have you confirmed it is she?"

"Our agent verified the physical resemblance to the extent he could, given the condition of the body. The embroidery and jewelry matched the description I gave him. I'm satisfied it is Selene."

"An unfortunate end for such a promising girl. I had hoped she would redeem herself and die penitent. I needed her accusations against Hypatia in my reports to the Augusta." Cyril steepled his hands. "However, we can salvage a small crumb of good from this sorry mess. Her story will be an example to the congregation of the need to resist pagan witches."

"Excellent. I will give the details to the presbyters. Should I draft a sermon?"

"No. I will compose this one myself. You may discontinue watching Calistus' home and servants. I need the parabolani to help us discreetly remove the Nitrian monks." Cyril reached for pen and paper then hesitated. "Arrange for one of the deacons to visit young Phillip and offer God's solace. With his father incapacitated and sister dead, he might be confused or angry."

"It will be done, Your Grace. What of Orestes and Hypatia?"

Cyril chewed on the end of his reed pen. "We must be more circumspect concerning the Prefect." He looked sharply at Hierex. "We don't want another attack on his person."

The little man fidgeted. "I didn't know the monks would be so volatile."

"I should have." Cyril sighed. "They nearly killed my uncle, decades ago, over a matter of doctrine. That was why he sent me to study with them for six years, so they would know me, and I them, when I took the Bishopric."

Cyril shook his head. "The monks are too dangerous to use in the city. My flock resents their rampages. We must wage a more subtle campaign; drive a wedge between Orestes and that pagan woman. If opinion turns against Hypatia, Orestes will have to abandon his public regard for her or risk losing the support of the populace. If he does forsake her he has no one but me to come to."

"Either way, Orestes becomes ineffectual as a governor." Hierex' eyes gleamed. "I will see to it."

Cyril waved his hand in dismissal. "Keep me informed."

"PHILLIP!" SELENE RAN TO HER BROTHER. He picked her up and swung her around as if she were a little girl, then put her down, gasping, skin pale. Selene put her hand to his sweating forehead. "No fever, but you shouldn't exert yourself so soon after an illness." Her face collapsed. "I don't want to lose you, too. How is father?"

"No better." He tucked her arm in his, and they trailed to the sitting room. "I don't know what keeps him alive."

"I want to go to him. There is nothing I can do, but I want to see him one more time. And Rebecca?" Seated beside him on a couch, Selene looked into her brother's shadow-filled face.

"Rebecca tends our father as if he was her own, but still refuses to marry me." Phillip scrubbed his cheeks and knuckled his eyes. The action didn't erase the marks of illness or pain from his countenance. "I don't know what to do."

"Rebecca has suffered many losses—her mother, brothers, nearly her life— at the hands of Christians." Selene snuggled closer, head on his shoulder. "She needs to heal, as do we all. Give her time and trust that whatever happens, happens for the best."

"How can you say that, with what you've gone through?" He gathered her to his chest. "How is it for the best that you are hounded by the Patriarch, and must live in a shadow world, cut off from your rightful place in society? My little sister is dead, and it's all for the best," he said bitterly.

She hugged him back. "I know it seems strange, but this necessity helped me see what is important in my life. Stripped of my past, I have the opportunity to make my own future. I will never again be Selene, daughter of Calistus, with all the protection and obligations of a young woman born to my station. I will take on new obligations, but of my choosing."

"It's a hard world for a woman alone." Phillip laid his cheek on her hair. "You need the protection of a brother, the support of a family."

She pushed him away at arm's length. "You will always be my beloved brother. But I am no poor ignorant woman, burdened with children, abandoned by her husband. I have an education and skills. I can make a living, possibly find happiness." Her eyes glistened with unshed tears.

Desperately, Phillip said, "Orestes told me he offered you shelter as long as you wanted. It would be an easy life and out of danger." Phillip's eyes slid away from hers. "You will be dead. No shame will attach to our family. I could visit as often as you wished."

"Do you believe I could be happy here? I can't marry Orestes, and living as a cloistered concubine would be little better than taking a cell in the desert." Selene shook her head. "You, who are closest to me, should know food, safety, companionship are not enough. I need to make a difference, make things better, if only in small ways."

"You've changed, little sister." Phillip could not hide the worry in his eyes. "You've grown up in ways I never expected. It's just that…you, Rebecca, Father… in so short a time is difficult."

"I know. I lose you all too." Selene stiffened with resolve. "I won't let Father die without me. I will visit him. Tonight."

"No, Selene, it's…" Phillip saw the look in her eyes. "What time?"

"I'll be at the servant's entrance shortly after dark. Tell Father I'm coming home."

SELENE PULLED THE CLOAK OVER HER HAIR, hiding her face in deep shadows. Demetrius led her the back way through the garden to the servant's quarters and out of the mansion's grounds. Nut juice darkened her face and hands, well-placed smudges of kohl deepened lines from nose to mouth, other lines created wrinkles in her smooth brow. She took on the gait that comes with the burdens of age.

Orestes had told her it was too soon to go out, and much too soon to go to her father's house. She threatened to leave undisguised if he didn't help. The hurt in his eyes and bitterness of his words haunted her. "I knew I couldn't keep you safe here forever." He'd laughed harshly. "We're a fine pair of fools, you and me. May God look after you, because I can't." He had stomped out of the room before she could say good-bye.

Demetrius opened a small door in the side of the wall and passed her a key. "You'll need this to return, Mistress."

"I don't know when I'll be back. Tell Orestes..." she hesitated, "tell him I'll stay safe."

She slipped out of the servant's entrance and down the steep hill. People hurried to their homes and evening meal. With her old woman's hobble, she blended with the crowd, keeping a watchful eye. After several minutes, she realized a well-built youth, with something of the soldier in his bearing, trailed her.

Selene's heart thudded in an erratic rhythm. Did Cyril's people still hunt for her? Or did the youth see an easy target for robbery? She ambled across a square and ducked into a crowded tavern. The young man followed and casually surveyed the crowd.

Selene snagged a servant by the sleeve. "Do you have a latrine?"

The harried woman hooked a thumb over her shoulder. "Out back."

Selene slipped out. Tables and benches crowded the patio, lit by oil lamps. At the far end of the garden, a small building announced its purpose by its odor. A tree next to it overhung the wall. She glanced back. No sign of the nosy young man. Selene scrambled up the tree to the top of the wall and down to the alley behind. From there she made it to her father's home with no shadow but her own.

Selene knocked on the kitchen door. The scuff of sandals preceded the door opening. Lamp light flickered on Rebecca's face. Selene sidled through with one last glance over her shoulder at the empty alley. She pulled back her hood.

Rebecca's eyes went wide. "Selene, is that really you?"

Selene held out her arms. They embraced; then Rebecca pulled back to look her over more carefully.

"I thought I'd never see you again. When we heard you had escaped, I hoped you'd left the city. The Bloody Patriarch's men turned this place upside down. I practically threw them out of your father's room. They scared poor Aaron out of the last of his wits. He dreamed for days that the 'bad men' came to take us away. When Orestes gave me your message…"

Selene chuckled. "Slow down, my friend. We will talk, but first I must see my father."

"Of course." Rebecca hugged her again. "I'm so happy you're safe."

"We need to be careful." Selene gently disentangled herself. "You never know who might be listening at keyholes. Someone told Cyril of things in our household." Her voice caught. "Did you hear of Mother Nut?"

"Another life I hold the Patriarch responsible for." Rebecca's moist eyes became flinty. "I have my suspicions about who told tales. I sent her home to her family. The rest of the servants are in bed. But you're right, we shouldn't tarry." Rebecca led Selene out of the kitchen, toward the private quarters.

"Have you been caring for Father alone?"

"One of the other servants watches when I have to leave. I've been sleeping on the floor. Phillip is there now."

"Good. If any do see me, tell them I'm a nurse Phillip hired to help you."

They arrived at Calistus' door. Phillip sat by the bed, a lamp in the corner burning low. He rose and embraced his sister. "There's no change. He hasn't eaten or drunk in days."

Selene hardly recognized her father. Flesh had melted away, leaving pasty gray skin stretched tight over bones. His breath came in shallow irregular gasps. Selene sat in the chair her brother had vacated and picked up her father's skeletal hand.

"It's Selene, Father. I've come home to take care of you."

Selene thought she saw her father's lips twitch, more likely an illusion caused by the flickering lamp light or eyes blurred with unshed tears.

"We'll leave you alone." Phillip ushered Rebecca out.

Selene took a sponge from a bowl by the bed and squeezed water into her father's mouth. It ran down the sides of his face. She wiped off the moisture. Deprived of doing anything substantive for her father, Selene found herself humming a lullaby; one her mother had sung to her.

The night crawled by, filled with memories of her father and brothers. Sometimes she spoke aloud, asking if Calistus remembered the time she got stuck in the fig tree, or she scared Nicaeus by putting a snake in his bed. Sometimes she sat in silence, or crooned nonsense words. The quiet watch and long day eventually overcame her.

AS THE WATER CLOCK STRUCK THE HOUR, Rebecca shook Selene awake. "He's gone."

The hand Selene held was cool and dry. She checked her father's breath and pulse, lifted his eyelids.

Selene had dreaded this day for over a year. She thought she had shed all her tears, and was surprised by the clenching pain that shot from her heart to close her throat with an iron grip. She drew a ragged breath. Tears oozed down her stained cheeks.

Generation, growth, and decay—the inevitable cycle of mortal life. She knew the process intimately, had wrestled with loss both expected and unexpected. This empty husk was not her father. His absence, a sharp pain, she knew from experience, could be blunted by time.

Selene crossed his arms over his chest and kissed her father one final time. "I'll tell Phillip."

"He's in your father's study. I'll stay with the body." Rebecca touched her arm. "I think he knew you were here. That's why he held on so long; waiting for you."

"Thank you, Rebecca."

Selene went downstairs to her father's office. Several lamps made the room bright as day. Phillip looked up, started, and rose to his feet. "Father?"

Selene moved into his arms. "He's gone." Phillip clenched her tight and bent his head into her hair. She felt his breath shudder as he stifled sobs. "He's out of pain now, brother."

"I know." Phillip released her and rubbed his stubbled face, erasing any trace of tears. He went to a pitcher sitting on a side table. "Would you like wine?"

She nodded.

"I kept hoping for a miracle." Phillip handed her a cup. "Each time I walked into his room, I expected him to sit up and greet me. I knew it wouldn't happen, but I couldn't help myself." His gaze turned inward. He crashed his goblet on the desk, slopping red wine over the papers, staining them like blood. "He's been sick a whole year and what did I do? Gad about the city, playing the spy.

Acting the fool is more like it. He needed me home and I spent my time in taverns. I avoided my responsibilities—as he always accused me."

"Father knew you did important work. He took pride in your friendship with Orestes."

"Much good it did him, you, or Orestes."

"Father had a disease of the heart. Nothing you did could have prolonged his life or cut it short. And your relationship with Orestes saved my life." Selene set down her goblet to take his face in her hands. "Don't blame yourself. The pain of losing Father causes such morbid thoughts. I know. I tell myself it's a blessing; he's released from the agony of his failing body. That's why it hurts so. I don't want his death to feel natural, accepted. I want to howl at the moon, twist God's arm, and make Him give my father back."

Phillip sighed. "You feel angry and I feel guilty. We make a fine pair." He sopped the wine from a pile of ledgers and notes.

"What are those?" Selene asked to distract him from his self-abnegation.

"Account books, tax receipts, civil levies." Phillip's mouth turned down in a bitter line. "Father was in worse straits than we thought. He owes thousands of talents, and guess who holds most of the notes?"

"Not Ision?"

Phillip nodded glumly. "He's been buying them since your inquest. I'll have to sell almost all the land and, in these bad times, will not get near their worth. With the rents gone, I can't afford this house and its upkeep, much less my civic obligations."

"Surely you can get more time on the notes." Selene grasped her brother's arm. "Next year's harvest might be better."

"One good harvest won't save me. Besides, why would Ision wait, when he could have both land and harvest?"

"I had no idea." Selene gripped his arm. "Phillip, what will you do?"

"Frankly, I don't know. Tonight I'm too tired to figure it out." He laughed, slightly hysterical. "At least Father regularly paid the funeral association. We won't have to sell anything to bury him."

"When will you have the funeral?"

Phillip chewed his lower lip. "Monday, next."

"When is my funeral?"

"Good God, I forgot." Phillip looked shocked. "That poor girl's body is still at the mortuary. I promised someone to fetch it when the arrangements had been made." He sat and gulped more wine. "I guess we can have a double funeral. Given our family's disgrace and lack of financial resources, we can be forgiven if it's a small gathering."

Selene yawned. "It's nearly dawn. I should leave before the servants wake." She kissed her brother on the cheek. "I'll be there."

He opened his mouth to protest, then closed it without comment.

CHAPTER 40

ENTERING HER ROOMS, Selene nearly tripped over Demetrius. He sat up groggily.

"Mistress Selene. Are you all right?"

"Perfectly safe, Demetrius." She stripped off her outer robes on her way to the bedroom.

The slave rose to his feet, wincing. "And your father?"

"He died before morning."

"I'm sorry, Mistress." Demetrius followed, picking up her things. "Would you like a bath?"

"Demetrius, you must read minds!" She repaired to the cosmetics table to rub her face with lotion. Little of the dye came off. "I'll have to soak for a week to get this off my face and hands."

"Then you won't be going out again?" Demetrius asked neutrally.

"Not until the funeral, next Monday."

Demetrius drew her bath. "I'll bring breakfast, Mistress."

LOUNGING IN THE COOLING WATER, Selene started when Orestes arrived with a tray. A mottling of blue, yellow, and green still showed where his bruises healed.

"Demetrius told me about your father." Orestes set the tray down on a table. "Calistus was a good man. He will be sorely missed in the council. I trust you journeyed home and back without incident?"

She hesitated. "A young man seemed inordinately interested in me, but I eluded him." She told him about her shadow and how she lost it.

"So that's what happened." Orestes smiled. "Phoebus was most upset. I upbraided him heartily for letting an 'old woman' outsmart him."

"You had me followed?" She looked at him accusingly. "Didn't you know it would frighten me?"

"I care for you and want you safe." He scratched his jaw. "And I underestimated your ability to take care of yourself—again. I never thought you would spot him."

She harrumphed and stood to retrieve a drying sheet.

Observing her two-toned body, he broke into strangled guffaws. She snatched the sheet, wrapping it around her. "Go away. I don't want you to see me like this."

"I've seen you naked, or have you forgotten so quickly?"

"No." She blushed. "I mean, I don't want you to see me looking like a piebald animal."

"My dear, if you wore the spots of a leopard or the stripes of a zebra, you would still be beautiful." He looked her over critically. "That golden mahogany suits you. With red henna in your hair, your own brother might not recognize you."

"I'll try that. It's difficult being an old woman." She squeezed water from her hair and sat at the dresser to comb it.

"Besides, no one would believe I keep an old woman as my lover. It's time you have servants to care for you. Poor Demetrius is running himself ragged, waiting on you and functioning as my secretary." Orestes picked over the fruits on the tray, choosing a ripe fig. "Where would you like to be from? Cyrene? Or maybe Thebes?"

Selene stared into the silver mirror. "I'm not sure how long I'll stay here, Orestes."

His eager smile retreated and his voice grew guarded. "Demetrius told me..."

"...that I won't be going out again until Monday," she interrupted. "That doesn't mean I want to live here permanently. There is little for me here."

"I see." His mouth tightened. "I promised to help you in any way necessary. Please let Demetrius know and I will authorize it." He turned on his heel, arms stiff at his sides.

"Orestes, wait!" Selene grabbed at her slipping sheet. "Curse it! I didn't mean it like that. Please sit and eat. I'll dress and we can talk. I feel at a disadvantage, nearly naked while you're fully dressed."

He nodded and sat. In a cedar chest, Selene found a sky-blue gown of thin linen, less revealing than most, and pulled it on. She had misjudged the depth of Orestes' passion, and the prickliness of his pride. Selene had reckoned his concern for her to be more political than personal; his reluctance the night they made love, that of an honorable man with a friend's sister. Now she thought his reticence masked a more personal pain.

The breakfast tray remained untouched. Selene sat at Orestes' side, close enough to feel the heat radiating through his linen tunic. She twined a strand of damp hair around her finger. "Who do I remind you of, Orestes, that I trouble you so?"

His shoulders stiffened; then he slumped forward, hands dangling between his knees. "Selene, you are so young. You will have many loves in your lifetime. I am over twice your age, and know the pain love brings. I would spare you that if I could."

For the first time she noticed the flesh sagging slightly around his jowls, the generous silver threading his hair. She hesitantly touched his shoulder.

"Would you spare me the joy as well? For that is what I would miss if I could not love."

He shivered.

"Are you chilled?" Selene asked in concern

"No. Where I grew up, people say sudden chills come from someone walking on your grave. The tribes of Britannia have many superstitions."

"The wild people of the Misty Isles. You told me of them the first night you came to my father's house."

"I grew up in the south of Britain in a Christian home, but fell in love with the daughter of a druid. She was fair, with hair the color of burnished copper and eyes like the sky on a bright summer's day. She ran the fields like a wild mare and smelled of honeysuckle." He gazed into the distance.

"What became of her?" Selene asked, reading the answer in his face.

"We were young and foolish. We felt our love pure and timeless, that all would bow down before it. Our fathers felt differently. Mine enlisted me in the army to serve in Gaul. Her father arranged a marriage. When I returned to Britain, a year later, I found she had drowned herself, and our unborn babe, months after I left."

He clenched his hands till the knuckles turned white. Selene caught her breath at the anger in his emerald eyes.

"I loved no one but Rhianon. If I had fought harder to stay with her...but she was lost to me. I poured my heart into service, forsaking all thoughts of love and happiness." Orestes unclenched his fists and, sliding his hands down Selene's bare arms, gently traced the play of muscles under her skin. "Then I saw you dancing. Your youth, passion, and hope for the future inflamed me."

"I was too weak to save Rhianon, but thought I might right the wrongs done you." He took both her hands in his and gazed into her eyes. "For one night, I thought I could. You made me feel young and strong. The next day, that cursed monk struck me down. I grow older, my power wanes. I cannot restore you to your family, and you will not let me keep you safe, so there is no joy in my feeling for you, only pain."

Better with action than words, Selene pulled his head to her breast. He circled her waist and relaxed into the comfort of her embrace. She tried to rekindle the reckless freedom of the night they made love. It eluded her. His loss and hers mingled to create a different bond, based on human compassion; the ability of a woman to ease a man's sore heart.

ORESTES DID NOT TRY to prevent her from attending the funeral, having Demetrius go so far as to arrange for her "apprenticeship" with a troop of professional mourners he hired for the occasion. She dyed her hair dark red and stained her body honey-brown. With kohl ringing her eyes, Selene hardly recognized herself. Taking no chances, she stayed in the background at the funeral, observing through her mandatory black veil.

"Not much of a crowd, eh, dearie?" One of the women near her dug an elbow into her ribs. "And for a councilor and all!"

Selene mutely nodded.

Only Lysis and three others represented the councilors. Hypatia and the imposing Haroun attended from the Museum. Selene missed old Auxentius but, if someone told him of her death, he probably forgot it within minutes. Phillip had insisted Orestes stay away; it would be unseemly for the Prefect to attend the funeral of a declared witch. Antonius, pale and haunted, stood in a corner, drinking far too much wine.

It hurt to realize the extent of her family's isolation.

"Have you ever done one in this neighborhood before?" Selene's companion asked.

"No. This is my first engagement."

"Well, don't judge by this." The woman sniffed. "We usually get fed at the funeral feast. Sometimes there's enough to take home. But I heard tell there'd be no feast today. Lucky the patron that hired us paid triple."

The tiny gathering, mostly servants, settled as Phillip called them to order. He spoke at length of his father and his accomplishments, stopping twice when tears choked off his words. The professional mourners lamented softly. Selene, released by her role, freely wailed.

Phillip spoke more briefly about Selene. It chilled her flesh to hear her brother's confession of love and admiration, and to know he knew she heard him.

Antonius shook with suppressed sobs.

It gradually dawned on Selene that this truly was farewell. The initial boldness of her action had carried her through the days, but now she faced the irrevocability of her decision.

Her life was gone; smashed like a fragile vase, never to be repaired. She would never return to this house, read to her father, tease her brothers, gossip with Rebecca.

Selene moaned, trembling in her black veil.

"Don't moan, dearie," the woman beside her admonished. "Wail, like this." She gave a soft ululation, rising and falling like music.

The breath caught in Selene's chest. All that came out was a squeak. The mourner shook her head and continued her accompaniment.

Hypatia stood next and gave a ringing oration, expressing her sorrow at the passing of "two such fine citizens and friends; a father and daughter of warm heart and pure spirit; loving, kind, and always giving."

Selene barely heard the words.

The bodies occupied plain limestone coffins, lids firmly in place. When Hypatia finished her remarks, Phillip signaled servants at each corner to raise the coffins and start the procession.

Selene and the professional mourners took up their tambourines and chanted in a descant, following the minuscule crowd. They traversed the city, under a threatening sky, to the southwest gate, and the necropolis beyond the walls. At the tomb entrance, she drifted to the side in a mock show of concern for a perfectly good sandal lace. Calistus, and his false daughter, were to be laid to rest in an ancient tomb with several generations of ancestors. If God were just, his soul would be reunited with that of his beloved wife and lost children.

Regret sliced through Selene. A stranger's bones, a girl whose life ended too soon, took her place beside her father and mother.

With a flash of bitter insight, Selene realized she couldn't stay in Alexandria. Life would be too cruel, seeing everyday what she couldn't have, living in the shadows. Orestes had been right. She should start her life over. But where?

She tried to pray to the wise merciful God of her childhood, but the words wouldn't come. She didn't know what to pray for. Her father's soul? Her prayers would not sway God's justice. Good fortune for her and her brothers? God had paid scant attention so far.

At last, she prayed simply for the strength to carry on.

She raised her head and pushed back the veil. A single ray of sunshine bathed the tomb in golden light. Selene closed her eyes and let the sun kiss her face, feeling the warmth penetrate to her bones and the light lift her spirit.

Voices echoed up the stairs from the tomb. She pulled her veil back over her head. The interment service had been brief; there was no elaborate banquet to keep the mourners at the grave site. Selene fell in with the professionals as they collected their fee from Phillip. She squeezed his hand to let him know it was she. Tears coursed down her cheeks. He held her hand a moment longer than necessary to pass the coin.

She stood wailing with the women in black until the other mourners straggled out of sight. The woman who instructed her, took Selene's elbow and escorted her to the side. "That was unprofessional, dearie, not to go into the tomb. It made us look bad."

"I'm sorry. I think my uncle was wrong in recommending me for this apprenticeship. I'll tell him I'm not suitable."

"Not everyone can do this." The woman patted Selene's hand sympathetically.

The small party wound its way back to the city walls, where they dispersed. Selene repaired to a public fountain, where she washed her tear-stained face with her veil.

Two boys played nearby, but avoided the solemn woman dressed all in black. Selene overheard the older boy teasing the other, daring him to approach "the scary lady." She heard the scuff of small bare feet sneaking behind her. At a light touch, she whirled around, crying, "Aiee!" The boy's eyes widened in delighted terror and he scampered away with squeals of triumph.

Selene laughed. The boys reminded her of Phillip and Nicaeus as children.

With a yearning so intense it knotted her stomach, Selene wanted to see Nicaeus. If she couldn't be near Phillip in the city of her birth, at least she could have the comfort of one of her brothers in her new life. She resolved to ask Orestes to arrange for her passage to the Thracian border.

Her course settled, Selene decided to attend a final lecture by Hypatia. She mused on the twists her life had taken since, over three years ago, she'd set out on the same errand in a very different disguise.

Selene entered a major crossroads square where a man jostled her elbow, bringing her out of her reverie. A shrill voice, filled with vitriolic passion, rolled across the crowd. Selene turned to see a man in the sober robes of a presbyter inveighing against evil.

The throng felt wrong. Mostly male, it contained far fewer men of stature, and many more with rough clothes or hardened looks, than Selene expected. It seemed more a mob waiting to riot than a public seeking knowledge. The holy man, whom someone addressed as Peter, exhorted the people to beware of demons and witches.

A chill crawled up Selene's spine.

She looked around. A familiar brown figure stood several feet away. Hierex nodded as Peter's voice rose and thundered. He scanned the crowds, nodding in seeming satisfaction. Selene froze like a rabbit in the open, then broke off her gaze. When she glanced back to see if the Prefect's secretary had noticed her, he was gone. A name, dropped by the presbyter, caught Selene's attention.

"Hypatia is the snake in the path of the Prefect's and Patriarch's reconciliation. This city is torn apart as she beguiles those in power through her satanic wiles."

Ice gripped Selene's bowels.

"The first to fall victim was the governor. Orestes came to us a Christian, but that foul practitioner of the black arts convinced him to stop attending church. Hypatia is an abominable messenger of hell devoted to magic, astrolabes, and instruments of the dark arts. She must be stopped!"

Alarm lent urgency to Selene's flight.

She edged her way out of the crowd and ran toward the forum, Hypatia's usual lecture spot. Tripping on her cloak, she dropped it to the street. She soon shed her encumbering outer robe, and hiked up her light tunic. Her legs flashed brown as she raced through the crowds, dodging carts and stray cats.

People frowned at her as she rushed by. Several shouted. Selene didn't waver from her course.

It had been months since she ran so freely. Pain stabbed her side. Selene gasped for breath as she skidded to a stop at the entrance to a colonnaded plaza. A much smaller crowd dotted this area. She spotted Hypatia dismounting from her chariot on the far side, and took off again.

"Selene?" An incredulous male voice made her hesitate.

Antonius.

Hoping he would think he was mistaken, she dropped her tunic hem and walked away at a brisk pace. After a few steps a rough hand closed on her shoulder, jerking her around. She lowered her eyes and brushed at his hand. "Please, Sir, I must get back to my sick child. Don't delay me further."

Antonius put his hand under her chin, tipped her head, and inspected her countenance. A joyful smile blazed across his face. "Selene, it is you. I thought I saw a ghost. But I would know your running, your face anywhere. It's burned into my heart."

He reached to embrace her.

"Not here," she hissed. Antonius' arms dropped to his side. His eyes grew round with hurt. Giving up her pretense, she grabbed him by the wrist and started to sprint across the plaza. "We must warn Hypatia."

"Warn her of what?" he panted as he tried to keep up.

"A churchman is inciting a crowd against her. I fear they mean her harm."

"But how did...?"

"Later!"

She pushed forward at a faster pace. People complained as she jostled her way through a final screen of people. Hypatia had yet to start her lecture. Selene rushed to her teacher's side.

"Lady, you must leave at once."

Hypatia turned her unflappable countenance to Selene. Only a raised eyebrow acknowledged her surprise at seeing the student whose funeral she had just attended.

"Why should I disappoint my followers?"

"You are in great danger. The presbyter Peter preaches against you, inciting a crowd to riot. He accuses you of practicing the black arts."

"I see." Hypatia's face looked grim as she straightened to her full diminutive height. "If this crowd has been incited by words, they can be dissuaded by words. Let me reason with these people."

"They have no *reason*. These people are driven by hate and violence." Selene put every ounce of pleading she could into her voice. "Please, Lady, do not tarry. I fear for your life."

A commotion broke out on the side of the plaza. An angry mob boiled into the open space, sweeping the students before them.

"There's the witch!" someone shouted.

CHAPTER 41

Antonius swept Hypatia, protesting, into his arms and carried her to the chariot. Selene ran behind, shouting, "On your life, Lady, we must flee!"

The mob, seeing their prey about to escape, stampeded across the plaza, shouting.

Hypatia, seeing the murderous nature of the rabble, grabbed the reins and slapped the bays, shouting "Hie!" They took off at a canter. Selene and Antonius gripped, white-knuckled, the edges of the careening car. The leaders of the crowd peeled off to block their path.

Hypatia first attempted to go around, then through, the mob. A man in church robes leaped in front of the horses, waving a white cloth and shouting. The animals reared, squealing wildly. The man grabbed the bridles and pulled the horses to a trembling stop. The animals' eyes rolled white. Bloody foam trickled from their mouths where he yanked on the bits.

The mob swarmed in from all sides, led by a goodly number of parabolani. Selene kicked a man in the face, sending a spray of blood from his broken nose. Another grabbed her tunic, pulling her off-balance. She crashed to the floor of the car, banging her chin in the awkward space, pain shooting to the top of her skull.

Antonius struggled above Selene. He pushed one attacker off the car and into the crowd, sending them reeling. Another clambered over a wheel to punch him in the lower back. Antonius gasped, half turning. The man kicked him in the shoulder, sending him sprawling on top of Selene.

Men reached into the back of the chariot. Two pinioned Antonius and pulled him from the car. Another dragged Selene from the chariot by her legs. A dirty hand throttled her while another twisted her arm behind her back. Selene's sight began to darken. She thrashed in panic at the loss of air.

"Stop!" Hypatia's magnificent voice rang out.

The man released Selene's throat. She stood trembling; gasping for breath; arm still pinned.

"You know me." Hypatia scanned the crowd, looking into individuals' eyes, until they wavered. "What do you seek? I have given freely to this city over most of your lives. Ask what you will of me."

The throng milled uncertainly.

"You!" Hypatia pointed at the man holding Selene's arm, then to the ones pinioning Antonius. "Let those children go. They are innocents." She spread her arms as if to embrace the crowd. "My fellow Alexandrines, God watches and judges our actions. Go back to your homes. Don't stain your souls with murder and riot."

Hope bloomed in Selene's chest. The most famous rhetorician in Alexandria could surely tame this beastly crowd.

"Stop her mouth!" Peter strode forward, pointing at Hypatia. "The sorceress bewitches us with her words. She uses magic to turn us from the path of righteousness. In Christ's name, listen not to her lies!"

Selene's newborn hope faltered.

Hypatia turned toward Peter, voice ringing with passion. "Who advocates violence in the name of the Prince of Peace? Surely you urge blasphemous acts. I seek only safe passage for me and my students."

"Witch!" Peter's face twisted with hate. "Bind her, before she imperils all our souls!"

One of the parabolani invaded the chariot, pinioning Hypatia's arms. A second stuffed a filthy rag in her mouth. The crowd roared its approval. Selene, aghast at such treatment, let out a low moan.

"To the church," Peter shouted.

"Yes, let her stand before God!"

"To Caesarion! To the church!" The mob chanted. "Death to the witch!"

The man clutching Selene's arm marched her to the sprawling complex of buildings surrounding the Caesarion. She passed through the familiar streets as if in a nightmare. The confused roar of the mob pressed on her ears, till the din took on the aspect of a distant storm—noise felt more than heard.

Most passersby melted into the side streets, turning faces away. A few joined the rabble; mouths stretched wide in demons' howls. Selene kicked out, but was cuffed for her efforts. She clung to the faint hope that the city guards would stop the mob.

That hope faded as they passed the docks.

Mariners swelled the ranks to an intimidating number. With grim purpose, the throng passed between the towering obelisks guarding the entrance to the Caesarion and entered the church precincts. Selene's heart sank. She feared she would never come out of the church alive.

Two men dragged her up the low sweeping steps, into the church proper, and to the left of an altar graced with gold candlesticks and a jeweled crucifix. She had lost a sandal; the pink marble felt cool to her bruised foot. Acrid sandalwood incense almost overcame the stench of the mob bent on blood. As many as could, stuffed themselves into the soaring nave of the church, their malice crowding out any feeling of peace and holiness.

Peter stood between the altar and the silk-cushioned Bishop's chair. He prayed with arms outstretched, head slumped to chest. The mob quieted.

Hysterical laughter bubbled into Selene's throat. She choked it down, but not before the ruffian on her right clapped a broad hand over her mouth, hissing, "Quiet, witch."

Selene's captors forced her to her knees, head bowed, arm still twisted behind her back. Fiery pain settled into her shoulder joint, distracting her from older bruises. Selene rolled her eyes. She could see nothing through her cascading hair on the right, but glimpsed Antonius held in a similar excruciating position to her left, his pale face marked with blood from a cut over his eye. Hypatia stood pinioned in front of the Bishop's chair, hair straggling down her back, white scholar's robes askew, face impassive.

Peter finished his prayer and strode to Hypatia. "All-seeing God watch over us as we destroy this abomination. Protect our souls from Satan's taint."

Hypatia's captors dragged her to the doors screening the choir, directly across from Selene. Two parabolani yanked the philosopher's arms taut, lifting the diminutive woman off her feet with the force. Hypatia grimaced in pain as a distinct popping sound announced at least one dislocated shoulder. The men lowered her so the tips of her toes barely reached the floor.

Peter stood before Hypatia, made a two-fingered warding sign, and ripped the robes from her body. Hypatia's wrinkled skin shone white in the dim light. She glared at her tormentors.

Selene gasped and averted her eyes. Her captor grabbed her chin and turned her face toward the horrific scene, whispering, "You're next, witch."

A mariner heaved a net bag next to Peter. The scent of dead fish and brine battled the musk of the frenzied crowd. Peter reached into the bag and pulled out a razor-edged clamshell. He struck Hypatia on the breast. The wound gaped, blood spattering the floor. Peter struck again, crying, "In Jesus' name, we scourge this demon."

Hypatia took that blow, and the next, and the next, without taking her gaze from Peter. With each stroke, he grew more frenzied; blood covered his face and ran down his arms. It pooled at Hypatia's feet. At last, the older woman's eyes wandered and filmed. She slumped in her captors' arms, flesh hanging in shreds.

Peter howled. "See what fate awaits the wicked!" Several of his followers snatched clamshells and joined in a frenzy of rage, mercifully screening Selene's sight as they hacked at the body.

In this holy place, desecrated by profane acts, Selene piled God's indifference on the scales of justice and found Him wanting. Her bitter curses blended with the roar of the mob as they dismembered Hypatia's body and passed the parts around as if they were the relics of a saint.

Someone shouted, "Burn the body!" Others took up the chant.

The mob headed for the doors of the church, dragging Selene and Antonius. She sent him a despairing glance as the parabolani paraded the bloody shreds of her former teacher before them.

The streets were quiet. The harbor battened down for a late winter squall. The hushed calm before the storm flattened the water, turning it from a deep blue to iron gray.

The mob headed through the ruined Imperial Bucheron, toward the Gate of the Sun. Peter led the way with Hypatia's head impaled on a spike, her long hair streaming before blank eyes.

Selene struggled, vainly hoping to earn a deathblow. She did not doubt the imminence of her death; she only wanted it to be quick. She knew she couldn't face the end as stoically as Hypatia, and feared the pain to come. One of her captors clouted her on the head so that her vision blurred and stomach roiled, but not hard enough for merciful oblivion. Despair settled in her soul like a smothering fog.

Shouts of the crowd deafened her as they arrived at the east gate. The guards prudently gave way. The mob streamed into the open space between city wall and canal.

Parabolani appeared with wood for a pyre. Their captors pulled Selene and Antonius to the fore to watch the green faggots being lit. Sooty smoke spiraled into the sky, followed by a sickly flame.

Selene mouthed the words "I'm sorry" at Antonius. He smiled at her, she imagined, the way the Christian martyrs smiled before consigned to the circus or the cross.

It took the fire time to grow from small licking flames to a roaring conflagration. The wind picked up, sending a shower of sparks across the throng. The mob seemed smaller in the open space. Perhaps some had fled after Hypatia's murder.

The crowd quieted as Peter shouted, "What we did today is blessed by God. Pray to Him to save your souls from such as the black sorceress. Ask for the strength to smite His enemies and destroy them in His name."

With a final prayer of deliverance, Peter tossed Hypatia's head into the flames. Others followed suit, roaring each time a limb or unrecognizable lump of flesh crashed onto the pyre, sending sparks curling to the heavens. The fire burned higher, reeking of scorched meat.

The heat dried the sweat and tears on Selene's face, but did not chase the chill from her bones.

Toward the end of the gruesome ritual, someone shouted, "Her disciples! Throw them on the fire."

Others took up the chant. "Burn the witches!"

Her captors tightened their grips.

Selene heard a horn close by, and the shouts of military orders. The crowd milled in confusion as a cohort of mounted guards sliced through them.

Antonius struggled and broke loose. One of his captors sprawled on the ground.

Her guards relaxed their grips slightly. Desperate hope lent Selene new strength. She kicked one captor in the knee. His howls of pain were lost in the shouts of the battle going on about her.

A horse charged the trio. Her captors released her arms to flee. Selene threw herself out of the path of the horse toward the fire, fleeing to the other side. Antonius followed closely, limping.

Two men moved toward them on the right. A third circled the fire on the left to cut them off from the canal. Selene could outrun the men to the water, but she wouldn't leave Antonius.

One lunged at him. They wrestled to the ground, Antonius astride his chest, hands about the man's throat, madness stamped on his face as he squeezed.

A spindly mariner lunged at Selene with a long knife. He feinted to her right. She dodged, letting him veer toward the fire.

A parabolani swung at her with a cudgel. She put up her left arm to block the blow from her head. Selene heard the sickening sound of bone splintering as pain scorched her body and numbed her mind. She stood rooted to the spot, her arm dangling useless at her side.

Her attacker threw her a venomous look as he fled at the sound of hooves.

Selene slumped in relief, then turned at a shout of triumph behind her. The first man again charged her with the knife.

Antonius threw himself between them.

She screamed; an otherworldly sound she didn't recognize as coming from a human throat.

Antonius fell back against her. The knife stuck out of his gut, his hands clasped around the hilt. She staggered to the ground, cradling Antonius as best she could.

Horses snorted and soldiers shouted as they chased down the remnants of the mob. The mariner escaped beyond the fire.

Selene knelt at Antonius' side, ripping his tunic into bandages with her good hand and her teeth. Leaving the knife in place, Selene pressed the cloth around the wound, but the blood soaked through as fast as she could replace the bandages.

"Selene?" Antonius coughed; red foam bubbling from his lips.

"I'm here."

"Are you safe?"

"I think so." Selene looked around. The fire burned low. She sat back on her heels, wiping her face with her good hand. "The guard is chasing the mob. No one's near us."

"Good." Antonius clasped her hand. "It's getting dark."

Selene, tears runnelling the soot and blood on her cheeks, looked at his pale face, felt his thready pulse, and lied, "You'll be all right, Antonius."

He coughed again. "I don't think so." He looked up at her. "Selene, my love. It's enough you're alive and safe." He gasped for breath. "I couldn't bear the thought of this world without you."

"Don't talk, Antonius." She held his head in her lap. "Save your strength. You have to get better. You have a son to care for."

"My father can raise my son. I only wanted you." He lifted a bloody hand to her cheek. "For once my love has been a boon to you, not a burden." His wandering gaze focused on her for a moment, begging.

"I love you, Antonius," she whispered, knowing she could not save him.

He gripped her hand and smiled as the light fled from his eyes.

Selene bowed her head, letting her hair curtain the sight of her tears from any passersby. Antonius' many faces flashed across her mind. A red-faced boy, racing her across the beach. A youth, eyes alight and mouth passionate with a first kiss. A man, haggard with grief over her death, sowing the seeds of his destruction with wine.

Selene forgave Antonius his misplaced love as she cradled his still form.

At the sound of horses' hooves, Selene raised her head. Her arm throbbed at her side with an intensity that sent dark streaks across her vision. At least the ends of the bone had not broken the skin.

Horses stomped all around her. A dappled gray snorted at her hair.

Orestes dismounted, reached down and lifted her to her feet. "Thank the Good Lord you are still alive." His face showed no surprise, but the pallor under his tan and tight lines about his mouth betrayed his fear. His sharp gaze swept her body, taking in her injuries. "How badly are you hurt?"

She mutely indicated Antonius, swayed, and collapsed against his chest, sobbing. "He saved my life."

Orestes held her until her shudders subsided, then pulled a scarf from his neck and fashioned a sling for her injured arm. She winced as he tied it in place.

Orestes knelt to examine the body at her feet. "I'm sorry about young Antonius." He sighed. "Did you love him very much? Is that why you risked all? To let him know you were alive?"

She shook her head and hiccupped. "No. We met by accident. I don't know why he was in the agora. Maybe he was going to a tavern, or just didn't want to go home after my funeral. I was running to warn Hypatia when he recognized me."

"Hypatia? What about her?" Orestes gripped her shoulders. She gasped in pain. He dropped his hands.

"You didn't know? I thought that was why you were here."

"I heard the Patriarch's parabolani had captured a witch and rioted in the streets. Because you were abroad after the funeral, I feared you were their captive. What about Hypatia?"

Selene's lips quivered as she described her teacher's murder.

"Hypatia's dead?"

Selene nodded; eyes finally dry of tears.

Orestes trembled, from rage or grief, or both. He lifted his face to the roiling sky, neck corded, arms clenched at his side. He let out a barbarous howl; as if his heart ripped in two.

Selene backed away from the savagery etched on his face.

CHAPTER 42

O RESTES STOOD BEFORE THE OPEN WINDOW, looking at the quiet square. A soft spring breeze wafted the smell of rose blossoms through his offices. He breathed deeply, savoring the sweet scent as a momentary lift in his bleak mood.

He watched two soldiers stop a man and question him about his presence in the square. The detained man expressed anger in his wide gestures and aggressive posture.

Orestes sighed. The populace grew restive after six weeks of martial law, as did he. His initial fury over Hypatia's death had moderated to a cold anger. The leading citizens dithered, neither condemning nor condoning the violent murder, waiting to see which way the wind blew from Constantinople. These people didn't deserve to have such a great lady as their champion for so many decades.

He turned back to his desk, piled high with petitions to lift martial law and requests for reparations due to lost business.

Demetrius entered with a letter marked with the imperial seal. "A packet arrived from Constantinople, Master." Demetrius handed the letter to Orestes. "Perhaps it contains news of your petition."

Orestes slit the wax with his thumbnail, quickly scanned the letter and crumpled it in white-knuckled rage.

"They're denying your petition, Master?"

"Yes." Orestes slumped into his chair. "The Augusta has consolidated her power. I have no patron left in the court. The new Praetorian Prefect

Aurelian—with their majesties' approval—denied my petition to compel Cyril to turn over the murderous presbyter."

Orestes sat gloomily looking at the missive.

Demetrius said, with uncharacteristic distress, "They will do nothing?"

"They have granted the council's request to reduce the number of parabolani to five hundred." Orestes snorted. "The bloody bastards are barred from gathering in public forums or invading council rooms and magistrates' courts. But nothing about Hypatia. That noble lady's death will go unpunished."

Orestes threw the crumpled sheet across the room. "Cyril's won. There's no more I can do."

CYRIL SMILED AS HE READ the letter from his deacon in Constantinople.

Peter's unexpected violence had shocked Cyril with its savagery. He had feared imperial retaliation, but God was on his side. The death of a pagan philosopher received short shrift at court—as it should. Hypatia was dead, and the tighter Orestes gripped the city, the more resistant it became to his cause.

Cyril said a silent prayer of thanksgiving. His vision had come true. Alexandria belonged to the Patriarch of the One True Church. The attack on Orestes, and Hypatia's murder, gave him profound insight into the power of his office. He needed to think carefully how to use that power to the Church's advantage.

Hierex entered the office and bowed. "It's time, Your Grace."

Cyril looked out the window. "So it is." Orestes could not forbid the Easter celebrations.

Cyril eschewed the gold-embroidered purple and white robes of the Patriarch, to go among his flock in the rough garb of a penitent for this joyous celebration of the Resurrection. He and Hierex wended their way to the courtyard, where other church fathers joined them. Paulinus, his dour chief steward, stood with the official almsgivers, counting coins. He and Cyril had forged an adequate, if prickly, working relationship since Theophilus' death. Contributions to the church poured in daily, keeping Paulinus and his accountants busy.

Cyril's new Archdeacon greeted him with a kiss. "Your donkey is ready, Holy Father."

Cyril mounted the docile beast, feeling awkward as his legs dangled to the ground. Hierex led the donkey from the courtyard. Hundreds of monks and clerks emptied out of the buildings to follow in their wake, chanting, "Hosanna." Citizens lined the broad streets carrying palm branches, which they threw to the ground before Cyril passed. Spring rains had washed the blood from the streets and soot from the walls. Flowers and colorful banners festooned the buildings.

The procession made its stately way to the forum. A huge crowd cheered as Cyril entered and paraded around the square. Someone started a chant and others took it up, booming, "Cyril, blessed of God." On the second round the chant changed to, "Cyril, a true ascetic." On the third, it changed again to, "Cyril, the new Theophilus."

Tears blurred Cyril's eyes. His heart swelled.

His people bowed in adoration of their Patriarch.

DEMETRIUS WATCHED HIS MASTER observing the Easter procession. As the crowds cheered Cyril, Orestes' face hardened into a grim mask, a slight tick by his left eye the only movement.

After Hypatia's death, Demetrius had seen his master grow withdrawn and bitter. Lady Selene, having lost both her teacher and her friend, reached out to comfort Orestes, but he continually rebuffed her. Demetrius felt that, if they could share their grief, they might heal one another, but Orestes' bitterness and disappointment ran too deep.

He touched Orestes' sleeve. "Master, come away from the window. It does no good to watch the Patriarch's spectacles."

"Don't use that pitying tone with me." Orestes rounded on Demetrius, eyes flashing. "I won't have it."

Demetrius stepped back and bowed deeply. "I most humbly beg your pardon, Master."

As quickly as it flared, the anger left Orestes' eyes. His shoulders slumped. "I should beg your pardon, Demetrius. You've been an excellent servant and do not deserve my harsh words. Come, I have something for you."

Orestes turned his back on the street and strode to his desk. He rustled among the papers and pulled out a scroll embossed with the Prefect's seal. Orestes handed it to Demetrius with the first genuine smile he'd shown in weeks. "This is long overdue."

Demetrius took the scroll in trembling hands and read the flowery script—his manumission and a generous stipend to live on. He looked up at Orestes with moisture fogging his vision. "Thank you, Master."

"No longer 'Master,' Demetrius. It's a small enough reward for your faithful service." The smile disappeared from Orestes' face. "If I had listened more intently to your advice…"

Demetrius kept a discreet silence. He found no solace in 'might have beens.'

Orestes composed his face. "You are free to leave today, if you wish. However, I hope you stay for a few weeks. I'm resigning as Prefect and would value your assistance in concluding my affairs."

"Of course." Demetrius bowed low. "I've waited twenty-seven years for my date grove. I can wait a little longer."

PHILLIP LAID OUT HIS FATHER'S MEMORIAL FEAST for the beggars in the cemetery. The wretched hoard snatched the good warm bread, fought over the roasted peahen, and swilled the beer, but Phillip smiled. The Church frowned on these feasts for this very reason—they celebrated the body, not the spirit.

Phillip's smile turned bitter. If he could snub the Church, he would. He saw no reason to believe in a Church that dismembered great scholars, hounded his sister into exile, and murdered Rebecca's people.

The thought of his gentle love—her modesty, loyalty, and tenderness—spread warmth through his chest. His eyes sparkled and breath quickened. He knew Rebecca would not approve of his bitterness—it poisoned his life. She showed more Christian charity than many who professed to be Christian.

She also refused to marry outside her faith, causing him no end of heartache.

Phillip sauntered to the entrance of the family tomb. He leaned his forehead against a smooth white marble column. "Father, what would you advise? Should I stay in Alexandria? Should I fight to restore our family to prominence?"

Cyril's triumph guaranteed it would be an enormously difficult task. If Phillip stayed in Alexandria, his sister would be alone in the world, an exile, and he would have to forgo Rebecca's love. Calistus had always demanded much of his oldest son, and Phillip felt he disappointed more often than he pleased. "I know our family name was important to you, Father, but I don't think you want a life of exile and lovelessness for your children."

Looking around the cemetery, Phillip came to a decision. He would take Selene, Rebecca, and her brother Aaron to Judea. Away from the city of his birth, Phillip could flout the Imperial law against Christians converting to Judaism. With the small portion left from paying off his father's debts and the generous gift from Orestes, they could start over.

He would study to become a Jew. He and Rebecca would be married.

Phillip let out a whoop, disturbing the bedraggled feasters. As they looked at him with suspicion, he shouted, "Raise a cup of beer to me. I'm going to be married!"

Several tentatively lofted their cups and gave a ragged cheer. He left them the gift of food, dishes, and baskets, and hurried away to tell Rebecca of his decision.

As he neared the cemetery exit, Phillip spied a familiar figure—an athletic older man with heavily lined face, followed by several servants with baskets. "Lysis?"

Antonius' father squinted at Phillip, then brightened when he recognized his old friend's son. "Phillip, my boy, how good to see you."

Phillip smelled the rich aroma of roasted lamb and the biting tang of pickled pork. "I see the beggars will eat well today. I left a feast of bread and fowl."

"Yes, I imagine they fared poorly during Orestes' martial law." Lysis' face became shadowed. "This is the first time I've been able to visit my son's tomb since his hasty interment. I want to give him a true funeral feast."

A baby cried. One of the servants quickly hushed the child.

"Antonius' son?"

"Yes. A lusty boy." The old man's shoulder's straightened as he said, with pride, "Ision and his money be damned. Honorius will grow up a credit to our family. I'll see to that."

The baby howled, probably in hunger. The child's cry tugged at something inside Phillip. He suddenly thrilled at the thought of children of his own. Rebecca would be a wonderful mother. He needed to get home quickly.

Phillip clasped the older man's arm. "I'll not keep you from your mission. Good fortune to you and the child."

SELENE CURSED HER WEAKENED ARM as she tried to fold a robe. Six weeks with her arm in a splint had tried her small store of patience. She dreaded the thought of another month before she regained full use.

Selene's few possessions lay scattered across her bed in Orestes' suite: a few tunics, an extra pair of sandals, a sturdy cloak, her mother's jewelry, her medical bag, and three precious volumes of texts. She glanced anxiously into the sitting room, realized it was still early, and returned to her task. Selene finished sorting as Demetrius arrived with visitors.

"Phillip!" She ran to her brother, then spied another standing behind him. "Rebecca! I'm so happy we get to say goodbye."

"You know I could never let you leave without seeing you one last time." Rebecca's lips trembled. "You don't have to do this alone, you know. Please come with us to Judea."

Selene had promised herself no tears at this parting, but moisture leaked from the corners of her eyes. She sniffed and dashed the unwanted tears away with the back of her good hand.

Both put arms around Selene and escorted her to the sitting room. Demetrius discreetly stayed behind to attend her packing.

"You aren't going to make this easy, are you?"

"Did you expect us to let you go into the world alone without a fight?" Phillip put a protective arm around Rebecca and said solemnly, "We have enough from father's estate and Orestes' gift to purchase a small farm or business. You can practice medicine in Judea as well as anyplace else."

Rebecca took Selene's hand in both of hers. "We want you to come with us. We are going to a new place, where none know us. We can tell others you are my sister, for that is what you truly are."

A shadow crossed Selene's face. "I cannot go with you."

Disappointment twisted Phillip's mouth. "In the name of Jesus and his holy mother Mary, can you tell me why?"

"Is this proper language from a prospective Jew?" Selene laughed as Phillip colored.

"A life-time of habit is hard to break," he mumbled.

Rebecca paled. "Is that why you won't go with us? Do you disapprove of Phillip's conversion?"

"Oh, no, Rebecca," Selene cried. "I love you both and would not let such a thing come between us, ever!" She shook her head. "This has to do with me, not you."

"Is it Orestes?" Phillip's face brightened. "Are you going with him?"

"No. Orestes has chosen a different path. One, I fear, that will lead to his destruction."

"My friend has changed much in the past weeks." Phillip sighed. "He keeps me at a distance and has relieved me of all my duties. He's been generous in providing me with letters and references to his acquaintances in Judea. I had held out hope he might care for you in your exile."

Rebecca added, "Orestes does not look well."

Selene nodded, worry lines creasing her forehead. "Grief eats his heart and failure his soul. He won't let anyone comfort him, but tries to bear all his pain alone. He is resigning his office and retiring to his estates in Gaul. I fear for his health and peace of mind."

"That does not explain your refusal to join us," Phillip said.

Selene walked to the window and looked across the lush garden, warm sunshine bathing her face. A short time ago, nothing could have driven her from her home, but so much had happened. So many deaths. There was nothing to hold her to this city except fear of the unknown, and that held little terror for her in the wake of the last several months. Instead, the unknown future beckoned with possibility. She needed to move on, but exchanging the deserts of Egypt for those of Judea did not appeal to her. She turned back to her brother and her heart's sister.

"I want to leave this part of the world. I want to see other lands, perhaps touch snow or trek through a forest. I am free now to do as I wish. Besides, Nicaeus deserves to know the truth about what happened here. I'll go first to his post on the Thracian border. Write to him when you're settled, and I will get the word. Then…" she shrugged, brave words masking a tremulous doubt "… maybe Constantinople, maybe Gaul."

"Oh, no, Selene," Rebecca cried. "Not so far away as that?"

Phillip gathered Selene in his arms, but did not argue. "When you are ready to stop wandering, come to us," he whispered in her hair. "We wouldn't want our children to grow up never knowing their aunt."

Rebecca joined the embrace, tears streaming. "Stay safe, sister, and remember you will always have a home with us."

SELENE WANDERED THE EMPTY ROOMS RESTLESSLY. Movement still soothed her. She would never attain Hypatia's serenity. Her teacher could sit for hours working out a math problem or writing a treatise on the stars. The memory sent a sharp pain through her chest. Sometimes the sense of loss throbbed like an open wound, but more and more lately it felt duller, subdued, distant.

Someone cleared his throat.

Selene turned, a shy smile crossing her face. "Orestes, it's good of you to see me off." Demetrius had concocted a story about a new mistress, but any servant with half an eye knew Orestes rarely visited her, and then only for a few moments, occasionally, before he went to his office.

At first Selene had not minded. Her arm caused her pain and she considered her bruised face and body ugly. She needed time and solitude to heal. But as the weeks went by, Orestes continued to be politely correct to her, refused to confide his own pain and loss. Selene concluded he was too deeply wounded for her to heal. A wound of the body she could treat, but curing this sickness of the soul eluded her.

Orestes handed Selene a packet of papers. "I've prepared travel documents, drafts on my personal accounts for funds, and letters of introduction to important people in Constantinople attesting to your medical skills. I've said you are a freedwoman so your station more befits your profession. My acquaintances can help you set up a practice or gain a position in one of the hospitals for women."

Selene set the papers aside without looking at them. "Have you nothing else to say to me?"

Orestes looked stricken. He dropped to one knee, took her hand and bowed his head over it. His voice came harsh and halting. "I hope, my dear Selene, you can find it in your heart to forgive me someday."

Confused, Selene dropped to the floor in front of him and looked into his face, eyes wide. "For what? You've been a steadfast champion and firm friend to my family."

"I underestimated Cyril from the beginning. I thought him young, inexperienced, without support in the Church." His eyes filmed with tears. "Had I been more astute, you and your family would be secure in your home. Had I been more able, Hypatia might be alive today."

"You did what you thought best at the time. Whether your actions hastened or retarded Cyril's success, we have no way of knowing. I don't need to forgive you, Orestes. You need to forgive yourself. I fear for you, if you don't."

His shoulders shook with stifled sobs. Selene prayed her words helped heal his heart. He collected himself, rose, and helped Selene to her feet. She looked deeply into his eyes, and saw bitterness and self-loathing—no self-forgiveness.

Regret for what might have been and sadness at her failure—and his—pervaded her soul.

Orestes clasped her to his chest. She clung to his strong body and sheltering arms. He stepped away from her, echoing her thoughts, "If things had been different..."

Knowing there was nothing more she could do, Selene touched his haggard face and whispered, "I hope you find peace, my friend."

"Maybe...in time." He clasped her hand in both of his, his sight turning inward. "I have a strange feeling we will meet again, Selene. My mother's people were renowned as seers. Maybe I see truly."

"I hope so."

Without tears, she retrieved her hand. Selene gave Orestes a final smile, turned and walked through the door without looking back.

AUTHOR'S NOTE

HYPATIA, CYRIL, ORESTES, HIEREX, Archdeacon Timothy, Ammonius, and the presbyter Peter did exist and participate in these events, although I used "literary license" in portraying their physical appearance, dialog, and the details of their relationships. Selene, her family, friends, and servants are entirely fictitious. I created them to show how the decisions and actions of the powerful are played out in ordinary people's lives. All the major events—the riots leading up to Cyril's affirmation, the consolidation of the Christians, the Jewish trap and consequent expulsion, the attack on Orestes, and Hypatia's murder—as well as many minor events, are documented in primary sources.

I first came across this fascinating story of ambition, power, and political assassination in 1980 while attending Judy Chicago's groundbreaking feminist art exhibit "The Dinner Party" where Hypatia, the Lady Philosopher of Alexandria, had a "plate." Captured by the inherent drama of Hypatia's life and death, I embarked on a journey to bring her story to modern readers. During the next seventeen years, I haunted libraries, bookstores, and the internet looking for more material to fill out the sketchy and conflicting details available.

Hypatia's life had captured the imaginations of many before me and had become a metaphor in literature for the brilliance of the Classical Age, and her death one of the coming Dark Ages. Most stories painted a legend of a beautiful, virginal young woman cut down by fanatical monks. She was particularly popular in the Age of Enlightenment and it's Edward Gibbon's (flawed) version of her life from *The Decline and Fall of the Roman Empire* that is best known today. In recent times Hypatia has evolved into a feminist icon: a woman mathematician and scientist, celebrated for her rationality and intelligence; destroyed by superstitious, barbarous men. She appears in several biographies of women in science and mathematics.

Sorting through the hyperbole was difficult. I consulted dozens of books and hundreds of articles, but relied most heavily on the research of Maria Dzielska, a Polish classical scholar in her *Hypatia of Alexandria* published by Harvard Press in 1997. Professor Dzielska does a masterful job in reviewing the literary heritage of Hypatia's story and evaluating primary sources to present a more realistic, and much less biased, historical picture. Professor Michael A. B. Deakin has recently added to our knowledge of Hypatia's mathematical skills in his *Hypatia of Alexandria: Mathematician and Martyr* published by Prometheus Books in 2007. A bibliography of the most useful works can be found on my website at faithljustice.com.

Patriarch Cyril appears in the record as a Machiavellian character more enamored of power than of God. His contemporaries lauded his political acumen. His earliest acts were to eliminate those factions that opposed his appointment, including other Christian sects and the Jews. Later he fomented riots at ecclesiastical gatherings and bribed those close to the Emperor to get his way in doctrinal disputes. There is no doubt he significantly affected Church policy for many years and was made a saint and Doctor of the Church based on his doctrinal scholarship. He makes another malevolent appearance in *Dawn Empress*, my story about the life of Empress Pulcheria.

There is no proof that Cyril ordered the death of Hypatia. Primary sources both condemn him on the basis of jealousy and exonerate him on the basis of mob violence. I chose the interpretation that he wished to discredit Hypatia, but, in his youth and inexperience, underestimated the extent of his power. However, given the bloody times and lack of repercussions for Hypatia's death, he probably was pleased with the outcome.

Little is known of Orestes other than the dates of his administration, his admiration for Hypatia, his claim to baptism, and the attack by the Nitrian monks. There is some controversy over whether he survived the attack, but Dzielska believed he did, and was either recalled or resigned after Hypatia's death. I created a background and early history for Orestes that enhanced my story.

I included in the story a number of places from recent archeological digs such as the glassmakers' shop, theater, classrooms, tombs, monasteries, and cisterns. Most of the cisterns of Alexandria were filled in, but when is unknown. I chose to have them available for Selene's escape. I visited surviving cisterns in Istanbul (Constantinople) and used them as my model—and yes, you could boat through them! Other minor events, such as the couple divorcing because of demonic influence and the fire-walking priest, are taken from recorded incidents, but not necessarily during this three-year time period.

The Museum, of which Hypatia was a member, was one of the great learning centers of antiquity, and attracted scholars from all over the world to study philosophy, mathematics, science, nature, literature, and medicine for nearly five hundred years. The original buildings were part of a magnificent palace complex, which took up nearly one-third of the land inside the walls of Alexandria and contained The Great Library, scholars' living quarters, classrooms, a zoo, and gardens with exotic plants. War and nature battered this complex. Queen Zenobia of Palmyra conquered Egypt and attacked Alexandria in 269. Emperor Diocletian laid siege to, and ravaged, Alexandria in 298. A major earthquake in 365 sent most of the palace district into the sea. However, there is substantial evidence that the Museum and its library continued—in considerably reduced circumstances—in other buildings, possibly in the vicinity of the Caesarion, where a series of lecture halls have been excavated.

Scholarship didn't disappear with Hypatia. There were many philosophers (some pagan) holding public chairs in Alexandria after her death, and at least one other woman (Asclepigenia, daughter of Plutarch) taught philosophy in Athens.

I hope you enjoyed this 10th anniversary edition of *Selene of Alexandria* and seek out my other books. I have a companion non-fiction book called *Hypatia: Her Life and Times*. While researching Hypatia's story, I fell in love with a number of fascinating women including the Theodosian Empresses: Placidia, Pulcheria, and Athenais. They were women of grace and power with compelling stories. I told Placidia's story in *Twilight Empress* published in 2017. *Dawn Empress* about Pulcheria's life is out in 2020. Both books are available in all formats. I hope to have Athenais' story out by 2023 at the latest—"God willing and the creeks don't rise!"—as my mom used to say.

Please let me know how you feel about the story and characters by writing me at faith@faithljustice.com. Tell me what you liked, or didn't. Or visit me on the web at faithljustice.com where I have lots of free content. Sign up for my very infrequent newsletter and get a free eBook set in the *Twilight Empress* world as well as advance notice of free audio books and other giveaways. Although my daughter had to drag me into the social media scene, you can also find me on Twitter (@faithljustice) and Facebook.

Finally, I need a favor. I'd love a review of *Selene of Alexandria*. Loved it, hated it—please share your feedback at your favorite book review sharing site. No need for a literary critique—just a couple of sentences on what you liked/ didn't like and why. Reviews can be tough to come by these days, and having them (or not) can make or break a book. So I hope you share your opinion with others.

Faith L. Justice
Brooklyn, NY
November 2019

Thank you for reading *Selene of Alexandria.*

GLOSSARY

agora—an open space serving as an assembly area and a place for commercial, civic, social, and religious activities

Atalanta—a character in Greek mythology, a virgin huntress, who agreed to marry only if her suitors could outrun her in a footrace. Those who lost were killed. Hippomenes asked the goddess Aphrodite for help, and she gave him three golden apples. Every time Atalanta got ahead of Hippomenes, he rolled an apple to the side of her, and she would run after it. Hippomenes won the footrace and married Atalanta.

civitas—the rights and obligations of a citizen, including taxes for civic upkeep

dalmatica—the standard overgarment of upper-class men and women, made from a single long piece of fabric, stitched together along the sides and up the sleeves, with a hole cut for the head; decorative trim could be added to the hem, sleeves, and neckline; the quality of the cloth and the richer levels of ornament indicated the social status of the wearer

decurion—a Roman cavalry officer in command of a squadron

dux—the highest military office within a province and commanded the legions; the governor had to authorize the use of the dux's powers; once authorized, the dux could act independently from the governor and handled all military matters (root for later titles such as duke)

frigidarium—cold plunge, one of three pools available at Roman baths

Hippolyta—Queen of the Amazons. Theseus abducted her or she fell in love with him and betrayed the Amazons by willingly going to Athens where she wed Theseus, being the only Amazon to ever marry

litholater—"stone worshiper"; slur used to describe Patriarch Theophilus because he built so many churches

Logos—in Christology, the Logos (Greek: "Word", "Discourse", or "Reason"')
is a name or title for Jesus Christ, seen as the pre-existent second person
of the Trinity; derives from John 1:1, which in many versions of the Bible
reads: "In the beginning was the Word, and the Word was with God, and
the Word was God."

medica (feminine)/medicus (masculine)—Latin for physician, doctor, surgeon;
of or belonging to healing, curative, medical

Mithras—a Persian god adopted by the Romans; particularly popular with the
Roman army; considered a mystery cult, members were sworn to secrecy
about the rites

modius—a bushel-shaped headdress worn in representations of certain deities
such as Serapis and Tyche; a Roman dry measure of about a peck or nine
liters

parabolani—"persons who risk their lives as nurses"; members of a
brotherhood who, in early Christianity, voluntarily undertook care of
the sick and burial of the dead, knowing they too could die; generally
drawn from the lower strata of society, they also functioned as attendants
to local bishops who sometimes used them as bodyguards and in violent
clashes with their opponents

philoponoi—radical Christian students, sometimes given to violence toward
pagans

Rhakotis—the original Egyptian village where Alexander the Great laid out
Alexandria; poor neighborhood in Alexandria primarily inhabited by
native Egyptians

Sema (or Soma)—"body" in Greek; the main north-south street in Alexandria;
Alexander the Great's tomb was originally placed somewhere on it, but it
was moved and the location lost by the 5C

Serapeum—temple to the god Serapis; a Christian mob destroyed the
Serapeum of Alexandria in AD 385

Serapis—a syncretistic deity derived from the worship of the Egyptian
gods Osiris and Apis and also gained attributes from other deities,
such as chthonic powers linked to the Greek Hades and Demeter,
and benevolence linked to Dionysus; promoted by the first Greek
Pharaoh Ptolemy I as a means of uniting the native Egyptians with the
conquering Greeks; later popular with Romans

Thautmasios—"Admirable" martyr name given to the monk Ammonius after
    his execution for attacking the Prefect Orestes

Theseus—the mythical king and founder-hero of Athens who won the
    Amazon Queen Hippolyta for a wife

Tychaion—temple dedicated to the goddess Tyche

Tyche—Greek goddess (Roman equivalent: Fortuna) the presiding tutelary
    deity who governed the fortune and prosperity of a city

ABOUT THE AUTHOR

FAITH L. JUSTICE writes award-winning novels, short stories, and articles in Brooklyn, New York. Her work has appeared in such publications as *Salon.com, Writer's Digest, The Copperfield Review*, and the *Circles in the Hair* anthology. She is Chair of the New York City chapter of the Historical Novel Society, Associate Editor of *Space and Time Magazine,* and co-founded a writer's workshop many more years ago than she likes to admit. For fun, she likes to dig in the dirt—her garden and various archaeological sites.

CONTACT FAITH ONLINE:

Website/Blog: faithljustice.com
Twitter: @faithljustice
Facebook: facebook.com/faithljusticeauthor

Discover these and other books by Faith L. Justice. Available in print, eBook, and audio in all the usual places.

HYPATIA: HER LIFE AND TIMES

Who was Hypatia of Alexandria? A brilliant young mathematician murdered by a religious mob? An aging academic eliminated by a rival political party? A sorceress who enthralled the Prefect of Alexandria through satanic wiles? Did she discover the earth circled the sun a thousand years before Copernicus or was she merely a gifted geometry teacher? Discover the answers to these questions and more in this collection of essays on Hypatia's life and times.

TWILIGHT EMPRESS (Theodosian Women #1)

Twilight Empress tells the little-known story of a remarkable woman: Placidia, sister to one of the last Roman Emperors. As Gothic Queen then Roman Empress, Placidia does the unthinkable: she holds together the failing Western Roman Empire; a life of ambition, power, and intrigue she doesn't seek, but can't refuse. Her actions shape the face of Western Europe for centuries. A passionate woman as well as an empress, Placidia suffers love, loss, and betrayal. Can her intelligence, tenacity, and ambition help her survive and triumph over scheming generals, rebellious children, and Attila the Hun?

DAWN EMPRESS (Theodosian Women #2)

After the Emperor's unexpected death, ambitious men eye the Eastern Roman throne occupied by seven-year-old Theodosius II. His older sister Princess Pulcheria faces a stark choice: she must find allies and take control of the Eastern court or doom the imperial children to a life of obscurity—or worse! Beloved by the people and respected by the Church, Pulcheria forges her own path to power. Can her piety and steely will protect her brother from military assassins, heretic bishops, scheming eunuchs and—most insidious of all—a beautiful, intelligent bride? Or will she lose all in the trying? *Dawn Empress* tells Pulcheria's little-known and fascinating story. Her accomplishments rival those of Elizabeth I and Catherine the Great as she sets the stage for the dawn of the Byzantine Empire.

SWORD OF THE GLADIATRIX (Gladiatrix #1)

An action-packed romance that exposes the brutal underside of Imperial Rome, *Sword of the Gladiatrix* brings to life unforgettable characters and exotic settings. From the far edges of the Empire, two women come to battle on the hot sands of the arena in Nero's Rome: Afra, scout and beast master to the Queen of Kush; and Cinnia, warrior-bard and companion to Queen Boudica of the British Iceni. Enslaved, forced to fight for their lives and the Romans' pleasure; they seek to replace lost friendship, love, and family in each other's arms. But the Roman arena offers only two futures: the Gate of Life for the victors or the Gate of Death for the losers.

THE RELUCTANT GROOM AND OTHER HISTORICAL STORIES

Dive into this collection of historical shorts by an award-winning author. You'll find stories of heroism, love, and adventure such as a panicked bachelor faced with an arranged marriage, a man battling a blizzard to get home for his child's birth, a Viking shield maiden exploring a New World, and a young boy torn between love for his ailing grandmother and duty to an empress. Whether set in imperial Rome, colonial America, or on the ancient Silk Road, these stories bring to life men and women struggling to survive and thrive—the eternal human condition.

TOKOYO, THE SAMURAI'S DAUGHTER

(Adventurous Girls #1)

Most noble-born girls of Tokoyo's age learn to sing, paint, and write poetry. Not Tokoyo. She's an adventurous girl, the daughter of a samurai in fourteenth century Japan. Her father trains her in the martial arts. When he is away, she escapes to the sea where she works with the Ama—a society of women and girls who dive in the deep waters for food and treasure. But disaster strikes her family. Can Tokoyo save her father using the lessons she learned and the skills she mastered to overcome corrupt officials, her own doubts, and a nasty sea demon? (Middle grade, illustrated fiction)

RAGGEDY MOON BOOKS

raggedymoonbooks.com

Made in the USA
Monee, IL
10 December 2022

20799793R00213